LIBRARY DIST. R-5
CHEYENNE WELLS, CO.

S0-DTD-079

	DATE DUE		
1994			
1995			
1996			
JAN 27			

LIBRARY DIST. R-5
CHEYENNE WELLS, CO.

HS

X

THE MIND BREAKER

By the same author

THE PAWN
EASY MONEY

THE MIND BREAKER

by Arthur Mather

Mn 074254

WESTMINSTER PUBLIC LIBRARY
3031 WEST 76TH AVE.
WESTMINSTER, CO 80030

DELACORTE PRESS/NEW YORK

Published by
Delacorte Press
1 Dag Hammarskjold Plaza
New York, N.Y. 10017

This work was first published in Great Britain by
Hodder and Stoughton.

Copyright © 1980 by Arthur Mather

All rights reserved. No part of this book may be reproduced
or transmitted in any form or by any means, electronic or
mechanical, including photocopying, recording or by any
information storage and retrieval system, without the written
permission of the Publisher, except where permitted by law.

Manufactured in the United States of America

First U.S.A. printing

Designed by Laura Bernay

Library of Congress Cataloging in Publication Data

Mather, Arthur R.
    The mind breaker.

    I. Title.
PZ4.M4249Mi 1980   [PR9619.3.M29] 823   80-16242
ISBN: 0-440-05294-7

THE MIND BREAKER

September 30, 1982

Vilas Daiton
Sheraton Centre
Seventh Avenue
New York City

Dear Vilas,

I have read your letter, and my reaction has been a mixture of skepticism and tremendous excitement.

Please do not be offended by my skepticism. You must understand that this is something new to me, and unexplainable, therefore I must proceed with caution. I have put your report to the council of the brotherhood, and they are more skeptical than I.

But we all know that you are a dedicated freedom fighter of long standing, and an invaluable contact in America, and past experience has proved to us that you are not prone to making wild, exaggerated claims.

If what you are saying is possible, then it comes at the right time for all of us. Resistance to our guerrilla tactics of hijacking and kidnapping is stiffening all over Europe, and there is a strong feeling amongst the council for a change of direction. There is general agreement that any further pressure must be directed toward America and we intend to shift the main drive of our operations to that country. If we can bend America to our will, then the rest of the world must follow.

But I must have personal proof of your claims to present to the brotherhood, and I must also be assured that you can positively locate the subject. Otherwise it is all speculation.

I will be in America within two weeks, and I will expect positive answers from you by then. Details of my arrival will follow.

Do not be deterred by my cautions, because I have implicit faith in your judgment. If your claim is true, then it opens the door to possibilities beyond our wildest dreams.

A plan is already evolving in my mind to put the subject to maximum use.

Yours in brotherhood,
HADAFFI

It was a crisp fall Sunday afternoon, so Daiton decided to walk the few blocks from Sheraton Centre up Fifty-first Street to Fifth Avenue.

He wore casual clothes, not sharp enough to attract attention, but a good faceless blend of jeans and jacket.

He cut along Rockefeller Plaza, casting a momentary glance at the white rectangle of ice already sheathed in place on the skating rink. A sprinkling of enthusiasts in bright-colored clothing twirled over the surface, some with partners, cutting rhythmic graceful circles, others plodding in solitary contentment around the outer edges of the rink. The rasping sound of the skates drifted up to him.

He didn't stop, but turned away into the Plaza, his mouth twisted into a disdainful sneer. Adults who refused to grow up, playing at children's games. Grimly determined to shut out reality. The world teetering on the verge of collapse, and they preferred to lose themselves in their mindless gyrations.

He shrugged his shoulders and quickened his pace, striding briskly past the multicolored flower beds toward Fifth Avenue. Solitary individuals spaced out along the benches either stared at him vacantly or pored over their newspapers. Pale sunlight filtered into the canyon, brightening the pastel colored flowers with a soft sheen. He came to the end of the Plaza and turned left onto Fifth Avenue without slackening pace, threading his way easily through the sparsely peopled street. He was a dark, well-built, good-looking young man of twenty-eight, with a mass of ink-black wavy hair, and an equally black moustache set beneath an aquiline nose. He had been told that he looked like Omar Sharif, but he always shrugged away the reference with a gesture of contempt. Still, he was very aware of the likeness, and although he would have vehemently denied the accusation, he had consciously adopted small mannerisms that heightened the resemblance. He listed his occupation as an insurance salesman, but he sold little insurance. He paid taxes like every other American, but his sources of income would not have stood up to any close scrutiny. His permanent residence was in San Francisco, but chance had brought him to New York, and chance was keeping him there.

He crossed over at Forty-seventh Street, and headed east. He just managed to beat the red light, and the horn from an impatient taxi driver blared raucously at him. He ignored it. That was New York. If one missed a heartbeat for every impatiently blasted car horn in New York, then one would be very quickly dead. He had a feeling of well-being, of confidence. Hadaffi trusted him. He could understand Hadaffi's doubts, but he wouldn't let him down; he would find the subject, and he would prove his claim. And now that he believed that the subject was so vulnerable it would be easy to apply pressure to him.

He took a piece of paper from his pocket and checked off the numbers until he came to the building. There was a narrow lane at the side, as he had been told. He turned into the lane as if he belonged, pacing himself with a firm, confident tread, because that was the best way not to be noticed. He came to the side door at the rear of the building, stopped, and took the key from his pocket. It felt cold and small in his palm, but it had cost him a thousand dollars. Perhaps in the future the owners of the building might find it more profitable to pay their janitors better. He slipped the key into the lock, and glanced up toward the lane entrance.

A few people drifted past, but no one paid him any attention. He went swiftly into the building, closed the door behind him, then made his way along a small corridor, up several steps, right through another door, and found himself in the main foyer. Gleaming chrome, black marble, and red highlights. Ahead of him on the main wall a large abstract mural by an artist unknown to him, in a style he found incomprehensible. To his left a bank of elevators, black doors framed with chrome. At the end of the elevators an unmanned floor-polishing machine, abandoned like a broken-down car. That bothered him. Somewhere there would be an operator, taking a leak, drinking some coffee, stealing a nap.

He shrugged. There were always small risks to be taken. He chose the elevator closest to him and pressed the button, and the door glided open immediately. He stepped in quickly, and pressed the indicator for the thirty-fifth floor. It rose effortlessly with an efficient whine, and the thirty-fifth floor was only seconds away.

He stepped out into the hall, and paused. The carpet was dark brown, and deep, absorbing his weight like a resilient sponge. He buttoned up his jacket, and smoothed out the sleeves. It was a nervous, unnecessary action, and he recognized it for what it was. He padded cautiously along the hallway until he came to door number 1127, and stopped. There was a small, elegant nameplate set in the door at eye level. MARK CLEMENTS. GYNECOLOGIST. He put his hands on the door, then paused to turn his head in a slow semicircle until his eyes had absorbed every detail of the hallway. He included his hands in the last-minute reconnaissance. The hairs on the backs of his hands lay unruffled, strand on strand, like grass on a windless plain. Not a tremor. Complete control. His mouth trembled in a half smile at a sudden flash of memory, of a training field, far away, long ago, with Hadaffi at his side. He a callow youth, only wanting to serve, ready to die. If you don't fear death, then you fear nothing, Hadaffi had told him. It is the greatest advantage you will ever have. Your enemy fears life, therefore he fears death.

He shook the memory away. He took the thin metal blade from his pocket, inserted it into the lock, and manipulated it skillfully until he heard the latch click open. He stepped quickly inside, and closed the door gently behind him.

He was in a small reception room, polished desk ahead of him with a matching chair. The desk top dressed neatly with a small typewriter, telephone, intercom, note pad. The texture of the carpet had changed subtly in socioeconomic terms from middle class to upper class. To his right was a line of stylish couches, and above them, set tastefully on the wall, the usual framed prints. Behind and slightly to the right of the desk was another door, which he presumed led to the doctor's consulting room. To his left another couch, and at the end of the couch a filing cabinet. It was exactly as Nerida had described it to him. The large window above the couch on his left looked out over a typical New York landscape, a geometric pattern of towering spires, mellow with soft color from the fall sun.

He crossed quickly to the filing cabinet and took a blade similar to the one he had used on the office door, and with the same speed and expertise opened the cabinet. When he saw the list of patients' files he knew it was going to take him a lot longer than he had anticipated. He knew the date of Jo's visit to see Clements, and he knew her personal particulars, but he was sure she would have used an assumed name. But if he was lucky she may have given her true Christian name.

It took him an hour, an hour in which the words on the cards began to blur and run together, and his fingers lost their nimbleness, stumbling into each other like weary runners, missing files and forcing him to go back over the same ground. But he disciplined himself to complete the set task. He had committed himself to Hadaffi, and to lose at this preliminary stage would be ridiculous. He would lose face not only to Hadaffi, but to the entire brotherhood if he failed to prove his claim.

He began to feel a sense of isolation from the rest of the world, shut off, almost timeless. He glanced through the window, noting the shadows on the multiwindowed steel giants had subtly changed direction. The longer he stayed the greater the risk of being caught, but it was impossible to force the pace.

Then suddenly he found it. The right date, the right particulars, the details of her pregnancy. And also some luck, because she had used her real Christian name. Jo. Jo Newman. The surname Newman meant nothing because he was certain it was phony. It was Jo Leica all right. He felt the adrenaline beginning to flow, pumping anticipation and excitement back into his bloodstream.

He took the card across to the desk, extracted a piece of notepaper from his pocket, and copied down the address. There was a deep, warm sense of achievement glowing in his belly. The next stage would be more difficult, but this was an enormously satisfying trigger for what was to come.

"What the hell are you doing in my office?" asked the voice.

Daiton spun around quickly. Not fast enough to throw him off balance because he was too experienced for that, but with the controlled swiftness of a supple animal.

He was a very ordinary-looking man standing by the door, fiftyish, spectacled, balding, sagging flesh around his neck like a man who has lost weight fast. His casual clothes were well cut, and Fifth Avenue.

Daiton saw immediately that the man had made a bad mistake by closing the door behind him. Perhaps he'd failed to see Daiton until he was inside the room, closing the door automatically from habit. Or maybe he had assumed the intruder was a mirage, a trick of the light.

Daiton felt very calm. He was conscious of his pulse,

but the rhythm was scarcely disturbed. He suddenly realized it had been a long time since he had done any front-line work. Too long. Well, Jo was going to change all that.

He smiled disarmingly, playing it cool.

"Dr. Clements?" he inquired casually.

The doctor stared back at him and a tinge of red flowed up out of the wrinkled folds in his neck, staining his face. He sensed in Daiton's friendliness a retreat, a meekness, a chance to take the offensive.

"I said, what the hell are you doing in my office?" he demanded. His eyes swung across to the filing cabinet. "And what the hell are you doing with my filing cabinet?"

Daiton put Jo's file carefully down on the desk, then shrugged, extending his arms with the palms of his hands turned to the ceiling. The disarming smile remained painted on his face, and he tried to make it look too fixed. The man was being very stupid. One did not question a burglar. Not in New York. One ran or screamed. It was unfortunate, but he had counted on no one coming to the office on a Sunday. And there was nothing he could say to this man. Nothing he could explain. Not about Jo. Not about his being there. That would only betray him, the entire plan would dissolve to nothing. All he could offer the doctor was silence. Permanent silence. And the offer would have to be enforced quickly, because at any moment the man would suddenly realize how foolish he was being, standing there alone, challenging him.

Daiton eased himself forward several steps. He didn't lift his feet, but slid through the deep pile underfoot. He kept the smile firmly in place.

"Central Intelligence, Dr. Clements," he said

smoothly. "I know this looks bad, and I hope you will accept our apologies, but there was certain information we needed urgently from your files."

The color in the doctor's face deepened, and his eyes flickered warily around the room. He placed one foot surreptitiously behind the other in a preparatory running stance, and one hand pawed blindly behind him for the door handle.

"Central Intelligence?" he queried suspiciously.

Daiton shuffled himself forward a few more steps. Hadaffi would not approve of this, but if he let the doctor off, the game would be over before the first move had been played.

"Yes," continued Daiton. "I know we should have contacted you, but this information was vitally urgent for us, Doctor. It simply couldn't wait."

The doctor's fingers located the door handle.

"You have identification?"

"Of course," answered Daiton easily.

He put his hand into his jacket and made as if to fumble for some identification.

"You have no right to break into my office like some ordinary thug off the streets," said Clements. "You can't do that sort of thing. I have my rights. If you wanted something that urgently, all you had to do was ring me at home. I'm in the phone book. All you had to do was ask, and I would have come to the office immediately." He hesitated. "I'm waiting to see your identification," he persisted.

Daiton kept fumbling in his pocket, still moving toward the doctor. There was a break in the doctor's voice that Daiton recognized. Fear. Suddenly felt. Suddenly recognized. Clements didn't believe a word of what he was claiming, now he was stalling until he could extricate himself from the situation. He saw the doctor's hand groping at the door handle. The bird was getting set to fly, the time for pretense was over.

They both came to the same conclusion almost simultaneously. Clements half turned from Daiton as he wrenched the door handle into the opening position, but he'd dallied too long, the other man was too close. Daiton closed the intervening space between himself and the doctor in three quick, lithe strides. Clements had no time to utter a sound. One muscular arm encircled his neck like a steel band, his mouth sprung open like a released trap to emit a scream that died somewhere in his belly, his spectacles slid down over his face and spilled soundlessly to the floor. A frantic spasm of panic took control of his muscles, jerking his body with the violence of an epileptic seizure. The knife came out of Daiton's pocket in one smooth action, and in an instant was planted deep into the doctor's back. The muscular contortions abruptly stopped, a wheezing gurgle rolled out of his throat, then he was dead.

Daiton held him for a moment, leaving the knife embedded until he felt the slack weight of Clements on his arm. He had been a long time out of front-line action, but you never forgot. It was like learning to swim, or ride a bicycle: when the moment came to do it again there was an automatic reflex response.

He jerked the knife out, released his hold, and let the body slide limply to the floor. The doctor sprawled over on his back, taking in a sightless survey of the office ceiling, and a rivulet of blood oozed out of his mouth and dribbled onto the carpet. A few inches from one outstretched hand lay the fallen spectacles, arms drooped down in a neat, waiting fold.

Daiton didn't move for a moment, but stood looking down at the body, expressionless. He felt nothing for the man. The moment of satisfaction he'd experienced from locating Jo's address was gone. It was a bad start. It had to be done, but it meant police, inquiries, all the things it was necessary to avoid at this early stage. He shrugged. Perhaps Hadaffi would regret the killing, but he would approve of Daiton's positive action.

He stirred himself back into action, bent down, and wiped the blood off the knife on the sleeve of the dead man's coat. He put the knife back in his pocket, crossed to the desk, picked up Jo's file, and replaced it in the filing cabinet. He relocked the cabinet, took a handkerchief from his pocket, and began to wipe around the office in an attempt to erase any fingerprints. After a few moments he gave it up with a shrug. He had no criminal record, so how could they trace him. He had one last look around the office, stepped over the dead man without bothering to give him a second glance, and went cautiously out back into the hallway.

He saw no one. Not in the hallway, not in the elevator, not in the foyer. The floor-polishing machine was gone, mute evidence that some other being shared this mausoleum with him, but there was no sound of the polisher operating anywhere. He went swiftly out through the side door, back up the lane, and onto the street. No one took the slightest notice of him.

He strolled casually down Fifth Avenue, his sense of urgency diminished, the murdered man already dismissed from his mind. Some of the lost elation at locating Jo's whereabouts returned, and he whistled softly one of the old brotherhood tunes. He had a cup of coffee on Seventh Avenue, then returned to his room at Sheraton Centre.

He stood for a while, studying his reflection in the mirror, and some niggling doubts about the killing returned. Perhaps it was not good after all to resemble a

famous actor, because it made him too easily remembered. He would shave off the moustache. He nodded
at his own reflection, his mind decided. After it was
done he would contact Nerida through the usual code;
he would need her help to complete the next stage.
Under normal circumstances he would have used Oxley, because it was risky calling Nerida away from
Washington too often. But he had grave doubts about
Oxley now. About his loyalty. Any member who expressed such a strong desire to leave the brotherhood
was suspect, and dangerous to use. Certainly on anything as important as this. He would have to resolve
that situation when Hadaffi arrived in America.

No, Nerida would have to come with him, and it
would be good to see her again, good to feel her body,
good to have sex with her. It was not that long since
she was last in New York, but that had been a rush
visit, and left no time for love. This time it would be
different. He would make sure it was different. It was
unfortunate that duty to the brotherhood forced them
to operate in different parts of the country, and there
was always a risk of them being seen together by someone who might recognize her. Love was one thing, but
duty to the brotherhood came first. So they would have
to be cautious.

October 5, 1982

Daiton flew to Lexington and by prearrangement
met Nerida at the motel. He never forgot how
beautiful she was, and even after a short time, it was
always a fresh joy to him. She was five years younger

than Daiton, but she more than matched him in her ferocious dedication to the cause. Daiton knew the fuel for that dedication lay in her childhood years in the Palestinian camps, although she never mentioned the subject.

She was dark like him, with regular features, long black hair, olive skin, and white, even teeth which she used like a trademark for she seemed to laugh a lot, although Daiton knew there was little humor in the expression. But the flash of her open mouth was like an advertising sign for a sex therapist.

She was not tall, only five feet four inches, and her body was perhaps too thickset, set off by well-shaped legs which seemed a trifle thin for her torso. But if there were slight physical imperfections they were lost in the vitality and energy generated by her personality. Men looked at her black eyes, at her flashing teeth, at her well-formed breasts, and all they wanted was to take her to bed. And if she was good in bed, with a marvelous abandoned sexuality, it was a wise man who remembered her dedication to the brotherhood, because she was equally adept at transporting a man to heaven through a savagely planted knife in his back as through the bliss of his groin.

They greeted each other warily in the foyer of the motel, for there were always prying eyes, even in Lexington, and after the killing in New York Daiton was doubly cautious. He allowed a warm smile, a gentle clasping of hands, a touch, a welcoming gesture. And later in their room he briefed her with quick, impatient efficiency, aroused by the nearness of her, the heavy-bodied scent he knew so well.

She was enraptured at the news of Hadaffi's coming, but he told her nothing of the killing of Clements. She had laid the groundwork for him weeks ago, by her faked visit to the doctor's rooms on Forty-seventh Street, memorizing the layout for him. It was enough for her to know that he believed he had been successful in locating Jo Leica. Or he thought he had. Tomorrow would be the proof of that.

But after the briefing there were other things to prove. That nothing ever changed during their periods of separation. Others might use her body in the cause of the brotherhood, but only for him was there real love, real desire, real passion. Over and over throughout the night she strove to prove with her mouth, and her body, and her hands, that no one else could diminish the passion she felt for Daiton.

And if he failed partially to shut his mind to the other man who had access to her body, it was a weakness from loving her too much.

The next morning he hired a car, and drove at a steady pace out along Highway Seventy-five until they came to the Daniel Boone Parkway. He turned along the Parkway until they reached Manchester, then branched onto the mountain road until he reached Gooseneck. From there he decided he would be navigator, and turned the wheel over to Nerida. She followed the murmured instructions given by Daiton from the map in his lap, and if the passion from the previous night lingered over them like a fragrant perfume they dulled their senses with a firm discipline, for this was important business.

At Wooton they swung right onto the winding road leading to Pine Mountain, and the nerves in Daiton's stomach began to churn with anticipation. Anticipation mingled with indecision. They were so close now, yet he had no idea what he would say to Leica when he found him. How long had it been? Three years? He really didn't want to see Jo, or Brett, not face to face. It would be enough for him just to know they were there, then the rest would be up to Hadaffi.

They stopped in Sylvan for a light lunch and some coffee. They spoke to no one, and no one spoke to them. A young fair girl with a spotty complexion, plump like a mountain melon, served them in the diner with mono-syllabic grunts and brazen curious stares.

They ate in silence, and occasionally Nerida put her food aside to let her fingers stray across the table to rest lightly on Daiton's arm. But he was too deep in his thoughts to respond, and after a while she gave all her concentration to her meal. They finished and paid the spotty girl on the way out, a wordless exchange of money and grunts.

Nerida took the wheel again, and they left the town and wound on into the hills, with Daiton poring over the map. He was looking for a small byroad now, and it was possible that it was not even marked on the map. He had considered asking the plump girl in the diner, but he had hesitated to feed her already obvious curiosity.

It was a beautiful day. A thin haze of clouds hung in the sky like transparent white chiffon, filtering the heat of the sun, and the countryside glowed in the gentle warmth. The tall close-knit pine trees hugging the contours of the mountains shivered in the light breeze, coating the slopes with multiple shades of green. The gradient in front of them increased, and the car responded with an effortless purr.

Daiton lifted his head from the map and glanced around, stroking his fingers impatiently along his upper lip. It was strange to feel no hair there after so many years. The erased moustache had scarcely aroused any comment from Nerida. You don't make love with your moustache, she had flashed at him with her teeth. He smiled absently at the memory. "How much further?" asked Nerida.

He shook his head, and pointed ahead through the windshield.

"There should be a small side road just ahead," he said.

"It is marked on the map?"

He nodded his head affirmatively.

"Yes, I've found it. It shouldn't be far now." He glanced across at her. "Are you getting tired of driving?"

She shook her head without answering. They continued to climb. Daiton glanced out across the panorama of curving hills and forest to his right. There was no other sign of habitation; they could have been the only two people in the country. Jo and Brett had really gone to a lot of trouble to hide themselves. Perhaps they could have stayed hidden forever but for his chance sighting of Jo in New York. And following her to that doctor's office. He wondered who had sent her to New York from somewhere like this isolated part of the world. She'd obviously been having some problem with her pregnancy. Well, that would be nothing compared to the problems she and Brett would have from Hadaffi, if everything worked out as planned.

Nerida was driving slowly, but they almost missed the side road. It was not much more than a track, with a weatherbeaten sign almost covered by the undergrowth. Nerida braked abruptly to a halt, throwing Daiton forward in the seat. She leaned across the steering wheel, and peered uncertainly at the raddled sign.

"Pearidge Road," she murmured.

Daiton threw the map over onto the rear seat, and leaned across her to confirm the name on the sign.

"That's it," he grunted. "That's the one we're looking for."

She slipped the car into reverse, and eased back along the shoulder of the road to obtain a clearer view up the side track. It was deeply rutted, and in some parts almost overgrown.

"It's not very wide, Vilas," she said doubtfully. "Do you think I can drive the car along there?"

Daiton hesitated a moment, then indicated the track with his hand.

"Well, let's see how far we can get. Stay in the center of the track, and see if we can make it up to the crest of that rise. Maybe I can see a house or something from there."

She nodded without conviction, and reversed away and back from the shoulder of the road to give herself enough maneuvering room to turn the big car. She eased it forward cautiously, her foot nervously alternating between brake and accelerator.

"Maybe you should do this," she muttered.

"You're doing fine," he encouraged her.

Ahead of them, running up the track, Daiton could see recent tire tracks imprinted on the dusty gravel surface.

"Someone's been along here very recently," he observed.

Nerida nodded without answering, concentrating on her driving. The car was almost as wide as the road, and the bushes at the verges seemed to resent the disturbance, beating against the sides of the vehicle with an angry swishing sound. They came to just short of the crest, and she braked to a halt and cut the motor.

"The road's narrowing even more, Vilas," she complained. "If we go any further, we're going to find it difficult to get out again."

Daiton looked around, and gave her a curt nod of agreement. They sat for a moment in the car without speaking. Reflections from the surrounding forest quivered in the polished hood of the car. It was very quiet. The breeze riffled at the tops of the trees, and the forest moaned softly. Nerida glanced at him curiously, but Daiton didn't move. Now that the time had arrived, now that the experiment had to be made, the nervous little flickers in his stomach returned, and he struggled for composure. Something like Clements back there in New York he could handle without a tremor; it was real, physical, something you could take hold of, sink a knife into, if that was the way it had to be. But Leica was something totally different. It was grasping at shadows, grappling with apparitions that teased the mind.

He thought back three years to San Francisco and Stanford University. Only he really knew what Leica was capable of achieving, had seen it happen to other people. Maybe it wouldn't be like that for him, maybe Leica would recognize him quickly, see him as a friend perhaps come to offer help, to bring him news, counsel him. They had parted badly, but only because Leica was a fool not to see the value of what Daiton was trying to do.

He levered himself stiffly from the car with arthritic clumsiness and closed the door softly behind him, as if fearful of disturbing the forest. He stooped over and smiled at Nerida through the window, and she smiled back.

"I'll just wander up to the crest and see if I can see a house," he said.

"Good luck, and take care," she answered.

He paused a moment, and studied her solemnly. Her mouth drew back, and the white teeth gleamed at him. She doesn't really understand, she had no idea; he hadn't even known her when he'd worked with Leica, he thought. He'd tried to explain, but it was impossible to those who had never seen it happen.

He walked steadily away from the car, picking his way carefully around the corroded surface of the track, sliding here and there in some loose patches of gravel. He felt he had himself under control now. In some way it was like the business with Clements, because it was something he had to force himself to do. The crest was only fifty yards away, and he reached it quickly, then paused and waved back to Nerida. The road turned sharply right, and down to a small valley. He went around the turn, shutting the car from sight, and went only another hundred yards before he saw the house. He felt the queasiness come flooding back to his stomach again. It looked like the sort of house that Leica would live in. And Jo. A mushy picture-postcard structure of two stories, white window frames, and vertical earth-colored boards. It had some of the fairy-tale sense of unreality that he associated with Leica. Set back off the road amid the trees, in perfect harmony with the forest, as if it had been planted there and grown like a natural form.

He slowed his pace to a crawl. The surface of the track was even worse now, badly water-scoured with deep scars each side. And narrower. The trees on either side leaned forward protectively, touching overhead to form a green cathedral. The tire tracks still showed ahead of him, running up toward the house. In a carport beside the house he could see what looked like an old Mustang coupé. He brought himself to a halt, and stood watching the house uncertainly. The atmosphere of serenity came to him with the strength of a powerful aroma. Was this where Leica had fled to cut himself off from the world, to cut himself off from reality? Now the world had need of him, and his peculiar talents. The world of the brotherhood.

He stood watching for some time, deciding on his method of approaching Leica. Because now he was finally here, there was no time for guesses. He had to be absolutely certain Leica was there.

Something buzzed past his ear, and he shook his head impatiently. It buzzed again, this time much closer, almost into his eye. He glanced down at his arm, and saw it was a bee, nuzzling into a fold in the sleeve of his jacket. He hated bees; he'd been stung once on the head, as a boy, and had never forgotten the painful experience. He shook his arm vigorously to dislodge the insect, but instead it was joined by another, and then another, coming from the direction of the house, until there were enough to form a small swarm on his arm. The shaking of his arm had no effect at all, and he hesitated to brush at them with his free hand for fear of being stung. Then the air around him seemed to be full of them, tiny angry bullets, darting about seeking a target, the aroused sound of their buzzing filling his ears. He began to panic, backing away from the house. He broke into a stumbling act, struggling to free himself from his jacket, hoping they would stay with the jacket and leave him in peace.

Then they came down on him like a cloud, a swarming, stinging nightmare. His mouth flew open in an involuntary scream, and they swarmed into the orifice, injecting their venom into the walls, stabbing agonizingly at the tender flesh of his tongue. They thrust at his tightly clenched eyelids, tiny wings beating against his lashes, voracious for the watery softness of his eyeballs. They beat at each other for the sensitive tenderness of his eardrums, filling his head with a sound like the high-pitched scream of a buzz saw. They crammed into his nostrils as if determined on suicidal suffocation, choosing death as a means to extend his agony. He'd never known such pain, it was like the thrust of hundreds of sharply pointed needles, all administered simultaneously, and he blundered back; back down the road in panic-stricken blindness, his hands stretched out in front of him. He didn't know how long he ran. He fell, he struggled to his feet, he fell again, he smashed into a tree, the world grew gray, then black, the needles less sharp, then he fell for the last time, praying for death, and lost consciousness.

When he opened his eyes he was lying on the road with his head in Nerida's lap. The smile was gone from her face now, replaced with troubled concern, and she was stroking his forehead, watching his face anxiously. He moved his arms, and felt his fingers stirring at the coarse gravel surface of the road. He lifted his head and saw the car only a few yards behind Nerida. He could feel no pain, no agonizing stings, see no bees. He moved his tongue warily around in his mouth, but there was no discomfort, no swelling.

"My God, what happened to you?" asked Nerida soberly.

He levered himself up on his elbows, and stared around at the surroundings. The breeze pulled out of the trees and washed refreshingly over his face.

"The bees," he muttered. His throat felt dry, and the words cracked with the effort of speaking.

Nerida sat forward, and helped to lever him into a sitting position.

"What bees, Vilas? I didn't see any bees. You came running down the road screaming like a madman, and falling over every few yards. What on earth happened to you up there? You've been unconscious for nearly ten minutes. I didn't know what to do. I couldn't lift you into the car, and I was frightened to go on up the road for fear of what you'd found."

He didn't answer. He sat forward with his arms resting on his upraised knees, shoulders hunched, trying to quell the sudden throbbing in his head. Then he pawed at his face, searching for swelling, for punctured flesh. But his skin felt as smooth and unruptured as when he had shaved that morning. He lifted his hands, and submitted them to examination, but they were the same. There was no sign of any pain-induced swelling from beestings.

"How does my face look?" he asked haltingly.

Nerida looked at him questioningly.

"What do you mean?"

"Exactly what I'm asking. How does it look?"

She shrugged. "Fine. You're very pale, but your face looks just the same. How did you expect it to be changed?"

"No marks? No swelling?"

"Vilas, there's nothing," she assured him. "What are you talking about?"

That was enough. He knew now. He held out a hand to Nerida, and waved it impatiently about in the air.

"That's all I wanted to know. Help me up, Nerida. I feel as weak as hell."

She struggled with her small stature to help his bulky physique into a standing position. He was unsteady on his feet, and he stood for a moment, leaning on her to test his balance. Then laboriously, like an aged man, he began to brush the gravel from his clothes. His jacket was at her feet, and she picked it up and helped him shrug it back on. He knew all right. The bastard. It was the first time he had personally had the experience of what Leica could do, and it would remain in those special recesses of his mind reserved for traumatic nightmares for a long time. Perhaps forever. But Leica had betrayed himself. There was no one else in the world who could have done that to his mind. He lived in that house all right. And so did Jo. Hadaffi would be pleased, because now the plan could evolve from speculation to reality. His nightmare was over, but Leica's was just about to begin.

October 20, 1982

Frank Carmody was in a sullen mood. He was due at the White House for an appointment with the President at seven thirty in the morning, and it was already seven forty-five when he turned off Wisconsin Avenue onto M Street. It was difficult to justify being late when Georgetown was so close. His boss, Martin Schyler, head of Central Intelligence, would not be amused. Schyler was much too preoccupied these days with worrying if Carmody was trying to edge him out of his job, and it made life difficult for Carmody. Perhaps Schyler was justified in his suspicions, but it meant that every minor infringement by Carmody was blown up into some drama. Like this morning. There was a briefing session with the President at eight thirty, and Schyler always liked to have his head crammed with every minute detail before he went into a briefing.

He shuttled the car about through the traffic like a nervous rabbit, and received a cacophony of blasting car horns from both directions for his audacious driving. He took a deep breath, and squeezed the car back into line to the accompaniment of another horn blast. He shrugged with resignation. Schyler would have to wait. It was another thing about the Middle East, and surely there was little that was fresh to communicate about that constantly seething dish of maggots.

But Schyler was always apprehensive about being tripped up by the President on some minor detail he wouldn't be able to answer. So every microscopic detail was always dissected right up until the last moment before the briefing. The last thing Schyler would want would be to have to defer to Carmody during the meeting. In his present nervous state he would see the President as interpreting that as a sign of incompetence.

It wasn't that Carmody had some great master plan to take over from Schyler, but after all the man was only a stopgap head of Intelligence. The sudden resignation of the former chief had taken them all by surprise, and at the time Schyler had seemed the only alternative to the President. But the appointment had come late in Schyler's career. Too late. He was aging. And while others had seen it as a temporary appointment, Schyler was savagely determined to make it permanent. By every means possible.

He was a man in his mid-sixties. Carmody was thirty-eight and cleverer than Schyler. It wasn't an ego-inspired judgment, but he knew he was. And he found it difficult to conceal, so that his every action was examined through paranoid blinkers, and interpreted accordingly.

His lateness this morning would probably be seen as

part of some plan to undermine Schyler with the President. Which certainly wasn't true. Schyler had nothing to do with his sullen mood, or his lateness, or the fact that he had slept badly last night, and overslept this morning.

And it was so childish it infuriated him. It was Angela. He'd been married eleven years, divorced three, but he'd never loved anyone like he loved Angela. Six months ago he'd been looking for an assistant, and she'd been recommended by someone at the Treasury. He hadn't even been considering a female appointment, but the recommendation had been so high, he'd decided to interview her. Over Schyler's objections.

The sparks had started to fly from the moment their eyes met. Singeing sparks. You could almost smell the aroma of scorching flesh. An overwhelming sexuality that almost smothered him. His immediate reaction had been not to hire her, not with those sort of distracting looks, but under questioning her intelligence proved as sharp as her appearance, and her security clearance was approved. So he took her on with a niggling sense of guilty apprehension, rationalizing that her looks might help him around the Agency anyway.

She was superb in the job. She could second-guess him almost before he had the original thought. She grasped at details that he found boring and time consuming, and fed them back to him with the accuracy of a computer. And she loved him. He could rationalize forever, but he knew those preliminary sparks would generate enough heat to start an inferno.

It broke all his rules about interoffice relationships, yet surprisingly it seemed to work. In the office and around Washington it was all efficiency and dedication, but at night, in bed, at their apartment, it was sexual ferocity at a level he had never experienced before. She engulfed him. She raised him to her level, to heights of sexual athleticism of which he had not believed himself capable.

When she was there. She had family problems. A mother and father in New York always ill to the point of dying. Or so they claimed. It would send her flying off to New York at a moment's notice, sometimes for several days at a time, and it infuriated him. It was childish, stupid, and selfish, but he couldn't seem to help himself. He tried to conceal his feelings from her, but not with a great deal of success. It was bad enough to miss her at the office, but at home it was somehow more acute. He knew she tried to make up for it by the intensity of her lovemaking when she returned, and that only filled him with guilt. He guessed deep down he was insecure about holding on to a woman like her, suspicious that maybe there wasn't a mother and father, but another lover.

Why couldn't she just leave it all to the hospital, or the doctors, or whatever? Or bring them to Washington?

She had left yesterday morning, promising to be back by night time, but she hadn't shown. Not all night. And no phone call. So he had drunk coffee, roamed about the apartment, watched some dreary old movies, thought about Schyler, tried to study the Orloff file, tossed around on a lonely bed, then finally dropped off to sleep only to miss his wake-up call. If he wanted to commit himself to a deep analysis of the relationship he guessed that through all her sexual passion there was something deep in her personality that he had failed to reach yet. Something very private, very secretive, that he was not supposed to recognize. That frustrated him also. So maybe his sullen attitude was only a reflection of his suppressed insecurity about her. He rejected the thought, squeezing it out of his mind. He caught part of his reflection in the rearview mirror, and grimaced. He wasn't such a bad-looking man. Dark, with a few tinges of early gray around the sides, regular features with perhaps his nose a trifle long, over six feet tall, articulate, a law degree, a comer. It wasn't a bad package. Maybe a little too ambitious, a shade too ruthless in his climbing. But that was an inheritance from his father. Get on, get on, get a degree, get the right contacts, push, push, climb, climb. Well, Christ, that's what it was all about, the only thing he had to watch was not to get taken off by a heart attack at forty-eight, like his father. That was a strange funeral. Lots of acquaintances paying their last respects, but no friends. He had tried to think who the friends were, but no names had come to his mind. Plus the only thing he had seen in his mother's face was a strange expression of relief. That had infuriated him. She owed him something more than relief. It had made him realize that the only influence his mother had ever had over him was bearing him. And that had ceased the moment he had freed himself from her womb. Somehow his memory of her was a nebulous grayness, a shape that fed and clothed him, almost reduced to transparency by the force of his father's personality.

He shrugged at the memories, because they answered none of his questions about Angela. Why he should be so hung up over one woman, even if she was only twenty-four, and the most sexually dynamic beautiful creature he'd ever fucked? Well, he guessed that was part of the answer. He was flattered and insecure, and deliriously happy, and sullen, all at one time.

He could always think about trying to go back to
Nora. He smiled sourly at the memory of his former
wife. Even after three years there was still a bleep of
anger signaling in his mind. It had been the classic old-
style middle-class relationship, progressing from high
school groping romance, to youthful marriage, to busy
young man on the move, really moving, running, and a
wife who couldn't understand the frantic haste.

Couldn't see it was all for her, only felt neglect, boredom, frustration. And she made no effort to keep up, to
run with him, to push, to urge. Made no effort, socially,
intellectually. But for all that, he couldn't let her go.
He rationalized loyalty and responsibility, but there
were no children, it went deeper than that. Emotionally,
he needed her. Needed someone to love. Someone to be
there, just there, even if there seemed little common
ground where they could meet.

The trouble with you, Frank, is that your father set
fire to your ass, and you're going to give yourself ulcers
trying to run away from the flames. Give her credit, she
had a colorful way of expressing herself, but Christ, that
sort of remark set fire to his resentment, because he
knew it was intuitively accurate, and he always cut back
at her with an answer implying intellectual inferiority.
Educational inferiority. Which was a shit of a thing to
do. She'd given up her chances for him, and she was
actually as smart as hell, it was simply that she'd never
disciplined her mind to any direction. So she laughed
at what she termed his toadying, sneered at his fastidious wardrobe, the acquired gourmet expertise. The maneuvering and acquisition of contacts was an inexplicable game to her, and his irritation for her naivety was
matched by her contempt for what she mistook as his
shallowness. So the relationship frosted over, turned
brittle, and cracked apart.

Yet he still couldn't let go, so she did it for him, packed a bag, and informed him crisply from the door that her lawyer would be in touch.

It was crazy, they had nothing, yet he felt as if part of him had been physically amputated. Yet he'd always had that trait about his possessions, human or inanimate. Never let go. Hang on. Run, pursue, acquire, but never let go what you'd rightfully won. That was the way of the world, the way of Washington; he hadn't made the rules, but by Christ, he'd made them work for him. And now Angela filled his emotional needs like an overflowing cup, and he'd never let her go either.

He forced his mind back to his driving, and the displeasure he would encounter from Schyler.

The traffic had dispersed enough for him to cut up Seventeenth Street at a reasonable clip, and he was parked by five minutes after eight. Schyler's car was already there as he expected, and he squealed his tires as he swung the car into the vacant space alongside.

By eight after ten he was in the small office reserved for Schyler's use at the White House; Schyler wasn't there. But Angela was, lounging on the settee at the side of the mahogany desk, an envelope in her hand.

He dropped his briefcase down on the floor, and gawked at her. Her legs were crossed with a brief flash of upper thigh, and even that was enough to set the nerve ends in his groin tingling with schoolboy anticipation. She shook her long dark hair, and her beautiful teeth flashed a welcoming smile.

"Aren't you glad to see me, Frank?" she smiled.

He wanted to put his arms around her, to kiss her, to hit her even. But nothing like that ever happened in the office. Not ever. He forced a smile.

"Hell, of course I am, Angela. It's quite a surprise to see you here, that's all. When did your plane get in?"

"Early this morning. It was too late to go to the apartment, so I took a cab to the office." She waved the envelope in her hand toward him. "This was on your desk, and it seemed important enough to bring it over."

She rose from the settee with all the grace and poise he knew so well, and held out the envelope to him. "You can see it's marked for your urgent attention."

He stepped toward her and she moved forward to meet him, close enough until their bodies brushed. It was the closest contact he could ever remember her making during office hours.

"I missed you," she whispered.

The rancor in his mind dissolved with the rapidity of hot steam. "And I missed you," he muttered.

He held himself there for a moment, enjoying the feel of her, then he backed away, and indicated with his hand toward the desk.

"Where's Martin?" he asked.

She grinned at him.

"He's stepped out for a moment. There seemed to be a little steam coming out of his ears."

Carmody grimaced wryly.

"I thought there might be. I'm late. Seems like I missed my wake-up call this morning."

She arched her eyebrows at him.

"We'll have to do something about that, won't we?" she murmured.

He smiled back at her uncertainly. She was making up for last night, but he wasn't used to her in heat around the office. He decided to break the mood, and turned his attention to the envelope. Special delivery from New York. He tapped the envelope reflectively against his chin, debating whether to open it before the briefing.

"How are your parents?" he asked casually.

"They think my father has cancer," she answered soberly.

"I'm sorry," he said. "When will they know?"

He came to a decision, and slit open the envelope.

"In a few days, I guess," she said.

He nodded absently, wishing he could appear more sympathetic.

The letter was code-named "Moccasin." The undercover agent in New York. He'd been expecting to hear from him. Angela seated herself back on the settee, watching him with a half smile on her lips while he absorbed the contents. He read it through several times, and let a soft-draw whistle escape from his mouth.

"I take it that it's something important?" asked Angela.

Carmody put the letter slowly back in the envelope, and nodded slowly. The "Moccasin project" was something between him and Schyler, and he'd never discussed it with Angela, and this was no place to do it.

"Very important," he muttered.

She waited, still with the half smile on her face, but he didn't elaborate.

"Something for the President to see?" she persisted.

He nodded soberly.

"It certainly is. And as quickly as possible."

"Then I did the right thing in bringing it over."

He smiled at her.

"You know you did."

"Anything I can help with?"

He pursed his lips thoughtfully before answering. He didn't want to offend her, he took her into many of his confidences, but he couldn't risk breaking Moccasin's cover. The fewer people who knew, the better. "We'll talk about it later," he concluded lamely.

She grinned at him with an impish expression.

"Promise I won't tell," she mocked him gently.

He shifted uncomfortably on his feet, but didn't answer her. She looked incredibly lovely. She had on a gray suit he hadn't seen before, and tan textured boots that enhanced her legs. In between coping with cancer she must have done some shopping on Fifth Avenue. She had the darkest eyes he'd ever seen on a woman.

Schyler bustled into the room, and stopped short when he saw Carmody. He was a large, thickset man, about Carmody's height, but running into fat. A large head squatted firmly on military shoulders, heavy jowled, bushy brows like a protective cover over surprisingly blue eyes. A tiny nose seemed somehow incongruous, almost lost amid the other craggy formations in his face. Smiles did not flow easily into the arrangement of lines and fattening contours, and he was left with a semipermanent expression of fierce concentration. His clothes had been bought before the onset of overweight, and he refused to face the reality of his thickening body, so he always gave the impression of wearing a size too small. He was either approaching, on, or beyond the age of sixty, but there was no visible sign of any slackening desire to hold on to his position.

He turned the expression of fierce concentration on Carmody, and consulted his watch, raising his arm in an exaggerated fashion.

"For Chrissake, where have you been, Frank? We're due in with the President in a few minutes. We agreed to meet here at seven thirty."

Carmody spread his hands apologetically.

"I'm sorry, Martin, it was just one of those things. I don't know what happened, but I just didn't get my wake-up call."

Carmody faced Schyler's scowl with bland innocence. He could almost hear the wheel clicking over in his superior's brain, and he waited for the subtle innuendos, the hints of disloyalty. Failing to keep appointments wasn't his usual thing. He couldn't recall the last time it had happened. Angela cleared her throat delicately, and Schyler glared past Carmody at the beautiful body draped on the settee. Whatever he was going to say, he changed his mind, strode across to the desk, and picked up a sheaf of papers.

"Perhaps you should buy a new alarm clock," he muttered in passing.

He paused in front of the desk, the papers tucked under his arm. "There are some details here concerning the Minoud initiative I think we should have gone over first. There are some fresh reports of an assassination attempt that is in the pipeline now, and could be financed by other sources outside the PLO."

Carmody twitched his shoulders with irritation.

"Martin, we've been all over that for the last few days. There is nothing more I can say, except to agree with your own thoughts."

"That's beside the point. These things have to be talked through again and again. That way it's possible sometimes to get a fresh insight."

Carmody shook his head wearily. Last night's lack of sleep was going to make it a long, long day.

"Well, let's put it to the President, Martin. Let's see if we can get a fresh insight from him." He paused, and looked down at the letter in his hand. "And there's something else, Martin. This letter came to me this morning, and it's bloody important. I think we should discuss it with the President at this meeting."

Schyler looked blankly at the letter.

"Is it on the agenda?" he asked.

"No, it isn't, but I think we should include it."

"Is it to do with the Minoud initiative?"

"Well no, but . . ."

"The repercussions?"

"Fuck it, no, but . . ."

Schyler shrugged and bustled past Carmody toward the door. Carmody could see he was going to steam for the rest of the day over his lateness.

"Then we haven't got time to discuss it now, Frank. It'll have to be brought up at a later date."

"It's a communication from Moccasin, and it won't wait," said Carmody determinedly.

Schyler didn't break his stride, but went out through the door like a train with its throttle jammed open.

"Then I think we should discuss it first," he cast back over his shoulder. "Come on, I don't want to keep the President waiting."

He left Carmody standing with his mouth open. He snapped his lips shut with a gesture of determined defiance, stuffed the letter into his suit pocket, and shot a bleak glance toward Angela.

"Christ," he grunted sourly.

Angela smiled back at him. She knew Carmody would buck Schyler over the letter, and the confrontation would be interesting.

"Good luck," she said. "Do you want me to wait here, or shall I go back to the office?"

"No, you go, and I'll see you there later." He raised his hand in an exaggerated gesture of farewell and sidled toward the door in Schyler's wake.

"If you hear an explosion from the President's office, you'll know what's happened," he grinned.

The President was as usual affable, attentive, courteous, and capable of making shrewd assessments of the material under discussion. He knew Schyler, knew he was capable of half-truths, evasions, and deception if he could get away with it. Schyler gave the standing of the CIA in the Washington power game a high priority, and if that clashed with the national interest, then sometimes the CIA came first.

But President Manningham knew his staff, knew how to get the best results out of them. Some men got their best results from a mixture of bullying and fear, but he had a much more subtle understanding of the human animal that secured much more effective results. A tactician, a negotiator, a numbers man, a superb political manipulator. Plus roots humble enough to make the people feel as one with him. Onetime Marine, onetime law student, onetime corporation lawyer, now-time elected representative as the nation's "finger on the button" man.

He listened carefully to Carmody, he deferred courteously to Schyler, and he missed nothing. He advised, he sought advice, he made judgments, and in most things he calculated in the context of the voting public, and how many votes each decision would bring him in the coming election. If it sometimes seemed an exercise in cynicism to Carmody, then he had to remind himself that he was involved in a cynical business, that votes meant power, and without power nothing was possible.

Occasionally when he stirred restlessly in his chair he

could feel the letter in his pocket, and he knew when the right moment came he was going to bring it to the President's attention. Schyler was going to blow a fuse, especially after his lateness foul-up, but it would serve the impatient bastard right for being pigheaded.

It took an hour, and a pause when it seemed that everything had been discussed, then Carmody seized the chance and took the letter from his pocket. The action caught the attention of both Schyler and the President, and Carmody saw a light crimson abruptly brighten his superior's face.

The President stared curiously at the letter.

"Do you have something else, Frank?" he asked. He glanced at his watch. "My next appointment is almost due."

"It's probably something we can discuss in another context, Mr. President," interjected Schyler hastily.

Carmody directed his eyes toward the President, ignoring Schyler.

"Unfortunately it's something I haven't had a chance to discuss with Martin, Mr. President, because this letter only came into my hands just before our meeting. But I think it's so important, we should discuss it if possible."

The President sensed the tension between the two men, and glanced quizzically at Schyler. The Intelligence chief sat ramrod in his chair, staring at Carmody, his mouth set down in a tight line that blotted out all lip formation. One day, thought the President, in the not very distant future, it will be Carmody in charge of briefing me on Intelligence, and it would be unwise to disturb the coming relationship. He smiled disarmingly at Schyler.

"If Frank is so disturbed about something, perhaps

we should listen for a few moments, eh, Martin?" he cajoled.

Schyler nodded stiffly, the color still in his face.

"As you wish, Mr. President," he muttered.

The President nodded for Carmody to proceed.

"This information comes to us from one of our best undercover men, Mr. President, and I would like to read it to you."

The President nodded agreement, and Carmody cleared his throat dryly, and proceeded to read in a slow, deliberate monotone.

"I have made further contact with the source as discussed with you previously, and the payment has been made. I have no doubts that the following information is accurate. Hadaffi, the terrorist leader, has entered the United States, as of Wednesday the sixteenth of October, but the informant does not know his whereabouts.

The informant is certain that he is here to organize an intensive terrorist campaign, to be carried out within the United States, although he does not know what form the terrorism will take. Hadaffi evidently has some plan for a form of terrorist activity which he believes will be more successful in America than in Europe.

The informant fears for his life, and obtained the information at great risk. He wishes to break with the organization, but needs more money. For a further payment he will try and obtain a description of Hadaffi's present appearance, plus his location, and some details of the form the terrorism is to take. If the payment is high enough I believe he may be persuaded to give us the names of those heading the organization in this country, and we may conceivably catch them all in one net.

I am proceeding on these lines through the usual funding process."

There was a prolonged silence. The President placed his hands in his lap, interlocked his fingers, and studied them solemnly.

"You can personally vouch for the credibility of the undercover agent concerned?" he asked Carmody.

"The best, Mr. President. He has kept me informed at all times. The agent first obtained a lead overseas that a branch of the terrorist organization was operating in this country, and followed it to New York. He has been skillful enough to make contact with a man within the organization prepared to inform for a price. I suspect the information that a man like Hadaffi has slipped into the country is as much a surprise to him, as to us."

"Has the FBI been informed?"

"We thought it best not to confuse the operation, Mr. President," put in Schyler blandly. "The information first came to the notice of Central Intelligence and at this delicate stage we thought it best to keep it within as small a circle as possible."

The President toyed with the thought for a moment. The information foreshadowed great potential danger to the electorate, and he wouldn't want anything disturbed by interservice rivalries. He leaned back in his chair and stared at the ceiling, as if seeking answers in the configurations of the decorated cornice.

"Hadaffi," he murmured. "That butcher. It's terrifying to think that someone like that is loose in the country." He turned to Schyler. "You knew about this, Martin?"

"Not about this last communication, Mr. President,"

interjected Carmody hastily. "The organization of the undercover agents is my responsibility. But certainly Martin knew the course our agent was following."

"You certainly did the right thing in raising it straightaway, Frank," said the President gravely.

"I guess we have to take into account the credibility of a paid informer," grunted Schyler sourly.

"If this agent is as reliable as Frank says, then I think some action is vitally necessary, Martin," said the President testily.

Schyler saw that he had stepped out onto soggy ground, and scrambled back for a firmer footing.

"I certainly agree, Mr. President," he added hastily. "I was merely pointing out that we don't want to create a panic situation. If this information was to become public it could bring air traffic in the country to a standstill."

"If that's what Hadaffi has in mind," said Carmody.

"I thought that's the sort of thing we could expect, Frank," said the President. "You think he may have something else in mind? Maybe the kidnapping of industrial leaders?"

Carmody spread his hands.

"I would only be guessing, Mr. President. But our agent seems to think it may be a totally new form of terrorism. Something we haven't considered as a possibility."

The President's fingers pawed uncertainly at his mouth, and his brow furrowed into deep lines of concentration.

"Martin, you're right about not creating a panic situation, but we should certainly warn airline security that we suspect a special threat may be building, and they should double their precautions." He paused, musing, his face deeply troubled. "Frank, is there any photograph at all of this man Hadaffi in existence that we could circulate, no matter what the quality? We don't have to say who he is, merely that he is urgently wanted for questioning on a criminal charge."

"It may be useless if Hadaffi has changed his appearance dramatically," grunted Schyler.

The lines on the President's forehead cut deeper furrows, and the corner of his mouth twitched with annoyance. Carmody read the signals and grinned inwardly. Schyler was having difficulty controlling his chagrin, and his mouth was pushing him out onto a defeatist's ledge.

"There must be limits to what a man can do with his appearance, Martin," he said curtly. "Is there a photograph or not?"

Carmody cleared his throat. "We have a blow-up of a small section of a shot taken of Hadaffi in a group in Iran. The photographer was later murdered and the film destroyed, but one small print survived. The blow-up lacks detail, but it's better than nothing."

"Then distribute copies where you think they will be most effective, Frank," said the President. "And take any other measures you think might be helpful in running this man down. A man like Hadaffi is capable of creating chaos in the country, and with an election due soon I don't intend to allow that to happen." He paused. "Within a small coterie I think this information should be given to our other enforcement agencies," he added heavily. "We need all the help we can get."

There was a pause. Schyler cleared his throat disagreeably, and charged in over rocky ground again.

"With due respect, Mr. President, I think that would create more problems than it would solve. It's our baby, and I think we should handle it. If you want, we can let the other . . . agencies . . . merely think it is another criminal wanted for questioning."

The President opened and shut his mouth several times. He glared at Schyler. "We'll let it stand, and review the situation within forty-eight hours," he gritted. He paused for effect. Carmody knew he was letting them know that there were political implications involved for him, and if they didn't fix it, then he would get someone else who would.

"We may receive another communication from our undercover man by then," put in Carmody soothingly.

"I hope so, Frank," grunted the President. "I also want you to handle this personally." He turned abruptly to Schyler. "I think that might be a good idea, Martin. Frank is in touch with the undercover man, and I think he should act directly. We're going to need some quick decisions, and I wouldn't want the process to get snowed under by any administrative tangles." He turned back to Carmody, and nodded curtly. "Right, Frank?"

Carmody nodded back wordlessly. He could almost feel the heat simmering from Schyler's direction. His heart bumped uncomfortably. If he could nail Hadaffi before he did any damage, then anything was possible. Schyler's job. Any job he wanted. But it would leave him hanging by his ankles if he failed. Maybe it would be safer to drag Schyler back into the mire, and share the responsibility. The thought stayed in his mind, refusing to transmit to his tongue. No, the hell with it. It had all the risks of a shortcut through thorns, but it was worth the chance.

"I'm sure that's the best way to handle it, aren't you, Martin?" asked the President.

It was more of a blunt statement than a question, and it left Schyler no room to maneuver.

Schyler nodded agreement, his jowls quivering.

"Of course, an excellent idea, Mr. President," he choked.

The President rose abruptly to his feet, brushed nervously at a few loose strands of hair, and consulted his watch.

"I'm overdue for my next appointment, and I wouldn't want to give anyone the impression that we've got some insoluble problem on our hands in here."

The other two men rose with the President, and he shook hands warmly with them both, Schyler first, then Carmody.

"I have every confidence you can resolve this, Frank," he effused. "I want you to keep in constant touch. A daily report on your progress. If you strike any problem that you consider might require an interpretation on policy, then don't hesitate to consult me." He hesitated, fingers to his chin, pondering if there was anything else to add. "I will have to take some people into my confidence, but I'll leave it as long as possible, hopefully when we have something more concrete on Hadaffi." He extended his arms outward in an impatient, shepherding gesture. "Thank you, gentlemen, now I have to go."

Carmody and Schyler strode back to the office enveloped in a poisonous silence. Carmody scanned his mind in an effort to find the right word to penetrate the atmosphere. He was sure that Schyler thought what had happened in the President's office was part of a carefully conceived plan to discredit him. Fuck him, it had just happened that way. It wasn't his fault if Schyler had made an idiot of himself with the President. In any case he was certain he could handle this thing over the terrorist better than Schyler, and obviously, so did the President. But he would still have to work with Martin, defer to him in some things, because after all he still controlled the Agency. It was a final thought that at last activated his tongue.

"I thought we might grab some lunch over at the Jockey Club later, Martin, and talk this thing over," he ventured tentatively.

He put special emphasis on the "thing," so that Martin would know that it was their relationship he wanted to discuss as much as Hadaffi.

"I didn't think you would have any time for lunch today, with all you've got to do," observed Schyler tartly.

Carmody swallowed, and tried again.

"I can have all the preliminary work done by then, and I should have time for lunch," he said, with forced brightness. "It might be productive for both of us, Martin."

Schyler didn't answer. They came to the office door, and the big man paused, with his fingers resting on the handle.

"I'll get on back to the Agency, and see you at lunch," Carmody tried again.

Schyler looked squarely into his face, and the nostrils in his small nose distended as if Carmody had just expelled the most evil-smelling fart in history.

"Go fuck yourself, Frank," he said quietly.

He went through the door and shut it firmly in Carmody's face.

Early morning over Pine Mountain had given all the promise of a fine, sunny day, but a bank of gray clouds had rolled in from the west like a snowball gathering momentum, and by noon the sky was the color of slate. The wind increased in strength, swirling over the pine-encrusted slopes, rolling the branches back and forth like breaking green waves. Intermittent showers began to fall, spattering against the roof of the car, and it gave Hadaffi a comforting feeling.

He glanced at Daiton, but his companion was lost in his own thoughts, staring out across the mountain as if hypnotized by the gyrations of the wind-beaten pines.

"Are you sure she has to return this way?" he asked quietly.

Daiton didn't turn his head to reply, but nodded slowly.

"It's the only way," he answered with assurance.

Hadaffi tipped his head with a gesture of satisfaction, crossed his arms in front of him, and shrugged down into the seat. He glanced down the road. They were well placed, mid-point on a wide curve of the road, with the car reversed into a small culvert, almost hidden from any passing traffic. For now he was totally reliant on Daiton.

He was dark like Daiton, not as tall, but broader, with wide powerful shoulders. He was difficult to recognize now for those who had never seen him without a heavy beard. It brought his features into sharper focus, the hawklike nose, the wide, thick-lipped mouth, the small dark eyes, never still, never trusting, always wary. He was older than Daiton by at least twelve years and his hair was thinning in front, with tufts of gray-streaked color surrounding his ears.

He had been a gregarious child until he had been forced to accompany his parents, two older brothers, and a sister into the Palestinian camps. When he was ten his mother succumbed to tuberculosis. Grief shadowed his smile, but in 1952 when his father and older brother failed to return from an Israel raid, the smile vanished, never to return. He was sullen, unapproachable, vengeful. If the world was determined to give him no justice, then he would make his own laws, and administer them. He had a quick mind, a talent for leadership, and an avid appetite for knowledge. At fourteen they taught him how to handle a submachine gun, and at fifteen he murdered his first Jewish family. A man, his wife, and three children. He felt nothing. He sprayed the room with bullets until they collapsed into blood-soaked bundles, and nothing stirred in his belly except hate. He knew the history of their persecution, but he was only concerned with his own. The only thing the world really understood and respected was violence. At sixteen he fought in the 1956 war, and was wounded. His remaining brother was killed.

He put aside two years of his life to try and heal the wounds to his body and his soul, and his mind. His body responded well, as did his mind, but there was no soul to be found. No humanity, no compassion, no love. He read Marx, Engels, and Lenin. He admired Stalin for his unswerving ruthlessness, and at eighteen he went to Moscow, to become one of their most diligent students. At twenty they sent him back, convinced they had forged a loyal tool that would be responsive to their every wish. They were wrong; he was too clever for that, he hated too fiercely to be anyone's tool, and cunningly he used the Moscow connection for his own purposes. Guns, intelligence, organization.

When he returned, his sister had married a Jew. It took three months for him to track her down, and listen patiently to her pleading for tolerance, and love, and understanding. They were words that had no meaning for him, words that had been exorcised from his vocabulary. He shot her in the head, three times, then went looking for her husband, but he never found him.

Discipline was imperative, and even one's own blood was not exempt.

In the sixties he created the brotherhood, and expanded its activities into the international field. Talking was useless, negotiation was weakness, violence and terror were the only possible options. Let the fools spout their meaningless platitudes in the United Nations; he knew that terror was the only thing they really understood. Assassination, hijacking, kidnapping, intimidation. He was a brilliant organizer, an awesome leader. An aura grew around him that inspired all those who responded to his call, because he was able to transmit to them his total disregard for death. The individual was expendable, only a temporary tool. What mattered was the brotherhood, not life or death.

That was his ultimate weapon. To those in the West imbued with a fanatical impulse to hang on to life, the sight of men with an equally fanatical impulse to destroy their lives in their cause was unnerving. Unnatural. Terrifying.

In the seventies things did not go well for Hadaffi. The capitalist countries fought the hijacking with a strength of backbone he did not believe they possessed. There were bad moments. Entebbe. The Sadat initiative. Only his hatred kept him going, because it was now part of his permanent emotional structure. Not in an explosive, irrational form, because to people who met him he was reserved, quietly spoken, introverted. But his hatred was like a built-in food supply, nourishing his strength, directing his organizing ability, steadying his killing hand. And it kept his emotional level pointed in the right direction. If there were sexual needs, then they were to be met coldly, without involvement.

In the late seventies he became concerned that the terrorist movement was fragmenting around the world, and he brought his organizing ability to the fore to try and correct the situation. The Bader Meinhoff group in Germany, the Japanese Red Army, he embraced them all to draw them together in one tight, well-knit unit. There had been some resistance from some of their own, small-minded, petty leaders, but it had been comparatively simple to kill them. The brotherhood had been killing for a considerably longer time, and they did it more efficiently. All that mattered was the existence of one unified force to confront the world.

And then Daiton's letter. The mind raced, the nerve ends tingled at the enormous possibilities. America. To bring this giant to its political knees would be the coup of the century. He had wanted to believe Daiton about this man Leica, he believed him enough to enter America with forged credentials, a risk he would not have contemplated six months ago. He wondered how many it might be necessary to kill to achieve the miracle.

This was Hadaffi. This was the man waiting on the road outside the town of Sylvan on Pine Mountain. Waiting for Jo Leica.

When the examination was completed Jo settled herself down in front of Dr. Weber's desk, and waited for him to complete writing on her card. He finished the last word with a theatrical flourish, and laid his pen carefully down on the desk. He smiled, and peered at her over his glasses.

He looked like someone who had been plucked out of a cliché television series about a country doctor. That's exactly what he was.

Sylvan's one and only doctor, a specialist in everything from an ingrown toenail to a coronary, but certainly no hack.

Benign, white-haired, elderly, he regarded Sylvan as

some sort of active retirement, but no one knew exactly where he had practiced before coming to the mountains.

Jo leaned back in the chair, placed her arms carefully across her swollen belly, and smiled back at Weber. It was a smile crowded with warmth and friendliness. She was an attractive woman of around twenty-seven. Not beautiful in the accepted sense, but with a combination of attributes that left a striking impression on the mind.

Tall and fair, with long blond hair, the willowy slenderness of her body was now temporarily disturbed by a five months' pregnancy. But it was her face that left such an imprint on the memory, because each individual feature taken in isolation would fail any standard beauty test. The nose was too thin and long, the eyes too wide and spaced, the jaw too bony. Yet somehow with all the imperfections placed together in the right proportions, they complemented each other. Combined with a natural warmth, the end result was memorably attractive.

"Everything's just fine, Mrs. Newman," smiled Weber. "There's not a thing to worry about. I expect you'll go on and have a normal pregnancy, and go for the full term."

She nodded with satisfaction. She liked the doctor, and she disliked the deception of the false name, but even up here in the mountains Brett was wary of using the name Leica. She regarded it as paranoid on her husband's part, but it was she who had insisted on having the child, so she had to respect his wishes.

"Maybe the visit to the New York specialist wasn't necessary after all, Dr. Weber?" she queried gently.

His eyebrows lifted, and sent lines rippling up his forehead to wash against the line of his white hair. He pursed his lips, and gave a small shrug of his shoulders.

"Maybe not, Mrs. Newman, maybe not. But I don't think one should take chances with this sort of thing." Absently he picked up the pen again, and drummed it casually on the top of the desk. "Okay, everything has turned out fine. The tests were negative. But isn't it better to know for sure that your baby's okay, for your own peace of mind? Would you like not being quite sure for the next three or four months if your baby was normal or not?"

She nodded agreement.

"What else can I say but agree with you. Of course you're right, and my husband thinks so too. It was worth the peace of mind. And the man you sent me to in New York, Dr. Clements, was very thorough."

Weber smiled again, stopped his drumming, and put the pen down. He decided to say nothing about Clements's being found knifed to death in his office. It was very unlikely that the news would ever filter into this region. He liked this woman, and he didn't want to risk upsetting her.

He changed the subject quickly, and flipped over his desk calendar.

"Well, everything's going so well, I don't think there's any reason for you to come and see me again until the . . . ah, let's see . . . how about the twenty-fifth of November?" His glasses slid further down his nose, and he peered at Jo benevolently. "Is that all right with you, Mrs. Newman?"

She stood up, patting at her hair. She tried to button up her jacket, but the reach of the coat failed to encompass the swelling, and she gave it up with a giggle.

"I think I'm going to need a fuller jacket," she said.

"It looks like it."

Her eyes flickered down to the calendar.

"I'm sorry, of course the twenty-fifth will be fine."

"Of course that always goes with the proviso that there's nothing troubling you in the meantime," he warned. "You can always call me, you know. Any time at all." He eyed her with a shrewd glance. "I can't contact you, can I? You have no telephone out there?"

She hesitated a moment. No, Brett wouldn't allow that. He thought it was dangerous, just one more way they might be traced. Maybe one day.

"No, we haven't," she smiled finally. "Ah, we prefer the solitude, Doctor. You know . . . away from things."

Weber gave a shrug that indicated it was none of his business.

"Well, perhaps you should think about having one installed now," he urged. "It would be a good idea while you're pregnant. Away from things is fine, it's what I like myself, but sometimes civilization is very necessary. Unless you want your husband delivering the baby."

She shrugged noncommittally.

"No, but I'm sure he could do it."

Weber rose slowly from his desk. The fall mountain air didn't do his back much good. "I'm sure he could, I'm sure he could," he murmured offhandedly. He went around the desk, crossed the floor of the small office, and opened the door for his patient.

Jo gave him a farewell smile as she crossed in front of him. "Well, maybe I'll talk to my husband about it," she said.

He patted her on the arm. "Tell him I insist," he grinned.

Outside the day was washed in a deep tone of gray. Overhead the tightly bunched clouds slickered past, hightailing before a strong southern wind, spattering the town with a passing shower. The large drops beat against the iron roof of the verandah with a staccato drumming sound. A truck passed with its tires hissing on the wet road, sloughing muddy water across the sidewalk.

She went quickly to the Mustang, clumsy in her pregnancy, head down against the rain. She started the car, reversed carefully away from the curb, and drove away at a steady pace. Maybe she could drive herself into town to see Dr. Weber for a few more months, then she was going to have to ask Brett. She knew he hated coming into Sylvan, but the hell with it, he was just going to have to make the effort.

She was soon out of the town, following the winding curves toward Pearidge Road, doubly cautious on the wet surface. The wipers smudged with each sweep, blurring her visibility. They needed replacing, like so many other things around the house. There never seemed to be enough money. It was ridiculous, they couldn't go on hiding forever. For three years she had stuck with Brett, bowed to his every whim, understood his paranoia, comforted him. Because she loved him. She shared his hatred of having his talent ill used, but after three years she was certain that hiding away from the world wasn't the answer. Sooner or later he was going to have to put aside his fear, and go out and face the world, and say this is my talent, my unique talent, and I'll use it the way I think is right, not the way you think is right.

He was the only man she had ever loved, and maybe that was unique in itself.

She was still a student of twenty when he had first come to Stanford University. She with her sights set on biochemistry, he already famous at thirty, proclaimed by some as a genius. With life so well ordered, so much a predictable progression from point to point, and cosseted by her parents, she wondered if her life would just go on and on in the same pattern, like an endless stroll along a pale-gray passage. Then he had noticed her. Unbelievably sharp blue eyes behind myopic lenses that never left her face. She was in turn unbelieving, cautious, flattered, then helplessly in love. Where some saw only arrogance, she knew there was gentleness, humility. He needed a shell, because he operated on a level that only a few could comprehend. Including herself. She recognized his unique talents without question, but she could only vaguely understand their application. Maybe Daiton was the only other one who understood, but that had ended in an explosive row.

She had married Brett at twenty-two, then there had followed two difficult years of watching him withdraw, become secretive, morose, wary of his own strange ability. Then the cataclysm. Run, run, hide, vanish, and she went with him unquestioningly, wandering from motel to motel, from city to city, from pseudonym to pseudonym. Until they had found this hideaway in the mountains, and only then had Brett felt safe.

And for a time it had been idyllic, until the feeling of the long gray corridor had come back to her again, that this was no temporary seclusion, but a permanent way of life, and she wanted more than that. Children for one thing. That would be her first lever; her determination for once was equal to his, and eventually he gave way.

She swung the car gently into the wide curve that led up to the Pearidge Road turnoff, and smiled secretly to herself. After the child was born it would need education, all sorts of things, that would require contact with the outside world. When there were more than just the two of them to consider, she was sure she could needle Brett back to the reality he was going to have to face one day.

Dulled by her musing, visibility blurred by the inefficient wipers, she failed to see the other car reversing out of the culvert until she was almost on it. Panic bubbled up over the foetus, and caught in her throat, and she swung the car violently to the right, her foot scrambling for the brake pedal. She hit the brake pedal with too much force, and the car slewed sideways on the wet road surface. The rear bumper caromed off a tree perched along the side of the road, and propped the car around until it was facing back down the mountain. It rolled forward slowly until the wheels locked against the gravel shoulder and forced it to a halt.

She cut the motor with trembling fingers. This was the finish of her driving down into Sylvan, especially in this sort of weather. It was too dangerous for the baby. From now on, Brett would have to do it, like it or not.

She crouched there for a moment, waiting for the trembling to subside, conscious of the sound of footsteps coming from behind the car. The idiot. She was shaken, but not too upset to let loose a verbal barrage at the other driver.

The hot words were already in her mouth, waiting to explode, when the door of the car was wrenched open and the man put his head inside.

"What the hell . . ." were the only words she managed, before she recognized Vilas Daiton. The moustache was gone, but there was no mistaking the man she'd known for two years, who had been an assistant to Brett at Stanford.

The words died, but her mouth stayed open, and she was no longer aware of any trembling.

He held out his hand, and gave her a strange, crooked smile.

"That was rather a clumsy way of stopping your car, Jo. I hope you're all right?"

"Vilas!" she said stupidly.

He smiled again, the same smile she remembered so well, and all the memories of his ingratiating phony sincerity came flooding back to her. Somehow she felt afraid, and she slid one hand from the steering wheel and down over her belly in a protective gesture. Over his shoulder she could see the body of another man, his face hidden by the roof of the car.

"What are you doing here?" she demanded. Even as she said the words she thought of Brett. Incredibly, for all their caution, Vilas had found them. How? Why? The questions tumbled around in her mind. She felt the baby under her hand, and her anger stirred again. "Christ, I don't know what you're doing here, Vilas, but you damn near killed me. Can't you see I'm expecting a baby?"

He shrugged, and the hand stayed out, extended toward her.

"Congratulations," he said coolly.

She stared down at the hand, then up into his face again. Fear niggled at her once more.

"It's been a long time," she said hesitantly.

The rain came again, sprinkling over the roof of the car like the light patter of birds' feet.

His smile had gone. "Three years."

"Yes, three years," she echoed stupidly.

It all seemed terribly unreal, like a dream, not actually happening, just a vision of Brett's insecurity.

"This is not a social call, Vilas," said the voice from outside the car. It was deep, heavily accented.

Vilas nodded, and his extended hand moved forward and grasped her firmly by her wrist.

"Get out," he ordered.

She tried to pull her hand free, but he held her tightly.

"I'm quite capable of driving on, thank you," she protested. "There's nothing wrong with the car."

"For Chrissake, Vilas, get her out of there," demanded the other voice impatiently.

Vilas increased the pressure on her wrist and began to drag her across the seat of the car. She tried to hang on to the steering wheel with her free hand, but he reached across and wrenched that loose too. She was very afraid now. She had never liked Vilas, but this was something new, something unexplainable, total confusion.

"Let me go, you fool . . . you must be mad," she screamed at him.

He released one of her hands and struck her hard across the face with the back of his hand. She stopped struggling and went very white, very silent. She was frightened for the baby more than for herself. The thought came to her that somehow he wanted to hurt Brett and was going to do it through her. But why? Surely not after an argument that had taken place three years ago.

He stepped away from the door opening and beckoned curtly to her. She slid across the seat and clambered awkwardly out onto the road. The other man was standing, watching them. He was older than Vilas, thickset, and balding. Wide thick-lipped mouth, and a hawk nose with large dark glasses perched across the bridge.

"I thought you said you knew her well enough not to have to use force," he said irritably to Daiton.

Daiton shrugged.

"She always was a difficult bitch," he grunted sourly.

Hadaffi made a swift gesture toward the other car.

"All right. Get her in the car. I'll watch her while you take hers. You know the plan. I'll wait for you at the end of the road until you've finished."

Vilas hesitated. It was the only part of the plan he didn't like, and it had been Hadaffi's idea. He remembered the trauma of the bee fantasy, and he shuddered.

Hadaffi reached out impatiently and grasped Jo forcefully by the arm, and moved her quickly toward Daiton's car. She stumbled over the loose surface at the side of the road, but the firmness of his grip prevented her from falling.

"Come on, Vilas, move yourself. I'll take the woman to the car. We can't just stand around here as if we're having some sort of roadside picnic. Some other car might come along. Hurry, man."

"Please, tell me what you want?" asked Jo weakly. "Don't hurt me."

Hadaffi ignored her, thrust her into the car, then clambered in alongside her.

Daiton slid himself behind the wheel of Jo's Mustang and restarted the motor. He gunned the engine several times to reassure himself that it was still performing well enough for the short journey. His hands felt clammy on the steering wheel, and his body dragged down into the seat as if trying to resist a sudden surge of gravity.

It was all right for Hadaffi. It was one thing to tell him what Leica was capable of, but experiencing it was something else again. He took the envelope from his pocket and laid it carefully on the seat beside him.

He put the car into drive, swung around, and drove slowly on up the mountain toward the entrance to Pearidge Road. In the rearview mirror he saw Hadaffi perform the same maneuver with his car and follow along about a hundred yards behind him. He could see Jo crouched alongside him. He grinned sourly to himself. Snooty bitch, she hadn't changed in three years—even when he worked with Leica she wasn't reluctant to let him know she didn't think he was quite good enough for her precious husband. She made sure he was never quite close enough to Leica to perceive how it was all done. There was a certain amount of pleasure in seeing her cringe. Christ, what a pale imitation of a woman she was compared to Nerida.

He came to Pearidge Road and slowed for the turn. He shuffled himself nervously about in the seat, and he felt his face begin to flush from the fast-running beat of his pulse. It was a delicate moment, and he had to make it work, because the entire operation depended on how carefully it was done. He would leave the car at the top of the rise and then he would run. Christ, how he would run, and all the time he would be listening for the buzz of some murderous insect around his head.

Brett Leica looked up from his book at the clock and stirred uneasily. He never tired of rereading Russell's *Principia Mathematica,* and time always passed swiftly, but he saw with a start that Jo was an hour late. She hadn't said anything about shopping in

Sylvan, and it was unlike Weber to keep her very long if it was only for a routine check.

She had been late before, but never this late. The car wasn't in top condition, and he hoped she wasn't having trouble with the wet roads.

He put the book down on the side table, unwound himself from the deep lounge chair, and stood up. He was a tall man, six feet four, thin and gangling, with large feet. A bony structured, thin pointed face, sharp blue eyes sheltered behind myopic lenses, and a wide generous mouth, capable of creating a smile loaded with charm. He was thatched with a shock of carelessly cropped fair hair. He was wearing jeans, sneakers, and a multicolored lumberjack shirt. He was thirty-eight years old.

He berated himself silently for not watching the clock more carefully. He closed his eyes and pressed his fingers to his temples to try and perceive any threat, but he had insufficient information. But he received enough perception to increase his uneasiness. He looked about the room. It was partly his room with its books, but more of Jo's room with its charm and color. Timbered, comfortable, a good room to live in. At least he had thought so for two years until he had sensed Jo's discontent. The baby had been the result of that confrontation, but he knew she really didn't understand his fear. And that was his fault, because there were things he hadn't told her, not only about the pressure from the CIA, but from other countries as well. Pressure that could have placed her in danger as well as himself. He'd never proved it, but he suspected he had Daiton to thank for a lot of that.

He wandered absently around the room, not too sure what action to take. That was typical. The original indecisive man. The only firm decision he had ever taken was more running away from a decision. Maybe because decisions had never seemed to be necessary. It was as if his subconscious mind had followed a set plan independent of his conscious intellect. It set him apart. People don't really like very bright individuals. They try to pretend, but most times they treat them like beings from another planet. It had been like that at primary school, at high school, at UCLA, at Stanford. Eggheads, think-tank operators—shake their hands, treat them cautiously, and shun them outside the place of learning. Maybe that's why he had found Jo so different, because she was his friend before she was his lover.

He turned around in circles, and some of the anxiety he'd experienced over the last three weeks began to return. It was the man he'd seen at the end of the road three weeks ago. He had been convinced it was Daiton. Christ, Daiton. The last man he would want to discover his hiding place, and for a moment he had panicked. And the surge of panic had been followed by one of the most intense bouts of concentration that he'd allowed himself in months. It had filled him with guilt, because he had a good idea of what must have happened to the man's mind. The more he thought about it, the more apparent it was how stupid he had been to imagine it was Vilas Daiton. How ridiculous, after three years. Probably a trick of the light through the trees.

But it had put his nerves on edge, made him difficult to live with, because he hadn't told Jo about the man, hadn't wanted to alarm her. Those last two hours he had spent reading Russell had been the first time he had really been able to relax in weeks. And now Jo was late, to irritate the raw edges again. He wondered if he should walk down to the main road and watch for the car. He decided to postpone that for the moment, give her a little extra time to appear, while he made a cup of coffee. He went into the small kitchen off the living room, selected a cup, took the coffeepot from the upper shelf, and placed them on the bench by the sink. He had a strange swirling in the pit of his stomach that almost equaled in intensity that of the night he had decided to disappear from Stanford. He turned on the tap over the sink, and glanced out the window. The rain had passed, but a pattern of translucent drops shivered on the glass.

He stood there, transfixed, as if his body had assumed the metallic form of the sink, letting the water run unattended from the tap. It was Jo's car, down at the end of the curve where the track went around to the main road. He could only see the front half, but it was the Mustang all right. He wondered why he was just standing there? Why he wasn't like any other proud husband with a pregnant wife, rushing out the door to find out what had happened? He stood there, fighting off the chilling icy fingers trickling up the backs of his legs, niggling his spine. He groped for the tap without taking his eyes off the car and turned off the water. It was suddenly very quiet. The sound of his heart drummed in his ears. The wind swished at the pines by the side of the house, and the water-laden branches sprayed the roof with sporadic showers. He put his head to one side and listened intently to the sounds of the house, hoping that maybe the car had broken down, and she had walked the last stretch of road. There was nothing: not the bright, firm step he knew so well, nor the sound of her husky voice.

He shook himself free of the window and forced himself out of the kitchen. It was absurd just to stand there, but his feet dragged as if chains had suddenly been secured about his ankles.

Perhaps all those unvoiced suspicions of a lifetime were true. He was really a coward. He was afraid to go to the car. For all he knew Jo could be sitting in the car, ill, waiting for him to come and help her. But he knew it was more than that. There was something terribly wrong, and his mind went back three weeks again to the man at the end of the road.

Maybe he had been right after all, and it had been Daiton.

He went out of the house, closed the door gently behind him, and walked slowly along the track toward the car. He wanted to run, with his arms outstretched, calling her name, but he couldn't do it. There was a tingling sensation down each arm, numbing his fingertips.

The wind knifed through the trees, cooled by the dripping forest, chilling him. He reached the car, but he knew there would be no one inside. There was a bad dent on the rear guard, just above the bumper, and he bent and ran his fingers over the area without really knowing why. Perhaps she'd had an accident and someone had taken her into Sylvan. But why would they bring the car back, and just leave it parked here?

He opened the door, and saw the envelope. He picked it up, closed the door, and stood for a moment with it in his hand, leaning against the car, looking up at the sky. The wind threw a few drops of water over his lenses, blurring his vision. He took them aimlessly off his face and cleaned them on his shirt. The end of three years' seclusion. Three years of peace. He didn't know who or why, but he was certain that's what it was all about. He made himself open the letter, just as he'd forced himself to come to the car. He replaced his glasses and held the letter up to the dull light. It was short, and written in a neat hand that was vaguely familiar.

" 'We are holding your wife captive,' " he read. " 'We wish to talk to you, and will come to your house at ten o'clock in the morning. Do not interfere with us when we approach your house, do not attempt to harm us, play no tricks with our minds. If you attempt to do this, your wife will be killed. We say this to you in all seriousness, so you will not delude yourself that it is an idle threat. It goes without saying that we do not believe for one moment you would be stupid enough to go to the police.' "

It was unsigned. He folded up the letter, and placed it neatly back in the envelope, not even conscious of his actions, as if he were in a trance. He closed his eyes and put his head back on the roof of the car. It was over. Whoever had written the letter knew all about him. It was ironic; for all his attempts to vanish, finally, it was Jo's life he had put at risk. More than Jo—now it was the baby as well.

She was the only thing that had made the last three years possible, and life without her would be meaningless. So he would have to do what he was told, because nothing was worth any harm coming to her.

He had never felt so totally helpless in his life. The only answer to come was who his supposed new masters would be, and what they would demand from him. The CIA? The KGB? Or whoever?

Nausea swept over him, and he crouched down by the side of the car and vomited on the road.

As usual after an absence, Angela made the night a memorable exercise in originality, imagination, exhaustion, and survival. And Carmody loved it all. It had been a frantic day and he felt the need of relaxation, although whether Angela's sexual voraciousness came under the heading of relaxation was debatable.

At such times she demanded little of him except an erection, although what direction she was coming from, and where it actually finished up, he was never too sure. She made him feel as if his body were some type of unique temple at which she wanted to worship, with her mouth, with her tongue, with her hands, or any cavity he desired.

There was a whore he'd known once in Mexico City who came a reasonably close second, but then that had lacked the spark of love that he had with Angela. She finished teasing him with her mouth and came up over him, straddling him with her legs while she eased him slowly deep into her. She sat there on her folded knees, rocking gently, her magnificent breasts glowing in the soft lamplight, a half smile on her face, her tongue flickering out and back and forth across her lips until they took on a sheen like highly polished veneer.

Crooning softly to him with a continuous purr, "Does that feel good . . . Is it good fucking me . . . ? I love the feel of your cock in me . . ." on and on, and him lying there, eyes half closed, nodding his head, like a small boy let loose in an ice-cream shop, told he could eat the shop empty.

When he came it was like a blast from Cape Kennedy, and he would have gone straight to the moon like any other rocket except that she held him down like some gorgeous anchor, quickening her pace to drain every last dreg of shuddering orgasm from his body.

He dozed for a while, holding her cupped in his arms. It was incredible she could be like this with him in bed, and so efficient and businesslike in the office. He was lucky that it worked so well, because he knew this sort of passion carried over into the office would be a disaster. Especially now, the way things were with Schyler.

He fought off the drowsiness, and thought about the thing with Hadaffi and Schyler. Angela stirred beside him, breathing deeply, her mouth against his neck, one arm across his chest, one leg curved over his legs.

Carmody had spent a busy day, but everything had gone well. Special people had been briefed, the blowups of the photograph had gone out with the carefully worded message that he was wanted urgently for questioning. There had been a politely worded request from the FBI for more information, and he had referred them to Schyler. It was his idea to hog the Hadaffi business for Intelligence, so he could do all the stalling. Not that that could go on for very long. The President would see to that. He had no great faith that the photograph would achieve anything, the quality was so poor, it looked like any man with a thick black beard. It was pretty certain that the beard would have been shaved off before Hadaffi attempted to enter the country.

He had thought of going to New York to try and see Moccasin, but that would have been dangerous, and he would only attempt that as a last resort. He didn't want to take the risk of breaking Moccasin's cover, not when he was so close to finding out who was heading up the brotherhood organization in America. But he would need the information fast to satisfy the President. Nothing mattered but satisfying the President, not now when he was within striking distance of Schyler's desk.

He had sent a coded message to Moccasin's pickup point stressing the urgency, but he knew the undercover man would merely burn it. He knew the urgency as well as Carmody, but the cable would look good on the files of the operation.

Everything had to look good on the files of this operation, because the President would be studying them, and he wanted to make sure that Frank Carmody looked bloody good.

"Do you feel fit enough to try again?" Angela murmured against his neck.

He thought about that for a moment.

"You want to kill me, is that your plan," he teased her. "The sort of sex you deliver, my darling, needs to be taken in spaced-out doses."

"Chicken," she muttered, licking at his neck.

"You're a runaway female fucking machine." He grinned.

"As long as you're the one I'm fucking, why should you complain?"

"I love you," he said. "Go back to sleep."

"I love you too, but I don't want to sleep."

"I can't keep up with you."

"You're not trying hard enough. You need more training."

"Bullshit."

There was a short silence while she ran her fingers over his belly with a soft drumming action.

"Noel Zambretti has come to work in our section," she said softly.

It sounded like a throwaway remark, delivered in a

drowsy monotone, but he knew her better than that. Zambretti? That creep. He didn't know a great deal about the way he operated except that he was a relative of Schyler's, and the word around the Agency was that Schyler used him as some sort of hatchet man.

"Christ, when did that happen? How come I wasn't informed?"

"You're being informed now."

"By whom?"

"By me."

Carmody levered himself up on one elbow and stared down at Angela.

"What the hell is that supposed to mean?"

She looked back up at him with dark, serious eyes, her hair strewn around her head like a black halo against the white pillow. He'd never seen anything more beautiful.

"There was a memo from Schyler to me this afternoon. You were too busy for me to break it to you, so I waited for the right moment. And this happens to be it."

He fell back on the pillow and stared up at the ceiling.

"Bloody Schyler. I won't have someone spying on me in my own office, then reporting back to Schyler. What did the memo say?"

"He's come in at Schyler's request as a temporary assistant to help you over the present crisis."

Carmody placed his hands behind his head, his brow creased with irritation, love momentarily forgotten.

"That's Martin. About as subtle as a ten-ton truck. Schyler's furious that the President put me in charge of this thing over Hadaffi. He thinks I'm going to try and shut him out. I've got enough on my hands without watching someone like Zambretti out of the corner of my eye every time I make a move."

"You can't get rid of him?" ventured Angela tentatively.

"Not without a hell of a row. If Schyler's put it out in memo form, that makes it official. I wouldn't want the President to get a whisper that Schyler and I are involved in some personal row right in the middle of trying to track down Hadaffi."

Angela rubbed her hand across Carmody's chest in a soft, consoling gesture.

"Can he really do any harm?" she asked.

Carmody shrugged, not quite knowing how to answer. It had been half in his thoughts to let Schyler know his decisions only after they had been made. That way there was little risk of interference. He was irritated that Schyler had read his mind so easily.

"I don't know," he grunted surlily. "I just don't want to be hog-tied by any interference from Schyler. This is my assignment. Zambretti goes running back to Martin with every little tidbit, I'll have him breathing down my neck every chance he gets." The irritation seeped into his bloodstream, increasing his body heat, and he spread his legs, probing for the cool areas of the sheets. "It's just like the devious bastard to send the memo through you, instead of direct to me. Christ, I had every intention of letting him know what was happening," he added self-righteously.

"You must have upset him badly in the briefing this morning," Angela ventured.

Carmody snorted derisively.

"Stupid bastard, it was his own fault. I tried to tell him how important the communication was from Moccasin, but he was so intent on playing schoolmaster and punishing the late student, he wouldn't listen. I knew I was right to bring it up at the briefing, and the President agreed with me. That's what really got under Martin's skin."

"He thinks you're after his job."

"Nonsense," Carmody lied.

"He's trying to protect himself."

"He's going to do himself a lot of harm using someone like Zambretti."

There was a short silence while Carmody fumed. Maybe Angela had thought this was a good time to break it to him about Zambretti, but she'd made a casualty of his lust. Her fingers slid down his chest, over his belly, paused for a soft exploratory tease of his pubic hair, then enclosed his testicles with a gentle sensuous message. He put his hand down, and pressed his fingers into her wrist.

"Not right now," he said gently.

She slid her hand away, back up to his chest, and smiled at him.

"I've upset you?"

"Not you."

"Then Schyler's upset you?"

"He should have told me. He should have discussed Zambretti with me."

"He knew you'd refuse."

Carmody grinned in spite of himself.

"And how."

"What do you want me to do?"

He craned his head around and looked down at her. She was being marvelous, and he was behaving like a stupid shit. Fuck Zambretti. He wasn't going to stop him from sitting behind Schyler's desk before this was all over.

"Shut Zambretti out. Keep his nose out of the files," he said.

"That won't be easy. After all, he is my superior."

He grinned at her and kissed her gently on the forehead.

"I know you, darling. You'll find a way."

"He'll try and pick my brains."

"Tell him no more than you have to."

Her hand stopped roving across his chest, and her fingers drummed out a short, sharp tattoo.

"That won't be difficult," she said dryly. "I don't know very much."

Carmody was silent for a moment. He slid his arm under her head and drew her close, his fingers massaging her arm in almost a compensatory movement.

"You know about Hadaffi."

"Only because you needed me to work with you. To get out the prints, to get all the special telexes out to the airlines."

He extended the area of his massage, along her shoulder, and down to the softly rising curve of her breast.

"I trust you implicitly," he murmured.

"I know."

"It's not necessary to tell you about Moccasin. It's not a matter of trust. It's just safer for him if as few people know about him as possible."

"I know," she repeated mechanically.

"He gave us the information about Hadaffi."

She nodded. "I guessed that much. He must be a valuable man."

"Very valuable. With luck he'll have a lot more valuable information within the next few days."

"That's good," she said with irony. "Then we won't

have to talk about him in bed as well as all day at the office."

He lifted himself up on one elbow again, and grinned down at her. She was right. No woman as beautiful as Angela deserved to have matters of state intruding into the bedroom. He tried to put Hadaffi out of his mind, because there wasn't much else he could do right now. Whatever devilry the terrorist was planning, they would know soon enough. He leaned down and took her nipple gently into his mouth, teasing with his tongue. She put her hand behind his neck, and pressed his face into her breast.

"That's more like it," she breathed. "There're lots more interesting things we can do than talk about Hadaffi and Moccasin."

When she was sure Carmody was soundly asleep, she slipped quietly out of bed and went into the bathroom. She closed the door noiselessly and turned to cross to the shower, when she caught her reflection in the mirror above the hand basin. She paused and went up to the mirror until there were only a few inches separating her from the reflection. She shook her hair until it fell back into place behind her shoulders. Then she lifted one hand and placed her index finger in the center of her forehead, and traced the outline of her face down over her nose, over her full lips, over the curve of her chin, down the sweep of her neck to her breasts. She was lucky. It was easy with a face like that, and even intelligent men could be such fools. Cultivate a man's ego, and anything was possible. Give me a job, give me a recommendation, give me a security clearance, trust me, love me, it was all possible.

If she shut her mind, and in that she'd had a lot of practice.

She had sold herself for a loaf of bread when she was ten, and she couldn't even remember the face of the man fucking her, because she had been too busy appeasing her hunger with the bread. Shutting her mind to one section of her anatomy while she satisfied the gnawing pangs of hunger in another.

Such a situation would be beyond the grasp of someone like Carmody. Inconceivable. And she would have still been there without the help of the brotherhood, who recognized the potential of her beauty, rescued her from the dung-heap, so that she could flower. Flower for them.

So the pretense with Carmody came easily to her. What would have been incomprehensible to him, unacceptable to his ego, was commonplace to her. His mind would flounder at the thought that all that passion, all that warmth, all that subservience, was manufactured. And if there were times of difficulty, then she was equally adept at fantasy. It was Vilas, not Carmody, who was in her; her orgasms, her moans, were for Vilas, because the image of him was always alive in her mind. And Carmody's moans of Angela could easily be switched in her mind to Daiton's moans of Nerida.

Perhaps she could even stir the enmity between Carmody and Schyler over Hadaffi. It was better if they consumed energy fighting with each other, rather than trying to trace Hadaffi. The advent of Hadaffi was her first big chance for the brotherhood, and she wanted to do well. Twelve years ago they had sent her to America, with instructions to infiltrate, and wait, that some day they would need her and her time would come.

Well, her time had come, and she wasn't going to fail them.

She moved from the mirror, went to the shower recess, stepped in, and turned on the water. She stood with her head back, eyes closed, letting the hot spray sluice over her body, cleansing away the touch of Carmody.

Tomorrow, somehow, she must get word through to Vilas, because the suspicions he had expressed to her had been right. There was a traitor in the brotherhood. An informer. The special delivery from Moccasin had come from New York, and perhaps that confirmed all of Vilas's thoughts about Oxley. So he must be warned as soon as possible. The information the CIA already had about Hadaffi's being in the country was unfortunate, but not disastrous. Sooner or later it would have been necessary to let the government know in order for the plan to work.

But any further betrayal would threaten them all. Hadaffi's whereabouts, Daiton's leadership of the brotherhood in America, her involvement, even the plan to use Leica. That must never be allowed to happen.

She stepped out of the shower and dried herself quickly. She hoped Daiton was returning to New York so she could contact him. There was no way Carmody would accept an excuse about her visiting fictitious ill parents again in New York, and it would be risky for her to try right now.

She went back into the bedroom, still naked, and paused by the side of the bed. Carmody was deep in sleep, stretched out on his back, his mouth open slightly, snoring. She shrugged. He was not a vicious man, even likable, but ambition sometimes made him stupid.

She hunched her shoulders and rubbed at her arms, feeling chilled. She went to the wardrobe, pulled out one of the drawers, and pawed around for a suitable nightdress. Her fingers came into contact with the thirty-two revolver at the back of the drawer, and on a sudden impulse she took it out, and looked at it. She balanced it in her hand, feeling the weight. Carmody had given it to her months ago, for her protection, after a prowler had been reported in the area. She hoped it would never be necessary to use it on Carmody. But if it ever had to be done in the cause of the brotherhood, then she would do it.

She had killed before when it was necessary, but it was a distasteful part of her dedication.

Next morning the rain had cleared over Pine Mountain, and the sky was scrubbed free of clouds into a bright, shimmering blue. The day was alive, as if sloughing off a passing depression. Possums skittered briskly along the branches; orioles called joyfully to each other as they winged precisely through the trees; the entire forest rustled with life. A light breeze tickled the pines, and myriad spots of sunlight danced in a jiggling pattern over the road. Pools of water spotted along the track up to the Leica house threw off shafts of sunlight, sparkling like diamonds. The house was a serene picture of peaceful escape.

Serenity was far from Brett Leica's mind. He had

thrown himself down on his bed last night without bothering to undress, because he knew sleep would be impossible. He couldn't remember the last night he had spent without Jo. At least for the time he could be reasonably sure that she was unharmed. Only the morning would tell him how long that would continue. He missed her badly. They were two of a kind, perhaps unique, inasmuch as neither of them had formed any deep relationships before meeting. More understandable perhaps for her, because she had only been twenty, but he was eleven years older. Maybe not a virgin physically, but psychologically so. Most people were uncomfortable with him, and she had been the first to see him merely as a human being, not some mathematical genius, set apart on some outer-space intellectual asteroid.

The thought of any harm coming to her because of him took his nerve ends and tangled them into a skein that formed a permanent ache in his belly.

At five in the morning the effort of trying to lie in one place had finally beaten him, and he had spent the rest of the time wandering about the house, fortifying himself with endless cups of black coffee.

He had watched the day come to life, the hush before first light he loved so much, the twittering gossip of the birds, the black mass of the surrounding forest gradually evolving into individual shapes of trees and rocks and bushes. And he tried to find some courage. Not the sort of courage he'd sometimes found in a whiskey bottle, but real courage. Decisive courage. To face this awful reality about Jo. He couldn't run anymore, he couldn't hide anymore, there was no place to go.

Around about eight he showered and shaved to try and bring some alertness back into his mind, but the ache persisted in his stomach. Food was out of the question, and he made no attempt to prepare anything.

Right at ten o'clock he heard the sound of a car pulling up outside the house, but he made no attempt to peer through the window or go to the door. He sat down in the easy chair, facing the door, waiting for the knock. When it came it was firm and decisive, but he didn't move from the chair. A muscle twitched involuntarily in the side of his face, and he put his fingers quickly to the spot and stilled the tremor.

He had left the door unlocked, and there was a pause until it swung widely back into the room. Two men stood in the entrance, backlit by the morning sun, one taller than the other, but slim, while his companion was thickset. Leica lifted his head, squinting into the light, his vision momentarily fuzzed.

"May we come in?" asked the thickset shape, his heavily accented voice sharp with sarcastic irony.

Leica gestured nervously with his hands, and the two men stepped inside, the taller of the two shutting the door behind him. It was only then that Leica saw it was Daiton. Both men were casually dressed in jeans and open shirts.

The other man Leica had never seen before. Older than Vilas, balding, with a hawk nose and thick-lipped mouth, dark glasses hiding his eyes. He scarcely glanced at Leica, but went carefully around the living room, his head never still, taking in every detail. Daiton remained where he was, stopped only a few feet in front of Leica, grinning awkwardly at him.

Brett stared back at him, expressionless, striving to control the trembling of his mouth, brought on by the sudden upsurge in his pulse rate.

There was no doubt in his mind now that it had been Vilas Daiton he had seen three weeks ago at the end of the road. Somehow it made him feel better about what he'd done to him.

"A long time, Brett?" said Daiton silkily.

"Where's Jo?" demanded Leica huskily.

"Safe."

"That doesn't tell me a damn thing." He tried to instill some aggression into his voice, but he was betrayed by the quiver in his larynx that he couldn't control.

"Safe," Daiton repeated.

"You lousy shit," Leica choked.

Hadaffi turned abruptly on the other side of the room and gestured impatiently with his hands.

"We have not come here to trade insults, Leica. That will only consume energy and time, and we have little to spare. I am here to deal only in reality."

Leica turned and looked at the speaker. The man was totally in control, completely calm; there was an aura about him he found quite terrifying.

"Who are you?" he demanded sullenly. "What reality?"

"Who I am is irrelevant," said Hadaffi. "All that is relevant is the reality that we have your wife. She is in a place not far from here. It is important that we make daily contact with the people holding her, I assure you, for her safety. If for any reason we don't make that contact, if for example we were to have an unfortunate experience similar to the one you . . . ah . . . inflicted on Vilas some weeks ago, then she will be killed. Quickly and with great efficiency." He paused for effect, and strolled across to the bookshelves and let his finger run idly along the titles. "That is the only reality you must be very aware of, Leica. It is the only reality you must never forget."

Hadaffi paused again, and the room fell silent. Daiton moved away from facing Brett and dropped himself down in a chair. He made no verbal attempt to usurp Hadaffi's role as spokesman.

Leica ran his tongue nervously around his lips. They had the feel of dried toast. There was something he didn't understand here: this wasn't CIA, or KGB. This was something else, perhaps something more frightening.

"I don't know what you're talking about," he muttered.

"I am not interested in any stupid stall. I have just indicated to you the reality you face. You do know what I'm talking about."

"Things have changed in three years," said Leica.

Daiton snorted derisively, but said nothing.

Hadaffi sighed and leaned against the bookshelves. He took a small cigar packet from his pocket, extracted one, lit it with great deliberation, and expelled the smoked toward the timbered ceiling.

"Brett Leica," he said slowly. "Born 1932, of middle-class parents. Father a bookseller, mother a teacher. Both dead. A brilliant mathematician in the making from the first day at school. Graduated UCLA and offered a post at that university as an electrical engineer to specialize in quantum physics. Filled the post brilliantly. Then to the Stanford Research Institute to work on long-range policy analysis or futurology in the military, scientific, and industrial field. Again performed brilliantly. Became interested and fascinated in the field of psychic research, and eventually specialized entirely in this area." Hadaffi paused and drew heavily on the cigar. He glanced across at Leica through a fine haze of smoke, but Leica was leaning forward with his elbows on his knees, staring at the floor. "I hope I'm not boring you, but this seems to be necessary," said Hadaffi bitingly. Leica ignored him.

"Did a vast amount of research into psychic technology, hypnosis, psychotherapy, and psychokinesis. Especially psychokinesis . . . the ability to manipulate physical or biological objects by mental powers alone. Achieved results so startling in this area, that only a few people were aware of what was going on . . . your wife . . . and Vilas, one of your assistants."

Leica lifted his eyes to Daiton with a look of acid hostility, but Vilas shrugged and looked away.

"Even you, I understand, were disturbed by what you were capable of doing with your mind. Daiton is right, that is the misgiving of a weak man," continued Hadaffi. "So you put nothing down on paper, no notes, no reports, and then it all leaked out. They all wanted you, the CIA and the KGB, all for their own purposes. There were pressures, threats, not only on you, but on Stanford."

"I have you to thank for that, you bastard," Leica threw at Daiton.

Hadaffi raised his hand in the air and cut smoke trails with his cigar.

"Oh, no, not quite, Leica. It was Vilas's intention to drive you in one direction, our direction. It misfired. He wasn't anticipating you would just vanish with your wife. But Vilas had seen with his own eyes what you could do, the effect you could have, the distances your powers could cover. So he never stopped looking, Leica. And he finally found you."

"I gave you your chance to work voluntarily three years ago," cut in Daiton savagely.

Leica shook his head wearily.

"We're not going to have that fight again, Daiton. I was trying to do something worthwhile with my mind. You wanted to destroy things."

"You might have a brilliant mind, Leica, but you're an idiot," Daiton sneered at him.

There was another pause while Hadaffi toyed with the books again.

"I'm glad you don't intend to dispute what I've just said," he grunted.

Leica shrugged. What was the use, Daiton had briefed him well. He felt like a piece of bait staked out in open ground, not too sure which wild animal was going to eat him. He waited for the crunch.

He was afraid. He wished he could convince himself that it was only for Jo he was afraid, but he knew it wasn't true. He was afraid for himself. Scared shitless.

"When do I see my wife again?" he asked hollowly.

"That rather depends on you," said Hadaffi.

"What do you want? What do I have to do to get her back?"

Hadaffi raised his hand and indicated Leica with the cigar. Some of the ash shook free and rained finely on the floor.

"If I am to believe everything that Vilas has told me, you have a unique ability with your mind, Leica. I never like to see a unique talent rusting away."

"There was nothing rusty about the bastard's unique talent three weeks ago," gritted Daiton angrily.

Hadaffi shushed him with the cigar.

"Enough, Vilas. As I understand it, there are limits. You do not, for example, read minds. You need certain information to become . . . shall we say . . . operational."

Leica's tongue swept across his lips again. His throat felt clogged with sawdust, and he longed for a drink, but it seemed dangerous to lift himself out of the chair.

"Perhaps," he muttered.

Hadaffi laughed unpleasantly.

"Leica, we are not here to discuss a 'perhaps.' We are here in actual fact to discuss the possibility of your wife continuing as a living human being. Do I have to keep reminding you of that?"

Leica looked down at his hands, and rubbed the palms slowly together.

"No."

"What happens?" asked Hadaffi.

"What do you mean?"

"Exactly that. What happens? Why did Vilas believe he was being stung to a torturous death by bees?"

Leica stopped rubbing his hands and glanced up at Daiton.

"Is that what happened?" he asked.

Daiton nodded grimly.

"Ah, I see," interjected Hadaffi. "You didn't know?"

"Not always. It would depend on what past experiences your mind had absorbed. Consciously or subconsciously. Daiton probably had a bad experience one time with some bees."

Hadaffi turned to Daiton with raised eyebrows, and the other nodded slowly.

"Fascinating," murmured Hadaffi. "You are able to regenerate a past experience from the mind of the subject, and convert it into a nightmare . . . a waking nightmare, of overpowering intensity. Perhaps an experience the mind had already suppressed?"

"Something like that," answered Leica sullenly.

"But it is not in your power to be selective. The psychokinesis you apply provides the spark, but the mind is forced to select its own particular fear to exploit . . . to disable itself."

Leica shrugged without answering. There was something animal about this man questioning him, something frightening, but he had an intelligent mind. A well-read mind.

"But," persisted Hadaffi. "Some people lead a very sheltered life. They hide in their own self-made holes away from the world. Would there be such fears lurking in their minds from a past experience?"

"There are just as many suppressed psychopathic fears hiding in the mind as there are real unfortunate experiences. More. No one of us is free from them," said Leica.

It was all being dragged from his mouth, piece by piece. Information that Daiton had never known, that he had only shared with Jo. He was pouring it out to this man, motivated by fear, and hating himself for it.

"You can vary the intensity?" Hadaffi continued.

"Yes."

"How?"

"By . . . by the length of time the psychokinesis is prolonged."

Leica could feel himself beginning to sweat profusely. He pawed at the beads of moisture sliding down his face onto his neck, and shifted uncomfortably from the dampness at the back of his legs. The strange thought came to him that perhaps this man was merely interested in knowing how it was done, and when all his secrets had been exposed they would leave him in peace, and Jo would be returned.

"You put Vilas under intense psychokinesis the other week?"

"Yes."

"But you didn't prolong it?"

"No," answered Leica hesitantly.

"He would have died if you had continued?"

Leica squirmed in his chair from the heat of the grilling.

"Maybe," he admitted.

Hadaffi paused and drew on his cigar again. He took it from his mouth and studied Leica thoughtfully, while smoke seeped from his nostrils.

"You are an interesting enigma, Leica. It would seem that you have . . . ideals . . . about the use you can put your mind to, but all you have produced is a killing machine. I think perhaps you are just a . . . phony. I realize the necessity at times to kill people, but I do not try to fool myself as you do, behind a veil of sanctimony. You tried to kill Vilas. You would have killed me if I had not taken your wife."

For the first time Hadaffi provoked a response from Leica that momentarily dispelled fear.

"That's not true," he said angrily. "I am just on the fringes of my capabilities. There are all sorts of possibilities . . . the ability to cure mental disorders, to cure inoperable brain diseases. Many things."

"But in the meantime you'll just have to settle for the ability to destroy the mind," said Hadaffi dryly.

"It's more than that," persisted Leica.

"Then why did you run away? It is not necessary to convince me, but there must have been other people."

Leica opened his mouth, then shut it again, and retreated back into sullen silence.

"Maybe you're a coward also, eh, Leica?" said Hadaffi softly.

There was silence, and Daiton stirred irritably in his chair. Hadaffi was taking too long, he was amusing himself playing with Leica, all this information was unnecessary. It was time to instruct Leica in what was wanted of him.

Hadaffi extinguished his cigar. He returned his attention to the bookshelves, withdrew one of the books, and idly leafed through the pages. It was the Talmud.

"You are Jewish?" he said over his shoulder, without turning to Leica.

Leica hesitated over the truth. He sensed the truth was dangerous.

"Yes," he said finally.

Hadaffi made no verbal response, merely nodded. He was amused. Somehow it made the entire situation more interesting. The fact that Leica was Jewish was no deterrent against using him as a tool, and then discarding him just as easily. Practicality must always take second place to emotional hatreds. He'd made that mistake with his sister, and it had accomplished nothing except the satisfaction of some immature vengeance. Hitler had destroyed Germany by eliminating instead of using the vast reservoir of Jewish talent. That was stupidity. Their destruction could have been accomplished after victory. But there would be a certain enjoyment in killing Leica when he was no longer needed.

He replaced the Talmud, and moved along the shelves, tapping his finger against some of the other books.

"Marx . . . Leibniz . . . Nietzsche . . . Russell . . . John Dewey . . ."

He turned to Leica, and gestured to the books. "You are interested in ideas, Leica?"

Leica had returned to studying the floor in front of his chair. He wanted this to end, the agony over, so he would know what they wanted from him. What he had to do to make Jo safe.

"Yes," he muttered.

Hadaffi swept his hand around the bookshelves.

"You think these men of ideas have changed the world?"

"What about my wife?"

"I'm interested in knowing what you think about these men, Leica."

Leica shook his head with a gesture of despair.

"Yes, yes," he replied.

Hadaffi lifted his hand like a schoolteacher admonishing a student.

"Then you are a fool. Bookshelves by themselves are for collecting dust and cobwebs. These are scribblers, dreamers, impotent in converting their ideas into reality. Ideas don't live in printed pages. They explode on the world when they are transmitted by people like me. Like Stalin. Like Mao Tse-tung." He indicated Leica with a contemptuous wave of his hand. "Not by people like you, afraid of the world the way it is, running away to hide in funk holes in the mountains. You know what you have been waiting for, Leica? To be used. To be used, like an inanimate, inert mechanical tool. If not by me, then by whoever else comes along with a talent for exploitation."

"I do not care for this sort of 'explosion,' " said Leica.

Hadaffi snorted with disgust and banged his hand against the side of the bookshelves. Enough. He knew enough of this man. He had nothing to fear. He strode across the room and positioned himself against the table, to the right of Leica.

"It is important that I see evidence with my own eyes of your . . . shall we say 'talent.' There are other people I have to convince."

Leica braced himself. The preliminaries were over, the skirmishing finished. Now he would know.

"In what way?" he asked grittily. His throat seemed to have swollen, narrowing the passage, making words painful.

"Daiton assures me there are practically no limits to your range?"

"Well . . . within reason."

"What does that mean?"

"I don't know. I've never fully extended myself."

"Across this country?"

"Yes."

"To another country outside America?"

Leica shrugged nervously.

"Perhaps. I think so."

Hadaffi held out a hand toward Daiton and gestured impatiently.

"The material, Vilas," he said.

Daiton took a large envelope from inside his shirt and laid it on the table beside Hadaffi. The terrorist took the material from inside the envelope and spread it around, then he gestured for Leica to come to the table. Leica unwound his lanky frame from out of the chair and stumbled toward Hadaffi. There seemed to be no strength in his legs, as if the muscles had softened to the consistency of jelly. He stopped and leaned forward, examining the contents, his knuckles firmly on the tabletop to support his trembling limbs. There was a photograph of a man in his thirties, a map of New York, a piece of notepaper with writing on it, and several photographs of a building from various angles.

Hadaffi picked up the photograph of the man, and held it up to Leica's face.

"You are to subject this man to intense psychokinesis." He put the photograph down and jabbed his finger down on the map of New York City. "At eight o'clock tomorrow night we have arranged for him to be at this location in New York. The Taft Hotel, on Seventh Avenue." He cast his hand back and forth across the table with an impatient sweeping gesture. "He will be on the fifteenth floor, room one five two three. Here and here are several photographs of the hotel taken from various angles for identification." He tapped his finger down on the notepaper for emphasis. "And here is the precise latitude and longitude of the Taft Hotel." He stepped back, placed his hands on his hips, and looked searchingly at Leica.

"If I am to understand Vilas correctly, you require this type of information to position the subject. Is that right? Is this sufficient?"

Leica picked up the various pieces and sifted them aimlessly through his hands. He tried to think of some reckless, daring answer, but nothing came to his tongue.

"Yes, it's sufficient," he mumbled instead.

Hadaffi nodded with satisfaction.

"Who is the man?" muttered Leica.

"Irrelevant."

"There is nothing irrelevant about killing a man."

"There is about this man. You would not like him. He is an irrelevant individual. The world has scarcely recognized his existence, and his passing will not even be noticed."

"I have never killed a man before."

Hadaffi shrugged, and folded his arms across his chest. Daiton shuffled his feet and glanced about the room, impatient to be gone.

"You have put volunteers through extreme psychokinesis," he said curtly.

"I stopped that."

"You have killed experimental animals."

"That was necessary, but no more."

"Then consider this man an animal. It will be an accurate assessment."

He paused, staring at Leica as if to make certain there was nothing he had forgotten. Outside the sun streamed over the treetops, striking through the front window, showering reflections off his dark glasses.

"Daiton and I will be in the same room as the subject to observe," he added. "I will allow you until nine o'clock. If nothing has taken place by then, I will instruct your wife to be killed by nine thirty." He paused for effect. "Is that understood?" he said bluntly.

Leica nodded dumbly.

"We will be in contact," said Hadaffi. "And I must remind you of one thing you must never forget. It has been arranged for one of us to contact the people holding your wife by telephone at eight o'clock every evening. If for any reason we fail to make that contact, your wife will be killed. Instantly. There is no way you can know where she is. If you are tempted to be stupid enough to use psychokinesis on any of us, it would be an automatic death sentence on your wife. Remember that."

Leica offered no rebuttal. The sleepless night and the tension had reduced him to a state of leaden weariness. He slumped back into the chair, and put his face in his hands. The skin on his face felt damp and clammy against his palms. He stayed that way until he heard the door shut, and then the sound of the car starting up and fading away down the road.

He put his head back and let himself slide deep into the chair until he was staring blankly at the ceiling. Perhaps he should go to the police. What would that achieve? He would have to make them understand, believe, and how was that going to save Jo? Perhaps after he had killed this man they would leave him in peace, Jo would come back, and he could go on living in the mountains. Every instinct told him that such a thought was stupidity, but it was all he had to cling to.

Maybe the man he had to kill *was* irrelevant. He was most likely a criminal, maybe even a murderer. He allowed himself a sardonic smile at the attempted rationalization. Since when did he appoint himself executioner of the world's undesirables?

And Daiton was not quite right. He had made an advance since the early days, and it was possible to make a contact with Jo. But it would take time, more time than he had to spare, working out gradually from the house like expanding radio waves. Even then only with a remote chance of success.

For the first time in a long while he felt the urge to talk to his father. Not that he would have received any advice, but it had always been a comforting thing. His father had been a small scholarly bookshop owner, charming, kindly, but vague in the way of a man immersed for most of his life in the printed page.

"Poppa, I have a problem."

"A boy like you. What possible problem?"

"The other kids don't talk to me at school."

"That's not a problem. They probably have nothing interesting to say." That was the solution: wait for the problem to go away, or pretend it wasn't there.

"Poppa, I want to play on the baseball team, but they won't practice with me."

"The hell with them. They're only jealous of your grades."

"Poppa, Nina Jewel goes down on all the other boys after school, but she only laughs at me."

He didn't really ask that one, but it hurt more than some of the others. It was his first experience of being shut out of an exclusive club. The Nina Jewel cock-suckers club.

And then his mother.

"Henry, our boy has a problem."

"What are you talking about, Emma. The boy is brilliant. Look at his job, look at his salary."

"The boy is twenty-six and not married."

"He doesn't need a woman, he gets all the satisfaction he wants from his work. When he wants a woman, he'll get a woman."

"Henry, the boy has a problem."

"Emma, you have a problem."

Just like that. Dismissed. Vanquished. He was a de-lightful old man, who saw the world through marvelous simplistic eyes. He could demolish a problem with a sentence in a way that left no room for argument, but the problem was still there.

"Father, I have a problem. This unique talent that I have tried to explain to you. There are people, ruthless people, who are trying to force me to use the talent in a way I think is wrong."

"Whose talent is it?"

"It's my talent."

"Then tell them to go away."

"Father," he said patiently, "it's not as simple as that. These are very powerful people. They can make life very unpleasant for me, even dangerous."

"You are wrong, Brett. It is as simple as that. Tell them to go away."

He dragged himself out of the chair and shuffled across to the window. There were intermittent tire tracks on the road where Daiton's car had lurched through some of the scattered pools of water. He almost needed the evidence of those prints to prove to himself the reality of what had just taken place. That it was real, not one of his own created nightmares. Words wouldn't make this problem go away. Not his father's words. Not his words. He was going to make the problem go away by killing a man, and if that's what had to be done to save Jo, then he would do it.

Hadaffi drove back to their motel at Manchester, where they had set up headquarters to be close to Leica. They had talked about staying at Sylvan but rejected the idea. It was too dangerous staying in a small town. Small townspeople observed, and talked, and gossip travels fast through the mountains.

There was a call waiting for them from Fardrin in Connecticut. There had been a contact from Nerida in Washington. The CIA knew that Hadaffi was in America, and the information had come from an undercover agent operating in New York. That meant there was an informer in the brotherhood, a dangerous informer who could destroy them all. Fardrin believed that it was Oxley, and had placed him under intense surveillance. At the moment there was no danger. A bad photograph of Hadaffi had been circulated, but it meant nothing. The real danger lay in the leakage of any more important information.

In a way Hadaffi was pleased. It justified the action they had already taken in relation to Oxley, and just in time. If Fardrin was watching Oxley, there was little chance he would get the opportunity to pass any more information before eight o'clock tomorrow night.

He and Daiton checked out, drove out to the airport, and took the first available flight to New York.

There was confusion at every major airport in the country. Schedules became impossible to keep, passengers' tempers became short, and airlines staffs strove to keep their cool with a courtesy that gradually deteriorated from patient warmth to icy detachment.

The problem was that no one really knew what was going on. Or why. Every major flight suddenly became subject to a rigorous security check double that normally expected. Bags were opened on the slightest pretext, suspicious bulges in passengers' clothing firmly inspected, tempers flared, irate travelers switched airlines, only to discover the same situation existed wherever they purchased a ticket.

Planes were searched, then searched again; pilots swore at hostesses; tearful hostesses harangued ground staff; ground staff flared at administration; and the hapless passengers milled around in the reception areas like shoppers at a retail store sale who had arrived to find all the bargains gone.

Of course, it couldn't continue. The new security checks defined in the directive to the airlines needed time to implement; it was impossible to superimpose them like one hat on top of another. By four in the afternoon the major airlines had decided. To hell with the directive, because they couldn't get their planes off the ground in time, and there was stacking over every airport in the country. It developed into some gigantic aeronautical traffic jam. The airline administrations took a deep breath and went back to normal operation procedures, then set their planners to work to figure out some way to make the new directives work without fouling up the system.

If there were any kinks, then the federal agency would have to sort out the problem. They had planes to fly, and schedules to meet, and passengers who demanded that they get flown from point A to point B in a certain specified time. And if there was a surplus of crazy bomb-planters and hijackers around as the directive hinted, then they would have to hope for the best, because they needed breathing space to make it all work.

After all, the percentages were on their side. If the crazy bastards they were being warned about knocked half a dozen planes out of the sky, the chances of being one of the unlucky ones were still pretty remote.

Nick Oxley went through Times Square, crossed Forty-second Street, and headed up Seventh Avenue, threading his way through the pre-theater crowds. He glanced nervously at his watch. It was seven forty-five. If he was a few moments late, then they were just going to have to wait, because he couldn't force his legs to hurry. He was nervous. Perhaps tonight's meeting was nothing more than Daiton had suggested, a chance for him to meet Hadaffi, to talk about the brotherhood, about their plans in New York.

He had not the slightest desire to meet Hadaffi, or anybody else connected with the brotherhood anymore. All he wanted was out, but it would have been dangerous to refuse. He had been forced to cancel his appointment with the agent, though, and that was an irritation. He had decided to feed out the information a little appetizer at a time, because he was sure that way there was more money to be made; keep him dancing, allowing him just a small nibble of the carrot each bite.

He would need all the money he could get, for there were only a few corners of the world where he could be totally safe from the brotherhood.

Then seeing Fardrin in New York this afternoon had disturbed him, made him doubly cautious. What was Fardrin doing in New York, when he was supposed to be out on the farm in Connecticut, helping to guard the woman? He put his hand inside his coat pocket, and reassured himself by the feel of the gun. If things got rough, then he knew how to handle himself. Hadaffi had an awesome reputation, but his body was no more immune to the force of a bullet than anyone else's.

Oxley was a small man. Thin-faced, wide-eyed, with jutting pointed chin, and sandy hair brushed forward to hide approaching baldness. He was about forty, a Marxist, a joiner—clubs, groups, anything, just so long as he belonged somewhere. But the brotherhood was too dangerous, they were crazy people, they saw people as bugs who could be stepped on and squashed at the slightest provocation. He had no intention of waiting around to be squashed.

He edged past a small crowd watching a group of musicians performing in a doorway. The flashing signs overhead threw a kaleidoscope of colors from their instruments. One of them had an overturned garbage can, and was energetically thrashing out a pounding beat with a set of drumsticks. There was an open hat on the ground in front of him, with a few pathetic coins inside.

Oxley grinned sourly as he passed by. At least selling information to the agent was more rewarding than playing music on the streets of New York. And this little tidbit he was passing on would give them quite a shock. The revelation about Daiton he would keep until next time, because for that he would demand quite a sum.

He came to the Taft entrance and was about to pass through to the foyer when the girl stopped him. She put her body right in front of him, blocking his path. They were like that in New York, aggressive as hell. She was black, nice dress, nice boots, a small bowler hat perched jauntily on the side of her head.

"Want a girl for tonight, sweetie?" she inquired throatily.

He grinned at her. She was a looker, and he hadn't beaten a girl as good-looking as this one in a long time. It was a pity she had no idea what she was going to miss.

"Some other time," he said.

"Fifty dollars. I'll come up to your room right now."

"Some other time," he repeated.

"Everything you want, baby," she murmured. "Come on, tell me your room number. I'll go down on you, you can do what you want with me. The best fifty dollars you've ever spent."

"Fuck off," he said.

She stepped a little closer, and licked at her mouth.

"Half an hour, that's all, sweetie. You can afford that much time, can't you? I'll give you half an hour that you'll never forget."

He reached up and took off her hat, and with a quick flick of his hand sent it spinning out into the flow of traffic along Seventh Avenue. It vanished under the wheels of a passing cab.

She stood looking at the honking traffic for a moment, then stepped back out of his path.

"You lousy white shit," she said softly.

"Get lost," he grunted. He moved past her and into the foyer and across to the elevators, picking his way around the stacks of tourist luggage gathered for transportation.

He stepped out on the fifteenth floor and poked his way around the corridors until he found room 1523. He paused at the door long enough to give the gun another reassuring squeeze, then knocked loudly.

"Come in," a voice called.

He recognized Daiton's voice, and he opened the door and went inside.

It was a pleasant room. To his left a double bed, bedside table, and a lamp. To his right a clothes closet, a chest of drawers with the mandatory television set perched on top, and a hand basin. Farther along a door, obviously to the shower and john.

Daiton was standing by the window, one hand on the sill, watching him, a soft smile on his face. There was a chair behind him. Across from him were another two chairs, one unoccupied, the other occupied by a balding thickset man who he presumed was Hadaffi. Both were dressed casually in slacks and jackets. It was five minutes after eight o'clock.

"Come in, Nick, come in," said Daiton warmly. He gestured to the other man seated in the chair. "Nick, I want you to meet Hadaffi. As I told you, Hadaffi, Nick is our number one connection in New York."

As Oxley moved forward Hadaffi levered his bulk out of the chair and both men met over a hand clasp in the center of the room.

"I've heard so much about you, it's great to finally meet you in the flesh," Oxley effused.

"You're a very important man to us," murmured Hadaffi. He indicated the chair alongside his. "Please, Nick, make yourself comfortable."

Oxley bobbed his head nervously and went across and perched himself primly on the edge of the proffered chair. Hadaffi strolled across and seated himself by his side. Everything seemed friendly and relaxed.

Daiton produced a bottle of Old Grand-dad from somewhere, and three glasses, which he set up on the bedside table. There was silence except for the *glop, glop* of the pouring whiskey. When he had finished, he handed out the glasses, first one to Hadaffi, then to Oxley.

He raised his own glass in a toasting gesture.

"To success." He smiled.

Oxley and Hadaffi raised their glasses in response, but Oxley merely sipped cautiously at his drink, while the other two men drained theirs dry.

"You seem a little cautious of our success, Nick," Hadaffi observed.

Oxley twisted the glass around in his hands with agitated fingers.

"No, no, of course not," he said quickly. He patted at his stomach. "I've an ulcer that plays up a little. I have to take my liquor very slowly."

"How unfortunate for you," said Hadaffi, with exaggerated solicitude.

Oxley smiled stiffly and took a longer sip. He waited.

"We have great plans for America, Nick," said Daiton. He took Hadaffi's empty glass and went across to the table and refilled it, then his own.

"Great plans," he continued. "And you're a very important part of that plan. New York is the financial hub of America, of the world. We need money, and this is the place to obtain it. Hadaffi will show us the right kind of persuasion we have to use to open the purse strings of this wealthy establishment city." He went across and handed the refilled glass to his chief. "Right, Hadaffi?"

Hadaffi merely nodded a smile and took the glass.

"I was wondering when you were going to take me into your confidence," said Oxley, managing an offended tone.

"We need you, Nick. No more of that resigning from the brotherhood nonsense," said Daiton affably.

"Certainly not. You took me too seriously, Vilas."

"I thought it necessary to ask. We have security to worry about."

"I was upset. You didn't take me into your confidence. I knew nothing. Not about our great leader here, not about any plan. I was beginning to believe you had lost confidence in me."

Vilas sat himself down on the edge of the bed, drinking more slowly this time.

"Nonsense, Nick, of course I have every confidence in you. But you must understand our security problems. It was important to get our leader into the country with as few people knowing as possible. No one else knew, Nick. No one. It would have been fatal if Hadaffi had been stopped by customs officials. You understand that, surely?"

Oxley nodded slowly. Something caught his eye at the base of the door leading into the room, and momentarily distracted him. It was a damp stain spreading rapidly into the carpet from somewhere outside in the passage.

Some careless maid must have knocked over a bucket of water, or something similar.

"You do understand, Nick?" Daiton asked again.

"Yes, yes, of course," said Oxley slowly. "What is it you expect me to do to help?" He turned to Hadaffi, and swirled the remaining whiskey around in his glass. "My only wish is to serve, Hadaffi. I don't have to tell you that. With my life, if necessary."

"We hope that won't be necessary," murmured Hadaffi. "Although I'm deeply touched by your loyalty." He took off his dark glasses, and the black eyes skewered through Oxley like a rapier thrust. Oxley took a deep gulp of his whiskey, more than he intended, and the liquor burned in his stomach. His eyes went back to the stain by the door, fascinated.

It was spreading now with increasing rapidity. The stain passed under Daiton's feet, but he didn't seem to notice. It was more than water from a bucket, it was almost as if some crazy fool had left a hose running in the passage.

Daiton reached into his inside pocket and took out a piece of paper. He spread it out on the bed and ran his finger up and down a typed list of names.

"These are the people we will need to concentrate on in New York. It may even be necessary for you to make the initial contact, Nick." He looked up and frowned with annoyance. "I'll need your attention, Nick," he said acidly. "I don't expect you to give up your life right now, but I would like you to listen to what I have to say."

Oxley pointed his glass at the stain on the floor.

"Someone seems to have started a flood out in the corridor," he said, with forced humor.

Daiton looked searchingly at the floor, then glanced up at Hadaffi with a strange intent expression of curiosity. Hadaffi leaned forward, craning his neck to see the spot Oxley was indicating.

"Yes," said Daiton hesitantly.

"I think someone should call the desk downstairs," said Oxley.

"I'm sure it will just go away eventually," answered Hadaffi.

Oxley didn't answer. From somewhere outside he could hear the sound of surging, fast-running water. Like the sound he'd heard the night the house got swept away. Christ, he'd almost forgotten the terror of that nighttime awakening. He must have been only four years old.

Daiton was reading off a list of names, and companies, and financial connections, and kidnapping, but it was only an indistinct burr in his ears. There was a roar from somewhere like a wall giving way, and water came spurting furiously into the room from around the edges of the door, and welling up in small waves from beneath the skirting boards.

"Jesus Christ," spluttered Oxley. He jerked himself upright from the chair, dropping the glass. It splashed down and bobbed around like a miniature glass boat enjoying a sudden sense of freedom in the water already ankle-deep around his feet.

"Christ, let's get the hell out of here," he shouted.

Neither of the other men moved; they just sat there, with the water sucking at their feet, soaking their shoes and trousers. A copy of the *Times* slipped off the bed and was quickly swept to the far wall and held there by the force of the water. Oxley came to the conclusion that his companions were mad. The water was rising with unbelievable speed, and by the time he floundered to the door it was up to his knees. It was cold and saturated with mud like flooded river-water.

"Are you crazy, Vilas . . . and you too, Hadaffi? Some pipe has burst somewhere. Let's get out of here."

But they just sat there like wooden dolls, waiting to be swept away, as if it were some sort of game, both with maddening expressions of intent curiosity. Fuck them, he concluded, they could make their own way. He didn't understand the water; it made no sense at all. How in Christ could a room on the fifteenth floor of a hotel suddenly flood? But there was no mistaking the evidence of his own eyes, or the bite of the cold water on his limbs. He could find out the answers to those questions later; for now all he wanted to do was get out of the room. But the door wouldn't budge. Maybe it had swollen already with the water, but it was jammed tight, immovable to any force he was capable of exerting. He began to panic, because there was no sign of the flow of water easing, and it was already over the waist. He dragged the gun out of his pocket and tried to fire at the lock of the door, but somehow it slipped out of his fingers and disappeared into the water. Objects bobbed around in the water like dropped leaves in a pond, pillows, papers, cases. The whiskey bottle caught against his coat until the water wrenched it free and sluiced it across the room to clink repetitively against the wall on the other side.

He floundered back to the bed and put his face close to Vilas, and shook him violently by the shoulders.

"Help me get out," he roared.

It was ridiculous. Vilas merely sat there, not moving, the same crazy expression on his face. He was still sitting, with the water almost up to his neck. Hadaffi was the same, still sitting in the chair, with the water bubbling almost at his mouth. He began to think he was losing his senses, that this wasn't really happening, the meeting had never taken place, he was asleep, fighting to return to consciousness before he drowned.

Even as he watched, the water swirled up past Hadaffi's mouth, over his nose, blotted out his eyes, then with one final wave, covered his head.

He gave up on both the door and the men. For some reason beyond his comprehension they had both executed themselves, inexplicable suicide.

He forced himself across the room, with the water now almost up to his neck, sobbing, scrabbling for the window. How could he possibly drown in an upstairs room in a New York hotel? His mind tried to face the question, and jammed shut. Like the window. It was his last chance to drain some of the water from the room, and it was shut as firmly as the door. He cast around for something to smash the glass, then he was jerked off his feet and bumped around the room with the rest of the flotsam. The roar of the water drummed in his ears, and he struggled out of his shoes and trousers, trying to keep afloat. Beneath him, under the water, the bedside lamp still burned, a watery swaying yellow blur. Dimly he could perceive the shapes of the two other men, still sitting where he had left them, drowned, but not floating. Why hadn't they floated like him, been swept up by the water to join the other objects swirling over the surface with him? There were no answers, only the question of how to survive.

He was not a good swimmer, and he flailed wildly with his arms, thrashing at the water to keep afloat, trying desperately to subdue the panic that threatened to drown him. He kept telling himself that it had to stop, that it made no logical sense for the level of the water to keep rising at such speed. But it did keep rising. It took him up until his head was only a few inches from the ceiling of the room, and he knew then that unless he did something he was going to drown. Drown in a room on the fifteenth floor of the Taft Hotel, in the center of New York City.

Something tangled around his legs, threatening to drag him under, and he kicked out frantically until he was free. It was a bed sheet, winding up from the floor with the easy grace of a reptilian swimmer.

The window was his only chance, he was convinced of that. He gulped air into his lungs, put his head beneath the water, and propelled himself downward toward the floor. He felt his feet come into contact with the ceiling and he used it as a lever, pushing down with all his force.

It took him down past Hadaffi, still sitting in the chair, his sparse hair waving gently about his head like seaweed fronds, watching him with wide, staring drowned eyes, but still the same maddening expression of curiosity. He went on past, forcing himself toward the window, blinding fear pumping demonic strength into his body. He grasped at each side of the window with his hands, curving his body upward until his feet came into contact with the glass. Water began to seep into his mouth with the taste of rotting mud, and there was a burning sensation spreading across his chest. He felt his eyes beginning to distend as if the water were forcing them from their sockets, and he kicked out wildly, ignoring the risk to his bare feet. The glass gave way, spearing out from the point of impact in a series of jagged cracks, and he felt a sharp pain in his right foot as a trail of blood merged with the water.

He ignored it, he was going to live; one more blow

and the window would disintegrate under the force of the water, and he would breathe again, the searing pain would go from his chest.

The window burst outward with a sudden crack and the water boiled through the opening in a torrent. He felt his hands wrenched away from the sides of the window as the surge of water took hold of him, as if he were a helpless piece of cork, turning him end over end, hurling him through the smashed window. Something slashed along his left arm, so quick, so sharp, there was no sensation of pain. All he was aware of was that he could breathe again, and he swallowed hungrily at the night air.

He was falling, turning slowly, end over end, the water coming down with him like a tropical downpour, the sides of the building rushing past him. The wind beat against his soaked clothes, chilling his body.

He shut his eyes tightly. This was not reality, this wasn't happening, the experience was crammed with the illogical lunacy of a nightmare, and any moment he would wake in his Greenwich Village apartment, maybe with the black girl lying beside him, waiting with her hand on his belly. The conviction was absolute; he didn't even scream.

The lights of Seventh Avenue sped toward him, multicolored glowworms seeking sanctuary in his body. Maybe they would transform into flesh-eating monsters before his waking time. Only he hoped it would be soon.

The black girl was waiting, he was sure. He could feel her hand scratching impatiently at his belly, he would roll over and bury his head in her breasts to drown out the sounds of the honking car horns, then he would . . .

The intense concentration went on for thirty minutes, the longest that Brett had ever sustained, and it exhausted him. That night he finally slept, anesthetized by the effort, even undeterred by his longing for Jo. It was eleven in the morning before he woke, his tongue furred, and his head with the thick feel of an overdose of sleeping pills. He stumbled under the shower and stood there a long time, letting the water bring him back to life. He was certain he had been successful, because there was a sensation he had never experienced before. Right at the completion of the session something had switched off in his mind, jerking him out of the trance as if there had been an automatic response from the subject. A termination, a signal that the concentration was no longer necessary. It had taken him by surprise, because up until now he had always been in control of whatever length of time he felt he needed. It was new, and scientifically interesting, but it had filled him with guilt. Because he knew it meant that he was a murderer.

Maybe it could never be proved in court. What jury could ever be convinced? But he was convicted in his own mind. If the water had needled his body back into tune, it did little for the depressed state of his mind. Yet he knew if he had the option again nothing would change. He had been given the choice between Jo and a stranger, and for him it was no choice. But if Jo came back to him today, what would they do? It would be impossible to stay here. How would his father have made that problem go away, how would he react when confronted by Daiton and the man in the dark glasses?

So he waited for Jo, hoping against hope that they would keep their word about releasing his wife. He prowled the room, touching things that belonged to her, recreating in his mind images of their times together, even their arguments, which seemed so inconsequential now, as if remembering someone who was already dead. He picked up her jacket from where she had left it, still cast over the corner of a kitchen chair, fingering it to sustain his memories, the cup she always drank from, the paintings she liked.

He had never sentimentalized over her before, but the danger had aroused such an acute sense of loss.

Even the argument over her having the child seemed immaterial now. He relived the night of conception, the tenderness. Sex had not come easily for them at first, which had been a surprise for both of them: she because she expected experience he did not have, he because of a nervousness he did not allow for. But intelligence had quickly overcome that barrier; what pleased her, what pleased him, had been rapidly learned.

Noon came and passed, but he didn't bother to eat, he let coffee sustain him. It was slightly warmer than the previous day, and the sun shimmered through the trees, throwing a pattern of dancing bright spots through the window and onto the stained wooden floor. The former pools of water along the track had dried to the consistency of soft mud, and the pines along each side luxuriated in the warmth of the sun.

He was trying to force himself to browse through a book when he caught the sound of a car engine drifting up from the bottom of the hill.

He put the book down, listening as the sound drew closer. He didn't go to the window, or the door, but stood rigidly in place, his fingers trembling, his throat abruptly dried by the sudden acceleration of his heartbeat.

He waited until he heard the car stop outside the house, his eyes closed, picturing Jo coming through the door, one hand laid over her swollen stomach, and her smile bright but concerned.

He opened them again, and it was the man in the dark glasses. Somehow he experienced no great sense of surprise, because he knew he had been sustaining himself with fantasy, and fantasy and reality rarely become one and the same.

Beyond the man in the dark glasses he could see another man he did not know, standing by the car, but there was no sign of Jo.

The man nodded curtly as he stepped into the room and closed the door behind him. He glanced around the room, strolled past Leica, and paused at the entrance to the kitchen. He inclined his head into the room.

"Be a good host, Leica," he said. "Make me some coffee. We have a great deal to talk about, and coffee would make it more pleasant."

"Where's my wife?" asked Leica huskily.

Hadaffi inclined his head again toward the kitchen.

"Coffee first," he insisted pleasantly.

Leica could tell nothing from his voice. Even, controlled. He could have been a lifelong friend invited in for a game of bridge.

Leica swallowed hard, and put his hand down on the shelf to try and disguise the trembling.

"Go to hell," he said. The tone of his voice cracked

and Hadaffi smiled thinly, not fooled by the attempted bravado.

"You want to talk about your wife, I want a cup of coffee," he said firmly. He shrugged and spread his hands, offering the bargain.

Leica sullenly accepted the terms, strode across the room, brushed past Hadaffi, and went into the kitchen. He bustled about preparing the coffee, taking the cream from the refrigerator, setting out the cups. It was the game thing again. He would have to wait while the man proceeded through his preliminary teasing and needling, wait until he had decided to be direct. In the meantime the man was amusing himself making Leica play waiter to his whims. But there was a dullness in his chest concerning Jo. The monster was going to demand something more of him, and then more and more, and he would go on playing assassin, but it would take him no closer to recovering Jo. On those terms life would be unacceptable, both for himself and Jo.

He poured the coffee and took the cups back into the living room. The man was back by the bookshelves again, in the same position. It was like peeking in at a movie he had seen before.

He put the coffee down on the table, and Hadaffi waved a book in his direction.

"James Thurber," he said. "You did not appear to me a man who enjoyed humor."

Leica shrugged. He could have stated the same about his visitor, but he let it pass.

"You have your coffee, now I want to know about my wife. You said you would bring her back?" There was a pleading whine in his voice, and he despised himself for it. "Did I succeed with the man you wanted me to kill, or not?"

"Ah, yes, the coffee," said Hadaffi, ignoring Leica's questions. He made no attempt to pick up the cup of coffee. He decided he would leave it there to go cold. That was part of the game.

"Would you be surprised to know that I enjoy reading Thurber?" he asked.

Leica said nothing. He left his own coffee where he had placed it on the table, untouched.

"Would you believe that I saw my first copy of Thurber in Moscow?" he said. "I have no idea how it got there. The Russians do not understand Thurber. I do. He saw so clearly the stupidity of your country, why it would inevitably collapse in on itself. I always find it reassuring to read Thurber, but there is so little time."

Leica had no interest in ludicrous interpretations of James Thurber.

"Fuck you. Why are you here?" he burst out. "I did what you asked, you promised my wife would be returned. What happened in New York? . . . did I fail?" A sudden fear jammed in this throat. If he had failed, then they would have killed Jo. "My wife is still alive?" he whispered. Even as he asked the question he knew he would have no way of knowing if the man would answer him truthfully. Maybe she had been dead all the time.

"No, you did not fail," said Hadaffi suddenly. "She is still alive. Would you like to know what happened to the man . . . the subject?"

Leica's head drooped down toward the floor, and he shook his head slowly.

"No," he whispered.

"Not even for scientific interest?"

Leica didn't respond.

"Very interesting," continued Hadaffi. "I have never

seen a man act like that. He was quite mad. He rushed around the room, he screamed at us, he threw himself down on the floor and threw his arms around as if he was trying in some crazy way to swim." Hadaffi smiled. He was enjoying himself. "From what I could gather of his crazy chattering, I think he believed he was about to drown."

Leica tried to shut his ears. He didn't want to know, he didn't want to know what sort of man he was, he didn't want to know how he had died, because he had enough guilt without any details.

Hadaffi went on with the torment. "He kept asking Daiton and myself to help him get out of the room. I have rarely seen that sort of fear in a man's face. He took off his trousers and shoes, then he smashed the window with his bare feet. He bled quite badly. Then he threw himself out the window." He paused and changed his mind about the coffee. He picked up the cup and sipped slowly. "Ah, that's good, Leica," he said patronizingly. "We were on the fifteenth floor. He must have been pulp after he hit the sidewalk." He shrugged. "We all die eventually, Leica. Some of us deserve to go in a more unpleasant way than others. This traitorous fool did, believe me."

In spite of himself, Leica absorbed the words, and he was appalled to realize that there was a detached part of his mind scientifically taking in every detail for analysis. Was that what he had become? Was he really just another scientist divorcing himself from the reality of creating horrendous weaponry? Well, no more. Like his father, he determined to make the problem go away.

"Stop playing your stupid shit games with me," he demanded harshly. "Tell me what you want. Tell me when I'm to get my wife back. Or get out."

Hadaffi scowled. He put the cup down firmly on the table, and the coffee slopped over into the saucer. The game had to be played on his terms, to his timing. He took an envelope from his pocket, extracted a photographic print, and laid it on the table in front of Leica. His finger jabbed down forcefully on the print.

"This is your next subject for psychokinesis," he said bluntly.

"You said the last subject would be all you would demand from me," said Leica, refusing to look at the photograph.

"I lied. This will be the last one."

"You are lying again."

"Perhaps. But the same terms apply. If you want your wife to live, then you must do as I say."

"You intend to make me become a mass murderer."

"I am not asking you to murder this man," grated Hadaffi.

"Then what are you asking?"

"Sufficient psychokinesis to terrify the man into a state of subjection." He stabbed at the photograph again with his finger. "Look at the photograph," he demanded.

Leica looked down at the print, and air seemed to bubble up from his stomach, blocking his throat, making words difficult.

"You're mad," he said weakly. "You can't be serious?"

"I have never been more serious in my life."

"You are asking the impossible."

"Then you are going to do the impossible."

Leica picked up the photograph with trembling fingers, then threw it down again.

"This is Thomas Manningham, President of the United States," he said.

"Exactly."

"What the hell are you hoping to achieve, putting the President under psychokinesis?"

"That is irrelevant for you. You are merely my tool, Leica. The psychokinesis must be prolonged enough to create terror, but not fatal. Like you inflicted on Vilas."

"I might disable the man."

"The hell you should care, Leica. Wasn't it his agents that drove you into hiding, hounded you?" Hadaffi sneered. "You could look at it as some sort of poetic justice. Your chance to get even."

Leica shook his head vigorously. Maybe he should feel like that, but he couldn't. This wasn't getting even, this was destroying the basis of governing the country. He hated all of them, the CIA, the KGB, the military, but this wasn't the way to do it. And this wouldn't be the end of it. He was being asked to terrorize the President now, but what about the next time? They were going to demand something from the President, and if they failed, what then? Kill the President. Then kill the one who took his place. Then the next and the next. That was chaos. Unacceptable. Perhaps he was a weak man, maybe even a coward, but he had to resist this, he had to find some of his father's simple strength.

"No," he said.

"You will do it," insisted Hadaffi.

"No."

"You are a fool, you owe them nothing."

"No," said Leica again.

"You are sentencing your wife to death."

Leica hesitated, his head down, white-faced, hands clasped. Was life acceptable on these terms? If not for him, then did he have the right to make a decision for Jo? What would she want him to do? She was probably hidden away somewhere without the slightest idea of what it was all about. He closed his eyes and tried to imagine someone coming into a room where she was, and shooting her to death. The baby dying in her stomach without ever knowing life.

"No," he whispered. "No, you ask too much."

Hadaffi's reserve snapped. His arm brushed across the table, catching Leica's cup of coffee and sending it shattering to the floor.

"Your life also, Leica," he snarled.

"No."

It was the only word he could find, it was his only strength. If he kept repeating it over and over, demanding no more of himself, then perhaps he could endure, not think about the consequences.

"There are worse things than death, Leica."

He didn't answer.

Hadaffi stood up away from Leica, his brows knitted tightly with anger.

"I can make it worse," he grated. "I will tell you who I am, then perhaps you will realize that I will carry out any threat I promise. You have to believe that." He paused, waiting for Leica to look up.

"I am Hadaffi," he said.

A shaft of sunlight sparked off the window, reflecting in Leica's face, and he squinted his eyes.

"Hadaffi?"

"Yes, Hadaffi."

"The terrorist butcher?"

"No, Hadaffi the liberation leader."

Leica blinked uncertainly.

"But I am Jewish."

"You are a tool for me to use. It does not matter if you are a Tibetan monk."

"You will kill me anyhow."

"Not if you serve me well. Your talents are too valuable."

Leica shook his head, and looked down at the floor again. He was lying.

"I am only asking you to frighten the President," wheedled Hadaffi, trying a new tack. It was a mistake, and he saw it immediately.

"No," said Leica weakly. It was more of a sentence than a statement, and maybe in the night he would wake screaming to change his mind.

Hadaffi stood looking down at him for a moment, then sighed with exaggerated regret.

"I had not expected stupidity from a mind as brilliant as yours, Leica," he said softly. He was back in control of himself. He was only wasting time, new tactics were required, and he would put them into action immediately. People never seemed to understand, never seemed able to comprehend, that in the cause of the brotherhood he was capable of anything, any cruelty, any suffering. It was unfortunate, but sometimes essential.

"I will be back in the morning and we will talk again," he said curtly. "There are two men outside in the car, I am going to get them to stay with you, just in case you may be tempted to do anything stupid. They are not great conversationalists, Leica, but they are very effective. They will not let you out of their sight."

He said no more, but walked briskly across the room and out the door. A few moments later Leica could hear him talking to the other men outside. He felt too weak to raise himself from the chair. Whatever thought he'd had about going to the police was lost to him now. He guessed Hadaffi was going to let him sleep on the thought of Jo's death. And his own. Maybe he was right, perhaps his sudden strength was all bravado, and during the night rationalization would decay his resolve, and he would find a reason for himself and Jo to go on living. He would see.

The room was comfortable and clean, with sleeping and toilet facilities, but someone had nailed heavy wire over the windows to create the appearance of a cell. There was even a television set which she watched listlessly, without really absorbing anything.

She tuned to the newscasts, but there was nothing about a pregnant woman being kidnapped; she was hardly surprised. While Jo found her kidnapping and imprisonment incomprehensible, she knew it wasn't a ransom, at least not in the accepted sense. If Brett hadn't gone to the police, then it was a logical conclusion that her disappearance had something to do with pressure being applied to him. Something that Vilas Daiton was responsible for. But would any of the government agencies go to such lengths to pressure Brett into working for them? She guessed anything was possible. Even Vilas's discovering the hideaway in the Kentucky mountains was a surprise she found hard to explain.

Some of her initial fear had dissipated since the actual kidnapping by Vilas and his companion on the road out of Sylvan. For a time she had been so terrified she had actually feared a miscarriage. It was not so much Vilas she was afraid of—she had always disliked and distrusted him, but she found it difficult to believe he would do her physical bodily harm—as much as the other man in the dark glasses. She had very quickly sensed that he controlled Daiton, controlled him to such an extent that Vilas would probably do anything the other man ordered. It was a more brutal Daiton than she remembered, acting like a small boy determined to show his elders what a big tough guy he'd become. That had certainly frightened her, but it was the menace of the other man that had stimulated uncontrolled trembling into her limbs. An aura, a feel about the man that she could sense like an animal smell. The curt orders, the responses of someone trained to violence, the cruel mouth.

They had blindfolded her, and then she had been driven for hours. She had lost track of time, lost track of direction, and somewhere she had been passed out of the hands of Vilas and the other man. New masculine voices to which she could attach no bodies took control of the car, and she went on and on in what seemed an endless drive. The new voices had paid her little attention, apart from a few muttered grunts when they gave her something to drink. She had dozed, on and off, worrying about the baby, worrying about Brett, trying to control her fear.

She had no idea where she was, except that it was out in the country somewhere. It had been dark by the time they had brought her to the house, and not until she was in the room had they removed the blindfold.

Someone had taken her arm in a firm grip, pinching the flesh, steering her first one way, then the other, with a steady flow of muttered instructions. That time the disembodied voice had been female, heavy, middle-aged, detached. She had been the first person she had seen when the blindfold had been removed, and the voice had matched the body.

Somewhere between fifty and sixty, gray hair tied back in a bun, lined face, flat Slav features, solid rounded body, with large breasts, and a mouth that had not smiled for a long time. She was dressed in a plain green dress, and flat, heavy shoes. She was the only person she ever saw. The only person she ever questioned. She knew there were others around the house because she heard voices, male voices, calling to each other, and sometimes she heard her warder answering them. Occasionally a car would drive up to the house, and the door would slam, followed by some inaudible conversation, then the car would drive away again.

When the blindfold had first been removed, and she had stood squinting about the room, trying to adjust to the light, the first question had come, the first of many to be ignored.

"Where am I?"

Nothing. The woman had merely stood there, staring at her, looking down at her distended belly.

"What am I doing here? Why have I been brought to this place? What do you want from me?"

Nothing. The woman had broken the stare and strode across to the windows, brushing back the curtains to show her the heavy wire. An unspoken gesture to show that the room was now a cell.

"You can see I'm having a baby. I must be treated well. Will you let my husband know that I'm all right?"

Nothing. A stupid question anyhow. The woman had crossed the room again in her heavy masculine tread, and opened another door to show her the toilet facilities.

"I want to see Vilas Daiton."

Nothing again. The woman had turned and lumbered out of the room.

She had waited for the worst, but nothing happened. By her watch she had finally dozed off around four in the morning, and that had taken her into a deep sleep. It was when she woke that some of her fear had gone.

Now that her mind was clearer, she was certain that she was being held to bring some pressure to bear on Brett. The only question was by whom?

But at least it made her relatively confident that for the moment she was safe. And so was the baby. Even in her predicament she felt a flow of sympathy for her husband. Poor Brett, it was all over. Her urgings for them to come out of hiding meant nothing now. He would be forced out of hiding, and on someone else's terms. She wondered how he would react. With strength, she hoped. He was a clever man, a brilliant man, and there was a gentleness there that most people mistook for timidity.

She had to admit there were times when she even saw it that way herself.

The woman brought her breakfast: eggs, toast, and coffee. The green dress had been changed for a gray color, and it made her look more like a jailer than before.

"How long are you going to keep me here? I need more clothes," Jo asked hesitantly.

The woman put the breakfast tray down on the table without looking at her, expressionless, her movements slow and cautious.

"I am going to smash the window, and tear away the wire," said Jo in frustration.

The woman folded her arms and stood looking at her with the same flat expression.

"That would be foolish." The voice from the previous night, deep and heavy with a trace of accent.

"Ah, you have a voice."

"Only when you need to be warned."

"Then why am I here?"

Nothing again.

"How long are you going to keep me here?"

Silence.

"Somehow I am going to escape."

The woman sighed, the heavy drawn-out hiss of air released when one is coping with a capricious child.

"It is important for you to realize that you are of no consequence."

"What does that mean?"

"It means you are being held here by people who are engaged in a game with a very high prize at stake. If you give no trouble, it is possible you will be unharmed. If you make trouble, they will kill you. It is as simple as that." She paused, and the sigh came again. "You are of no consequence."

Fear came back to Jo in a flood, like an ebb tide racing in over dry sand. She put her hands over her stomach in a gesture of protection.

"The government would never stand for that," she said shakily.

It was a probe, an attempt to see if there was any government responsibility, and it failed.

"We are responsible to no one," said the woman bluntly.

The baby moved under Jo's hands, and she felt a sudden rush of nausea. The breakfast tray suddenly looked like a dish of unpalatable maggots. Her vision blurred with giddiness, and she put a hand to her head.

"I don't feel well. I want to rest awhile."

"As you wish," the woman shrugged.

The woman left the tray and went from the room. The sound of a turning key clicked loudly from outside. Jo climbed on the bed and lay back on the pillow, her head turned toward the window. It was a beautiful morning. A thin line of white clouds straggled across the window, the only smudge on an otherwise sharp blue sky. Somewhere a dog began to bark, the sound brittle in the morning air, and she could hear the plaintive sound of a cow from a long way off.

She wondered if it was possible for Brett to contact her. She knew it was something he'd been working on for a long time, projecting out like a radar scan, he had tried to explain to her, but he'd had little success.

She closed her eyes and tried to emulate what she had seen him do, concentrating on an image of his face in her mind, on the house, on the mountains. Nothing happened except that over a protracted time she developed a splitting headache.

She gave up the idea in disgust. She knew it was crazy from the start, but anything was worth a try.

The baby moved again, and she twisted uncomfortably. She hoped her mother and father were going to become grandparents, although her mother would hate the tag of implied age. Not that she had seen them for three years, because that was another stricture that Brett had insisted on.

She dozed fitfully while the sun subtly changed direction through the window of her cell, the wire mesh casting eerie cobweb patterns on the walls.

When she woke the breakfast tray was gone, and her jailer was standing at the end of the bed with a man. He was in his mid-forties, heavily built, totally bald, with small features set into a large round head. Small eyes, small nose, small mouth. A thin gray moustache filled the space between nose and mouth.

She raised herself on her elbows, startled, and the woman shushed at her with her hands.

"What do you want?" asked Jo.

"You said you weren't feeling well this morning."

"I'm all right now. It was probably the journey last night."

The woman gestured to the man.

"This is a doctor. He is going to examine you to make sure you are all right."

Jo looked suspiciously at the man. He didn't look like a doctor to her. He was dressed in jeans with an old checked shirt. He didn't say anything after the introduction, but merely smirked at her.

"I don't wish to be examined. I'm perfectly well."

"It is not for you to say."

"I want you to leave me alone."

"We merely wish to make certain that you are well."

"I thought you said I was of no consequence."

The woman shrugged and placed her hand at the man's back, urging him forward.

"That's true. But for now you are of some value. You will be examined."

"I don't want that man to touch me. How do I know he's a doctor?"

The woman clucked her tongue impatiently without answering. She went quickly to the side of the bed and took hold of Jo's wrists and thrust her down forcefully against the mattress. She was incredibly strong. Jo arched her back trying to struggle free, but the woman's fingers were like iron bands around her wrists.

"You bastard," Jo breathed.

"I will pin your legs to the sides of the bed if you continue to struggle," said the woman. She thrust down with her arms, exerting extra pressure in warning. "Now lie still."

There was nothing Jo could do. She lay there with her eyes closed, praying for it to be over quickly. Her eyes filled and tears oozed out from under her closed lids and ran wetly down into her neck.

After it was over and they had left the room, she lay there exhausted, dabbing wearily at her wet cheeks with the end of the bed sheet.

She could hear them outside the door, talking in muted tones.

"Then we'll have to make other arrangements," she heard the woman say.

That was the only sentence she caught, the rest was an indistinct murmur, then she heard the sound of their retreating steps away from the room. She had no idea what the woman meant.

She turned on her side, facing the wall, and tried to control a sudden overpowering surge of resentment against her husband.

"This is a copy of the report I'm going to submit to the President," said Carmody. "I thought you might have a look at it first, Martin." He dropped it down on Schyler's desk top, but the Intelligence chief made no attempt to pick it up. It would have given him immense satisfaction to tell Carmody that he had already seen the report, that Zambretti had managed to funnel an advance copy into his office hours ago. But he maintained a poker face and let it pass.

"Why do you think I should see it, Frank? Do you want me to rubber-stamp your mistakes for the President?"

"I don't follow you."

"I hope there is a detailed analysis of the foul-up concerning the security directives to the airlines."

Carmody bit down on his lip, and colored slightly.

"That was unfortunate," he said with embarrassment. "It's going to take a little longer to make them completely operational than we thought. We're all working on the problem together. It should be running smoothly in a few days."

"Let's hope that Hadaffi doesn't take it into his head to blow up a few planes before then," said Schyler, with heavy sarcasm.

"As head of Intelligence I thought you would want to see it before the President," said Carmody, indicating the report. "The President asked me to keep him in touch, and that's all I'm doing. I thought you would want to come to the meeting with me."

Schyler picked up the report and made a pretense of leafing through the pages. It was nothing important, merely a recital of what had been done so far.

"No, I don't think it will be necessary for me to come at this stage, Frank. I have complete faith in your ability to handle any assignment the President hands you," he added with irony. "If by chance you happen to turn up something worthwhile, perhaps I'll come along then."

Carmody quelled a spasm of irritation. He was trying to do the right thing, observe correct protocol, but the bastard was determined to be as difficult as possible. If this was the way he wanted to play it, then he would be just as much of a bastard. Next time he'd made sure that Schyler saw any reports after the President.

"How's Zambretti fitting in?" asked Schyler casually, dropping the unread report back on the desk.

"Fine," Carmody smiled. The smile was a well-controlled mask, but it didn't fool Schyler.

"Plenty for him to do? He's a good man, he'll be a lot of help to you with this terrorist thing."

"I'll need all the help I can get. I've brought Rick Hamilton in as well. He's had considerable Middle East experience, he knows how these people think, and I believe he can offer valuable advice," said Carmody blandly.

It was Schyler's turn to hide behind a smiling mask. Check, and countercheck. Schyler was as aware as anyone else that Hamilton was a special protégé of Carmody's, someone who would be totally loyal. But Schyler still believed that he had the edge. Zambretti was a more devious man, more unscrupulous, more skilled in the game of interdepartmental politics.

"That's good, that's good," said Schyler offhandedly. He made a contemptuous gesture toward the abandoned report on the desk. "No need for me to go over that in any detail, Frank. You let me know when you've got a real line on Hadaffi, then we'll be in business. I've got enough to handle as it is." He paused. "I hope you can manage to straighten out the security mess with the airlines," he added maliciously.

Carmody retrieved the report from the desk with a deliberate, controlled movement, because he didn't want Schyler to see how much the needling had stung him. He probably failed in hiding his feelings from someone as shrewd as Schyler, but he felt compelled to try and keep some face. Schyler had seen the report, Carmody was sure of that.

It wasn't like Schyler to bow out of a briefing session with the President, but he guessed he wanted him to stew alone in the airlines mess. Fuck Zambretti, he was as slippery as a toad, and Angela was going to have to watch him a lot closer. At least now he had Hamilton to help her.

He tucked the report under one arm and stalked out of Schyler's office. He glanced back as he closed the door, and Schyler was already busying himself at his desk, as if the meeting had never happened.

"Trouble?" asked Angela, taking one look at Carmody's face.

"Just Schyler acting like a bastard."

"Oh," she said.

"I'll lay big money that that shit Zambretti got an advance copy of the report into Schyler. He scarcely looked at it when I took it in, but I'm sure he'd read it before."

She assumed a doleful, crestfallen expression to disguise her inward smiles. She thought Zambretti might take advantage of her contrived carelessness.

"I'm sorry, I'm being as careful as I can. I can't imagine how he could have got his hands on a copy," she said mournfully.

He gave her an encouraging smile.

"Don't worry about it too much. We're all going to have to be more careful until this thing with Hadaffi is over and we can get rid of Zambretti. It's going to be a lot better with Rick around the office." He frowned. "But if Martin wants to act like a bastard, then I can be just as big a bastard as anyone."

He looked up quickly, catching an expression on her face that was difficult to interpret.

"I don't want you to get upset about it," he consoled her. "Zambretti's as cunning as a weasel. If he pushes too hard, come to me."

Her mind had been on Daiton, a sudden flash, and she was momentarily flustered. She was wondering when it would all start.

She glanced quickly at her watch to cover her confusion.

"You're due with the President in twenty minutes, you'd better move," she cautioned him.

"Yes, thank you," he nodded.

He snapped open his briefcase and dropped the report inside and took a deep breath. Schyler had got him so uptight he was almost expecting a blast from the President over the airline business, and it probably wouldn't be like that at all.

He paused at the door and smiled at Angela.

"See you for lunch," he said.

"I'd like that, and good luck," she said soberly.

He tapped at the wall beside the door with exaggerated caution.

"Don't forget, the walls have ears," he grinned.

And it wasn't like he'd expected. It was worse than he'd expected. At least Schyler had made a pretense of looking at the report, but the President didn't even bother to go through the motions. Hadaffi was yesterday's issue, but this was another day. The polls were out, and Manningham's popularity had taken a nose dive. There were lots of reasons: inflation, unemployment, uncertainty, and he was looking for an issue, a big issue, something that would put him back on a white charger again with the sword of justice in his hand, and he didn't see Hadaffi in that category. There were elections coming, and he wanted something now. It wasn't that he wasn't interested in Hadaffi, or didn't realize the potential menace of the man's being in the United States, but even the whispered threat of the terrorist's presence he needed like a hole in the head. All he wanted was the man found, incarcerated, deported, anything, as long as he was gotten rid of. It was a brief, tight meeting. Public relations staff were waiting on the President to formulate ideas to try and reverse the opinion polls, or at least halt the trend.

Secretary of State Dan Wenkell sat in on the briefing, and Carmody gained the impression that the President intended to delegate any further responsibility for Hadaffi on to the dapper Wenkell. Not that Wenkell couldn't handle the situation. Poised, polished, from his distinguished graying hair to his carefully groomed gray moustache, Washington man-about-town woman-izer, charming, articulate, there was nothing in the political circus ring that escaped his attention. He was a perfect foil for Manningham's more down-to-earth conservative image. There had been a time when Wenkell's ever roving eye had lighted on Angela, and he had zeroed in with all the experienced instincts of a homing pigeon. For a moment Carmody had even considered encouraging the relationship, because it would have been a valuable listening post to acquire, but Angela had shown no interest, so he hadn't pursued the point.

"The airline problem is being corrected?" he asked Carmody. The voice was sharp and incisive, in contrast to Manningham's more deliberate, slow-formed questions.

"We asked too much of them too soon," said Carmody frankly. "We should have the situation under control within a few days."

"No results from the distribution of the photograph?" inquired the President.

"Nothing so far."

"How wide is your distribution?"

"Saturation."

"The FBI is working on the problem?"

"Yes. The photograph has been distributed through all the agencies with appropriate instructions."

"They know it's Hadaffi we're looking for?" asked Wenkell.

Carmody hesitated, and attempted to sidestep.

"Martin has been handling the interdepartment communication."

"But he must have told you, Frank. You do know?"

Carmody executed a fast shuffle to recover ground.

"Of course," he answered quickly. "Our previous discussions with you, Mr. President, indicated a certain caution in the number of people who should be made aware that Hadaffi is in the country. I think we were concerned about starting any panic. The FBI are looking for Hadaffi, as are other police departments, without really knowing who the man is. This originally came through an overseas contact to an undercover man in New York."

"I understand all that," said Wenkell testily. "But for Chrissake, let's get the man before he does any damage. Who the hell cares who gets him as long as it happens?"

The President held up a cautionary hand to Wenkell.

"I agree with you, Dan, I really do, but we were worried about Hadaffi's reputation, especially with the airlines. The history of Hadaffi's hijacking operations overseas would be enough to start a panic here."

"We don't seem to have done badly in that area ourselves," observed Wenkell dryly, "and without any help from Hadaffi."

"It's very difficult to keep tight security on anything like this," said Carmody.

There was a pause. Wenkell tapped his fingertips together and assumed an expression of studious concentration. The President glanced impatiently at his watch.

"We are conducting a search through our Middle East contact for a more detailed photograph of Hadaffi," added Carmody hopefully. "But the man has been extremely careful. The threat of immediate execution is a very forceful deterrent to anybody with any thoughts of trying to take a photograph of him."

"Nothing more from the undercover man?" asked the President.

"Not so far, although I think he's probably our best bet."

"You have been in contact with him."

"No," said Carmody hesitantly. "I considered it, but he knows the urgency as well as any of us. When he knows something, then he'll contact me."

"If they don't get him first," added Wenkell morosely.

Carmody didn't face Wenkell on that one, because he didn't want to contemplate such a gloomy forecast. Moccasin was the only real ace he held at the moment, and without him they were swinging punches at empty air.

"It's a little like sitting on an unexploded bomb," murmured the President. "I guess you need a lucky break, Frank. We all need a lucky break." He glanced again at his wristwatch. "And talking about breaks, I've got to break this one up because Alan Moody and his boys have been waiting for the last thirty minutes." He picked up Carmody's report and handed it across to Wenkell. "Have a good look through this, Dan. You may see something there that's eluding us at the moment. Frank can fill you in on any details that you may need." He rose abruptly from his desk, and shuffled his feet about in the carpet, anxious for them to be gone. "It may just be possible that your undercover man is wrong about the reason Hadaffi has smuggled himself into this country, Frank. Maybe he's just here to have discussions with his people without engaging in any terrorist activities."

"It sounds an unnecessary risk for him to take, Mr. President," answered Carmody doubtfully. "I don't believe my man could be that wrong."

"Well, it's a slim ray of hope for us to cling to," said the President. "Now if you'll excuse me, Frank, and you too, Dan . . ."

"I think it would be a good idea for Frank to take Eric Dalgety and Geoff Simpson of the FBI into our confidence over Hadaffi," persisted Wenkell. "I don't think it's wise to have them working in the dark. After all, it's much more than just an intelligence thing now."

The President nodded slowly.

"I think you're right, Dan. That was my first inclination when I heard about Hadaffi."

"What about the airlines?" asked Carmody.

"They're not fooled," grunted Wenkell. "They know something pretty serious is going on."

The President cautioned again with his hand.

"But they don't know it's Hadaffi," he warned. "I don't want them to know that. Not yet. You have to guard against that being leaked, Frank."

Carmody nodded agreement. Schyler was going to hate his guts for letting the FBI into the act, but if he didn't like it, then he would have to take it up with the President personally.

He drove back to his office slowly, thinking about Schyler. Events were taking him into a situation which was going to lead him into an outright confrontation with Martin, and he tried to erase any guilt feelings. If he was going to fight tooth and nail to hold him out, he was going to force himself to be more bloody-minded, because Schyler was quite capable of destroying him. Zambretti would help him do that. Perhaps he should apply more of his bloody-minded upbringing. Be a winner. It was an exhortation that still drove him from those early formative years. Catch the biggest fish, shoot the biggest deer, win the most races, take the most prizes. Schyler's job was the next biggest prize, and he had to have it. He wasn't too sure if he could explain why, but it was just the way things were with him. Angela was a prize. He loved her like crazy, but he knew enough of himself to know that she was another prize. To have those looks and that figure in his bed, to have her do anything to please him. To read the envy in other men's faces. That made for exhilaration. Satisfaction. Confidence that had an overwhelming appetite. He would beat Hadaffi, and he would beat Schyler—no more of this mealy-mouthed lip service to protocol. Why couldn't Schyler be satisfied; he'd headed up the section for twenty years. Why couldn't he go and sit in the sun somewhere and let nature take its course?

He wanted to be surrounded by trophies. He had Angela, as securely as if she were mounted and stuffed on a wall of his apartment.

Then he would have Schyler. And Hadaffi. But he knew the hunt had to go on. He wondered what trophy he would want next?

After Hadaffi had left the house, Leica spent the rest of that day, and that night, and until mid-afternoon of the following day living with shadows. They were both young men, dark, remote, with the lithe casualness of their age; and they gave him the feeling that he didn't exist. An uncanny sense of transparency. The uninvited guest at the society party who gets drunk and pisses on the living-room floor while the well-bred hosts go through the charade of pretending he isn't really there.

They didn't speak to him, they didn't make any gestures toward him, obscene or otherwise, yet one or the other of them was never out of his sight. They asked nothing of him, not to prepare a meal, not to show them around the house, nothing. But if he turned from the stove in the kitchen, one of them would be there; if he came out of the toilet door, one of them would be there, not watching, not obstructing, but just there.

It was unnerving, and in normal circumstances it would have been unbearable. But he stood it because his mind was full of Jo, and what he would say when Hadaffi returned. Because he still didn't know. The fact that he had sentenced himself to death was cataclysmic enough in itself, that he could somehow find within himself that sort of courage. But could he really do that to Jo? To his child? That night in bed the rationalizations had come crowding in on him, as he knew they would. They didn't want him to kill the President, just frighten him a little, and then maybe the President would acquiesce to whatever demands Hadaffi was going to make, and they would all go away.

But he knew that was ridiculous. Fairy-tale reasoning. Stupid enough in itself with what he already knew, what they had already made him do. But he was Jewish. From what he knew of Hadaffi, that would be reason enough for him to be killed without anything else.

But no matter how he turned and twisted, there seemed no way out of the maze. The President wouldn't be the end of it, there would be others, and on and on until he would feel like Eichmann, smothered in blood and piteously disclaiming responsibility.

Maybe if he destroyed himself, then they would let Jo go. There would be no reason to hold her once he was dead, and he was sure they wouldn't have given her any reasons for her imprisonment. But he could never be sure. And even the act of self-destruction would not be easy, with his two shadows constantly haunting him. There was no gun in the house, no poison. What would he do, hold his breath, fall on a kitchen knife?

So when he heard the car pull up again outside the house he had reached a stage of almost paralyzed indecision. Even when Hadaffi walked through the door, followed by Daiton, he really had no idea what he was finally going to say.

Hadaffi gave a flick of his hand, and the two shadows melted away, merging into the shadows of the room. Daiton was carrying a parcel, a smallish box shape wrapped in brown paper.

For a time no one spoke while Hadaffi made the lighting of a cigar into an elaborate theatrical gesture. He puffed on the cigar several times, then made himself comfortable in one of the large chairs. He blew a cloud of smoke in Leica's direction and eyed him coldly through the haze.

Leica remained standing, supporting himself with his buttocks against the edge of the table. Daiton stood also, clasping the box in his hands as if silently waiting for instructions.

Hadaffi cleared his throat and studied the white-ashed tip of his cigar.

"The communication to the President has been drafted," he began, his voice harsh with antipathy. "It will go tonight, detailing what we expect from the President." There were to be no games played today, Leica observed, no needling circular approach to a point of demand. The now-familiar accelerated beat of his heart that Hadaffi could produce at whim thundered in his chest.

"The communication will contain a warning," Hadaffi continued, "that unless our demands are met, the President will be subjected to a form of coercion that will threaten his life. He has until three o'clock tomorrow to accede to our demands or the coercion will take place." He lifted his hand and stabbed the cigar repeatedly in Leica's direction, as if he were hurling darts at a target. "At three o'clock tomorrow you will supply that coercion, Leica. There is no doubt in my mind that our first demand will be rejected, so the President will have to be taught a lesson. A lesson he will never forget. You will be the teacher, Leica."

Leica closed his eyes. Is this all there was to be—no other horrific form of pressure applied to him, merely a blustering aggression?

"No," he said. It was almost a whisper, but it seemed to reverberate around the room like the echo response to a scream. He was barely conscious of the word forming in his mouth, let alone the utterance. Something in his brain screamed, No, I didn't mean that. I want to take it back, I want to change my mind, I want Jo to live, but it failed to transmit words to his tongue.

He opened his eyes, and Hadaffi was standing, his mouth set in a strange crooked line, half sneer, half fury, his eyes so dark it was almost as if they had retreated into his brows. He turned to Daiton and jerked his arm in Leica's direction.

"Give him the box," he muttered.

Daiton didn't place the parcel directly into Leica's hands, but slithered over and dropped it down within reach. He didn't look at Leica.

"Open it," commanded Hadaffi.

Leica studied him blankly for a moment, then turned to the parcel and unwrapped it slowly with trembling fingers. He had no idea what they were trying to do to him.

"I thought you might finally come to see yourself in some heroic mold, Leica," said Hadaffi. "People like you generally do, and you always fail. A brilliant mind means nothing without a streak of ruthlessness to raise it to its full potential. You are merely ridiculous when confronted by someone like me." He paused, drawing on the cigar, watching Leica through narrowed eyes. "You seem to have no conception of how unique you are, Leica," he said softly. "Totally unique. The first of your kind. You could be anything, do anything, hold the world in the palm of your hand. And you run away and hide in this funk hole and let yourself become a manipulated oddity, because you don't understand the world. You don't see it the way it is, because you don't want to see it the way it is."

Leica took the lid off the box and stared down, transfixed, but every muscle in his body quivering. Tears boiled in his eyes, flooded over his face and mushroomed wetly down onto the table.

They had aborted his son. The foetus lay curled in the box with the unmistakable signs of masculinity that would never develop. The son he had believed he never wanted. This monster had torn it out of his wife's body and brought it to him in a cardboard box. The hot tears came in a flood. He had never cried before, not like this.

"Poppa," he called, the word involuntarily formed from anguish.

For the first time in his life, controlled, rational reason deserted him, and he went for Hadaffi like a mad dog. He only managed a few feet. One of the shadows materialized swiftly from across the room, and something struck him a stunning blow across the back of the neck. He crashed to the floor, his spectacles flew from his face, and he rolled into the wall, his ears filled with a roaring sound. He lay there, stunned, physically and spiritually, waiting for the fuzz to clear from his brain.

He propped himself up against the wall and tried to focus on Hadaffi, but he was only a blur without his spectacles. Someone handed them to him, perhaps one of the shadows, and he fumbled them back into position. Hadaffi came back into focus. He had not moved, his expression was one of detached curiosity.

"You animal," said Leica hoarsely. He didn't seem to have the strength to get to his feet. He sat with his back to the wall, his legs drawn up, his arms extended out along his knees, his head turned down toward the floor, moving slowly from side to side. The tears ran down each side of his face to a gathering point on his chin, and dripped to the floor.

"My God, my God," he repeated tonelessly, over and over again.

No one made any attempt to help him to his feet. They stood there watching him, waiting.

"What about my wife?" he mumbled.

"She is in excellent hands, and quite well," said Hadaffi. He paused, drawing again on the cigar. "I'm sorry, Leica," he said flatly.

Leica lifted his head and stared at him in disbelief.

"You're sorry," he said shakily. He shook his head again. "My God, sorry . . . you're sorry. You must be mad."

"Some things are totally necessary. They are not done for sadistic pleasure, but because they have to be done.

I am Hadaffi. You have to learn how dangerous it is to defy me."

The tears began to dry, and Leica looked back to the table, at the forlorn cardboard box carrying what would have been his son, their son. What sort of a monster could do a thing like that? His mouth trembled.

"All you do is write yourself down as another one of history's monsters," he muttered.

Hadaffi shrugged. He stepped past Leica and crossed to the bookshelves, the one place in the room that always seemed to draw him like a magnet. He ran his fingers back and forth across the stacked books with the sound of a twig caught in a spoked wheel.

"You have learned nothing here, Leica," he sneered. "Nothing at all. History is unconcerned with monsters, as you call them. Do you think history goes wandering over the battlefields asking the corpses if they objected to being massacred? All that matters is who won or lost. Do you think history looks at Stalin and asks how many Kulaks he annihilated, that it counts them? History only sees Russia now as a powerful nation. Do you think history is interested in your aborted child? It is only interested in what happens to the American political system. How it had to bend to the wishes of Hadaffi. For all your intelligence, for all your uniqueness, you are a fool not to know that."

Leica offered no reply. His arms fell away from their perch on his knees and dropped down beside him to lie parallel to the floor. It was as if a tube had been plugged in and drained away all his energy.

Hadaffi crossed back to the table and squashed out his cigar in the ashtray.

"You will apply psychokinesis to the President tomorrow afternoon at three o'clock. Not sufficient to kill him, but enough to thoroughly terrorize him." He paused. "If you refuse, tomorrow afternoon I will bring you another box. This time it will contain your wife's right hand. Then if you still refuse, her left hand will follow. And so on." He stood close to Leica and stared down at him, to emphasize his position of strength. "You know I will do it, Leica. You know now. I will do whatever I think is necessary in the interests of the brotherhood."

Leica closed his eyes and slowly nodded his head. There was no way he could possibly make this problem go away. It had beaten him, overwhelmed him. To die was one thing, but he couldn't let them do this horrific thing to Jo. He would pretend total subservience, and maybe a chance would come. He had no idea what it would be, but he had to cling to some shred of hope. He tried to imagine how she must be feeling, and it filled him with frustrated rage.

"I am waiting for an answer, Leica." said Hadaffi.

"Yes," said Leica wearily. "Yes, I will do what you ask."

Hadaffi nodded with satisfaction.

"Good, I thought you might. Who knows, Leica, the one session on the President might be all we require of you. Then we will leave you in peace."

He was lying. Leica knew that with certainty. Death was the only peace he would be granted, but quick death, not gradual dismemberment as he threatened Jo. That was all he could do for Jo. The promise of a quick death.

He glanced up and saw Daiton approaching the table, his hand extended to retrieve the cardboard coffin containing his son. The tide of his energy surged back into his body, galvanizing him into action. He came up off the floor with one powerful lunge of his long legs and swept up the box in his hands before Daiton could touch it.

"Leave that alone," he demanded fiercely.

Daiton hesitated in mid-stride and looked queryingly toward Hadaffi.

"Do you think I would let shit like you touch it?" snarled Leica.

Hadaffi shrugged.

"What do you want to do, Leica?"

"I will bury him myself. In the yard. In his home."

There was a short silence while Leica waited. Hadaffi finally gestured to one of the shadows.

"If that's what you want," he grunted. "But I insist on my attendants' being with you."

Leica carried the box in his hands and walked slowly from the room, the two shadows close on his heels. When they were gone, Daiton looked at Hadaffi, and dipped his head in the direction of the departed Leica.

"Do you think we can trust him?"

"To do what we ask . . . yes. To stay alive . . . that might be a problem."

"What do you mean?"

"It hasn't come to him yet, but he may contemplate suicide as a way out. He probably suspects we'll kill him anyway, and by killing himself it may forestall what we have threatened with his wife."

Daiton frowned and rubbed his fingers thoughtfully across his mouth.

"Then he will have to be watched carefully."

"Every minute of the day . . . and night."

"We can do that," said Daiton. "The boys are very efficient." He rubbed the palms of his hands together, thinking. "The letter to the President is being delivered through the Saudi Arabian embassy?"

"Yes. It would be unwise to give the slightest suspicion that we're aware they know I am in America. Best to let them think we are unaware of the Oxley leak. It has been leaked to the Saudi Arabians that I am in America, and they will pass it to their embassy. If our letter is passed through the embassy, the Americans will merely conclude it is an attempt on our part to make it authentic. That it is not just a crank demand."

Daiton smiled with satisfaction.

"It is all going to work, Hadaffi. I have a great feeling of confidence."

Hadaffi permitted himself a grim smile in return.

"Yes, it is, Vilas. I have the same feeling myself. I don't think the Presidency of the United States will ever be the same again after tomorrow."

Leica took the shovel from the toolshed and chose a position by the large pine at the bottom corner of the yard. He and Jo both loved the tree. Tall with a certain grandeur, it towered over its rivals.

There had been times on balmy spring days when they had spread a rug beneath the tree for a relaxed outdoor lunch. He laid the box reverently on the ground, and commenced to dig. The two shadows watched unmoving, expressionless. There was a cold fury through his body that seemed to begin in his belly and expand to his fingertips. He would survive, somehow he must survive, if only for his dead son's sake. He turned over the soil slowly, piling it neatly to one side, and the tears came again. He could go on and on in his mind, berating himself for the three years he had spent in the mountains, for running, for using Jo's love as a lever to make her stay with him. But wallowing in guilt would achieve nothing. He had to force himself to the reality that he was shut in by a set of circumstances he had created himself, that he had to dig himself out, as surely as he was digging his son's grave. And somehow he would bury Hadaffi. The day would come, he was certain of that. There was a feeling of courage growing in him that he had never known before, something that had seeded from the very first time he had said "No" to Hadaffi, and every hour he was conscious of it flowering.

The following morning Carmody briefed Geoff Simpson and Eric Dalgety of the FBI about Hadaffi, a recital of facts as they were known, and fears as yet unconfirmed. He studiously avoided any reference to the fact that the FBI had been kept in the dark concerning Hadaffi's identity, and if there was any resentment, neither of the two men gave any indication. He invited Rick Hamilton to the briefing, and made certain that Zambretti was out of the office. It was good to have Rick around. He needed someone he could trust, and Rick's loyalty was unquestioned. He was only twenty-eight, with a law degree like Carmody, good-looking, intelligent.

They thrashed around with a few ideas, but there was general agreement that there was little they could do at the moment but wait and see.

The present initiatives would continue, but there was a feeling that maybe the President was right, perhaps Hadaffi's illegal entry into the country was not a prologue to a campaign of terrorism. The thought was even beginning to take root in Carmody's mind that there was some truth in the theory.

They started early, and were through by nine thirty.

It was only ten minutes later when Carmody received a call from the White House. The President wanted to see him and Schyler immediately.

It was a silent drive to the White House. The message had only come to Carmody, and he'd been left in the position of relaying to Schyler that they were both wanted urgently by the President. It was a courtesy presence required of Schyler, and he knew it, and so did Carmody, and it charged the air in the car with particles of antagonism. Perhaps directing the message to Carmody had been an oversight on the part of Harvey Schultz, the President's aide, but to Schyler it was another point on the rising tally he had to repay Carmody.

They parked the car and went straight to the President's office like two total strangers with a determined commitment never to communicate.

There was quite a gathering.

The President was at his desk, flanked by Secretary of State Dan Wenkell and Harvey Schultz. Around the room were Bob Rand of the Secret Service, Chief of Staff General Mike Cooper, Secretary of the Treasury Mort Helder, and Eric Dalgety of the FBI.

Carmody raised his eyebrows in the direction of Dalgety, and the FBI man gave an embarrassed shrug of his shoulders.

"I got the message almost as soon as I stepped out of

your office, Frank," he murmured. "So I came straight here."

Carmody nodded without comment.

The President seemed relaxed, almost languid, in his chair, acknowledging with a smile everyone as they entered the room. But there was something mechanical about his smile, remote, and the fingers of his right hand drummed with a continuous beat against the desk top, signaling a tension he was trying to conceal.

"Any introductions needed, Harvey?" he asked pleasantly.

Schultz raised himself to his feet and glanced questioningly around the room. There was a brief hesitation, then an indication in the negative. Carmody had sat in on meetings with everyone except Bob Rand, whom he knew by sight, and Secretary of the Treasury Mort Helder, whom he also knew by sight but had never spoken to. He'd pick that up as the meeting went along, because he wasn't too sure how Helder fitted in. But he was certain of one thing, that they were all gathered there because of Hadaffi. Something very dramatic had taken place since yesterday to change the President's attitude, when he had seemed intent on shifting the Hadaffi problem onto Dan Wenkell's shoulders. For the moment the opinion polls were in a bottom drawer.

"I think we're right, Mr. President," said Schultz. He sat down again, awkwardly squirming into his chair. He was a portly young man, not much older than Hamilton, ex-Ted Bates advertising executive, pushing hard, rising fast. Someone to be watched warily.

Manningham cleared his throat, and the smile faded. He was everyone's picture-postcard impression of what a President should look like, almost the perfect composite portrait of authoritative paternalism. The graying hair; the stern, resolute face; the slow, precise speech. Nature had been kind in the aging process, and millions of television screens around the country had borne testimony to the fact that his was a face carved to perfection for political packaging. But if the opinion polls were right, somewhere the image had faltered.

"What we're about to discuss must not go outside this room," the President began carefully. He paused and looked around the assemblage. "I want to emphasize that before we begin, because this problem has to be resolved before a word leaks to the media." He glanced around. "Understood?" There was a solemn shaking of heads, like hens pecking for seed.

The President continued. "There are some people here who are already aware of the problem and have been working toward a solution. However, early this morning the problem advanced to another stage, and this is what I want to discuss with all of you." He clasped his hands together on the desk in front of him, interlocking his fingers. They were big hands. Strong hands. Once they had done heavy farm work, and the years of political living had not smoothed out the calluses. "Hadaffi, the international terrorist, has managed to enter the United States. This information was first passed through our Intelligence overseas, and later confirmed by an undercover agent in New York, who is still engaged in trying to trace Hadaffi's whereabouts in the country." He glanced across at Carmody. "Do you have any further information to add to that, Frank?"

Carmody shook his head.

"Not at this stage, Mr. President. The fact that we have so little information about Hadaffi's appearance is stalling us."

"Do we know why he's here?" asked General Cooper,

in his usual blunt, direct fashion. Cooper had been an army man in the Patton style, and he had carried over the same style into administration. It wasn't a style that encouraged friendships, but he could be tremendously effective.

"The information we received indicated that he was here to organize an intense campaign of terrorism in this country, although at this stage we don't know what form the terrorism is to take."

"Christ, I would imagine that would certainly include aircraft hijacking to start with," growled Cooper.

"We have been looking at that situation," answered Carmody.

Cooper was in the act of lighting a cigar, and he paused with the yellow-flamed match frozen in midair.

"The hell, that wasn't something to do with the foul-up I got caught in at Kennedy a couple of days ago?"

Carmody shifted awkwardly in his seat.

"I guess so, General, but I think we've managed to straighten that one out. Another few days, and things should be running smoothly."

The general stared at Carmody for a moment, then shrugged, and resumed the lighting of his cigar.

"How long has he been in the country?" asked Bob Rand. He was a big man, six feet five with matching bulk, around forty, balding, an ex-football player, a weapons expert. A bland open face belied his age. The chair seemed too small for him, and he sat awkwardly with his legs cast out in front of him, like holding anchors.

"Several weeks, from what we can make out," said Carmody. He hesitated, and glanced at the President. "There is an opinion that maybe he isn't here to organize terrorism, but to confer with colleagues. That goes against the information received from our New York agent, but it is a possibility."

"We can discount that possibility, Frank," said the President soberly.

Carmody moistened his lips and nodded slowly. If Hadaffi had made his first move, he wondered how the President had the information before him.

The President turned to Harvey Schultz and nodded his head. Schultz rose to his feet and began handing out photostat copies of a single sheet of paper to each person in the room.

"I thought we may have been briefed before this in the eventuality of any threat to you, Mr. President?" said Rand carefully.

The President thought about that for a moment. This was not the time to confuse the issue with political considerations of his own.

"There was a security problem, Bob," he smiled. "Although I certainly appreciate your concern. But as you can see by the note, there is going to be plenty of work for you from this point on."

"We thought it important to keep it tight within the Intelligence area for a time to try and minimize any panic that might arise from public knowledge of Hadaffi. Such as the airlines," cut in Schyler.

He had been sitting on the sidelines for a while, and it seemed important to make a contribution, to draw attention.

Rand didn't pursue the point, but there was obvious irritation which he made no attempt to conceal.

"The paper that Harvey is handing around is a copy of a note sent to the White House from Hadaffi. As you can see, Martin, there doesn't appear to be any airline involvement in Hadaffi's plans," said the President. "The note was delivered through to Harvey from the Saudi Arabian embassy. We believe it was done through the embassy to convince us of the authenticity of the note. The Saudi Arabians have positive information that Hadaffi is in this country, which they passed on to us with the note."

"That means the Saudi Arabians know of these preposterous demands?" asked General Cooper, throwing his copy down on the table.

"It came to them sealed, with a covering note from Hadaffi. Let's make an assumption that they left it sealed, and merely passed it through to the White House. It makes sense to me that Hadaffi would adopt a tack like this. He would want to be assured that his note is taken seriously, and there is no way he would know that we already know he's in the country." He looked across the table and smiled apologetically toward Carmody. "Frank, I know as you are heading up this project I perhaps should have had preliminary discussions with you over the note, but you can see by the timing that Hadaffi has set, it demanded an urgent meeting of those concerned." He nodded to Schultz as the aide resumed his seat, and picked up a copy of the note from the desk. "Thank you, Harvey. Now I want to throw the contents of this demand open for discussion for everyone."

Schyler snorted with disgust, and imitated Cooper, throwing his copy down on the table.

"This is nonsense, Mr. President. A stupid bluff, a feeler. I don't even understand the meaning of the note."

The President raised a soothing hand, and shushed Schyler.

"You may be perfectly right, Martin, but I would

like to establish a consensus of feeling about the demand. Let's go through it, and try and get general interpretation. Firstly, money. They demand five hundred million dollars to be paid into the Union bank in Zurich. Secondly, that the United States bring immediate diplomatic pressure to bear to have all terrorist prisoners released from any prisons where they are being held at the moment. Thirdly, that the United States stop all armaments to Israel and break off diplomatic relations with that country unless she agrees to return to her original 1948 borders and allow the Palestinians to reclaim what is rightfully theirs. That unless these demands are agreed to, a devastating form of coercion will be conducted against the President of the United States. As a demonstration that the President agrees to meet these demands, the five hundred million dollars should be paid into the Union bank in Switzerland by three o'clock this afternoon, otherwise the threat of coercion will be carried out." The President let the note slide out of his fingers and waft gently down to the desk in front of him. He put his hands to his face, and dry-washed his eyes. "There are details of the account into which the money is to be paid, but very little else." He smiled wryly at Schyler. "It would seem that I am Hadaffi's prime target, Martin, not any airline."

Schyler straightened up in his chair and gestured impatiently with his hands. He beat out a drumming rhythm with his forefinger on the discarded note in front of him.

"I wouldn't concern myself too much about any threat to your safety from this form of note, Mr. President," he grunted. "Apart from the political considerations, what does Hadaffi mean by 'coercion'?"

The President shrugged.

"I have no idea, Martin." He glanced around the room. "Does anybody else have any ideas about what this terrible thing is that Hadaffi is threatening me with?"

"I agree with Martin," said General Cooper. "This is bluff, Mr. President. And not very clever bluff at that. It makes no sense that these demands can be met by three o'clock this afternoon."

"That only refers to the money," said the President. He inclined his head in the direction of Mort Helder. "Is what Hadaffi is demanding possible, Mort?"

Helder shrugged. He was a quiet man, and probably the oldest in the room. A large domed head encompassing small features and large black spectacle frames perched on a slight, wiry frame. He had been around a long time, an adroit political manipulator. The President relied on his judgment.

"It would only take a phone call, Mr. President. A message of intent, and the procedures could be started immediately. I presume Hadaffi would have someone in Zurich who would notify him as soon as the procedures were in operation. Yes, that could be managed . . ." He paused and smiled gently. ". . . if the President had the slightest intention of complying with the demand."

"Which I'm certain you haven't, Mr. President," said Cooper dryly.

The President appeared not to hear Cooper, but turned his eyes in the direction of Carmody.

"Coercion? What do you think, Frank?"

Carmody paused, hoping for some shattering insight to lance into his brain, but nothing came.

"It's an unusual way to word some implied threat, Mr. President. It's unusual for this sort of demand not to be backed by some specific threat. To shoot someone . . . to blow up some building . . . to destroy some precious object . . . something. But coercion could mean anything. It's possible this note is only some sort of . . . come on . . . to gauge your reaction." He paused again and caressed his chin with his fingers. He realized how quiet it was in the room when everyone stopped talking. Everyone was watching him, waiting. It made him feel good. "But Hadaffi is no fool. We have to take his formidable reputation into consideration, Mr. President, and take your safety as our prime concern. This man is completely dedicated to his cause, totally ruthless. Human life means nothing to him. And he must know what your reaction will be. Quite apart from the money, the ramifications of the political demands are enormous." He paused again, and frowned, absently brushing with his fingers at the hair around his ears. "I don't know why he would make the demands in this form. It's almost as if he wishes this . . . coercion . . . to take place."

"I take Frank's point about your safety, Mr. President," said Bob Rand. "If there's the slightest threat, then the Secret Service should be mobilized for this afternoon at three o'clock . . . just to be ready."

"I'd agree with that," Eric Dalgety cut in quickly. "I have the same reaction as Frank when it comes to Hadaffi's reputation. I have no idea what he means by coercion either, but let's play it safe."

"Well, I agree with that also," admitted Schyler. "Of course we have to play it safe. We can turn the White House into an armed camp by three o'clock this afternoon, and that's what we should do. But I can't figure Hadaffi. He must know our immediate reaction to his note will be to throw an impenetrable security around the White House. What's he hope to accomplish?"

"I guess what he hopes to accomplish is in his note,"

observed the President dryly. He picked up the note again, not reading, but absently toying with it back and forth from hand to hand.

"Of course I am merely a politician, gentlemen," he said soberly. "In reality this note is a demand against the highest executive position in the United States, and as such is untenable. I have to admit that Hadaffi is a man with a formidable terrorist reputation, but I would be failing as President if I did not have the utmost confidence in the security forces of the nation to protect me. To protect this high office." He glanced around the table, his face set in tough, stern lines. "It would be beneath the dignity of a nation as powerful as ours even to concede the possibility of responding to this . . . this ludicrous attempt at international blackmail." He paused, his fingers tapping reflectively against his chin. "I don't intend this note to be seen by anyone outside this room for the moment." He turned to his Secretary of State. "Agreed, Dan?"

The Secretary of State, who had taken little part in the proceedings up until then, nodded vigorously.

"Yes, I do, Mr. President. I think it would be a mistake to widen the circle any further. But if there are extraordinary security activities around the White House this afternoon, it may be difficult to explain."

The President turned back to Carmody.

"What do you think, Frank?"

"Well, Mr. President, let's say it's an . . . ah, test run. An experimental operation to see how we would cope with some future crisis."

The President grinned, an infectious wrinkling of facial skin that had delighted television producers the length of the country.

"Fine. We'll do it that way."

"If this is all we've got to worry about from Hadaffi, then you can sleep easily, Mr. President," grunted General Cooper.

Schyler ducked his head in the direction of the general, with a hasty smile of agreement.

"Well, it seems I have a very personal stake in hoping both of you are right," murmured the President. He turned his attention back to Carmody. "Frank, you've been in this Hadaffi thing right from the beginning, and I think that's where you should stay . . . under Martin's guidance, of course. I want you to head up the co-ordination of the security operation around the White House. Work with Bob and Eric, and General Cooper. I know I can rely on you to have it so tight a mouse wouldn't get into the kitchen without knowing the password." He paused, and glanced slowly around the assemblage, moving from face to face for any last thought. "I can't imagine what Hadaffi hopes to achieve myself," he concluded heavily. "By coercion or any other way. It's certainly not the sort of activity we expected from him." He shrugged away the spasm of gloom as if discarding a coat, and rose to his feet smiling.

"Frank, I invite you and Martin to have a cup of coffee with myself and Dan at three o'clock this afternoon. Agreed?"

"Certainly, Mr. President," said Schyler.

"Of course," echoed Carmody.

"Then we can all have a good view of Hadaffi coercion from the window," said the President confidently.

The tension in Manningham that Carmody had sensed when he had first come into the room seemed to have dissipated, blown away like a passing fog. Perhaps merely sharing the burden had cleared his mind. After all, he was only human like the rest of them, and maybe the threat was against the highest executive position in the country, but it was also against him as a person. There had to be qualms he was holding down deep in his gut. He was sure if they caught Hadaffi the television screens around the country would blossom with images of the President. He was too shrewd a politician not to play something like that for all it was worth.

The President glanced quickly at his watch.

"Dan and I have another appointment right now, so I'd like to leave you gentlemen here to get on with your security arrangements." He indicated Harvey Schultz with his hand. "Harvey, you'd better stay here as well. You took delivery of the letter from the Saudi Arabians, and there may be details you can supply." He paused, thinking, his brow furrowed, then the smile came again. "As for me, gentlemen, I intend to pursue the day as planned. No cancellations; all appointments, meetings, and functions will proceed as scheduled."

"Just the same, I hope you will be staying around the confines of the White House, Mr. President?" inquired Bob Rand anxiously.

"Hadaffi's great coercion effort isn't supposed to happen until three o'clock, Bob."

"I think it would be a mistake to rely on a thug's word."

The President raised a hand and wagged it back and forth like a cautionary signal.

"I believe we should think of this man in another way, Bob. Thug isn't quite apt. If we were merely dealing with a man who has a formidable reputation as a criminal it would be simpler. Simpler for all of us. Frank is right. It's not only that these people have no respect for other human life, but they have very little respect for their own. We are not dealing with people who are prepared to risk their lives to carry out their threat. We are dealing with people who at this moment may have decided to die in order to carry out this . . . coercion. That is how strongly they believe, and it is from that premise we should plan to counter them."

"Exactly my thoughts, Mr. President, and that's certainly how we intend to plan the security," said Carmody stoutly.

"I just thought I'd make the point anyway," said the President quietly.

"I still hope you will be staying around the White House," persisted Bob Rand.

Dan Wenkell edged across to the door and held it open.

"We're going to be late, Mr. President," he murmured.

"Thank you, Dan, I'm coming now," said Manningham. He smiled at Bob Rand. "You'd make a great mother hen, Bob, and I do appreciate it, believe me. To put your mind at rest, no, I don't intend to stray from the White House today, but only because that happens to be the way my schedule is planned." He moved slowly toward the open door held by the Secretary of State. "Harvey will be arranging another meeting with you all just before lunch so you can brief me on the details of what you propose to do." He gave them a final nod of his head. "Thank you again, gentlemen. I have complete faith in your abilities to protect both me and the Presidency of the United States."

"You haven't a thing to worry about, Mr. President," said Schyler confidently, determined to be the last word from the gathering.

They both left the room, and for a moment there was an awkward silence, each waiting for the other to fill the vacuum left by the President. Manningham was like that; he had a presence that made him the natural dominating focal point of a gathering, and when he was gone it was as if some of the air had been sucked out of the room, and momentarily everybody paused to drag more oxygen into their lungs.

"Should we start with you, Bob?" said Carmody finally. He realized suddenly that they were waiting on him, because the President had appointed him to head up the coordination of the security. Alongside him, Martin squirmed irritably in his chair. "Your primary job is protecting the President," he continued, "so let's start with anything you have in mind, and we can work on from that point."

"Yes, let's start with Bob," muttered Schyler.

Eric Dalgety made an apologetic gesture of intervention.

"Just before we get to that, Frank, I'd like to ask Harvey if we can question the people at the Saudi Arabian embassy about how the note was delivered. Any postmarks? Any messenger identification?"

"I understand the letter came special delivery," said Schultz. "As for questioning the embassy staff, that may be difficult. I think they are embarrassed about being used like this by Hadaffi and want as little to do with it as possible. For all I know they may have hesitated about even sending it through to the White House." He shrugged, leaned forward, and picked up a pen in his pudgy fingers, and made a note on a pad. "I'll see what I can do, Eric, but I can't promise anything."

"The President's last few words concerned me," cut in General Cooper. He leaned back in his chair, his brow wrinkled into a tight frown, studying the end of his cigar as if the total security operation were revealed in the glowing ash. The tone of his voice seemed to have lost some of the blasé confidence expressed for the benefit of the President.

"I guess I didn't sound too concerned about this 'coercion' business at first, when I know the sort of security we can mount around the White House," he went on, "but when you think a bit more about the people we're dealing with . . . Christ, you can almost imagine a wave of assault troops storming across the White House lawns, not caring how many of them get killed as long as someone gets through."

"Then that's the sort of contingency we have to plan to meet, General," murmured Helder.

Carmody looked across with a start, realizing that Helder was still in the room. That was a mistake. The Secretary of the Treasury was an able man, but he had no place in the security planning. Still, it was hardly his place to order him to leave. He frowned, glancing around. But he couldn't let this go on, everybody chattering around the room. He was the President's man, and he was going to have to act like the President's man, with firmness. He clasped his fingers together into a double fist, and dropped them down on the table with enough force to attract attention.

"We can't all talk at once," he grunted brusquely. "I think we're all aware by now of the sort of fanatics we're dealing with, so let's take it from that point." Cooper bit down hard on his cigar and shot Carmody a malevolent look, but said nothing. "We have a lot to do, and only a few hours before we have to present the results to the President. I want to cover eventualities in all areas. An attack from the ground, an attack from the air, anything we can think of." He turned to Bob Rand again.

"Now I'd like to hear it from you first, Bob."

There was a moment of antagonistic silence, while Carmody stared down at the table, waiting. They were all men used to dealing from a position of power, and the President had dropped this upstart down on them from out of nowhere. He could almost hear their minds ticking over. Let him have his fling. The slightest thing fouls up over this Hadaffi business, and he'll come down to earth with the speed of a burnt-out rocket.

Bob Rand began to elaborate on the special plans he had for the Secret Service, choosing his words carefully, delivering them in his soft southern drawl.

It was a busy day for Angela, but that was good, because it helped to keep her explosive sense of exultation under control. Daiton had communicated the result of the last confrontation with Leica, and it was all going to happen. Along with Hadaffi and Daiton she knew instinctively that there was not the slightest possibility of the President's submitting to their first demand note. But it would be a different story once the President had been exposed to Leica's treatment. Maybe at this stage they thought it a simple matter to counter Hadaffi, but after three o'clock they would know better. Chaos. Fear. Impotent terror.

Not that she was unaware of the security preparations that Carmody was setting in operation, because he had contacted her with a list of instructions, people to telephone, arrangements to make, and it was all one huge joke. Let them circle the White House with a hundred helicopters, line Pennsylvania Avenue with sharpshooters shoulder to shoulder, fill the White House grounds with soldiers—it wouldn't make the slightest difference. How do you counter something like the power of Leica, something you can't see, something you can't hear? Suddenly everything seemed possible; she experienced the same surge of expectation as when Hadaffi first lifted her out of the dungheaps. Now it could be the same for all those not as lucky as she, still trapped in the manure she had escaped from.

And the thought that she might one day have to kill Carmody was now only an extremely remote possibility. And somehow she was glad, although why, she found difficult to explain. Perhaps for all that she loved Daiton, it was conceivable for some grain of feeling to grow from a constant sexual relationship. She shrugged it away. It was unnatural, something inexplicable to her, something she could never discuss with Daiton. So she plunged into the work while accepting the fact that as far as she was concerned it was a wasteful farce. But the constant bustle helped to steady her nerves, and it was always important to keep Carmody aware of how invaluable she was to him. She wondered how long Daiton would expect her to carry on this role with Carmody. Just as long as it was important to the brotherhood, she guessed. And to Hadaffi. For a time she had pondered over letting Daiton know about the preparations at the White House, but rejected the thought. They would only see it as she did, a comical farce. She wondered what Carmody's reaction would be when he saw what happened to the President.

At least she would have a restful night, because she was sure sex would be far from Carmody's mind.

Leica positioned himself by the window in the living room that overlooked the backyard of the house where he could see the pathetic mound of earth that marked his son's grave. The wind had caught hold of the cardboard box and whisked it up to a branch of one of the pines on the outskirts of the forest, and it swayed gently, white on green, in a hesitant gesture of surrender. He had left the shovel leaning against the tree, because by the time he had completed the grave it had seemed like a massive weight, too heavy for him to carry back to the house.

He could see it from where he sat, a mound of earth still stuck to the bottom of the blade. He had liked to work with his hands once, digging, carpentry, painting. He recalled the boat he had built when he was fifteen, the boat that was never launched, like so many other things. Making always seemed far more important than using.

He was using the grave to fortify himself, using it like a stimulant to help the tight knot of hatred growing in his belly. He was sure his son would understand. And Jo, wherever she was.

He was going to do what they asked, he knew that, because there seemed no choice, and there didn't seem any way he could make it easy for the President. But the impetus to suicide had left him. Gone like his mildness, and his compassion, and his cowardice, and his constant rationalization. These men belonged to a world he had tried to make himself forget existed, but he would survive to kill them, every one of them. Even the shadows he could hear behind him, murmuring softly to each other, the shadows that never left him.

Hadaffi had returned to the house at ten o'clock in the morning, but he paid little attention to his aides, and no words passed between him and Leica. Everything seemed to have been said. The terrorist prowled around the house like a chained bear, drinking countless cups of coffee, the only chore he commanded from his two shadows.

Leica ignored him, disdaining to turn his head from the window even when he had first entered the room. There would be no games today, no pseudophilosophical baiting, no prodding urgency that Hadaffi seemed to need to try and prove some intellectual superiority.

He listened for his footsteps, judging his position in the house by the sound, the heavy clump in the room where he sat, the muffled tread from the kitchen, the sharp echoing step coming down from the upstairs rooms. The man was never still, and Leica could guess that at the back of Hadaffi's mind was the nagging thought that at the last moment he might renege. That was what kept his feet moving, dragging him from room to room in an endless circle. If what Leica suspected was right, he had no intention of putting the terrorist's mind at ease. Let him sweat. Let him agonize. Let him feel anything that might be considered some form of pain.

Only once did the footsteps come to a halt, and then Leica could feel the presence of the man standing immediately behind his chair, could smell him, could hear the sound of his breathing, deep and controlled.

He must have shared Leica's view of the grave, and perhaps that was what stilled his tongue, because after

a few moments the sound of the footsteps were re-
newed, round and round, clump, clump, clump.

He wondered where Hadaffi and Daiton went when
they left the house, where they stayed. Surely not in
Sylvan; that would be too dangerous. Not that it was
important. All that was important now was survival,
and revenge.

He made no attempt to eat lunch, and no one asked
him. Around about twelve thirty he heard someone
clattering around in the kitchen, the pinging sound of
cutlery on plates, but he still didn't turn. He wanted
the sight of the grave never to leave his mind. A permanent imprint locked into every cell. The morning
dragged away. The early cloud dispersed, and the forest
took on various shades of brilliant green, shimmering
in the sun. It seemed so peaceful, so unconcerned.
Perhaps the earth should have stayed that way, har-
monious, every part coexisting with the other, not
fouled by human beings.

It was two thirty, and the knot in his belly was like
a dried pinecone, the edges sharp and cutting, when he
heard the outside door open again, and the sound of
Daiton's voice. He hunched back in the chair, not turning his head, but listening. Every time the door opened,
or a car drove up, he had the crazy notion that maybe
he would hear Jo's voice, but that's all that it ever was.
A crazy notion.

"There is nothing from Zurich," said Daiton.

There was a pause, and suddenly there was no sound
of footsteps.

"Numartz was in touch with the manager of the
bank?" asked Hadaffi.

"Yes. Nothing has been paid into the bank. No preliminary negotiations have been started. No one has
contacted the manager. Nothing."

There was silence again. Shoes shuffled abrasively against the wooden floor.

"I am not surprised, of course," said Hadaffi quietly. "It's what we expected. But now they will have to learn the hard way."

There was another pause, then the footsteps started up again, clump, clump across the room toward Leica's chair. Leica extracted a handkerchief from his pocket, removed his spectacles, and began polishing the lenses. He braced his elbows against the sides of the chair, trying to control the trembling in his fingers. The footsteps stopped, and he looked up at the blurred image of Hadaffi standing in front of him. He concluded the polishing with slow deliberation, then slipped his spectacles back into place. Hadaffi leaped into focus in front of him, grim set mouth, unsmiling. He wore a black turtleneck sweater that Leica had not seen before.

Hadaffi lifted his arm and tapped his finger slowly against his watch.

"It's two thirty, Leica," he grunted brusquely. "Time to prepare. I want this exercise to happen right on our scheduled time of three o'clock." He permitted himself a slight humorless grin. "It would be impolite to keep the President of the United States waiting."

He shuffled forward several steps until his physical bulk occupied the entire area of Leica's vision.

"Don't you agree that would be impolite, Leica," he sneered.

Leica pushed his chair back and stood up. The trembling was under control, but there was a dullness in his chest, a lead weariness in his legs, that was just as disturbing. He fought down an almost uncontrollable urge to strike the man.

"Yes," he muttered.

"Where do you need to go?"

"In the small study upstairs."

"I will come with you," grunted Hadaffi.

"It is not necessary."

"I insist."

"You may disturb my concentration."

"I will be a mouse. Is all the material you require in the study?"

Leica nodded. Hadaffi paused for a moment, waiting, then gestured toward the stairs. They went up together, Hadaffi in the rear, one hand forward on Leica's elbow, as if guiding him up the steps to the gallows.

B y two thirty Carmody was confident that everything had been achieved that was possible. The President had approved their plans earlier in the day, and a late meeting between himself and the other members of the security team had expressed satisfaction with the arrangements.

So far there had been little media concern, although Steuben from the *Post* had been wandering around asking what was going on. But there was a carefully prepared news release to handle that, and so far no awkward questions had been asked.

The operation encompassed three phases. Security inside the White House itself, which was the responsibility of Bob Rand and constituted the placing of heavily armed men in strategic positions inside the building.

Security outside the White House, but inside the

grounds themselves, by units of the army under General Cooper's supervision, with sidearms and machine-gun positions.

Security around the White House by the placing of motorized Marine assault units in the surrounding streets, in Seventeenth Street, Fifteenth Street, West Executive Avenue, and East Executive Avenue. Units were also drawn up in Lafayette Square.

Sharpshooters were also strategically placed along the approaches to the White House, under Eric Dalgety, from Constitution Avenue up to Pennsylvania Avenue.

Overhead two helicopter gunships would take up a constantly rotating surveillance over the White House, beginning at two thirty.

At first the President had seemed a little embarrassed by the scale of what Carmody proposed, but had finally given approval. Perhaps they were killing an ant with a sledgehammer, but it was better to play safe with someone like Hadaffi. Who knew what the fanatical bastard would try to make his threat a reality?

Carmody made a final tour of the preparations right at two thirty, accompanied by Schyler, and they were both well satisfied. For the moment, the enmity between the two men was held down to a low key; there had been too much to do in a short time for personal animosity, and Schyler was momentarily silenced by his involvement.

Right at two thirty the two gunships came burring in from Andrews Field, and immediately assumed a tight clucking formation around the White House, their side doors open, the black snub of their machine guns pointing down.

It seemed right, in view of the state of preparedness, that Carmody should be with the President at three o'clock, but as an extra precaution he arranged for a two-way transmitter to be in the President's office to keep in touch with Cooper, Dalgety, and Rand, in case they needed him.

By two forty-five both Carmody and Schyler presented themselves at the President's office. It was a seemingly relaxed Manningham that rose to greet them, hand outstretched in a warming gesture of welcome.

Wenkell was already there, draped casually in one of the chairs. He smiled and nodded, but didn't rise from his chair.

"Sit down, Martin . . . you too, Frank," said the President. He gestured toward the chairs and resumed his own seat. "The coffee will be here in a moment, and we can sit here and relax while Hadaffi tries to get himself through the ring of steel you gentlemen seem to have thrown up around me. I hope this isn't going to make us look slightly ridiculous."

"Well, it is only an exercise after all, Mr. President," smiled Carmody.

"Yes, but you know the boys from the press. They smell anything, they'll ferret around until they get at the truth. You don't know them like I do, Frank."

It was a reservation Manningham had failed to express before, and maybe it had something to do with the opinion polls.

"Well, I guess it's better to be overprepared than underprepared," said Dan Wenkell.

The President nodded agreement.

"You're right of course, Dan, and at least we're forewarned. It's not something out of the blue like it was with Kennedy." He glanced toward the window as the waffling sound of one of the helicopters beat down over the White House grounds. "You don't seem to have overlooked anything, Frank. I think congratulations are in order." There was a short pause, and Schyler cleared his throat dryly. "And of course to you also, Martin," the President added quickly.

The transmitter had been left on the floor propped against the side of the President's desk, and Carmody rose from his chair and picked it up. He held it up to the President.

"Just a precautionary measure, Mr. President. I hope you have no objections?"

Manningham gave an affable wave of his hand.

"Certainly not, Frank. I saw that before, and I guessed it was something to do with your operations."

"Just in case I have to contact someone outside."

"Understood. Understood completely. Good thinking."

The secretary came into the room with the coffee and poured for them. A smatter of lighthearted small talk drifted around the room until she had finished, and left the room. Carmody looked at his watch. It was two minutes after three. The President noted his action and followed suit.

"I have two minutes after three, Frank. Does your watch agree?" he asked. There was a general mimicry of the watch consultation around the room and a sage nodding of heads.

"Well, at least our friend Hadaffi isn't completely punctual," smiled the President.

"I don't think we'll see hide nor hair of him," said Wenkell confidently. "It would take a small army to make the slightest impression around here, and he's not likely to mount something like that. Forget him."

The President shrugged noncommittally. He lifted his cup and sipped at the hot coffee, when the door opened. He looked up with an irritated frown, because staff were under strict instructions not to disturb him. There was a small man standing in the doorway, carrying a medical bag, and wearing a white hospital coat. He opened his mouth to question the man, but somehow no words emerged from his throat.

The man was dark, Japanese, about thirty years old, and vaguely familiar. Manningham turned to the others in the room with an apologetic smile, but they seemed preoccupied with their coffee, completely unaware of the stranger.

Wenkell was saying something to him, but the words were scrambled like a record played at the wrong speed. A burring sound fluttered in his ears that had nothing to do with the helicopters circling overhead. For a panicky moment he thought he was on the verge of a heart attack.

He stared at the stranger, his coffee forgotten, and his vocal cords seemed paralyzed, making it impossible to order the man from the room.

He turned to the others for help, but they were smiling at him, chatting in some inane indecipherable language that made no sense.

"Good afternoon, Sergeant Manningham." The stranger smiled, with a slight bow from the waist. The accent was Japanese, but his English was very good.

The color went out of Manningham's face, his eyes widened, and the years suddenly rolled back. Back to 1944. Sergeant Manningham? He'd forgotten what it was like to be addressed as sergeant. And the memory of this man's face jolted back into his mind. But that was impossible, it was nearly forty years ago, and the man looked no older now than he had then. He blinked and squirmed in his chair, trying to move, to raise himself, but his legs seemed to be bolted to the floor. He'd gone mad. There was no other explanation. The Japanese doctor he and Shepherd and Luft had found in the camp when they were out on patrol on Guadalcanal. He forced his eyes shut at the onrush of those ferocious memories. They badly wanted information on that patrol, their unit had been ambushed a couple of times, and they needed to know where the Japanese troops were. And all they found was the Japanese doctor.

Shepherd had lost his brother in one of the ambushes, and he was determined to make the doctor talk. And Luft was with him. He couldn't stop them. Shepherd was an animal, and he'd never seen anything like that done to a human being before. The screams had stayed in his mind for a long time, the sight forever. Maybe he should have tried harder to stop them, but when they got back from the patrol with the information, it was all praise and promotion, so he held his silence. And so did Shepherd and Luft until they were killed on Okinawa and silenced forever.

He opened his eyes, hoping that what he'd seen was only a mental aberration and the man would be gone. But there were three of them now, the doctor and two taller orderlies flanking him. He looked beseechingly at Carmody, but the man smiled like an idiot, mouthing words he couldn't hear. A television program with the sound tuned out.

"It has been a long time, Sergeant," smiled the doctor.

Manningham couldn't answer. He was obviously locked into some sort of nightmare, perhaps brought on by strain. It had to be that. A man dead forty years couldn't possibly wander into his office in the middle of some crisis.

The three of them moved into the office and grouped

around the President. They seemed to be completely invisible to the others in the room. The doctor placed a gentle hand on his arm and put his bag down on the desk. Manningham felt beads of perspiration flood out over his face, as if he had stood under a shower.

"Retribution has been a long time coming, Sergeant," grinned the doctor.

"It was Shepherd and Luft," babbled the President.

His heart was pounding in his chest as if it would smash its way out of his rib cage, and every limb was quivering. He turned his eyes to Carmody, and to Schyler, and on to Wenkell. They had stopped their silent mouthing and were watching him with concern. Perhaps they can see them after all, he thought desperately. Perhaps I'm not mad.

"It was Shepherd and Luft," he repeated again.

"You were responsible."

"I tried to stop them. They went mad. You know that . . . you know I tried to stop them."

"You did nothing except become promoted, Sergeant."

"Damn you, that's not true. I tried. I did try."

"Yes, well we shall see," murmured the doctor.

He nodded curtly to the two orderlies, and they seized the President by the arms, lifted him out of the chair, and forced him down on his back along the top of the desk. From somewhere they produced straps and bound him tightly, one across his chest, one across his waist, and one across his ankles. He became like part of the desk.

"Jesus Christ, it was Shepherd and Luft. Fuck you, why don't you believe ·me? I couldn't stop them."

The doctor opened the bag and glanced at the President, still smiling.

"It seems that your friends are unable to stop me, either, Sergeant."

The President shook his head back and forth, feeling the sweat running into his collar.

"You're not real . . . you're not real," he groaned. "If I can just manage to go to sleep, you'll be gone when I wake up."

"But you are awake now, Sergeant," smiled the doctor.

The President grunted in reply and heaved furiously against the straps. The hardness of the desk top bit into his shoulder blades. A trussed chicken. Powerless. He stared up at the ceiling and tried desperately to grasp what was happening to him. Total recall. The smell of the island, the tang of the sea, fear, sweat, the agonized cry of a man zeroed by a bullet. The patrol. He could see Luft, could smell him, the sullen scowl. They both wanted to abort the patrol, both Luft and Shepherd, but he had forced them on. He didn't want any aborted patrol on his record, not with his eyes on a political future. There was a roaring in his ears, maybe artillery, or the wind lunging in from the sea, ripping at the palm fronds.

There was a nurse somewhere, yes there was, and Luft had chased her into the jungle and had come back buttoning up his trousers, the scowl momentarily erased. Until he saw the doctor, and Shepherd over him with the knife. Had he really tried to stop Shepherd, or had he thought how good a successful Intelligence report would look on his record?

He thought of Hadaffi. He was caught in some crazy other dimension, wafting between the past and the present. Was this what Hadaffi meant by coercion? Oh, Christ, Christ, this was madness, something was tearing his mind apart, and he was standing on the sidelines aware of the total illusion, yet helplessly entrapped. How could it be illusion? The doctor was real, the orderlies were real, Carmody was real . . . maddeningly real, sitting there across the room with a stupefied expression on his face. And Schyler and Wenkell, equally stupefied, equally inert.

He heard the clink of metal, and awkwardly raised his head, trying to focus along the length of his body.

"You're not real," he gasped hoarsely.

"Whatever you like to think, Sergeant."

The President's head bumped down on the table, his neck muscles weakening under the strain.

He strained up, trying again.

"Hadaffi sent you," he wheezed.

"I know no one named Hadaffi. Was he part of your patrol, Sergeant?"

The President swallowed forcefully, trying to control the fear rushing through his body. He could feel something cold and metallic along his leg, and the sound of scissoring material.

He levered his head up again.

The doctor was running the scissors up the legs of his trousers, cutting them apart. His breathing came in short, labored bursts, cramming his chest tightly against the straps.

"What are you doing?" he managed, before his head clumped down again.

"Repaying a debt, Sergeant."

"Tell Hadaffi I'll talk to him. Please . . . I'll talk to him."

"Hadaffi is a stranger to me. I told you that."

The President closed his eyes, and shook his head to drain the perspiration out of his lids. He turned his head toward Carmody.

"For God's sake, help me, Frank." He moved his eyes on past Carmody to Schyler and Wenkell. "Please, one of you, help me . . . call Bob Rand . . . call General Cooper."

It was hopeless. Infuriating. Incomprehensible. Carmody's lips were moving, but he was locked in a soundproof room. He heaved at the straps again, caught in a sudden fury that equaled his fear. For Chrissake, he was Thomas Manningham, President of the United States, and this couldn't be happening. The exertion exhausted him, and he lay still after a moment, staring at the ceiling. He heard the ripping sound of cloth and the metal touch of an instrument on his leg, and fear took possession of his body, swamping the fury.

"What are you doing?" he asked again. He didn't try and raise his head again, but delivered the question toward the ceiling.

"A service, Sergeant."

"A service?"

"This gangrene cannot be permitted to continue, Sergeant. It will kill you."

"Gangrene?" babbled the President. "What gangrene? I have no gangrene."

"You have forgotten your wound, Sergeant."

"That was only a scratch."

"Now it is gangrene. I would not be a doctor if I allowed it to continue."

"Liar, liar. Fucking liar. It was Luft and Shepherd. Don't punish me for what they did."

Panic garbled his voice, clogging his throat with phlegm. He was totally enmeshed in the illusion now, not conscious of Hadaffi, of Carmody, of anything except the terror generated by this manaic.

"You must realize we are cut off in this part of the island," said the doctor softly.

"Cut off?"

"Yes. You have sunk all our ships, Sergeant. Bombed all our supply depots into extinction."

"What supplies?" gasped the President. He made another attempt to raise his head, and glimpsed the smiling doctor framed between his feet. He raised his arms in a small gesture of apology.

"You must understand we have no anesthetics at all. You will have to be brave, Sergeant." He motioned to the orderlies, and they stepped forward, seized the President's exposed legs, and bound tight straps around the uppermost portion of the limbs. They stepped back, expressionless, staring toward the wall.

"No," screamed the President. "Luft and Shepherd. Please, Luft and Shepherd."

"No, Sergeant, you. You. You. Luft and Shepherd are dead. Only you are alive. Only you are their keepers, Sergeant."

"No," screamed the President again.

The doctor edged up along the desk until he was positioned beside the strapped legs. He raised the knife and held it up to the light, turning it slowly, sparking bright reflections.

"Even without your legs, you will still be alive, Sergeant. Not like Luft. Or Shepherd. Or even me, eh, Sergeant?"

He leaned forward, his face puckered in concentration, and began to cut. The pain swept up the President's body like a stabbing, jolting wave, palpitating his heart, flooding his mind, drowning the scream in his throat. A merciful black cloud swept in and numbed his mind.

"**I**s he conscious, Doctor?" asked Carmody.

Dr. Walters nodded solemnly. He was the President's personal physician, and it was a stroke of luck that he had happened to be in the White House. He looked quickly at his watch.

"I've kept him under sedation for three hours, and he still appears to be in a state of shock," he said quietly. He looked firmly from Carmody to Wenkell to Schyler. "He's been asking for Frank Carmody, and I'm afraid I can only let one of you go in."

Wenkell nodded agreement, placed a hand behind Carmody's back, and urged him forward.

"You'd better go on in, Frank. Someone is going to have to tell him."

Walters put a hand out to stop Carmody.

"Tell him what?"

"That's a security matter, Doctor," grunted Wenkell.

"I'm not so much concerned with security matters as I am with the President's health. That's my responsibility. I don't want him told anything that is going to add further strain to his condition," said Walters firmly.

Carmody hesitated, glancing uncertainly from Wenkell to the doctor.

"We're not even too sure what happened to the President yet, Dan." He turned to Walters. "What has he said to you, Doctor?"

Walters frowned and rubbed at his chin. He was a man in his sixties, round, smooth features, impeccably dressed, an expert surgeon. He fished with the President, he golfed with the President, he assumed he was a confidant of the President. Not this time.

"About his experience . . . nothing. I can only make deductions from what you've told me happened in the President's office, and from his condition. I would say he collapsed from a suddenly induced tremendous mental strain. What it was, he refuses to say at the moment . . . refuses to talk about. At least to me," he added, with sudden pique in his voice.

"Then it adds up," said Schyler, gravelly awe in his voice.

Wenkell shook his head.

"I can't believe it," he murmured. "I refuse to believe it."

Carmody patted his elbow and edged past the doctor. "Let me see what the President has to say first, Dan," he said.

Walters lifted an admonishing finger.

"No further strain, Mr. Carmody. He's gone through a tough time. I won't be responsible if you add to it in any way."

"I'll take it easy with him," said Carmody.

"Not a word to the press, Doctor," warned Wenkell. "Not a whisper. No one else except us three, and you, know what happened. Or at least know that something pretty terrible happened, even if we're not too certain what it was."

"You can trust me," said Walters stiffly.

Carmody went quietly into the room and stopped at the foot of the bed. The President was lying on his back, his eyes closed. His skin had the pink-gray pallor of a clouded dawn, his hair was neatly combed, and there were lines in his face Carmody had never noticed before.

His wife, Amelia, rose from the bedside chair and nodded to him. She was a handsome woman. Even in a moment of crisis she seemed to have the knack of being perfectly dressed for the occasion. Right now the shoes were a perfect match for the beautifully-cut gray dress. A political woman to her fingertips. Veteran of a thousand campaigns, the ultimate foil. Grace. Style. Charm. Worth fifteen percent of the vote on any election trail. Good family, good connections, sculptor-in-chief behind the scenes, carving the raw material of Thomas Manningham into the sophisticated President of the United States. A tiger. Her claws would be unsheathed, gleaming, at the results of the opinion polls.

"How is he, Mrs. Manningham?" asked Carmody cautiously.

"Resting."

"Has he said anything to you?"

"About what happened?"

"Yes."

She indicated the negative with her head. "Nothing, Mr. Carmody. Nothing at all." She cleared her throat nervously and absently brushed stray hairs from her forehead. Fatigue and anxiety had etched fresh lines in her face also. "What happened, Mr. Carmody? What did this to him?"

Carmody shook his head.

"We don't know."

"Is this something to do with Hadaffi?"

"I can't say. It's something we have to try and find out."

Her eyes widened, but she didn't press with any further questions. She gave him a wan smile.

"Then I'll leave you with him for a time. Don't press him too hard."

Carmody gave her a reassuring smile, and she swiveled

on her heels and left the bedroom by another door. Even the pressure of anxiety failed to undermine her grace and style.

Carmody waited uncertainly, still holding to his position at the foot of the bed. The window overlooked the White House grounds, a portrait in multishades of rich green. A weak, fading sun sprinkled patches of pale sunlight through the trees. Small groups of soldiers were still dotted around, but Carmody knew they were no longer needed. Cooper and Rand and Dalgety were pressing hard to know what the hell had happened, but Carmody had stalled until he had a chance to talk to the President. He knew they resented having to defer to him, but until the President countermanded the order, he was still in charge of the security operation. Cooper refused to call off the troops, and there was nothing Carmody could do about that at the moment.

"Hello, Frank," said the President. The tone was thready and weak, and lacked the timbre the nation knew so well.

"I'm glad to see you looking better, Mr. President," said Carmody.

The President managed a faint imitation of a smile.

"If this is looking better, then I must have looked like a corpse before," he whispered.

He shrugged himself up against the pillow and indicated with his hand the chair just vacated by his wife.

"Mrs. Manningham has just left the room. If you wish, I can call her back, and we can go on with this when you feel stronger?"

Manningham shook his head and indicated the chair again, until his hand dropped weakly down on the bed.

"No, Frank, no. I heard Amelia leave the room. It's better this way. I don't want her worried anymore, and I think it's important that we talk as soon as possible."

Carmody nodded, and seated himself in the chair. "As you wish, Mr. President," he murmured. Whatever the President had experienced, it had made him as weak as hell. He was going to have to take notice of Walters and not produce any shocks to worsen his condition.

The President let his head drop back on the pillow. Gray on white.

"Tell me, Frank," he asked softly.

"Tell you, Mr. President?"

The President rolled his head about on the pillow, ruffling the hair Amelia had combed so neatly into place.

"What happened at three o'clock? What did I do? What did you see me do?"

Carmody coughed nervously, hesitating. The President rolled his head around until he was staring at Carmody.

"Bo Walters is a good friend, but he can also be an old woman sometimes. I'm sure he told you to lay off me, Frank, but I have to know . . . and I have a suspicion it's important I know as soon as possible. Now, what did I do? In some crazy way it has to do with Hadaffi, but I stopped believing in ghosts a long time ago, and I want a rational explanation."

"I don't know if I can give you one, Mr. President."

The President carved faint circles in the air with his hand again.

"Try, Frank. Try hard. Don't think of me as the President of the United States for a moment. Think of me as a tough Marine, asking for the truth. Without the formalities. Without the bullshit. Tell me what I did."

"What we saw I can tell you. Rational explanations are going to be more difficult," said Carmody.

The President turned his eyes back up to the ceiling.

He caught at the edge of the blanket with one hand, rubbing the material gently between finger and thumb, a childlike expression of anxiety.

"Then I have to find one, Frank," he murmured. "Without a rational explanation this country has a deranged President, and that can't be allowed to continue. That can only mean resignation. Without a rational explanation, what happened to me in that room could only happen to someone who's lost mental control. And that could happen again." He rubbed his head wearily against the pillow. "Tell me, Frank," he urged again. "I want to be able to believe that Hadaffi was in some way responsible."

Carmody cleared his throat, choosing words. Which came first? The new communication from Hadaffi, or the events in the office? He decided for the latter.

"You appeared to be a man being subjected to intense fear," Carmody began carefully. "You sat in your chair with your body as rigid as concrete, your eyes wide, your face white. You seemed incapable of hearing anything we said to you. You screamed. None of us knew what to do." He hesitated. "You kept calling out two names . . . Luft and Shepherd. Does that mean anything to you?"

"Yes," murmured the President dully.

"You . . . you dragged yourself out of your chair, and stretched yourself out along your desk." Carmody paused, twitching his shoulders in embarrassment. "I know it sounds crazy, Mr. President . . ."

"Go on," persisted Manningham.

"Wenkell ran for help. Martin and I tried to get you off the desk. You screamed several times, then you lost consciousness." He stopped, suddenly conscious of his own tense posture in the chair, and forced himself to relax. "We got Walters, and you were brought in here . . . and that's about it. It was a terrifying business."

"Yes," said the President.

There was a pause.

"Do you think I'm mad, Frank?" asked the President.

"No, Mr. President."

"I wish I could be as sure as you sound. I'm going to tell you what happened to me in the office, because I think it's important for you to know. But first I want a good reason why you don't doubt my sanity"

"I think it had something to do with Hadaffi," Carmody stated.

"How? Why do you think that?"

Carmody hesitated momentarily, then plunged ahead. Wenkell was right, the President had to know, and as soon as possible.

"About two hours ago we received another communication from Hadaffi."

The President turned and stared at Carmody, and for the first time since Carmody had come into the bedroom, some of the old fire came back into his face. He dug his elbows into the bed and levered himself into a higher position on the pillows.

"Through the Saudi Arabian embassy?"

"No, this time direct . . . special messenger. Dalgety's following it up now."

"What did it say?" asked the President eagerly.

Carmody extracted a piece of paper from his pocket, and handed it across to the President. Manningham waved it off impatiently. "Read it to me," he demanded.

"It's addressed directly to you, Mr. President, but we thought it best to open it."

"That's all right, Frank. Just read it."

" 'President Manningham,' " Carmody began, " 'because of your refusal to meet our demands, by now you will have experienced the mental agony produced by being subjected to psychokinesis. I warn you that this mental coercion can be produced at will, and you are powerless to prevent it. Your entire armed forces are powerless to prevent it. Our demands still stand, and you have another forty-eight hours to comply. Unless you agree, you will be subjected again to psychokinesis, only of a more intense nature. This will continue until you accede to our demands.' " Carmody looked up and folded the paper over in his fingers. "It's signed Hadaffi," he concluded.

The President gaped at him.

"Psychokinesis? That's crazy. I've read about that. Isn't that something to do with a person being able to use his mind with enough power to destroy or incapacitate someone else. That's on about the same level as black magic. No one has that sort of power. Hadaffi's crazy if he expects us to believe that sort of mumbo-jumbo." His elbows slipped from under him, and he eased back into the pillows, exhausted by the outburst. "Maybe it was done some way with drugs?" he appealed hopefully to Carmody.

"It's difficult to see how any drugs could have been given to you here in the White House, Mr. President."

"Perhaps one of the staff?"

Carmody pursed his lips thoughtfully.

"But how could Hadaffi guarantee to produce the same effect in forty-eight hours' time?"

There was a short silence.

"Walters took a blood sample while you were unconscious," Carmody ventured. "It showed nothing, but there are other tests we can do, of course."

There was another short silence while the President moodily studied the bedroom ceiling.

"You believe this . . . psychokinesis, Frank? You, and Dan, and Martin?"

"We don't honestly know, Mr. President. We did a roundup of what expert opinion we could find in the last few hours. Psychiatric, psychological, chemical, scientific. They can't be sure either, although there is a consensus that there is progress being made in this area. They find it impossible to accept that it's been made to this extent, but they don't know. It's a no-man's-land."

"Then what you're trying to tell me, Frank, is that it's possible."

Carmody shuffled uncomfortably in the chair, trying to gauge the President's reaction.

"I wish I could give you a definite answer, Mr. President. Maybe it would help if you told me what the experience was like for you?"

The President hesitated, and closed his eyes. The gray pallor in his face seemed to intensify, and his lips moved soundlessly, as if he were having difficulty knowing where to begin.

"Have you ever had a really bad nightmare, Frank? I mean something that woke you in a soaking sweat."

Carmody thought for a moment.

"Not that I can recall, Mr. President. Not for a long time."

"This was a nightmare, but without any fragment of a dream quality. It was real. Do you know the first thing I did when I regained consciousness, Frank?"

Carmody shook his head.

"I sat up in a panic and grappled at the blankets to see if my legs were still there."

"Your legs?"

"Yes, my legs. Because I was convinced in my own mind that my legs had been amputated. That's what happened in my office. A man I knew to be dead, a man from almost forty years ago, a doctor, came into the office with two assistants, and began to amputate my legs ... without anesthetic." He paused a moment, his mouth quivering at the memory. "My God, it was terrifying, because it was so totally real. I could talk to him, he could talk to me. And you all just seemed to be onlookers. I couldn't communicate with you." He closed his eyes, and his cheeks seemed to hollow, making the bones stand out in sharp relief. "I could feel everything: the knife, the pain, the terror. That's why I thought I must have gone mad."

"Christ," Carmody breathed. "The doctor's name was Luft ... or Shepherd?"

The President wearily shook his head, creating a ruffling sound against the pillow.

"No, no, Frank. It was an incident from the war ... something I thought I'd almost forgotten about. I was out on patrol; Luft and Shepherd were two Marines with me. We came to this Japanese camp ... there was a Japanese doctor ... he was ... killed. That was the doctor who came into my office, as three-dimensional flesh and blood as you are sitting by my bed."

"Christ," muttered Carmody again.

There was a short silence, as if the President were gathering strength to go on. He took a deep breath and let the air filter out slowly with a soft hushing sound.

"Now you're telling me that it's possible Hadaffi could do this sort of thing to me again. I honestly don't know if my sanity could take that. It would push me over the brink, Frank. If I am to believe in the possibility of this ... psychokinesis, then I can't see any alternative to resignation. Under those conditions I couldn't perform as the President of this country."

"We're only guessing, Mr. President. We only had Hadaffi's word that a person does exist who has this incredible ability."

"Then we have to take his word for it at the moment, unless someone can come up with a credible alternative as to what was done to me. I think that still leaves me in a no-win situation, Frank." A wry attempt at a smile wrinkled over his face. "Considering the opinion polls at the moment, maybe now's a good time to bow out." There was a silence. The President lay still along the bed, his breathing scarcely discernible. His eyelids fluttered nervously, as if acting as a filter for his thoughts. "If Hadaffi is threatening a more intense form of . . . psychokinesis, then I'm sorry, Frank. What he is actually threatening is to destroy the mind of the President of the United States."

There was another pause. Faintly through the window came the cry of a muffled order, and Carmody could see a small group of soldiers gathering in the far corner of the grounds. Maybe Cooper had decided to call off the troops after all.

"The troops are still there, Frank?" asked the President, reading his thoughts.

"Yes, Mr. President."

"That was a waste of time."

"We had no way of knowing."

The President sighed and shook his head.

"You're right, of course." He turned tired eyes toward Carmody. "Should I resign? Can you stop Hadaffi within the next forty-eight hours? Or do you want an insane man as the political leader of this country?"

Carmody stared down at his hands, interlocking his fingers, considering a reply.

"I wish I could give you a definite answer on this

psychokinesis, Mr. President. I wish I could give you an alternative. Expert opinion says no, and maybe, in the one breath. They find it difficult to believe, and so do I." He hunched his shoulders and spread his hands. "But what else is there to believe? One thing is certain, though: your resignation wouldn't stop Hadaffi. Whoever took your place would be the next victim. You said something along those lines yourself. It's not against you as a person; this intimidation is directed, but against the Presidency itself. I can't tell you what to do, Mr. President. That's something you'll have to decide with people like Dan Wenkell." He hesitated, studying the gray face profiled against the pillow in front of him. "All I can promise is to bring every effort to bear that we possibly can, to get Hadaffi before the forty-eight hours are up."

"You're looking for one man in the entire country, Frank. And you're not even sure of what he looks like," said Manningham, with assumed confidence. "What can you do that you already haven't done, Frank?"

"Well, maybe this psychokinesis is a lead in itself, Mr. President. We've already commissioned an expert panel to start working on the problem. Maybe there's some way it can be neutralized. I intend to fly immediately to New York and contact Moccasin. He isn't going to like it, but he has to know that we're now in a state of crisis. We need any information urgently, and he's our only key to Hadaffi at the moment. If he's just playing along with a lead at the moment, then it has to be resolved immediately. We can't wait any longer."

The President nodded, with a slight tilt of his head. Only spirit was holding off exhaustion, the spirit that had won a hundred elections, bulldozed through a multitude of back-room deals. But major decisions would be impossible for him right now.

"I'll hang on as long as I can, Frank," he muttered. "I know you're right that any resignation of mine isn't going to stop Hadaffi, but the last thing the country wants is a mentally defective President. That's what it'll have if you don't stop Hadaffi. I know I couldn't take another experience like that."

He stopped speaking and lay there for a moment with his eyes closed. Carmody waited, but the interview seemed to be at an end, and he wanted to get to New York as fast as possible. He stood up away from the chair, shuffling his feet uncertainly.

"Will that be all, Mr. President?" he asked.

Manningham lifted one hand, then let it drop down on the bed again.

"Ask Dan to come in, will you, Frank. Ask him to contact the Vice-President and bring him along too. We'd better be prepared for any eventuality." He opened his eyes suddenly, and stared at Carmody. "Nothing to the press, Frank. Understand, not a whisper. Have they been around?"

"Just covering the activity around the White House, Mr. President. No one knows anything about this, I'm certain."

There was another pause, and the President closed his eyes again.

"Good," he whispered finally, almost as an afterthought.

Carmody began to edge around the bed, plotting his course as he made for the door.

"Are you sure you feel up to another meeting, Mr. President?" he asked with solicitude. He didn't want Manningham to resign. This closeness to the President was a once-in-a-lifetime eventuality, and if he could stay this close, the only way he could go would be up. Up out of sight. Up to the rarefied air. Up where he knew he belonged. He didn't like the Vice-President. If Manningham resigned, he would have to start the game from the scratch line again, and he didn't relish the thought.

The weary hand waved absently from the bed again.

"Must see them, Frank. Must force myself to see them. Decisions have to be made, and we haven't got that much time." He still didn't open his eyes, as if they were affected by the light. The hand came up again, only this time firmer, as if strengthened by a fresh thought. "This psychokinesis, Frank. The person who might have this sort of power with his mind . . . where would he be? In the White House? Outside the White House? In Washington? Anywhere?"

Carmody was at the door, one hand on the knob. He shrugged.

"I'm embarrassed at not being able to give you direct answers to so many questions that demand answers," he apologized.

"Don't your experts have any ideas?"

"It would depend on how sophisticated in the use of his mind the person had become."

The hand lifted from the bed, and described impatient circles in the air.

"Well . . . a few yards . . . a hundred yards . . . a mile . . . a thousand miles?"

Carmody hedged. "If there was such a person, Mr. President, and remember we're still only talking possibilities, there is a feeling that he could operate from . . . from . . . anywhere. But that's pure conjecture," he added hastily.

"Thank you, Frank," said the President heavily. There was a trace of irony in the thin voice, but there was little Carmody could do to ease the burden.

Whether it was intended or not, Carmody took the words as a signal that the meeting was over. He opened the door and paused.

"I'll send in the Secretary of State immediately, Mr. President," he said.

The President made no verbal reply, merely the same almost imperceptible movement of his head. His eyes were closed again, perhaps trying to shut out the memory of his horrendous experience.

When he went out, General Cooper, Bob Rand, and Eric Dalgety were standing in a tight talking circle around Dan Wenkell. There was no sign of Schyler. He went over and they opened up like a flower to the sun, folding him into the circle.

"I've brought them right up to date, Frank," said Wenkell, sweeping his eyes around the circle. "It's time they knew."

"You don't go along with this bullshit, surely, Frank?" said Cooper brusquely.

"I don't know what I go along with, General," Carmody shrugged. "All I know is that I've just listened to a man who had an experience that threatened his sanity. And if he's subjected to the same type of experience again, he will lose his sanity. All that means to me . . . to us . . . is that somehow we've got to get Hadaffi within the next forty-eight hours . . . or this country will have a new President. And then it will be his turn." He nodded curtly to Wenkell. "The President wants to see you, Mr. Secretary, and he would like the Vice-President to go with you." He glanced quickly at his watch. "I have a plane to catch." He switched his attention abruptly to Eric Dalgety. "Eric, I'll be in touch from New York. You know who I'm going to see. Concentrate on the psychokinesis thing as much as you can.

See if it leads you anywhere. Okay?" His eyes moved on, skewering around the circle, then out to the surrounding corridors. "Where did Martin go?"

Bob Rand shrugged.

"I haven't seen him for the last hour. He must have gone back to your offices."

Carmody nodded behind a poker face. Schyler was probably off somewhere conducting his own investigation. It would be a nice torpedo to Carmody's ambitions if he could nail Hadaffi first. Well, fuck Schyler. Moccasin in New York was the best bet, and that's where he was going.

Angela drove Carmody to the airport, listening intently to his description of what had happened to the President with a subtly constructed expression of distress, all the time savoring the warm glow of satisfaction in her stomach. It was marvelous. Daiton was right. Hadaffi was a genius. But as soon as Carmody was out of Washington she would call Fardrin at the house in Connecticut so he could let Hadaffi know immediately of the success of the operation. They would be elated. And it might be important for them to know that Carmody was flying up to New York to see Moccasin. She knew they had a lead on Moccasin's identity—not that she really believed that Moccasin knew anything, now that the leak through Oxley had been blocked, but it was best to play safe. If they knew who he was, then they should kill him quickly.

It was Monday, the sixteenth of October, a date for

the President to remember. The traffic was heavy, but moving swiftly. She turned the car across the Rochambeau Memorial Bridge and down onto the Parkway leading to the airport. It was a cool night, with low, ragged clouds weeping light rain over the city. Light reflections glistened on the Potomac, highlighting the fretwork pattern of the rain on the surface of the water. Ahead the airport was a tight cluster of glowing eyes, and the air boomed with the thunder of landing and departing jets.

Beside her Carmody was finally silent, wrung out with instructions, fears, and information. She saw no reason to break his silence, and filled the vacuum with planning her words to Fardrin.

She dropped him at the airport entrance, and they exchanged a perfunctory kiss, deadened by anxiety on his part and detachment on hers.

He expected to fly back that night, and his final parting words told her not to come and meet him, because he had no idea of what time, and she might as well go to bed.

She sat in the car for half an hour, watching the winking lights of a parade of jets climbing into the sky until they were blotted out by the low cloud. When she was sure Carmody had gone, she went to one of the booths at the airport and called the Connecticut number. She was delighted when Daiton answered the phone.

"Vilas, darling, how wonderful," she cooed. "This is Nerida. I had no idea you were back at the house."

His voice came back, low and cautious.

"Where are you calling from?"

"Washington airport."

There was a moment's hesitation.

"Let's be careful what we say," he warned.

"I always am, darling. You know that. Where is our friend? Still at the other house?"

"For the moment, yes."

"Then you should let him know that his operation has been an enormous success. His patient may never be the same again. Maybe panic isn't the right word for his friends, but very close to it. They have no idea what to do. They are waiting with a great deal of fear for his next visit. I think they may do what he asks."

"That's marvelous," answered Daiton jubilantly.

"I thought you might think that."

"I'll let him know immediately. One of his friends is waiting for news at the motel."

She paused a moment, gathering her thoughts.

"There is one other thing, darling. I thought you should know that Mr. Carmody has just left for New York to talk to Mr. Moccasin. Do you think you know who Mr. Moccasin is yet?"

"We think so, but we're not certain," answered Daiton.

"Do you think he might have some more information for Mr. Carmody?"

There was a burring pause on the other end of the line.

"I don't believe so," Daiton slurred. "But we have no way of being positive."

"It's dangerous to speculate about such a thing, darling," she said brightly. "Perhaps you should make sure."

"We know he has been talking to a street girl about Oxley. Oxley had evidently done some crazy thing with her hat, and it stuck in her mind. But she's being cagey with us. We are trying to get her to make a positive identification."

Angela paused before answering, her finger tapping thoughtfully against the receiver.

"Maybe Carmody can do it for you," she said softly.

"How do you mean?"

"You know Carmody by sight?"

"Yes, I saw him that time in Washington."

"You are watching the man you believe may be Moccasin?"

"We have taken that precaution."

"Then if he meets Mr. Carmody, that will give you positive identification, and your problem will be solved."

Daiton chuckled gently over the telephone.

"No wonder I love you. That's an excellent suggestion. I'll take a fast car to New York immediately."

"I love you too, darling Vilas. Perhaps in a day or two we can meet?"

"I hope so," he said tenderly. "I'd better leave you now, if I want to get to New York in time. Thank you for calling."

"I love you," she whispered.

She hung up the receiver and wandered slowly out to the car. What a fool Carmody was. He was trying so hard to impress the President, and he was going to run into another dead end in New York. She hoped a very dead end. Hopefully her time with him was almost at an end, and she could be with Vilas, perhaps forever. Surely the brotherhood owed her that much for the service she'd given them.

She started up the car and drove carefully out of the parking area, and back onto the Parkway. The rain was heavier now, and the wipers swished smoothly at the water beating against the windshield. She moved the car at a leisurely pace. She should go back to the office and talk to Rick Hamilton, but suddenly she felt weary of all the pretense, and it was a dangerous state of mind to carry back with her. A slip of the tongue was always possible if her concentration was down. Rick Hamilton could wait until morning. If Dalgety or any of the others wanted her, they knew she could be reached at the apartment.

She followed the river around to the Francis Scott Key Bridge to cut across into Georgetown. The rain pecking at the metal body of the car made a comforting sound. Cars plowed past on either side, throwing up a fine curtain of water. She wondered idly what time Carmody would be back, perhaps she should have a meal prepared that would be easy to heat. The thought suddenly jarred her. Why should she think like that? Why the hell should she care if he had anything to eat? Was it an automatic response to her contrived role as the passionate, caring lover?

It would be just as easy to pretend sleep when he arrived back, and not have to listen to some mournful tale of missed opportunities in New York. The thought opened the gates to a multiplying collection of niggling doubts she knew had been taking root in her mind. Doubts that she'd forced aside and refused to examine, tried to pretend didn't exist. But they were out now, caged rats suddenly reveling in freedom, and she drove slowly, forcing herself to a dispassionate survey.

America was changing her. Washington was changing her. Softening her. It wasn't something she could discuss with Vilas, because he would find it impossible to understand, knowing her background, and it would make him uneasy. No, she had to face it herself, resolve it herself.

She had grown to like all the pretty clothes, the good restaurants, the theater nights. God, she even felt difficulty in hating Carmody sometimes, when she should despise him, be contemptuous of his petty ambitions, his maneuvering against Schyler, his calflike devotion to her. And it frightened her. What had happened to the woman who had killed Eddington a few years ago without compunction? And later glowed in the praise heaped on her by the brotherhood. It had nothing to do with her love for Vilas, that was unshakable. It was the vehemence of her hatred that had softened. It made no difference to the way she acted, at least not yet; she still plotted against Carmody, betrayed all his confidences to Vilas, but what was once automatic now had to be thought about, even rationalized. That was stupidity. That was to risk everything. It would be fatal to have her resolve weakened, especially where Carmody was concerned. Even when she had first been given this assignment, she had known there would always be the possibility that one day she might have to kill Carmody. Now she twisted and turned away from the thought, drove it out of her mind.

She spun the wheel viciously, angered by her thoughts, and the car slewed wildly into Thirty-fourth Street. Oncoming headlights glared into her face as she hastily corrected, and the blast of a passing horn rapped against her ears. She slid the car into the gutter and braked to a halt. She cut the motor and leaned her weight against the steering wheel, staring ahead as the rain created an opaque screen on the windshield. She held her mouth down tight, concentrating. No, nothing must weaken her resolve over the next forty-eight hours. Nothing. Then maybe she could be rid of her association with Carmody, with Washington, fly back to the shelter that Vilas could give her, and let him dissolve all her secret doubts.

She didn't want to change, she told herself. It was important to do what she was doing, important for her, important for the brotherhood.

Maybe Vilas would seize the opportunity while he was in New York to kill Carmody along with Moccasin. She hated to admit it, but it would give her a sense of freedom if she never had to see Carmody again.

It would be dangerous to kill him right now; he was helpless and he knew nothing, and it would stir up a hornets' nest in the government to have their top Intelligence man killed. But it was worth thinking about, even if only for her own personal, selfish reasons.

She restarted the car and eased gingerly back into the traffic. Maybe it was worth another phone call to Connecticut. It would be too late to contact Vilas again, but maybe Fardrin could reach him in New York.

She drove cautiously, examining the thought, trying to come to some decision before she reached the apartment.

For a hooker she was a good-looking girl. A good-looking, sensual, sexy broad. Especially sitting naked on the bed like that, with her back against the wall, her legs apart and drawn up, her hole staring at him like the evil eye. Moccasin realized he wasn't playing the scene very well. He was trying to be pleasant, but he knew by the contemptuous smile flickering across her mouth that she was playing a line with him. He didn't have that much time before he had to leave for his appointment with Carmody, and maybe it would be easier to just belt the Christ out of this dame, until she told him all he wanted to know about Oxley.

He knew she was milking him, and he couldn't just let it run along anymore. She looked good, side-lit by the lone bedside lamp, her black skin glowing with a velvet sheen.

He was a good-looking black man, bushy black hair, trimmed black beard, dark soft eyes with an expression of innocence that gave false comfort to the girl. He was tall, with a muscular leanness, a strong sapling ready to test himself against any wind, to bend a little then spring back into position, made stronger by the ordeal. He was around thirty-four.

He was smart, smart enough to be anything he wanted. His father was a government clerk, his mother a teacher, and he was the family jewel, to be pointed out, admired, a source of inspiration. School was a breeze, learning was a parlor trick he picked up as a child. But he could never settle. He learned too quickly, and life became a bore unless you kept moving. He tried law, he tried truck driving, he tried crime, he played with black power, but they never quite trusted him, he seemed too much one of the others. The enemy. A white man in a black skin. He resented the implication, and he moved on. He was looking for excitement, for difference.

He really didn't expect to be approved when he applied to Intelligence, but he dazzled his interviewer and was accepted. But he didn't want the well-cut suits, or the well-ordered office; that was an extension of boredom. Undercover suited him; it delighted his palate for the sinister, the double-dealing. The intrigue.

No one was leaning over his shoulder, so he made up his own rules, because results were the only thing that mattered. He traveled. Several times he killed, but always in a cold, efficient way. He had run with the tough kids in Washington for a time, and he knew violence. They had decided he was too smart for them also, and he had drifted away. Perhaps one day Intelligence would begin to bore, and he would fade away again.

He rarely saw his parents. They would look at his unwashed jeans, his scrubby leather jacket, and ask about his law course with puzzled frowns, and he would smile their inquiries away. He knew they were disappointed because they thought all that learning ability was going down the drain, and maybe they were right, but he couldn't help that. He wanted variety out of his life, and he applied his smartness to that end.

He studied the girl on the bed closely. She would understand violence, she flirted with it every day of her life. He was probably right: a small dose of violence would achieve faster results than playing a gentleman. She mocked him again with her smile, opened her legs wider for his inspection, and wriggled her ass invitingly around on the bed.

"What's the matter, honey, can't you get it up? This is the third time you've come up to my room, and paid me money, but you never screw me. Never even take off your clothes." She pouted and slid her tongue out and over her lips in a slow washing movement. "All you want to do is talk about this guy Oxley." She put her hands on her upraised knees, and wagged her legs from side to side. "Come on, honey, I'm good, really good. Put it in. Get your money's worth."

"You don't have to take your clothes off," he murmured. "You know what I want."

"It's what I do best, and I feel I got to do something for the money. Stop playing snoop, and enjoy yourself?"

"I told you I wasn't a cop," he said irritably. "You promised you'd find out from the other girls about Oxley. I need to find him . . . fast. He owes me money. You know all about this. I don't have to go over it again."

"I told you I don't know the jerk. He was never a customer of mine. All he did was ruin a fucking good hat, the bastard."

"You're stalling me."

She widened her eyes in mock innocence.

"Why would I do that?"

"You said you were going to talk to some of the girls who knew Oxley. I've given you plenty of time. I've given you all the dough you're going to get. Now I want to know where I can reach him."

She lowered her eyes and snapped her legs shut, with a soft thwacking of flesh on flesh.

"I haven't had a chance to talk to them yet," she answered sullenly. "Some of them have been out of town. Maybe in the morning. Yeah, I know one of them I can see in the morning. She'll know. Then I can meet you again."

She was stupid and she was a liar. And he was being stupid. All another meeting would achieve would be another hundred dollars for her. She would play it forever as long as he kept paying. He went over and stood beside her.

"I want to know now. The dough's running out."

"Then you'll never know," she sneered back at him.

He smiled with his soft innocent eyes, and she relaxed. He put one hand gently along her neck, just beneath her chin, and the other at the back of her head. She smiled triumphantly, and her legs drifted open again.

"That's it," she murmured. "Take it easy. Enjoy yourself. I identified the guy for you, so let it go at that for now. I can talk to this other girl in the morning. Why rush things, honey?"

It was all a matter of timing. He snapped her head forward, then back again sharply, with the hand underneath her chin. Not enough to break her neck, but enough to make the result extremely unpleasant.

Her eyes glazed, and a rivulet of blood belched out of her mouth, and ran down into her neck.

He let her go and stepped back. An agonized cry choked up out of her throat, her head fell forward on her knees, she rolled over sideways, and spilled onto the floor with a dull, flat thud.

He stepped back to make room for her body on the floor, and stood looking down at her. He said nothing. She scrambled around on the floor, moaning, her limbs refusing to coordinate as she tried to raise herself up on her hands and knees.

"Jes, Jes," she choked, over and over again.

He strolled across to the small chair, sat down, crossed his legs, and waited. He consulted his watch. There wasn't much time left. He didn't want to be late, even though he hated the thought of meeting Carmody. It was too dangerous. He knew it, and so did Carmody, and he would have refused the summons if it had not been requested in such urgent tones. Something must have happened with Hadaffi to throw Carmody into a panic, and it made him feel that he was going to need this information about Oxley before the meeting.

The girl managed to get herself up on her hands and knees, and she stayed prone in that position for a moment, quivering like a terrified dog. A wave of spasmodic tremors rippled up her body, culminating in a retching sound in her throat as she vomited on the floor.

Moccasin stood up again, walked across to the girl, seized her under the armpits, dragged her into an upright position, and flopped her back on the bed. Her body looked marvelous. Black highlights against the white bedcover, but her face was distorted with fear and pain. She pawed at the blood around her mouth, leaving a smear of red over her cheeks and neck.

"Jes, you bastard," she murmured painfully. "You bastard, you bastard."

He took a knife casually from his pocket, leaned forward, and pressed the point against her throat until it drew a small globule of blood. Terror took over from her pain, and she backed off from the knife, shuttling backward across the bed on her elbows and buttocks like a terrified bug in retreat.

"Don't kill me," she choked.

"Oxley?" he asked quietly. "I'm not going to let you go on milking me for any more dough. I was willing to play along with you, but you're a greedy bitch. Now I want to know. I haven't got any more time left."

His tone was almost conversational, the innocence still in his eyes, only for her it was now an expression to be feared.

"You have spoken to the other girls," he stated.

She swallowed painfully, and another speckle of blood flared out of her mouth. She nodded agreement without speaking.

"You know where he lives?"

She nodded again.

"Tell me?"

She opened her mouth, and only a dry rasping sound filtered out of her throat. She tapped weakly at her neck with her fingers, and shook her head. Something had happened to her voice. He put the knife away and took a small note pad from his pocket, together with a pen, and threw them down on the bed beside her. "Write it down."

She rolled over on her side and picked up the pen. Her fingers stumbled, colliding with each other like strangers. Laboriously, as if the mere act of writing were painful, she scrawled out an address in Greenwich Village.

He leaned down and plucked it out of her hand, and put it in his pocket.

She flopped again onto her back, and lay there with her eyes closed, breathing in drawn-out fluttery sighs. The blood still dribbled from the corner of her mouth, but she ignored it. She stank of vomit and fear.

"If you tell anybody about this, I'll come back here and kill you. I want you to believe that. It's important for you to believe it. Do you understand me?"

She nodded slowly, her eyes still closed. Her body shuddered again, and her breasts moved and glistened in the dim light.

He paused at the door on the way out.

"Don't be such a greedy bitch next time," he advised.

It was a small bar along Eighth Avenue. Narrow, dimly lit, a bar running the length of the place one side, narrow booths hugging the other. The patrons were mostly black, draped along the side of the bar in repetitious anonymity, each man nursing his drink, using it to kill time. A soft murmur of conversation drifted up from the bar, but individual words were indistinguishable. The walls were a cracked, peeling blue. The bar was tended by a solitary, overweight black man with a polished bald dome, who seemed instinctively to know each man's drink without the necessity of asking. He wore a bright red shirt garnished with a natty blue bow tie, as if trying to inject some light into the dingy interior. He didn't bother to glance up when Moccasin came in.

Carmody was already there, perched apprehensively on a stool at the farthest end of the bar. He looked so uncomfortable and out of place, the undercover man found it difficult to suppress a grin. He slid into a vacant booth at the end of the bar and motioned with his head for Carmody to join him. Carmody lifted himself off the stool and slid into the seat opposite. He brought his beer with him and put it down heavily on the table, betraying his irritation. The beer slopped over the sides of the glass and formed a scummy circle on the table.

"For Chrissake, what sort of a place is this to meet?" he rasped. "Can't we go to your apartment?"

"I don't want to be seen going there with you," said Moccasin smoothly. "Even this is risky enough."

"What about a car? Couldn't you bring your car?"

Moccasin gave a determined shake of his head. "Too easy to be picked up by a bug. I've got a hunch someone is watching me. Nothing concrete, just a feeling, but I'm not taking any chances." He grinned without humor. "Except meeting you. This had better be good, Carmody. I've spent a lot of time and effort building up a cover, and I don't want it blown in one night by a fit of panic."

Carmody lifted his glass and sipped at his beer, staring across the rim at Moccasin.

"You sure we can talk here?"

"Yes. Keep it low, and you'd think you were in church. Everybody here makes a profession of minding their own business."

Carmody put the beer down on the table and interlocked his fingers around the glass.

"Believe me, this is no panic," he said soberly. "I need the latest you've got on Hadaffi, and I need it fast. Tonight. Has your contact fed you any more information?"

"My friend and big mouth Mr. Oxley has vanished," grimaced Moccasin.

Carmody picked up his half-empty glass and thumped it down on the table.

"For Chrissake, what do you mean, vanished?"

"Just that. I had an appointment with him a few days ago, and he never showed. I've been trying to get a lead on him and I finally managed to get his address tonight. Just before I came here. I'm going straight there as soon as we've finished." He took the piece of paper with the address from his pocket and laid it on the table in front of Carmody. "It's down in the Village."

"How do you know the bastard will be there?"

"I won't until I go there, will I?"

Carmody glared at him. He could pull rank on this insolent bastard, but that wouldn't help any, and he needed him too badly. Moccasin folded up the piece of paper and returned it to his pocket.

"I'll come with you," said Carmody.

"I can handle it. What's the rush?"

Carmody leaned forward across the narrow table until his head was almost touching the other man.

"The rush is that we won't have a President of this country in another forty-odd hours unless we nail Hadaffi," he whispered furiously. "That's the fucking rush."

The fat bartender materialized at the side of the booth, the overhead light reflecting on his bald dome. He had an overflowing glass of beer in his hand, and he thrust it aggressively down on the table. Carmody turned his head away and slunk back into the corner of the seat.

"You want your usual beer?" asked the fat man.

Moccasin pursed his lips and frowned, as if considering a reprimand, then shrugged it away.

"Sure, okay," he nodded.

They waited a few more moments for the bartender to waddle out of earshot. Moccasin took a few cautious sips of the beer, put it down, and studied Carmody gravely.

"And what the hell is that supposed to mean?" he muttered.

Carmody took a deep breath, leaned forward on his elbows, and poured out the whole episode about the President and psychokinesis. It sounded even more incredible to hear it repeated, but he left out no detail, speaking in deliberate earnest undertones. Moccasin heard him out in silence, with occasional sips at his beer.

"I know it sounds fantastic, but we have to go with Hadaffi's claim at the moment," concluded Carmody. "We have no other rational explanation to explain what happened to the President. Christ help us, and him, if it happens again. If it does, it won't end there. Whoever takes Manningham's place will get the same treatment. It's the Presidency itself that's at stake. I've got to get Hadaffi somehow." He looked pleadingly into Moccasin's face. "I guess it all sounds crazy to you?"

Moccasin didn't answer for a moment. He contemplated his beer, his fingers running aimlessly up and down the sides of the glass, his brows clutched together in concentration.

"No, it doesn't," he murmured slowly. "Not crazy at all. I believe there is a man who exists somewhere in this country who would be capable of that sort of psychokinesis."

Carmody stared at him, and a tiny adolescent flutter beat in his chest.

"Are you serious?"

"Of course I'm serious."

"For Chrissake, who?"

Moccasin took another sip of beer while Carmody's fingers chased each other impatiently along the edge of the table.

"It was about three years ago," began Moccasin slowly. "I was in Paris at the time, teamed up with Walt Murphy. We picked up a tip that the Russians were on to some guy back in California who was doing incredible things with his mind. I mean things out of this world. That was when I first heard of this psychokinesis thing." He wrinkled his brow and thumbed at the corner of his mouth. "The way I got involved, somehow the whole operation was taken over by the military. They evidently had ideas of their own about this guy because they pulled strings right on up to cabinet level so even Intelligence didn't know what was going on. Murphy and I flew back to California to see this guy. He was working at Stanford University outside of San Francisco." He paused for a moment and lifted his beer to his mouth again. He replaced it on the table

and dry-patted his lips. He was a frugal drinker. Carmody waited, his body rigid with anticipation, almost
no pulse, as if he'd stopped breathing.

"His name was Lett . . . Lead . . . no, Leica. That's
right, Leica. We got our hands on a whole dossier written
by some guy who'd worked with him. Lots of incredible
stuff. Killing monkeys at a range of five hundred miles,
just by using his mind. Other things at even greater
range. He'd used a few human volunteers as well. Not
killing them, but the results were just as staggering.
Disabling them mentally when they were half the
country away from him. They recovered all right, but
the inference was that he was only operating at half
power, so to speak. We approached the head of Leica's
department at first." He shrugged his shoulders. "I was
like you at the time . . . skeptical. I mean, what else
could you be? The department head was a guy named
. . . ah, Moslin. I think. He had a fair idea of what
Leica was doing, but without the details. It was all very
hush-hush. I got the idea he was a bit uptight because
Leica was keeping him in the dark about the details of
the experiments. But he wasn't too cooperative with us.
He couldn't stop us, but he obviously didn't want Intelligence agents prowling around the University. You
know the way it is. This guy Leica was something of a
genius, already famous in the field of physics. I'd say
he was about thirty-five then. Shy sort of guy, almost
timid. He was going through a hell of a time. Whoever
had blown his security had done a pretty thorough job.
They were all after him. The KGB, us, and God knows
who else. Man, did we put some pressure on him. The
whole bit. He had a young wife, can't remember her
name, but anyway Murphy and I decided to extend the
pressure to her." He shot Carmody a wry grin and

sipped another taste of his beer. "I don't have to fill you in on details. I mean, we didn't know what his politics were, for all we knew he was getting set to go over to the Russians, and we weren't going to let that happen." He rubbed the fingers of one hand musingly along his jawline, reflectively studying his beer glass. "That's when I stopped being skeptical, when I found out about psychokinesis. I was on my way to see her one night when it happened. I can't describe it to you. I'm not even going to try; all I can say is that it was something as horrendous as what happened to the President. I thought I was going to die. Matter of fact, I hoped I was, it was so bad. I'll never forget it. But it convinced me about Leica. I was hospitalized for two days. When I got out, he was gone. He and his wife. Vanished. They'd slipped right out from under Murphy." He frowned at the memory, and his fingers agitated each other around the glass. "It turned into a bit of a circus after that. We were all trying to trace him, but no one turned up a clue. He'd crawled into a hole and pulled the covers over."

"Wouldn't all this be on file somewhere?" asked Carmody.

Moccasin shrugged. "I made out a full report, but I have no idea what happened to it. It wasn't like the usual thing. Maybe it's buried somewhere in the Pentagon. I guess they had some special plan cooked up to use his powers. But once he was gone they hushed the whole thing up as tight as a drum." He drained the glass and put it down heavily. He paused, making circular patterns with his finger on a wet spot on the table.

"But from what you've told me about the President, he's working for Hadaffi. I wouldn't have the slightest doubt about that. I figured at the time we only knew a fraction of the real power he was capable of . . . and this confirms it." He shrugged again and folded his arms on the table. "I guess now we know about his politics."

"Not necessarily," grunted Carmody. "Hadaffi could be using some sort of pressure on him. He's ruthless enough to do it."

"It would have to be some pressure, but maybe you're right. He didn't appear the sort of guy who would put himself into this sort of scene. Although don't ask me how the hell Hadaffi would have found him. We tried hard enough, and all we drew was a blank."

"Do you have anything else on Leica?" asked Carmody anxiously. "Pictures? Descriptions?"

"No, and I could only give you a hazy description. Moslin at Stanford University could give you those details better than I. I had a sneaking feeling he may have known where Leica had gone, but we could never get anything out of him."

"Then I'll fly to San Francisco tonight. To Stanford University. If we can plaster a picture of Leica over every television screen in the country, surely someone would have seen him. Christ, this is just the break we've been looking for."

"You should have asked me sooner," said Moccasin tartly. "But I think you're hoping for miracles if you think a picture of Leica is going to work fast enough for you. You'll get a million false calls."

Apprehension sent Carmody's body wriggling about the tight confines of the booth.

"At least it's something concrete to go on," he said defensively. "Something positive. Maybe Moslin can give me some more personal information that can add to what you've told me. Some detail that may have been overlooked. Where Leica might be."

"You'd better call Moslin before you go flying out across the country. That was three years ago. He may not even be at the University anymore."

"Yes, I will, but just to make the contact," said Carmody. "I've got to talk to him face to face. The detailed information I have to get on Leica isn't going to come from a phone call."

Carmody's fingers drummed an uncertain rhythm along the tabletop. Which lead to follow? Maybe this Oxley had some additional information for Moccasin that would make flying to San Francisco unnecessary. But his disappearance didn't fill him with confidence. There was no guarantee he would be at the address. Maybe he was dead.

"I hope to Christ you're right," he said slowly.

"About Leica?"

"Yes. As you said, it's three years ago. It's possible that someone else could have developed the powers of psychokinesis to the same degree."

The lines in Moccasin's forehead crammed together with irritation.

"Anything's possible, Carmody," he grunted. "But at least I know that Leica is reality. I tell you it has to be him." He paused.

"What are we going to do about Oxley?"

Carmody linked his hands together and leaned forward intently, pressing tightly against the dividing table. His words came like a burst of rapid fire.

"I'll go back to the hotel and make the call to Palo Alto. You go on to Greenwich Village, and I'll join you there. What you find may determine whether I fly to San Francisco tonight or not."

Moccasin's eyes flicked open and shut several times in a mute gesture of assent.

"Then I'd better move," he grunted.

Carmody fell silent for a moment, not moving, his fingers caressing his chin in a gesture of doubt.

"Maybe I should go with you first to Greenwich Village?" he mouthed hesitantly.

Moccasin rejected the thought with a decisive shake of his head, raised his body, and began to ease himself out of the booth.

"No dice," he grunted. "Oxley would only clam up if you were with me. I'm the only one he'll risk talking to. You go and make your call, like you said."

He extricated himself from behind the table, raised himself to his full height, then leaned toward Carmody, one hand extended as if to stifle any objection. The dim light from the bar threw a soft yellow halo around his dark hair.

"I guess you're right," said Carmody slowly.

"I know I'm right," Moccasin answered. "I'm going to pay a quick visit to the john. Think about it while I'm gone." He formed his hand into a tight fist, the thumb raised in an insolent gesture of confidence. He waggled the upright digit at Carmody and grinned sourly.

"Okay?"

He turned quickly, with the sinuous grace of an athlete, and was gone before Carmody could answer.

Daiton was beginning to sense a feeling close to panic. Indecision was pinching the muscles of his stomach into a tight knot, producing an effect like a sharp cutting pain in his gut.

He had positioned himself at the bar where he could

observe Carmody and the man, and now he found difficulty in controlling the nervous tremor of his fingers around the damp glass of his untouched beer. He had to do something, and quickly. The man had talked to Carmody too long. About what, he had no idea, but he wouldn't feel safe until the man was dead. None of them could feel safe. And even better if he could kill Carmody too. But how?

Could he chance just walking up to the booth and blasting them both? Maybe that was the only way, but he'd have to make up his mind to do it, and do it fast. It wasn't the way he liked to operate. He liked to plan, to leave no room for error, the way he'd handled the doctor.

But there'd been no time for that sort of planning this time. He swiveled about nervously on the stool, bumping awkwardly against other drinkers draped along the bar. He ignored the flat, questioning stares, trying to force himself into decision. Maybe he should wait outside and try and nail them both as they came out of the bar? But what if they didn't leave together? He lifted the glass to his mouth in a pretense of drinking, slopping the beer clumsily over his fingers. Then he saw Moccasin extricate himself from the booth and move into the small passage at the rear of the bar, where the toilet sign was located. It was the catalyst that propelled him into a decision. Maybe this would be the only chance he would get. Perhaps it would destroy the opportunity to eliminate Carmody as well, but he was committed to the other man.

He slid off the stool and moved casually to the rear of the bar, forcing himself to a slow, unhurried pace. His commitment to action was like an analgesic, instantly stilling the tremor in his hands. Indecision was behind him now. There was only purpose and dedication, and a ruthless determination to silence this man.

He went past Carmody without changing pace, looking neither right nor left, completely relaxed. But once he turned into the narrow passage, he quickened his step. A mean single light in the ceiling threw muted shadows around his feet. He put out a hand and let his fingers run along the wall, and some of the peeling paint wrinkled away with the pressure.

Someone in obvious anger had wrenched the sign off the door, and there was crudely lettered MEN in white paint as a replacement.

He pushed down the latch, opened the door, and stepped inside. With a speed culled from experience his eyes swiftly took in the details of the toilet. The decor matched the passage, an indeterminate shade of peeling yellow. To the left there were two cubicles, the open doors revealing a lack of occupants. Ahead a dirt-encrusted window, framed with ancient pipes. To the right, two bowls and the man with his back to him, urinating in one of them. It was an ideal situation for the knife. He prided himself on his expertise with the knife; it was silent, and he was so quick, the man would hardly realize he was dead. He scarcely broke stride, because the man was already zipping up his trousers.

Four steps forward, one arm like a swiftly coiling snake around the man's neck, a momentary strangled grunt of surprise, then the knife was in, then just as quickly out again, and the man was dead. He stood back and let him slide down to join the scummy tile floor in a grotesque embrace. It was just like the doctor again, so fast, so easy.

He wiped the knife on the dead man's jacket, and went quickly out the toilet door without a backward glance. He strolled casually back down the narrow passage, past Carmody, not looking, his heart thumping, smiling at no one. He went on down the length of the bar, opened the door, and was swallowed from sight by Eighth Avenue.

Carmody waited. Impatience agitated his body. Restless hands prowled the table. His feet engaged in a constant shuffle dance, and he repositioned himself every few moments on the narrow seat. He realized his first intuition was right, and he wanted to make that San Francisco call, but he needed to move. What the hell was keeping Moccasin so long? Finally he got his feet and stomped into the toilet. It wasn't the first body Carmody had seen, but it was a sickening feeling to know someone so alive one moment could be dead the next.

The detective's name was Kowaski. Lieutenant Stanley Kowaski. The fact that the frail human body was not constructed to survive the murderous assortment of weaponry that some New Yorkers used on each other no longer filled him with awe. Not for a long time. The end result was always the same. Blood. The extinction of life. A corpse.

Never had the toilet in the Eighth Avenue bar been so crowded with people engaged in an activity other than the elimination of human waste. Uniformed police, detectives, a photographer with the inert Moccasin as a subject, ambulance attendants.

Carmody felt nothing but anger and frustration. How

dare the undercover man be so stupid as to get himself
killed when there was so much to do, so much still to
learn. It was infuriating. The fact that the man on the
floor had been an associate engaged in conversation
with him just a short time ago inspired no sense of grief.
Maybe he was forgetting to be a human being, but the
only thing in his mind was saving the Presidency, and
what it could do for him. Moccasin's death dragged him
into a whirlpool of indecision. Call the man Moslin in
San Francisco, just fly out to San Francisco on the off-
chance of seeing him, or take over Moccasin's role and
try and find Oxley?

The remark he'd made to Moccasin about getting another operative to handle the Oxley inquiry had been
thoughtless. He hesitated to widen the circle of agents.
It would take time to brief them with all the double-
talk required to hide the facts of the threat to the Presidency.

For the moment he was stuck here, and time was the
one thing he didn't have.

Kowaski examined Carmody's identification carefully
and jerked his head in the direction of Moccasin, now
being trundled out of the bar on a stretcher.

"One of your men, Carmody?"

"I'm afraid so."

The detective nodded, and fumbled apologetically at
his chin with his fingers.

"I'll have to check your ID through headquarters,
Mr. Carmody. Just routine."

Carmody shrugged compliance. His first instinct after
finding Moccasin had been to leave the bar quickly.
Calling the police was an added complication, but it
was better than being hunted, perhaps as a suspect.

He followed Kowaski's broad competent shape out

of the toilet, along the narrow passage, and into the bar. Two policemen were questioning the denizens of the bar, coping patiently with the monosyllabic grunted replies. Carmody jerked his thumb in the direction of the interrogation.

"You're not going to find the murderer or the reason among that lot, Lieutenant," he advised.

Kowaski shrugged his broad shoulders and moved in the direction of the telephone.

"Routine, Mr. Carmody. But I'm sure there's some highly complicated motive you're not going to talk to me about."

He reached for the telephone, and Carmody thought quickly. He didn't want the police checking back through Schyler. Martin might just be bastard enough to try and immobilize him.

"Ask your people to talk to Eric Dalgety, FBI in Washington," he asked urgently. He lifted his arm and squinted in the dim light at his watch.

"As fast as you can, Lieutenant. I may have to catch a plane to San Francisco tonight."

Kowaski nodded, and commenced dialing. He was pretty sure this guy's ID was okay, but experience automatically told him to check.

Carmody waited, fretting with his hands; trying to come to a decision. He wanted time to stand still, give him extra days, extra hours, extra anything. He felt an enormous sense of irritation. How the hell had one of Hadaffi's assassins managed to kill Moccasin right under his nose? That wasn't going to look too good when it got back to Washington.

It was maddening. But how the fuck had they done it? Was he next? Maybe that was the way it was planned, and they didn't get the opportunity. He felt a cold tremor, as if a chill breeze had swept in off Eighth Avenue and fingered his spine.

The image of Moccasin's body in the toilet suddenly filled his mind, and he swallowed down hard on a tiny knot of panic welling up in his throat.

By the time Kowaski turned away from the telephone he knew what he was going to do. He would be guided by what he found at Oxley's apartment. That would be his first move and he would have to move fast, but he would take it from there. He looked into the Lieutenant's flat Slavic face, and waited.

"Okay, Mr. Carmody," said Kowaski woodenly. "Seems like we're to give you every cooperation. Anything you want."

Carmody took the piece of paper with the Greenwich Village address from his pocket, and showed it to the detective. At least he'd had the forethought to take it from Moccasin's pocket before the police arrived.

"I'd like a car and a couple of your men to go with me to this address, Lieutenant. It'll be protection for me, because I have a hunch whoever killed this man may also try to kill me. There's a man living at this address I urgently want to interview. If I have to fly to San Francisco I may require him arrested and placed in protective custody."

"On what charge?"

"Think of something," said Carmody bluntly.

Kowaski shrugged. This was a world outside his orbit.

"If I decide I want you to hold him, keep him here until I can get a man up from Washington to question him." He paused and permitted a smile through a tight-lipped mouth. "All right, Lieutenant?"

Kowaski shrugged again. He was a man given to shrugging his way through the world. People behaved

the way they did because of the way they were, and
nothing he could do was going to change anything.

"Sure thing, Mr. Carmody," he answered politely. He
turned and beckoned to another detective at the other
end of the bar.

The detective's name was Nelson. Carmody never
learned the name of the uniformed officer. They were
coolly polite, but offered no conversation. The uniformed man drove fast, with practiced efficiency, the
detective seated alongside him, surrendering the back
seat to Carmody. The traffic was heavy, but offered little
opposition to the police car.

Carmody interlocked his fingers and sat forward in
the seat, unable to relax. He prayed Oxley was going to
be at the address. He hoped to hell they hadn't killed
him too.

They went down Sixth Avenue to a house on the
other side of Washington Square. A geometric jumble
of fire escapes patterned the front of the building. As
they stepped out another car cruised past, and someone
shouted something obscene at the police car. The police
ignored the remark. Passersby stared with curiosity, but
no one stopped. Cold air arrowed through the gaps in
the buildings, filling the streets with a sharp, chill wind.

The landlady was a smartly dressed blowzy blonde
about forty-five, overdecorated with makeup. Her wide
face glistened in the night light, and the heavily applied cosmetics crinkled under her apprehensive smile.

"I was beginning to wonder about Nick," she gushed
effusively. "I haven't seen him for a few days. His rent
is paid up until the end of this week, but it's not like
him to go off like this." She paused and eyed Carmody
warily. "Unless of course he's in trouble with the police? I don't really know him that well," she added
quickly. "I keep a respectable place here."

The police left the questioning to Carmody.

"I'm sure you do," said Carmody politely. "But perhaps we could see his room?"

It was a small room, sparsely furnished. A small unmade bed, settee, table, and chairs, all well used. A pile of old newspapers, books, prints tacked on the walls, a guitar leaning in one of the corners. He went across the room and opened the wardrobe. The police stayed by the door with the landlady, aloof and uninvolved. There was a surprising number of suits and casual clothes in the robe.

"I hope he's not in big trouble?" said the landlady.

Carmody didn't answer. Oxley was gone. Well, what did he expect. He knew if Hadaffi's gang had the slightest suspicion Oxley was selling them out, they would have killed him without hesitation. His mind jarred indecision again. The room had to be searched, gone over with a microscope, but by whom? Not the police. What was he going to do about Moslin in San Francisco? That lead was too valuable to let go. He sat himself down on the bed and gave himself a few moments of careful consideration.

"Do you have any photographs of Mr. Oxley?" he asked the landlady.

She shook her head.

"Perhaps you could give the police a description while I make some long-distance calls." He caught the sour expression crossing her face. "Of course I'll see you're reimbursed for the cost," he added. He turned to the detective and smiled apologetically. "I'm afraid it's going to have to be confidential."

Nelson nodded without expression, and the trio backed out of the room, closing the door gently behind them. Carmody picked up the telephone and called Palo Alto.

He gave them Moslin's name, the Stanford University connection, and crossed his fingers that the man was still there. He also told them it was an urgent police matter.

They were back to him with a line to Professor Arnold Moslin in a surprisingly short time.

"Professor, my name is Frank Carmody, from Intelligence in Washington. I'm calling you from New York. I need some urgent information about a man called Leica. I've been told you may be able to help me."

There was a crackling pause at the other end of the line.

"Brett Leica?"

"I don't know his first name, but I expect that's the man. He was involved in experiments in psychokinesis at your university."

There was another pause, then the cultured voice came back to him again.

"My God, you people aren't still on that, are you? That was three years ago."

Carmody pressed the receiver tightly to his ear, holding down his irritation. Now he'd located the man, he hoped he wasn't going to prove difficult.

"Professor, I'll short-circuit this as much as I can. I don't want to go over old ground about what happened three years ago. I know about that, and so do you. But I need all the information I can get about Leica in the shortest possible time. This is a national emergency."

"Oh, dear," said the voice with heavy sarcasm. "You people seem able to dredge up a national emergency every few days."

Carmody buried an obscene rejoinder in his throat before it had a chance to be heard. Fucking intellectuals. He made a supreme effort to keep his voice steady.

"Professor, I'm very serious about this one. I may even have to take you into my confidence, but not over the telephone. I want photographs of Leica, anything you can give me. I'm prepared to fly out to Stanford right now . . . tonight . . . if you'll see me when I get there. Do you have material on Leica you can show me? Photographs?"

There was another pause. Fuck him, thought Carmody, if he wants to be an intractable bastard he'd go over there with a search warrant and tear the University apart.

"Yes, I can give you that material, Mr. Carmody," he answered stiffly. Perhaps he had read the implication of Carmody's thoughts in his voice. "What time can I expect you?"

"I can get a flight around ten o'clock. Let's see, that should get me there some time after midnight, West Coast time."

"That's rather late."

"Professor, believe me, I've got a time problem. I have to get this information as quickly as possible. Where can I see you?"

"I'll have to go to my office to get the material."

"I can come there, or I'll come to your home. Whichever is best."

Another pause, and a clucking sound, as if the man were beating at the receiver with the tip of his tongue.

"I would have thought you still had all the information on your files from three years ago," said the professor.

"I don't know about that," answered Carmody patiently. "I wasn't involved three years ago. Believe me, it's much faster if I get the information from you. Now, where do you want me to come . . . to the university, or to your home?"

"Very well, come to my home, Mr. Carmody. I'll go to the University and get all the relevant material I can, and bring it to my home. Forty-five Mayberry Street. Have you got that?"

Carmody dragged a note pad from his inner pocket, and scribbled down the address. "Yes. Thank you, Professor Moslin. Thank you for your cooperation. I'll see you in about five hours or so."

He hung up quickly before the professor had the chance to extend the conversation. Whether he took the man into his confidence would depend very much on his attitude. If there was antagonism, then he would use all the force at his disposal. He had no time for any verbal byplay.

He called TWA and confirmed a flight out of New York at ten o'clock.

Then he called Rick Hamilton in Washington.

"Rick, I want you to come to New York immediately," he said. "I've traced the address of Moccasin's informant, but he's not here. He may be dead for all I know, probably is, but his apartment needs to be searched. I mean really searched. Torn apart if you like. There has to be something here that tells us something about Hadaffi. The man's name is Oxley. Nick Oxley. I can't do it myself, I have to fly out to San Francisco on a new lead that's just as important as this one. You're the only one I can call, so I need you here badly."

"What about Moccasin, can't he handle it?" asked Hamilton.

"No, Moccasin's dead."

There was a sharp intake of breath on the other end of the line.

"Christ, what happened?"

"I'd say Hadaffi is what happened, but I haven't got

time to talk about it now. I've got a flight out at ten o'clock, so I'm not going to be here when you arrive. I'll have a police car meet you at the airport, and bring you straight to this address. It's in Greenwich Village. Anything stopping you from dropping everything and running?"

"If there was, I've forgotten it. I'll leave as soon as I hang up."

There was a pause. Carmody ran his fingers nervously up and down the receiver.

"What's happening there?" he inquired anxiously.

"I get the feeling everyone is running around in circles. Eric Dalgety is flying some expert on psychokinesis in from Boston. They're all pinning a hell of a lot of faith on what you're doing, Frank."

Carmody's tongue flicked nervously over his lips. He wished they had more than an expression of faith to believe in.

"I understand the President is still talking resignation," added Hamilton. "There's some talk of spiriting him out of the White House to another part of the country, but I believe he's resisting the suggestion. I don't know whether that would achieve anything."

"Probably not," said Carmody. "How can you hide from something like this, something you can't see? Listen, the detective who will meet you at the airport is named Nelson. I'll be with a Professor Arnold Moslin at Stanford outside of San Francisco. He's a professor at Stanford University. He may be able to tell me about the man I think may be responsible for the psychokinesis. Soon as I get there I'll call you at this apartment, so stay here until you get my call. Get that?"

"That sounds like an exciting lead, Frank."

"No time for details now, Rick. Just get here as fast

as you can." He hesitated. "Let Eric and the others know what's happening. And Angela."

"What about Martin? Zambretti's hanging around here like a polluted cloud too."

Carmody paused a moment, clucking his tongue thoughtfully. He'd like to know what the hell Schyler was up to.

"Give him a vague impression of what I'm doing," he said coldly. "I can fill him in on the details when I get back to Washington. Unless you find something important enough to bring me back to New York, I'll fly straight from San Francisco to Washington."

He hung up, then called General Cooper.

"Frank," said the general anxiously. "What's happening up there? We're having trouble pacifying the President. Have you got anything I can tell him?"

"Rick Hamilton has some details, General," said Carmody brusquely. Hamilton would probably be gone by the time the general got around to seeing him, but he couldn't help that. "I have to take a fast flight to San Francisco, General. It's going to be the middle of the night by the time I get there, and I want to be certain of getting back to Washington fast, without having to rely on a commercial flight. Can you put a military plane at my disposal? And I'll want someone to meet me at the San Francisco airport, someone connected with the plan if possible. I'm leaving New York on the ten o'clock flight with TWA. Can you arrange that for me?"

"Of course, Frank, of course," gushed the general. "But Christ, San Francisco? What's going on, Frank? Can't you give me anything to give to the President? He's in a hell of a state of depression."

Carmody charged on, roughshod, over everybody:

generals, politicians, professors. The niceties of protocol were a luxury he could no longer afford.

"Talk to Hamilton, General. I don't want to miss the flight. Tell the President everything's going fine."

He hung up on the general, and sat for a moment on the edge of the bed, probing his mind for any forgotten detail. He glanced at his watch. He had half an hour. He stood up and went across to the door, suddenly aware of a leaden weariness dragging at his feet. He would get the police to circulate the landlady's description of Nick Oxley, but he had a strong hunch that the informant was no longer in the land of the living.

It was midnight, West Coast time, when the fasten-seat-belts sign flipped on in the 747. The flight had seemed as if it would go on forever, as if the pilot had taken a wrong turn and headed straight for the moon.

He had tried to sleep, but apprehension had fought a winning battle with his desire for unconsciousness. His mind refused dogmatically to switch off, and two separate visions kept stomping their way through his brain. In the first vision he stood forever within the President's charmed inner circle, bathed in light and admiration, the lone victor over Hadaffi. He'd pulled it off. He'd done it all. The super-Intelligence man, gathering the important bits and pieces around the country, assembling them into one comprehensive form, and hey presto. The end of the threat from Hadaffi. The President's personal advisor on all matters of Intelligence. Everything. Money, position, power, and the greatest screwing talent any man ever had the good fortune to live with, because Angela would stay with him. He might even marry her.

But the second vision kept crowding in, trying to erase the first. Nothing happened. Nothing went right. Oxley was dead, and that was the end of any lead in New York. Professor Moslin refused to divulge any meaningful information about Leica. This flight was a farce. There were no other leads, no directions. The forty-eight hours sped by, and the United States had an insane man for its top executive. And all the fingers pointed at him. Smartass. Egomaniac. Determined to play a lone hand, cover himself with glory, and instead he'd covered himself with shit.

And Schyler would be there, just to make sure the shit stuck. All the words. Disloyalty. Incompetence. Good-bye Carmody.

The two visions wracked at him all the way across the country. They had prevented him from sleeping, and he desperately needed sleep.

So he had to settle for endless cups of coffee, watching a fatuous movie, and staring dolefully through the window at the inky blackness surrounding the plane. Gradually pinpoints of light penetrated the blackness, growing in profusion until they were like a vast collection of diamonds spread out on velvet for his inspection. San Francisco.

He rubbed wearily at his chin. He needed a shave. He needed a fresh shirt, a shower. The impeccably dressed Frank Carmody looked more like he was dressed for the hoboes' ball.

Ladies and gentlemen, we are about to land at San Francisco, crooned the hostess, in practiced tones. He knew the routine almost as well as she did. He patted at his hair, adjusted his tie, and tried to smooth out some of the wrinkles in his suit. He should have gone to the washroom before the plane landed, but he would attend to that at the airport. He hoped there would be someone there to meet him. Cooper was an efficient man, and he trusted him, but there was always a first time. He dry-washed his face with his hands and tried to shake off the mood of pessimism induced by the flight. He did some time calculations in his mind. Stanford was about forty-five miles from San Francisco. Allow forty-five minutes to get there. No traffic worries at this time of night. Hopefully thirty minutes with the professor, then another forty-five minutes back to the airport. Providing there was no need for him to return to New York, he should be back in Washington by early morning. Angela wouldn't have waited up for him, and there was no point in ringing her now.

The roar of the engines turned down to a whisper quietness. The plane banked around, bounced a little, the music came on, loaded with soothing syrup. The lights on the ground raced to meet them, attached themselves to shadowy buildings, and they came down to a feather-touch landing.

He picked up his briefcase and placed it in his lap, rehearsing his approach to Moslin as the plane trundled across to the terminal. He stood up, self-consciously smoothing his suit again, and joined the file of people shuffling toward the exit.

Thank you for flying with us, smiled the hostess. She was pretty, very pretty. Christ, had she been with them on the entire flight? Nothing was registering in his mind, not faces, not surroundings, there was no room for anything else but Hadaffi.

He went to the reception desk, and there were two

air force men waiting. One a colonel, the other a sergeant. He went up to the colonel and put out his hand.

"I'm Frank Carmody. Are you waiting for me?"

The colonel nodded, smiled, and shook his hand. He was tall, well built, with handsome square features. Good eyes, good mouth, good nose, good jawline. He looked vaguely as if he had stepped out of a Steve Canyon comic strip.

"Colonel Dulard, Mr. Carmody." He gestured to the other uniformed man.

"This is Sergeant Fremont. He'll be driving for you."

The sergeant shook his hand. He looked more Mexican than his name implied; dark, with an aquiline nose and a large head. He looked a good twenty years older than the colonel. Six inches shorter, but rounded, with a barrel chest and long arms. The dark hair beneath his hat was streaked with gray. He would be a good man to have around in a tight situation. There was an easy familiarity between the two men.

"Our only instructions are to give you every cooperation, Mr. Carmody," smiled the colonel. "I have an F111 on standby here, fully fueled and ready to go to Washington, whenever you say the word."

Carmody nodded with satisfaction. The general had been busy.

"First thing I need is to be driven to an address at Stanford." He turned to the sergeant. "Do you know the area, Sergeant?"

The sergeant nodded, unsmiling. He looked like a very serious man.

"Yes, I'm a local, Mr. Carmody. Out to Palo Alto along the Bayshore Freeway. That won't take us very long."

"I think I'll leave you with the sergeant, Mr. Carmody," interrupted the colonel. "I'm the pilot who'll be flying you. How long do you think you'll be?"

Carmody glanced queryingly at the sergeant.

"Forty-five minutes to Stanford, Sergeant?"

The sergeant shrugged. "If we move."

"Do you think you'll need me?" asked the colonel.

Carmody shook his head.

"All I need is transportation, Colonel. It's up to you."

Dulard hesitated, then smiled.

"Then I'd better stay with the plane. There are still a few things to be attended to. I'll wait it out here."

The sergeant put out a hand toward Carmody.

"Then shall we go, Mr. Carmody?"

Carmody motioned with his head toward the washroom.

"Give me five minutes to throw some cold water in my face and tidy up a little, Sergeant?"

The sergeant inclined his head slightly, still unsmiling.

"Of course. When you're ready, Mr. Carmody."

He felt better after he'd dashed some cold water onto his face, although it did little to improve his appearance. The shave and shirt would have to wait, and his suit sagged like an elephant's skin. Maybe that would stress his urgency to the professor.

The sergeant was courteous but silent. Maybe he'd been told not to ask any questions. He drove with polished skill, fast but comfortable. A thin fog hung over the bay area, and the headlights thrust ahead of them in watery yellow circles. They were quickly out of the airport onto the freeway, and the car gathered speed as the sergeant's foot went down hard.

"I'll turn off around Redwood City and go down onto El Camino," said the sergeant over his shoulder. "It may be quicker that way."

Carmody shrugged and settled back into the seat. Whatever way the sergeant wanted, as long as they got there fast. At the moment all he wanted was sleep. Even Hadaffi couldn't halt the dullness creeping into his mind.

"You know Mayberry Street, Sergeant?"

"I'll find it, Mr. Carmody," said the sergeant confidently.

Carmody nodded wearily, closed his eyes, and put his head back. If the sergeant said he could find it, then he was sure he could. He was that sort of man.

The sergeant was gently shaking his shoulder. For a moment he had a flash that he was back in the apartment and Angela was gently shaking him out of bed. How nice to feel that warm, smooth, compliant skin again. He opened his eyes and stared owlishly at the sergeant. That serious, unsmiling face had very little in common with Angela.

"We're here, Mr. Carmody."

Carmody pawed at his face, and sat up. He brushed at his hair, and tried to swallow away the sourness in his mouth. The outside fog seemed to have crept in and settled in his mind. He shook his head vigorously, trying to clear his brain.

The car was stopped. There was a house he could see through the window, wide and low. Californian timber style, set off in a large profuse garden. He got out of the car and stood for a moment, breathing deeply.

There was a single light burning at the left extremity of the house. The fog cast circular vignetted crowns around the street lights.

"Do you want to come in, Sergeant? I may be able to get you a cup of coffee."

The sergeant returned a professional shake of his head.

"I'll wait in the car, thank you, Mr. Carmody."

Carmody hesitated, then shrugged. The sergeant was keeping his distance, and he supposed that was the way he had been briefed.

The man who answered the door was about sixty. He was wearing a deep-red dressing gown. Medium height, bald on top with white hair clinging about his ears, heavy glasses balanced on a small nose, wide mouth, gray moustache, loose skin hanging beneath his chin like a man who had lost weight. He peered at Carmody and smiled thinly.

"Professor Arnold Moslin? I'm Frank Carmody," said Carmody pleasantly.

The professor widened the door and indicated entrance with his hand.

"I've been expecting you, Mr. Carmody. Please come in."

He followed the professor along a carpeted passage to a room at the far end. He felt as if he'd spent the night sleeping in a hay stack and his clothes were full of straw.

"You had a good flight, Mr. Carmody?" He held open the door and ushered Carmody through.

They were in a small study. Timber paneling, a wall of books, a desk of matching timber, two comfortable lounging chairs. There was an open file lying on the desk. Moslin waved toward one of the chairs, picked up the file, and dropped into the other chair.

"Yes," said Carmody, without elaboration.

The chair enveloped him like a cocoon, inducing

fresh heaviness in his eyes. He fought it off. They sat facing each other as if the professor had deliberately created an adverse situation. Carmody hoped it wasn't going to be that way; he hadn't flown thousands of miles to be stalled by anybody.

Moslin nursed the file on his knees like a fragile vase.

"This must be very important for you to come all this way from New York on the spur of the moment, Mr. Carmody?" he said. His tone was polite, but distant, wary, with a tinge of hostility. He took in Carmody's appearance, his eyes lingering over his clothes. "You look as if you could do with some sleep. Can I get you some coffee?"

Carmody gave a negative wave of his hand. It was a terrific thought, but he didn't want anything to happen that would slow down this interview. There was no time for sparring, so he decided to be blunt.

"Professor Moslin, I indicated to you over the phone that this was a national emergency, and I believe it involves Brett Leica. I don't know the details of what happened three years ago, or your part in it, and I don't want to know. I don't believe it's wise at this time to take you completely into my confidence. I just want to stress how urgent it is that I find Brett Leica as soon as possible, that I learn as much about him as possible, and that you cooperate with me." He hesitated. "The office of the Presidency of this country is at stake, and believe me, I haven't got a great deal of time to play with." He paused, and waited.

Moslin cleared his throat loudly.

"I wouldn't want to see any harm come to Brett Leica," he said carefully. "He went through a horrid time three years ago, and I wouldn't want to be the instrument of its being repeated. He's a very brilliant man, Mr. Carmody."

Carmody sighed. The professor wasn't getting the message.

"I don't want him to come to any harm either, Professor."

"He won't work for you people, you know. I think he made that perfectly clear three years ago."

Fuck you, thought Carmody. He had not time for a lecture; he wasn't one of the professor's students, cut off from the world in the cloistered environment of a university.

"Professor," he said patiently, "Brett Leica as I understand it has a unique talent in the field of psychokinesis. I don't want him to work for Intelligence, for anybody. And I don't want to go over the history of three years ago. I have to find him. I have to know about him. I have to know, for example, if it is possible for him mentally to disable a man from a distance of hundreds of miles . . . thousands if you like, and at any given time.

Moslin gnawed anxiously at his lower lip.

"Brett was very secretive about his methods and techniques."

"But you must have had some idea, surely?"

Moslin nodded slowly.

"Yes, yes I did. From my understanding of what he was doing, yes, he was capable of doing that."

"You helped him vanish?"

"No. No, I was as surprised as anyone else."

"But you knew the pressure he was under?"

"Yes. I expected something was going to break, but I didn't know it was going to take that form. He simply disappeared with his wife."

Carmody leaned forward on his elbows and stared aggressively into Moslin's face.

"I want you to think about this very carefully, Pro-

fessor. Do you know where he went? Do you have
any idea, because I have to know. You're concerned
for Leica, I'm concerned for this country. That should
be your first concern too, Professor. Now, do you
know?"

Moslin leaned back in his chair. He lifted the file on
his knees and caressed it with his fingers. He looked
slightly affronted.

"My concern is the same as yours, Mr. Carmody, but
I don't have to think carefully about your question. I
don't know where Brett Leica is. I have no idea where
he is. He said nothing to me before his disappearance.
He said nothing to anyone. The only person who may
have had some idea was his assistant, Vilas Daiton, but
he disappeared also."

"At the same time?"

"No. A few months after Brett. But I questioned
him, and he also denied any knowledge of Brett's
whereabouts."

"Do you know where I can find him?"

"I'm sorry, I have no idea. He simply dropped out of
sight as effectively as Brett."

"He left no forwarding address?"

"Nothing."

"You have a description of him?"

Moslin paused, fingers to his mouth, and permitted
a slight smile.

"You know the actor Omar Sharif?"

"Yes."

"That would be the closest description I could give
you. It was something of a joke around the women in
the department. There was a resemblance."

A needle slid into Carmody's memory and triggered
a response. Where? He'd seen a face somewhere like

that, and nothing had registered. Merely a flash, but it had dropped a photograph reference into some remote cells in his brain. The bar. Christ, that was it, the bar on Eighth Avenue. Good God, could he have been the one who hit Moccasin?

Moslin waited a moment, then intruded into his thoughts.

"You think you may have seen him?" he asked.

Carmody shrugged disconsolately.

"What was his relationship like with Leica?"

"Reasonable, except toward the end."

"What do you mean?"

"They had some terrible row. It destroyed any personal relationship. I couldn't get anything out of Daiton, and both Brett and his wife refused to talk about it. There was no working relationship either toward the end; they were scarcely on speaking terms. I would have had to do something about it, but before I could . . ." He shrugged. "You know what happened."

Carmody rubbed reflectively at his nose. It was quiet. He wondered idly if the Professor was married. He glanced at his watch. It was nearly one o'clock. Some of his tiredness had evaporated with his concentrated questioning.

"Can you give me any personal details on him, as well as on Leica and his wife?"

"Not a great deal, he was something of a mystery man."

"But you do have something?"

Moslin nodded and stifled a yawn. He didn't like this aggressive, persistent man, and he'd long ceased to be a night owl.

"Yes, I have something," he admitted.

There was a short break in the conversation. Carmody's mind was beginning to race, adrenaline was beginning to flow. The level of his tiredness was dropping fast.

"I understand Leica was a very retiring sort of man. Almost timid?" he continued.

"Yes, I would say that's reasonably accurate. But a very kindly man. He adored his wife, Jo."

"Would you say he would ever lend himself to any violent cause?"

Moslin shook his head firmly.

"No, never. He just wasn't that sort of man."

"Do you know anything about his political beliefs?"

Moslin frowned, and the corners of his mouth twitched with irritation. Carmody could see the growing signs of annoyance, but he ignored them.

"I considered that to be his own business."

"Now it's my business," said Carmody crudely. "The government's business."

Carmody waited for the tremors of suppressed rage around the professor's mouth to soften away.

"He was, I suppose . . ." He hesitated. "The word is so often misunderstood by you people."

"Tell me anyway."

"He had what you might call . . . liberal views."

Carmody grunted, but made no comment.

"What sort of personal details can you give me about all three? I mean photographs? Parents' addresses? Anything?"

The professor hesitated a moment, staring at him distastefully, then propped open the file on his lap. He extracted several documents, stapled together at the corners, and held them delicately as if frightened they would tear. He handed them across, reluctantly, like a mother parting with her child.

"I think you'll find everything there that you need, Mr. Carmody. There are several very good photographs I managed to get from my office of Jo and Brett Leica. Unfortunately I don't seem to have any photographs of Vilas Daiton."

Carmody leaned forward and took the documents from Moslin. "Thank you," he said curtly. He sensed the antagonism, but brushed it aside. Perhaps if the professor knew just what was at stake he would be more understanding. The man sensed in some way that he was betraying Leica, exposing him once again to what he'd experienced three years ago. Perhaps in a way he was. If Leica was responsible for what was threatened against the Presidency, there would be very little mercy available.

"I wish I could explain to you how vital it is that I know these things," he said in a softer tone.

"You have a job to do," said Moslin offhandedly.

Carmody flicked quickly through the files. It was all there. Parents who could be interviewed, descriptions, backgrounds. He could examine it all in more detail on the plane. He looked at the photograph of Brett Leica. The sharp, thin, intelligent face. Nothing clicked in his memory. The same with his wife Jo. An attractive blonde, but he had never seen her before. She looked a good deal younger than Leica.

"Jo Leica was a scientist also?" he asked.

Moslin shook his head wearily.

"Not really. She came to Stanford as a student in bio-chemistry. Brett married her here."

"She was involved in psychokinesis with her husband?"

Moslin's smile was an expression of tolerance reserved for idiots.

"Of course she knew all about what he was doing, but only as an observer, Mr. Carmody. I don't think you quite realize how unique Leica's talent is."

"I have a fair idea," said Carmody dryly. He kept leafing over the files, memorizing details. He put them down on his lap and turned his eyes back to the professor.

"Professor Moslin, is it possible that there is someone else in America, or even in the world if you like, who could have developed psychokinesis to the same degree as Brett Leica?"

"Anything is possible, but I doubt it. In fact I would be almost sure."

"Almost?"

Moslin hesitated, and ran his fingers restlessly along the arms of the chair.

"Even though Brett didn't take me into his confidence as much as I would have liked, I know he was light years ahead of anyone else in this field. What others dreamed of doing, he did. Maybe the rest of the world will catch up to him in fifty years time . . . even a hundred. For the moment I would regard him as being quite unique."

There was a niggle there. A suppressed irritation. Carmody wondered if he misjudged Moslin's sense of guilt. Perhaps the professor's cooperation was in part a resentment at being excluded from Leica's confidential circle, even if he refused to acknowledge it to himself.

But Moccasin had been right. It had to be Leica. It was the only thing that made any sense.

"Did you ever see Leica at work? I mean did you ever see him actually applying psychokinesis? What he actually did?"

"Only in the preliminary experiments. To the outsider it merely looked like an exercise in extreme concentration."

"But how would he be able to concentrate on single individuals? From a great distance?"

Moslin shifted uncomfortably in his chair and shook his head. The lines of weariness cut deep into his face. He looked all of his sixty years.

"I can't help you there, Mr. Carmody. Only Brett can answer those questions for you. At that stage he had withdrawn from communication with me to some extent. It was Jo who kept me in the picture."

Carmody pursed his lips, and idly shuffled the papers around in his fingers. There was little more he could learn here, but the trip had been worthwhile. Very worthwhile. He searched for the glow of elation he should be experiencing, but there was no spark. He had the material, he had the photographs, but how could he make it all work for him in the time he had left? That was what blanketed any elation. Give them a week, even three or four days, and they could trace all the information in these files, and maybe assemble some form of pattern to follow.

The photographs were the only thing that had a chance of getting some sort of fast result. And that would require luck.

He lifted his wrist and checked the time. Hamilton would be waiting for his call in New York.

"I would like to call New York, if I may, Professor," he said.

Moslin rose from the chair and gestured to the telephone on the desk.

"Of course, Mr. Carmody. I presume you would like me to leave you alone?"

"If you would be so kind," Carmody managed graciously.

He picked up the phone and smiled as the professor began to ease himself out the door.

"And thank you for your help, Professor. Perhaps one day I'll be able to tell you how vital it was to me."

The professor hesitated, framed in the open doorway.

"Your remark about the Presidency?" he asked.

Carmody waited, the phone poised in his hand.

"Brett Leica is the wrong man to pose that sort of threat. It would have to be some sort of coercion, Mr. Carmody. Some very strong coercion."

Carmody smiled absently, anxious for him to be gone.

"Perhaps," he said.

Moslin closed the door gently, as if not to disturb a sleeping house, and Carmody quickly placed the call. The house was mute, as if straining to play the role of eavesdropper.

"Rick, this is Frank Carmody," he began.

Hamilton's voice came back, clear and sharp, as if he were in the next room.

"Frank, how was your trip? Did you find out anything about the man?"

"Yes, I have something. Valuable information, but the question is how to make it work for us, and quickly. What about Oxley?"

"Oxley's dead, Frank."

Surprise, surprise. Did he really expect anything else. What was another life to Hadaffi?

"You're sure?" he asked anyway.

"Yes. The police checked out the landlady's description, and it tallied with an unidentified body they'd had in the morgue for a few days. They got the landlady to go down and make a positive identification. Seems like he fell out of the fifteenth floor of the Taft Hotel a few nights ago."

"Fell?"

Hamilton voiced a short, dry laugh.

"Well, that's all the police can say at the moment. The window in a room on the fifteenth floor was smashed, but there was no one else in the room. Another man booked the room, but he'd vanished."

"Do they have any idea who it was?"

"Well, how many people pass through the Taft in a day? The police have asked around, but no one remembers anything."

Carmody paused, leaning his weight against the corner of the desk. Well, there was obviously no point in going back to New York.

"What about Oxley's apartment?" he said.

"I'm still going over it, Frank. Inch by inch. I'm afraid I haven't turned up anything yet. I've pulled his bed to pieces, cut up his mattress, and sifted through it wad by wad. I'm still hoping. I'm starting on his clothes now. All I'm going to have left is strips of rag by the time I'm through . . . But I'll find something."

Carmody paused and thought for a moment. Somewhere the house creaked, as if restlessly stretching in its sleep. He hoped Moslin hadn't gone to bed. He found it difficult to share Hamilton's optimism. Hadaffi had found out about Oxley's betrayal and taken the obvious steps. It was as simple as that, and probably meant it was now a dead lead.

He spread out Moslin's files on the desk. May as well get what he could started right away.

"Do you have a pad and pen with you, Rick?"

There was a moment's pause.

"I have now, Frank."

"I'm going to read you descriptions of three people. Two men, and a woman. Give them to the police, and have them circulate the descriptions right around the country. Fast as they can. Just say . . . ah, wanted urgently for questioning."

"You think these are the people responsible for the psychokinesis?"

"Maybe. I'm pretty sure one of them killed Moccasin anyway. Are you ready?"

"Let me have them."

Carmody read slowly, omitting nothing. Height, age, color of hair, everything he could find. It was a forlorn hope considering the time frame they were looking to, but anything was worth trying. He hardly imagined Hadaffi or Daiton, or the Leicas would be wandering around in the streets where they could be seen by police.

He finished and did a slow check through the pages to make certain there was nothing he'd missed.

"Fast as you can with that, Rick."

"It's going to hold me up here."

"I know, but I can't help that. I want those descriptions to have first priority." He clucked his tongue, his mind shuttling back and forth. He scratched thoughtfully at the fast-growing bristles on his chin and fought to keep his heavy lids from shuttering down over his eyes. The tiredness was coming back, and he didn't want to forget anything.

"You keep on going there, and if you don't turn up anything, you'd better go on back to Washington. I have a military plane ready here to fly me back, so we'll probably come in at Andrews Field. If you're there before I am, get those descriptions to Eric Dalgety as well." He paused again, aimlessly fingering the pages of the files on the desk. "All right then, Rick. I'll see you back in Washington. If nothing concrete works soon, I think we'd all better start praying."

He hung up, put the files and photographs into his briefcase, and padded silently out into the passage. Moslin emerged from another room near the entrance hall and held open the outside door for him. He smiled nervously.

"I hope your call was successful, Mr. Carmody?"

Carmody didn't believe for a moment he cared whether the call was successful or not. All he wanted was for Carmody to be gone, to have his presence out of his house.

The professor held out a limp hand, and Carmody shook it without enthusiasm.

"You're going back to New York immediately, Mr. Carmody?"

Carmody eased himself through the door.

"Washington," he said.

"Then I hope you have a good flight, and I hope I've been some help in resolving your emergency."

Carmody smiled without warmth, noting the fresh irony in Moslin's voice. The professor had had some fresh thoughts while he'd been talking to Rick on the telephone. Perhaps in his own mind he'd come to the conclusion he had betrayed Leica. Well, he could think what he liked. He patted at the briefcase as he went out the door.

"I'll get these files back to you as soon as I've finished with them, Professor, and thank you for your help. It's been invaluable."

Moslin nodded curtly. Carmody went down the path, framed by the light from the open door. The fog swirled around him, yellowed by the glow. The door clicked to, shutting off the light, before he reached the gate.

The sergeant was there to take its place, holding open the gate for him. He escorted Carmody quickly to the car, silent, asking nothing, their footsteps muffled by the fog.

"I'll get you back as fast as I can, Mr. Carmody," was all he said. Carmody made no reply. Perhaps he could sleep again on the way.

Carmody had never flown in an F111 before. He strapped himself into the seat alongside Dulard, following the colonel's instructions. The dim light from the multitude of dials threw a ghostly light into their faces.

"This plane is supersonic, Colonel?" he asked.

"Mach 2.2, Mr. Carmody. You're going to have to pretend you're my navigator."

"Then we should have a fast run across to Washington?"

The colonel shrugged. "Maybe four hours if the weather favors us. I won't be able to fly supersonic over this sort of distance. The afterburner would use up too much fuel. Don't worry, Mr. Carmody. I'll get you there as fast as I can, but I don't want to make any refueling stops."

Carmody nodded. The unaccustomed helmet and mask felt bulky around his face, but the seat fit snugly, as if molded into his body. They howled down the runway, and went straight up to forty-two thousand feet. The wings slid back into the subsonic position with a soft humming sound. It was an eerie sensation after being so accustomed to the feel and motion of a commercial jet. There was the identical feeling at this height of being motionless, poised over the earth as if strung there on a wire, but he felt closer to it in the F111. Part of it, as if he could touch it. The stars and the moon formed a clear, cold canopy overhead. That's where he felt with Hadaffi. With the President. With his own ambitious reach for power. Strung out on a wire, with empty miles beneath him. Poised, so that he could go either up or down. Something had to break for him soon. He'd worked too hard for it.

They allowed Leica early-morning exercise, but leashed, like a dog not trusted to return home. The two shadows followed, and Hadaffi walked at his side, a piece of thin, strong rope connecting Leica's left wrist to Hadaffi's right.

One of the shadows had returned early in the morning after spending the night away, with information that had sparked a jubilant mood in Hadaffi.

Leica could only suppose it was news of what had happened to the President in Washington. He could have tried to eavesdrop, but he didn't want to hear, didn't want to think about it.

He led the way, dragging Hadaffi whichever way the mood took him, up the narrow rutted track at the rear of the house. Their footsteps made sharp scuffing sounds in the still forest. The pine branches hung low with heavy dew, and birds fluttered their wings in the wet grass, performing their early morning ablutions with twittering enthusiasm, mocking him with their freedom. The sky was low with leisurely drifting clouds, colored deep gray with the promise of rain.

Everything in the forest around Leica seemed free and untrammeled, and it magnified his own situation. They never left him alone, not for a second. The rope holding him to Hadaffi like an unbreakable umbilical cord was evidence of their caution. Did they think he might try to bolt? To run for it through the forest?

Perhaps Hadaffi was looking into his mind, guessed he was trying to evaluate his life, and Jo's, against what they were forcing him to do.

But Christ, he'd been through that, over and over again, and he was no nearer a resolution than before he'd subjected the President to psychokinesis. Perhaps he would never be capable of a decision, but would go on and on for the rest of his life as Hadaffi's puppet. No matter how much his hatred for Hadaffi swelled and toughened, when it came to the crunch of deliberately having Jo killed, he couldn't face it.

Yet it had to be faced. He could twist in every conceivable direction, but the time was coming again, and quickly, and maybe this time they would demand he kill the President. Would he do it? When he sat down at his desk would he look up at Hadaffi and say no, cut my wife into small pieces instead? The morning was cold, but he could feel the warm sweat in the palms of his hands from the thought.

At night he lay concentrating fiercely, trying to force himself to that next stage of psychokinesis that would

enable him to contact Jo. He would send his mind outward, scanning, his body rigid with concentration,
soaked in perspiration. But he couldn't make it work.
He still needed precise information, a location to home
in on. He wasn't ready for a free scanning operation yet,
perhaps it would never come to him, no matter how
desperately he needed it now.

And what of himself, and the role Hadaffi was forcing
him to play? How would the authorities see his com-
plicity? How forgiving would they be, if by some miracle they caught up with Hadaffi? After all, he was the
one responsible for the President's nightmare, and if he
could guess correctly, panic in the government. He
could imagine their feelings, trying to cope with something they couldn't see, couldn't begin to understand.
Did that leave him totally in a no-win situation? If
Hadaffi didn't kill him eventually, then the government
would. Would they understand his forced compliance
over Jo, or just see him as a weak fool guilty of treason?
It was a depressing thought. God, there had to be a way
out for him somewhere.

They came to the crest of the hill, and Leica came to
a halt. The rope bit sharply into his wrist before Hadaffi
paused for him. The two shadows stopped just short of
the crest and stood waiting, their bodies drooped in the
relaxed posture of the young.

The house was below them, snuggled with perfect
harmony into the pines. Hadaffi's large dark car parked
in the clearing was the only rupture on the landscape.

"You would like to kill us all, wouldn't you, Leica?"
said Hadaffi. Leica recognized the jabbing mocking
intonation, the prelude to a niggling he had come to
know so well.

He refused to answer, but kept his eyes away to where the needle tops of the pine trees seemed to spike the low gray clouds.

"It would be so easy for you," Hadaffi persisted. "You have no need of a gun, or a knife, nothing except your mind."

He sounded very sure of himself, very sure of Leica, sure enough to indulge himself in some mocking amusement.

Leica turned abruptly and trudged on, dragging at the rope. A bird flew up out of the grass at the side of the track, startled, and swished off through the dripping branches.

"What a gigantic ego you must have, Leica," said Hadaffi, tolerantly increasing his stride to keep pace with his prisoner.

Leica refused to be baited. They walked side by side, Hadaffi's feet kicking idly at the loose clumps of dirt.

"People like you, so weak, so unimportant, you balance your lives against someone like the President of this country, against the political framework of this country, and you come to the conclusion that your miserable existence is more important." He snorted. "I find you incredible, Leica, absolutely incredible."

Leica held his silence. What was the man trying to do? Was the terrorist so sure of his subjugation that he felt completely safe in needling him?

"You make it easy for people like me, Leica." He leaned across and put his mouth close to Leica's ear. "It would be so easy. Think of what you've already done to the President, all those miles away, and what you could do to me." He jerked his head behind him. "To us."

Leica shut his mind, his eye firmly ahead of him down the track, remembering the times he had walked this same route with Jo. The early mornings when the sounds of the birds and the solitude had been the only things on his mind then. And Jo.

"Maybe you're really enjoying yourself, Leica," persisted Hadaffi. "Getting your own back for all they did to you years ago. All this prissy agonizing is merely a front for your own conscience. For me." He nodded his head, and his face creased into an ugly grin. "I could understand that. I can appreciate that. Why don't you confess deep down it was great to get back at them like that."

Leica tried to put more distance between himself and the terrorist, and the rope chafed at his wrist again.

"You're mad," he grunted sullenly.

Hadaffi laughed unpleasantly.

"Yes, I guess I am, to think like that about you." He waved his free hand contemptuously about in the air. "That's what makes us so different, Leica. If I were in your position, there would be no problem . . . no decision for me to think about. Who really cares about your wife? Who really cares about you? Do you think they're going to put up a memorial to you? So we cut your wife up into small pieces. Is the President going to shake your hand and give you a lifetime pension?" He cleared his throat with an angry rasping sound, and spat forcibly on the ground in front of Leica's feet.

"Not that you could destroy me, Leica," he sneered.

Leica failed to understand that observation, but he held to his silence.

"I have a mind also, Leica," continued Hadaffi. "An intelligent mind. A mind I have trained, disciplined. Maybe it does not have your unique talent, but it has more strength than you have ever encountered before."

There was a pause. One of the shadows had picked up

a long stick, and he beat aimlessly at the grass by the side of the track. Leica turned into the side track that would lead them back to the house, dragging at the rope. Hadaffi turned with him, smiling sourly, and the two shadows followed. He wondered what Hadaffi was driving at.

"You would not find me easy, Leica, I am not like normal men. I believe you would find me impossible." He bobbed his head sagely. "Yes, impossible. I could discipline myself to resist you. I'm certain of that."

He drifted over to Leica until he was close enough to nudge him with his shoulder. "Not that you would ever have the courage to try, eh, Leica?" He nudged him again, and Leica swerved away, stumbling through the grass, then emerging with his shoes gleaming with water.

"Why don't you try, Leica. It would be a revelation for you to discover you could fail. That there was a mind stronger than yours, one you would find it impossible to worm inside and stimulate your horrors. I would beat you, Leica. Not that you will ever find out, eh? What do you think about that?"

So that was it. God in heaven, it was a challenge. Leica turned his head and stared at Hadaffi for a moment, the sneering, contemptuous confidence, then looked quickly away again.

"Why don't you try, Leica?" Hadaffi needled. "Why don't you try. It would be worth having your wife cut up just to discover your own limitations. You could put it down to scientific observation."

He believed it. He really believed it. It was true that failure with psychokinesis never occurred to Leica now, provided all the circumstances were right; and there was no reason to doubt that it would be just as success-

ful with Hadaffi. The man didn't really understand
what the force was.

"You see my mind is superior to yours, Leica. I am
stronger than you." He jerked the hand in the air that
was anchored to Leica, dragging the other's hand up in
its wake. "You see, you are my prisoner, Leica. You
do as I command you, because I am stronger than you.
My mind would defeat yours, Leica."

Leica felt a trembling in his spine, and dared not
look at Hadaffi again. All the casual talk about cutting
up Jo was unnerving, and while it strengthened his
hatred, it weakened any resolution toward a decision.
Hadaffi laughed unpleasantly at his side. How he hated
the man. He had never hated anyone like this before,
had prided himself on his tolerance, on his ability to
accept people for what they were. But when had that
stopped? Not just now, but three years ago, that had
been the honing edge for the hatred he had developed
now.

"Perhaps the time will come," he said shakily. He
wished he could have implied some menace, some
threat in his voice, but fear vibrated his vocal cords.

Hadaffi laughed again.

"The only time that will come for you, Leica, is
when you deliver our next warning to the President.
And you must excel yourself this time. This time the
fear must go so deep the thought of not accepting our
demands would be inconceivable."

Leica slowed his step, and Hadaffi altered his pace
accordingly. Suddenly Leica had no desire to be back
in the house. Now it was a place of execution, not a
haven to hide from the world.

*"Father, the son you admire so much now has a new
profession."*

"What is that, my boy?"

"I am a professional killer, Father. I terrorize people to death."

"And do you enjoy the work?"

"Henry, don't question the boy so."

"Quiet, Emma. I have to show the boy that I'm interested in what he is doing."

"I despise the work, Father."

"Then you must stop doing it."

"But if I do they will kill Jo."

A thoughtful pause.

"Then you must do what you think is right, my boy."

Cop-out. It was always the same when he didn't know what to say.

His pace slowed to a crawl, and Hadaffi moved ahead of him, tugging impatiently on the rope. How long did he have? A day? Twenty hours? And where was Daiton? Was he with Jo? There was a numbness in his limbs that had begun to creep up his body toward his brain. Perhaps that was the answer. Perhaps he could apply psychokinesis to himself. That was an interesting thought. Then he would know nothing, would not be aware what they were doing to Jo. But that would be another cop-out, like his father's answer.

Carmody dozed intermittently, but he never fully lost the feel of consciousness. The same apprehensions that had kept sleep from his mind on the flight to San Francisco returned to plague him. The photographs and files sitting snugly in his briefcase should have provided some form of analgesic, but they only inspired fresh doubts. How to use them with the most effectiveness? How could they be made to work in the time he had left? Would coast-to-coast exposure of the pictures on television work, or would it merely alert Hadaffi, and drive him further underground? Maybe Dalgety would have some better ideas, or General Cooper. Or even Angela.

He watched the light filter into the sky along the eastern horizon, yellowing the sky, and coating the plane with a soft, warm glow. They thundered toward the brightening sun with the unerring instinct of a drawn moth. The clouds lay thick beneath them, wave on wave of ruffled deceptive solidity. It looked like the perfect place to put his mind at rest, to step out of the plane and find a soft fluffy curve to place his head, and sleep the day away.

He dozed again with a modicum of success, and when he opened his eyes again the plane was in a shallow dive, enveloped in clouds. He glanced at the colonel questioningly and received a grin in reply accompanied with a downward jerk of the pilot's thumb.

They broke through the clouds, and the geometric pattern of Washington lay below, blurred with a gray haze of drizzling rain.

They came in low over the Potomac, the jets hissing, over the Rosecroft Raceway, banked sharply, and dropped down accurately at Andrews Field.

When the plane had taxied to a stop, he clumsily removed his helmet and shook the colonel's hand. It was nine o'clock, Washington time.

"Thank you, Colonel," he said warmly. "Thank you for everything."

The colonel returned a Steve Canyon smile.

"My pleasure, Mr. Carmody. I understand there is someone waiting for you in the reception area."

Carmody nodded his thanks, and rubbed at his chin, feeling the bristles. He felt terrible, and he guessed he didn't look much better. He couldn't possibly meet with anyone feeling like this, he would scarcely be articulate. He would go to the apartment first, shower and shave, put on some fresh clothes, then call an urgent meeting. Maybe no one else had slept any better than himself. He supposed the President would be in that category.

When he got to the reception area it was Hamilton waiting to meet him, and his appearance was not much better than Carmody's. He was holding an envelope in his hands, his face white, grim, unsmiling, and something tightened in Carmody's stomach. An expression like that had to be a forecast of bad news. Maybe the President had sustained another attack during his absence.

They shook hands, then Hamilton gestured to one of the corridors.

"I've arranged an office where we can talk," he said brusquely.

Carmody nodded, and he followed as Hamilton led the way. Their footsteps beat hollowly in the corridor, and uniformed men drifted past with curious stares.

"What's been happening?" asked Carmody tentatively.

Hamilton shrugged. "I called Dalgety earlier from here, and he filled me in. Cabinet meetings. Controlled panic. The President's taken most of his inner cabinet into his confidence. He's asking for a range of opinions, but evidently he's still talking resignation. Of course everyone's against it on political grounds, but they don't have to cope with the psychokinesis if we fail to get Hadaffi."

"Did he say how the President was?"

"He's holding up. I guess he's a tough old warhorse, but I don't know what another bout with psychokinesis will do to him. Evidently some of the cabinet have rejected the idea of the psychokinesis thing out of hand, but no one has any alternative ideas. Dalgety says they're running around in circles, praying for miracles from us."

They came to a door, and Hamilton opened it and ushered Carmody through. It was a small office, carpeted, with regulation desk, two chairs, filing cabinets, framed color photographs of jet aircraft on the walls. A window overlooked the field, and Carmody could see men working over the F111 that had just flown him from San Francisco. He sat down at the desk, folded his arms, hunched his shoulders, and stared challengingly at Hamilton.

"Okay, Rick, what's up? I can tell by your expression it has to be something very serious. Is it something to do with Oxley in New York?"

Hamilton squatted down opposite him and opened the envelope. He took out the contents and laid them down on the desk in front of Carmody.

There were several typewritten sheets, a handwritten letter, and on the bottom a photograph. He put his hand over them and looked intently into Carmody's face.

"After I spoke to you from New York, I went back to work on Oxley's apartment. I cut everything to ribbons. Curtains, bedspreads, clothes. It took me a while until I found this sewed into the lining of one of his coats. It must have been the next piece of information he was going to feed to Moccasin. I guess he was running a typical piecemeal operation, to make the money string out." He lifted his hand from the papers and studied Carmody, his face troubled. "I'll leave the stuff with you to go through alone if you like."

Carmody's face creased into a puzzled frown.

"What the hell for? Do you have something urgent waiting for you back at the office?"

Hamilton hesitated, and shook his head. Ruffled hair fell down over his forehead, adding to the lines of weariness.

"No," he muttered.

Carmody put his elbow down on the desk and rested his head against his hand. He picked up the papers and went through them slowly. He got halfway and his mind seemed to jam shut, refusing further information. The words danced and jiggled in front of his eyes as if trying to hide, or to reform themselves into new sentences that he could believe. He put down the papers for a moment and stared at the photograph. It played the same tricks with his eyes as the words, the features shuffling around as if to disguise the reality from his brain. His fingers lost their grip, and it wafted away to settle on the desk. He pawed at his face, trying to erase the illusive mists playing tricks with his eyes, and read through the papers again. Then he went through them again. Then again, and again, until each word was imprinted into his mind.

He was vaguely aware that Hamilton was gone from the other side of the desk, and heard a gentle cough from behind him.

"Would you like me to leave you alone for a moment, Frank?" he asked quietly.

Carmody nodded slowly, scarcely trusting himself to speak.

"Maybe," he said huskily. Then, as if to excuse his show of emotion: "I'll want to talk to you about what I found in San Francisco."

He spoke so quietly he wasn't sure that Hamilton heard him. He waited until Hamilton was gone, then he raised himself from the desk as if freeing himself from chains, and went and stood by the window.

They were still at work on the F111. Across the field another jet rushed past, bellowing, lifted into the air, and went up like an arrow, trailing a plume of vapor.

The problem was that he had always needed love so intensely. To be wanted. To want to love. It was his Achilles' heel, held down deep inside his outer shell where no one could suspect its existence. Because he could be taken advantage of by the intense need. It was something he had cautiously revealed to only three or four people in his life. It made him vulnerable; it was something in conflict with his ambition, to be wary of, to be suppressed. But he had never suspected he could be as vulnerable as this.

He stood looking out the window for what seemed a timeless pause in his life. Men and planes occasionally crisscrossed the window, but his eyes refused to transmit the sight to his mind. There was no room for anything else but the conflict he had to resolve. Professionalism and ambition fought a battle with his emotions, and won. And as it went around and around in his mind, the victory turned sourly to revenge. But revenge with a purpose, because if he played it right, then everything could be resolved, and that would be satisfying irony. He checked his watch. He had a few hours to gamble with and it would be worth every second, because it could resolve all his doubts about the authenticity of Leica, about Hadaffi, about everything. If he played it right. He would lock the gate on tender memories as if they had never existed. Perhaps it would be a pretense, and shafts of longing would lance into his mind, but he would erase them. Like he would erase Schyler. And Hadaffi. And anyone else who stood in his way.

A tentative hand pushed open the door, and Hamilton put his head through the opening.

"I thought perhaps we should move, Frank," he said nervously.

Carmody beckoned him with his hand.

"I think we can make this work for us, Rick," he said. He picked up the papers off the desk and let them drop down again.

"I guess it's something of a shock, Frank. Who would have guessed?"

"We all make mistakes," said Carmody calmly. He seemed completely self-possessed, but when he tried to smile, something happened at the corners of his mouth, and the expression lacked conviction.

Hamilton eyed him cautiously, but made no comment. Carmody picked up his briefcase from the floor and put it down on top of the desk, to one side of the papers. He fumbled at the catch with fingers that refused to coordinate, that betrayed his inner turmoil, and finally threw the lid back with an oath.

He took the documents from Stanford out of the case, closed back the lid, and laid them on top. He tapped at them with his forefinger.

"These are the documents I picked up in San Francisco, Rick," he said. "They contain the descriptions I read out to you over the phone." He raised questioning eyebrows toward Hamilton. "You passed them on to the police?"

"Yes, but I wanted to speak to you first, before I gave them to Eric Dalgety. I haven't been back long from New York, and I came straight here." He pointed tentatively at the papers on the desk. "I figured you'd want to see that as soon as possible."

"Yes, you're right," said Carmody heavily.

"Which is the man you believe is responsible for the psychokinesis?"

Carmody picked up one of the photographs, and passed it across to his aide.

"That's him. Brett Leica. The description of the woman I gave you is his wife. The other man was an assistant to Leica at Stanford University. This was all three years ago, so it'll be a hell of a job tracking them down in the time we have left. That's why I'm sure I can make this other information work for us." He paused, frowning, and stroked at his bristly chin. "I guess it cost Moccasin his life, so we should try." He hesitated again, striving to force a clear thinking path through the jangle still in his mind. How could anybody be that convincing? How could anybody pretend that much passion? It was freakish, unnatural, crushing. He forced it away and tried to concentrate on revenge.

"It might be the best idea if they could be copied," he murmured. "I wonder if that could be done here. That way I could get you to take a copy on to Eric Dalgety. There are parents' addresses where they can be traced and interviewed. I think that needs to proceed quickly."

"What about Martin?" interjected Hamilton hesitantly.

"I think Eric would be more effective, and faster,"

said Carmody coldly. "I'll let Martin know what's going on once it's under way." He held out the Stanford documents to Hamilton. "I'm going to call Eric now anyway. There're a lot of things I have to talk to him about. Why don't you see if you can get these copied here? It will save time, and that's something we don't have to spare." He paused, thinking. *I love you,* said a voice. *I love everything you do to me, I've never loved a man like this before.* His mouth trembled and he closed his eyes, trying to block the words from his mind. He opened them again, suddenly embarrassed by Hamilton's stare. "Does anyone except you know that I'm back in Washington?" he asked harshly.

Hamilton shook his head.

"When I spoke to Dalgety I told him you were due back, but I couldn't give him a definite time. I haven't been to the office at all. Like I told you, Frank, I came straight here."

"What about Angela?"

"I didn't talk to Dalgety about her. But there's no way she'd know you were back yet."

Carmody checked his watch. It was after nine thirty, and she would probably be at the office by now. He waved Hamilton out of the office on his copying assignment and called Dalgety. Angela had been up half the night taking notes with him from the expert on psychokinesis he'd flown in from Boston. There was nothing more she could do until Carmody returned, and he didn't expect her back in the office until later in the morning. Carmody hastily cut off his flood of inquiries, told him he'd call back, and hung up. Then he dialed the apartment. Maybe it was better this way, instead of getting her back from the office. He waited while the call signal burred in his ear.

"Hello?" Her voice sounded sleeply, as if he'd dragged her out of bed.

"Frank," he said curtly. He ran his tongue around his lips, and swallowed dryly. He didn't want to sound abrasive.

"Darling, thank heavens you're back," she cried. "Have you been calling the office?" She sounded surprised to hear his voice.

"No, I didn't want to do that. I thought I'd call here first on the off-chance you might still be home."

"Eric Dalgety had me up half the night with some expert on psychokinesis. He called me last night and got me back into his office. I don't think we achieved anything. Where are you? What's been happening?"

He swallowed hard again, and steadied his voice.

"I'm at Andrews Field. I've just flown in from San Francisco."

"San Francisco?"

"I can't tell you about it now. Wait there until I get to the apartment."

"I was just about to leave for the office."

"Stay there. I need you there. I'm coming out right now. I haven't slept all night, I've been flying back and forth across the country, and I'm dead on my feet. It wouldn't be possible for me to speak to the President, or anyone else, the way I feel right now. I don't think I could even articulate my thoughts. That's why I haven't called the office yet, or the White House. I need a shower, a change of clothes, at least to make me feel human again. I'll call Dalgety from the apartment."

There was a pause on the other end of the line.

"Frank, is everything going to be all right? Did you find out anything?"

He smiled, a crooked line across his face that had no relationship to humor.

"We've got Hadaffi beaten," he said confidently.

There was another moment of silence. Then breathlessly. "Frank, are you serious?"

"Absolutely serious." A light film of moisture gathered on his forehead, and he dabbed at it with his fingers, feeling the dampness. He could hear the sound of her breathing in his ear, like the labored panting of an overstrained athlete.

"That's fantastic," she said finally. "What happened?"

"I can't talk about it now. I'll fill you in when I get to the apartment. Wait for me."

"All right," she said.

He waited a moment. *I love you*, said a voice, but it was in his mind, not from the telephone.

"It's good to hear your voice again," she said. She sounded far away, as if mind and vocal cords had temporarily disconnected.

"You too," he replied, and hung up.

He waited a second, his mind dragging like a slow-running clock. He was gambling, and he couldn't afford one single error. He blinked his eyes furiously. Fatigue and emotional stress made for a bad combination.

He called Dalgety again. He told him everything, to a mixture of shocked surprise and jubilation. Carefully, they laid plans.

He'd finished by the time Hamilton got back with copies made of the Stanford documents. He put the originals back in his briefcase, and instructed Rick to take the copies to Dalgety. The papers from Oxley also went to Dalgety. In a way, what he'd told Angela was the truth. He really wasn't in any condition to speak to the President. He hoped to hell the shower would wash some of the fatigue out of his system.

And he had one more fast call to make on the way to the apartment. He wasn't only gambling on a fast location of Hadaffi and Leica. He was gambling with his life. Thirty minutes ago such a thought would have been ludicrous, but anything was possible now. Anything.

Angela paced the apartment waiting for Carmody. It couldn't be true what he had intimated over the phone. How could he possibly have Hadaffi beaten? Maybe it had been a bluff, trying to bolster his own confidence? But that wasn't like Carmody. But how? Did Oxley tell Moccasin more than they had all imagined?

A dozen times she lifted the telephone to call the house in Connecticut, and put it down again. What was she going to tell them? Repeat Carmody's brash words? They would only laugh at her. Then what did Carmody mean?

She was still in a state of befuddled indecision when she heard the front door open and Carmody call to her. She patted at her hair, practiced a smile, disciplined her taut muscles to relax, and went to meet him.

He looked terrible. She was so used to seeing a fastidious dresser, she was momentarily taken aback by his scruffy appearance. But she went quickly to him, controlling her anxiety, and kissed him warmly. Soft mouth. Cloying mouth. Pushing tight, widening, enveloping. Erotic persuasion. He waited for her tongue, but it didn't happen.

He looked around the apartment with a sense of unreality, as if seeing it for the first time. The paintings, the trendy striped lounging chairs, the bar, the drapes. It was her room, not his. There was nothing here that mirrored anything about him at all.

She stood back and smiled at him.

"It's good to see you, but, darling, you look terrible. What a night you must have had. What would you like me to get you . . . coffee . . . a drink?"

He rubbed at the back of his neck, and ran his fingers through his hair, and grinned ruefully. He had the eerie feeling of having stepped into a Broadway theater watching a performance.

"Yeah, it's been quite a night, darling." He waved his briefcase in the direction of the bedroom. "I'm going to go in and get out of these clothes and fall under the shower. Maybe that'll make me feel better."

She smiled and patted his arm. Her heart had a faster beat, but it wasn't betraying her.

"What would you like?" she asked again.

He trudged past her toward the bedroom and paused, framed in the doorway.

"Make it a Scotch, thanks, darling."

She poured the drink while he went into the bedroom. She heard the sound of opening cupboard doors and the rattle of coat hangers.

"Don't you have some time to get a little sleep before you go to the White House?" she called.

"Afraid not," he answered her.

"Do you think you're going to be up to a meeting?"

"I'm going to have to try."

She dropped in some ice and swizzled it thoughtfully around in the glass. She framed the next words in her mouth, careful to make them sound just right.

"I can't tell you how excited I was by what you said

on the phone, Frank. I just hope it's as good as you made it sound. If it is, the President will be relieved."

"It is," called Carmody confidently. His voice was frayed with fatigue, but he sounded very sure of himself, and her heart gave an uncomfortable lurch. She picked up the drink, swallowed several times to try and erase the dryness from her throat, and prepared herself for the next encounter.

He was sitting on the bed when she went into the room, his coat lying on the floor. He was kicking off his shoes. Some fresh clothes were laid out neatly on the other side of the bed, and the briefcase was open by his side. She could see some papers and photographs inside the case. She handed him the drink, and smiled.

"How marvelous," she said. "I can't wait for you to tell me what it's all about."

He took the drink from her hand, and his face crinkled into a boyish grin, and for a moment the fatigue was gone. He closed his eyes and took a long, slow mouthful, then placed the glass on the bedside table.

"Thank you, that was good," he said.

She waited, one hand caressing the other, then smoothed at the blue dress, the one she had put on because she knew it was his favorite.

"You look great," he said appreciatively.

Pent up air came from her mouth with a hiss of exasperation.

"Frank Carmody, will you stop keeping me on edge? I've scarcely been able to keep still, waiting for you to get to the apartment and tell me what's happened. Have we really beaten Hadaffi? What on earth were you doing all the way across in San Francisco?"

He grinned at her again, dragged at his tie with one hand, and indicated the open briefcase with the other.

"It's all in there," he said triumphantly. "All the information I need about the man who is applying the psychokinesis for Hadaffi. And where to find him . . . and his wife. The only thing I don't know about him is why he's doing it, whether it's a political motive, or whether Hadaffi is using some form of pressure on him. Where he is, that's where we'll find Hadaffi." He rid himself of the tie and commenced unbuttoning his shirt.

Her pulse increased sharply, and she felt a nervous trembling in the muscles at the back of her legs. It threatened her composure, and she moved quickly to the small bedroom chair, and sat down.

Carmody leaned toward the briefcase, took out one of the photographs, and held it up for her inspection.

"That's the guy," he grunted. "Brett Leica, and his wife, Jo. He used to work at Stanford University outside of San Francisco. He's the only person in this country, probably in the world, capable of using his mind to create psychokinesis like that. I saw a Professor Moslin from the University last night." He dropped the photograph back into the case and resumed his undressing.

"How on earth did you find out about him?" she asked. For all her enforced discipline she failed to keep the breathlessness out of her voice, and she hoped it only sounded like suppressed excitement.

"A real break," said Carmody. "Moccasin knew about him. From a time way back." He slipped out of the shirt, threw it down on the floor, and shook his head ruefully. "And just in time. Someone killed Moccasin in New York just after he'd told me."

Angela shook her head and widened her eyes, not trusting her voice.

"We'll get the guy," grunted Carmody. He picked up the drink from the table and took another long swallow. He put it down again and rubbed at his mouth with his fingers. "I have a pretty good idea it was a former assistant to Leica. A guy named Vilas Daiton. I have a lot of information on him too. I gather he has a strong resemblance to the actor Omar Sharif. Don't worry, we'll get him all right . . . along with Hadaffi and the rest of them." He stood up from the bed, and began to shrug out of his trousers.

Some large object seemed to move up from Angela's stomach, blocking her throat, as if intent on strangling her. He knew about Vilas, too. It all seemed impossible. How could he have found out so much in such a short time. She couldn't look into his face, not without betraying the turmoil in her mind. She put her fingers to her face and felt the coldness of her skin. She suspected her color was suddenly a bloodless pallor.

She forced herself out of the chair and went and stood by the window so that Carmody's back was to her.

"I'm very proud of you," she managed shakily. Her voice sounded like a braying warning signal, but she had to say something. He failed to notice anything. "Martin will be furious," she added.

He threw his trousers over the bed.

"Yes, he will, but I can't help that. Serve the bastard right."

"Dalgety must be relieved . . . and the President," she murmured. She tried to keep her voice low, just enough to be heard. That way the tremor was less noticeable.

He swirled around on the bed, naked, and looked at her. She wanted to drop her eyes, to look away, but it was too dangerous, and she forced herself to meet his gaze. Again he failed to notice anything, her pallor, her nervousness.

"They haven't seen the information yet," he said. He smiled. "You're the only privileged one so far. Remember I told you over the phone, they don't know I'm back yet." He put one hand down and leaned on the bed. "I'll tell you what I want you to do. While I'm in the shower I want you to call Eric Dalgety. Set up a meeting with him and the President for say . . . midday. Tell him I'm back, with information that will stop Hadaffi. I'll want General Cooper there too, because we're going to need some assistance from the army to take Hadaffi." He waved his free hand at the briefcase. "Then I want you to take all this material to the office and have it copied . . . say half a dozen copies of each, and take them on to the White House. I'll meet you there later, because by then I'll have the final piece of information that will put the sealer on everything."

She nodded, and tried to smile in return. She leaned back against the window with her full weight, not trusting her trembling legs.

"What's that?" she asked faintly.

"I'm getting a call from Leica's parents at eleven o'clock. Moslin's spoken to them. They know where Leica is living, and they've agreed to tell me. I didn't tell you that Leica's been in hiding for the last three years. It's a long story connected with his incredible ability of psychokinesis, but I can't go into details now." He put his head on one side and studied her quizzically. "All right, darling? Can you attend to those things for me?"

She didn't seem able to move for a moment, and he frowned. "Say, are you all right, Angela? You don't look very well."

She forced a smile, patted at her face, and forced her self into motion.

"No, I'm fine, darling. I was up late myself last night, and maybe I'm a little tired . . . then this excitement on top of everything. It's marvelous and exciting, but I guess you've rather taken my breath away."

"We've been lucky," he smiled. "But I guess we needed some breaks." He scowled suddenly. "All except Moccasin. That was a bad business." He shrugged, and picked up his glass again. "I guess he knew the risks he was taking, but it's tough. Specially when he was such a top agent." He lifted the glass to his mouth and drained the contents. "Ah, that was good," he muttered.

She paused by the side of the bed, forcing herself to maintain a half smile.

"As long as you're safe," she said.

He grinned at her and handed her the empty glass.

"I take a lot of killing."

"Would you like another drink?"

"No, but I'd like you to make that phone call," he answered.

She nodded. She thought of kissing him, but the effort would have been beyond her and only another risk of self-betrayal.

She padded from the room, stiff-legged, trying to stifle the trembling in her body. She was going to have to stop him. Somehow she was going to have to rediscover her strength, her purpose, because there was no one else to help her—not Daiton, not Hadaffi, not anyone. She was going to have to do it, because now everything was at stake. The information Carmody had could destroy them all, and this was the moment for which she had been trained. The thing that she'd tried to put out of her mind, that was no longer a nerve-racking possibility but a demanding reality, had to be done. She tried to remember how it had been with Eddington. She couldn't recall this light-headed, almost feverish feeling, the trembling in her limbs, the dryness in her throat, the fluttery panic in her chest. If only Daiton were at her side. She put the empty glass on the bar and moved across to the phone. She could hear Carmody still pottering around in the bedroom, and the sound of a cupboard door opening and closing. Why in the name of everything she believed in was she so distressed? It had to be done. It was as simple as that. It had to be done. She repeated it to herself over and over, as if using it as a code to strengthen her resolve. It had to be done. It had to be done. If she allowed Carmody to take that information to the White House, it would be almost like standing by and watching them kill Vilas.

She didn't dial, but picked up the receiver and put it to her face.

She turned as Carmody put his head around the door.

"Won't be long," he said.

She nodded and waved him away.

"I'm just calling Eric now," she said.

"Tell him to pass on the message to Martin." He grimaced at her. "I guess he'd better be at the meeting."

He disappeared, but she still made no attempt to dial the number. She waited until she heard the bathroom door open and close, then she slowly put the phone down again. Perhaps she should wait until he came out of the bathroom? Perhaps she should wait until he was dressed and ready to leave? Perhaps she should wait until he was in the car? Perhaps she should call Vilas and ask if Leica could subject Carmody to psychokinesis? She shook her head vigorously and stirred herself away from the phone. She was stalling. The psychokinesis was nonsense; there was no time, no time for anything but silencing Carmody.

If only she could just take the documents and run, but he knew it all, it was in his mind. And she couldn't let him take that call from Leica's parents. She went slowly into the bedroom like a reluctant snail, her feet dragging a trail through the carpet. She heard the sound of running water from the bathroom and tried to hasten her feet.

What would she do afterward? How long before they started to look for Carmody? How long would she have to run? One hour? Two hours? Even if they found his body, they would never suspect her. Why should they? She could be with Vilas at the house in Connecticut before they even found him. Be with Vilas. She hoped he would be proud of her, although she would never let him know of her agonizing over the killing of Carmody.

He would find it difficult to understand, the situation would be so clear-cut to him. It would have appeared the same way to her once.

She pulled out the small drawer and took out the gun. When had she last taken it out and looked at it? Only a few days ago, although it seemed like another time, almost another life, when the thought of killing Carmody was only a macabre possibility. Did she really feel something for the man? When she considered her passion for Vilas, such a thought seemed absurd; but there was something there, she had to face that, something making her limbs quiver, her blood run like a flood.

She went across to the bathroom door, leaned her back against it and closed her eyes, the gun cocked in her hand. The sound of rushing water on the other side of the door pricked at her memory. It could almost be the sound of the torrent beating on the canvas shanty that had passed for home in the camp. God, how long ago? Hadaffi had rescued her from that, and the debt would never be repaid. She was still paying it now, here with Carmody.

She opened her eyes, pressed her lips together so tightly it distorted her face, and shut her mind. Reached out for an opaque blanket and closed out the light from her brain.

The sound of the water suddenly stopped, and the apartment was strangely silent. Now, said a muted voice. Now, now, now, or he'll return to the bedroom and you'll never do it.

She pushed open the door. He'd run the shower hot, and the room was enveloped in steam. The door of the shower recess thrust open, and a hand came through, groping for a towel. Nausea stirred in her belly, and bubbled into her throat. Give me strength, she prayed. Just for a few moments, give me the strength. She lifted the gun and pointed it at the open door of the shower recess, but her trembling threatened to ruin her aim so she brought up her other hand for support, her fingers like a claw around her wrist.

He stepped out of the shower, the towel in front of his body, patting at his face, and for a moment he failed to see her. And when he finally did, peering about through the haze of steam, nothing registered.

"I thought you would have gone . . ." he began, then stopped, staring stupidly.

She fired once, twice. She saw the towel jerk about in front of his body, the vacant look of death in his face, then he fell back inside the shower, out of sight.

All except one foot, hanging limply out of the door. She stood completely still for a moment, the gun still upraised in her hand. The sharp crack of the gun had seemed muffled by the confines of the bathroom. It seemed incredible he could be so quickly dead. If only Vilas could have done this in New York as she had hoped, instead of leaving her to face this trauma.

She didn't want to see Carmody, shrank from the thought of looking into his face. She had to move quickly now, gain control of herself. She stepped back into the bedroom, the gun still in her hand, closing the door softly behind her, and stood for a moment, trying to assemble her thoughts. She should drive to Connecticut in her car? What if someone accidently made a quick discovery of the body? They knew the registration of her car at the office. It would take her hours to drive to New York, and she could so easily be picked up on the highway. That was too risky.

It would be better to go to the airport, take a plane to New York, then maybe a rental car out to the Connecticut house. Or she could call Vilas to drive to New York and meet her at the airport. But somehow that seemed dangerous for Vilas. If there was even the remote possibility of her being picked up, she could expose Vilas to the same danger she was trying to protect him from.

The alternatives flooded into her mind like uncontrolled traffic, bumping and honking at her for attention, and she had no time to try and sort out the tangle. Maybe someone heard the shots? Maybe anything? She had to get out quickly, so she decided for the flight to New York, and the hired car, rightly or wrongly, because she had no time to be indecisive. Besides, she wasn't expected at the office until late.

She dithered momentarily about the gun. Take it with her, or leave it? Surely it was too dangerous to carry with her? She hastily wiped it clean, thrust it back in the drawer, and covered it over.

She took a large handbag from the wardrobe, checked the wad of money she had secreted there a long time ago for any such emergency, then went and took the documents from Carmody's briefcase.

She folded them into a tight wad and crammed them into her bag. There was no way to destroy them now, it would have to be done later.

All she wanted was time. Time to warn Vilas. To warn Hadaffi. Maybe all that Carmody had discovered could be rechecked by Intelligence, but by that time they could have Leica moved to a new location.

She glanced quickly around the room to make certain there was nothing she'd forgotten. She looked at the bed and had a sudden flash of herself and Carmody locked in sexual embrace. She thrust the image out of her mind. That was over. Somehow she'd allowed herself to soften, and it was a warning never to let her guard down again.

She saw no one around the apartment. She drove carefully to the airport, obeying every traffic rule to a degree of perfection, hunched over the steering wheel to try and alleviate the pangs of apprehension cutting into her stomach. No one stopped her. No one took any notice of her. There was an Eastern flight to New York which only gave her a twenty-minute wait, but it seemed like twenty hours as she fretted in the terminal, unable to sit, unable to stand still. A few men gave her surreptitious glances, but she knew those looks from experience and ignored them. Again she thought of calling Vilas. But he would come rushing down to New

York to meet her, and she didn't want that. Finally she did go to a booth to call him, but they were all occupied, and then she had a last call for boarding which left her no time.

By the time she was airborne some sort of peace and order had returned to her mind. It was foolish to worry. No one except herself knew Carmody was back in Washington, and it would take them hours before anyone thought of going to the apartment. And then once they found the body, more hours to try and retrace his steps back to the Stanford University man in California. And there was no Moccasin to question anymore, thanks to Vilas. Carmody had deliberately played a lone hand in his attempts to outmaneuver Schyler, so that worked in her favor. Everything was in her favor, the more she thought about it. And if every now and then the shots in the bathroom reechoed around in her mind, and the vision of Carmody's foot pathetically extruding from the shower recess joined in, then she could cope with that. Time would eventually eliminate that. And her love for Vilas.

Just out of New York she called the hostess and arranged for a Hertz car to be waiting at La Guardia. The hostess smiled, took her message, and went on down to the rear of the plane. She paused and smiled at a man sitting alone, and bent forward as if to engage in casual conversation.

"She has asked for a Hertz car to be waiting at the airport when we land," she murmured.

The man smiled back as if exchanging a pleasantry.

"What name is she using?"

"She's asked for the car to be booked in the name of Nerida Bergaze."

He nodded, and the smile never left his face.

"One of our men by the name of Norman Harte is waiting at the airport. See that he's informed about the car. He'll know what to do."

The hostess nodded and strolled casually back toward the front of the plane.

Some of Angela's apprehension returned on her arrival at La Guardia. Somehow it had seemed safer on the plane, out of sight, sheltered from the death she had left in the Washington apartment. Here in the airport lounge she seemed suddenly exposed, the target for a thousand eyes.

But she controlled her nerves, walked calmly at an unhurried pace, and forced an expression of composure on her face. She hesitated again, passing a telephone booth, over calling Vilas, but she didn't want to stop now. It was too public here, too many people, scurrying feet, cries of welcome, embraces. And guards. She longed to be enclosed, to feel safe as she had on the plane, and she knew that the car would give that to her.

The car was waiting, there were no problems, and she was quickly away. And she was right, the feeling of safety returned. She relaxed behind the wheel, and spun the car out into the flow of traffic.

It had been some time since she'd been out to the house, and she went slowly at first, letting her memory guide her. She followed the Whitestone Expressway out over the East River, connected onto the New England Thruway feeling her way, but once she was on the Connecticut Turnpike with Long Island Sound to her right, it all came back sharp to her mind, and she picked up speed. It was a gray day, with a strong breeze scudding in from Long Island Sound and washing over the car. Whitecaps decorated the surface of the water, never still, dancing, disappearing, reforming. She thought of

Carmody, sprawled in the shower recess, with the water dripping slowly onto his body. She shook her head angrily. That was done, it was over, it had to be done, and all that should be on her mind was Vilas. She created an image of Vilas in her mind as she drove until it swelled enough to crush Carmody out of her memory.

She turned off before Bridgeport, and went north through Upper Stepney, climbing, on past Sandy Hook, and she knew then that Roxbury was only a few miles away. The house couldn't be seen from the road, but she knew the dipping right turn into the valley. The hills glowed around her with red and green and yellow, a primping woman in full fall regalia. The gate was open and she drove through, and up the track leading to the house, noting Vilas's parked car with relief. At least that hopefully meant that he was at the house, safely back from New York. Everything looked so serene, so peaceful. The high gabled roof, the lattice windows, the wide skirting verandah, all nestled tightly into the trees at the rear. A thread of smoke drifted lazily from the chimney. It would be a nice place to spend a few weeks alone with Vilas when this was all over.

He was in the kitchen drinking coffee with a large gray-haired middle-aged woman she had never seen before, and she countered the look of astonishment on his face by swiftly crossing from the door and throwing herself into his arms. He put down his coffee and stood up from the table to receive her embrace. She put her arms around him and locked her fingers tightly behind his back, as if she never wanted to release him.

The woman said nothing. Vilas made no attempt to introduce her, but she made Nerida some coffee, then sat down at the table, watching and waiting, her face expressionless. There was a large combustion stove set

into one wall, topped with a motley collection of sauce-
pans, and it filled the room with a cheery warmth.

But it was a mixture of excitement and relief, more
than the stove, that produced the flush in Nerida's face.
For a moment she was almost incoherent, all the words
babbling out of her mouth in an uncontrolled torrent,
stumbling and slurring, until Vilas calmed her down
and insisted she drink the coffee first.

She took a few sips, but it didn't allay her sense of
urgency, merely gave her pause for breath, then the
words came, slowly and distinctly. A parade of expressions flowed across his face as she went through the
story: alarm at what Carmody had discovered, relief at
her successful role of executioner, and then finally
anger. Anger that she recognized in his face, without
understanding the reason. She took the documents from
her bag as added evidence, together with the photographs, and laid them out on the table smoothing out
the creases with quick, nervous strokes of her hands.

"You should have called immediately after you'd
eliminated Carmody," he said angrily.

"It wasn't easy for me," she countered. Her voice
sounded thin and fragile. The praise had not come, and
she was taken aback by his anger. He picked up the
documents without really seeing them, glanced over
the photographs, then dropped them back on the table.

"I had to get out of the apartment as quickly as I
could," she added. "I was . . ." The word frightened
came to her lips, but she bit it away. "I was anxious to
get to you as soon as I could. It seemed terribly important that you see them as soon as possible."

Vilas stood up away from her, his dark face wrinkled
into an ugly scowl, and began to pace the kitchen.

"I wish to God I'd managed to get Carmody along

with Moccasin," he muttered anxiously. "Then none of this would have happened."

"It'll be hours before anybody finds Carmody's body, Vilas," she consoled him. "Hours. He could lie there all day. Even then it will take them a long time to back-track to California and the man who gave Carmody the information. I'm sure we're safe."

"The hell we are," he said furiously.

Nerida looked away as the woman rose from the table and fed a fresh piece of wood into the stove. The flames crackled hungrily at the new timber. She hadn't expected this, not after the trauma of the murder, and the journey, building herself up to seeing Vilas, to being consoled in his arms. There was a flatness in her mind, and her hands toyed listlessly with the documents.

"You think I shouldn't have killed Carmody?" she asked dully.

"Of course not. He had to be killed, and quickly. But you should have called. If not from the apartment, then from the airport, or from New York. We've lost precious time. We're going to have to move Leica to a new location, and quickly."

"All I could think of was getting away, getting to you," she muttered.

He paused in his pacing to place a consoling hand on her shoulder, but his anger came through, and his fingers bit deeply, until she was forced to wrench away from the pain.

"Stopping anywhere to call you seemed unnecessarily dangerous," she countered sullenly.

"Danger is what you've been trained for," he shouted suddenly. "Do you think we had you placed in Washington as a pretty ornament passing on information? Of course it wasn't easy for you killing Carmody. But it's

what I expected of you. What Hadaffi expected of you."
He glanced at his watch. "What time did you say you
left the apartment?"

She shrugged, trying not to show her disappointment.
"I would say about eleven o'clock."

"If you had called then, I could have taken a plane
to Hadaffi and he would have the information by now."

She said nothing, but continued staring at the fire.
The woman across from her made a gurgling sound in
her coffee.

"It's almost four o'clock now. Carmody has been dead
almost five hours. They won't call in from the motel
in Manchester until eight o'clock. That's a set proce-
dure every day. I couldn't get to Hadaffi before then, so
we'll just have to sweat it out until the call comes in."
His tone was quieter, resigned.

She looked up at him, and her mouth trembled.

"I did what I thought was right," she murmured.

A weak smile shone to her through the fog.

"I know," he said softly. "And you're probably right.
By the time they find Carmody it will take them hours
to backtrack. And it will mean a long time before anybody makes contact with Leica's parents. But we need
that time. Desperately. Now we've come this far we
can't let anything stop us."

He paused behind her and put his hands down on
her shoulders. This time there was no pincered grip,
but a softly smoothing caress.

"You did well with Carmody," he murmured.

The woman gurgled in her coffee again, but Nerida
ignored the implied derision. She leaned back and put
her head against Vilas, savoring the feel of him. Everything would be right now. Even Carmody would
eventually be blotted from her mind.

It was Dalgety who had suggested that Carmody replace the bullets in Angela's gun with blanks, and Carmody had gone along with the idea more to humor him than anything else. You don't sleep with a woman for that long without learning some minute fragment of her personality. Maybe she had emotionally fooled him in a way that had crushed him, but he was sure she was no killer. Maybe she was Hadaffi's tool, maybe all that warmth and passion had been contrived, unbelievably contrived, but she was no killer. That was the only thing he had left to believe about her. And that had vanished with ego-crushing finality in the bathroom of the apartment.

Yet what had he expected? The whole idea was to panic her, to make her run, and had he really believed she would leave him luxuriating in the shower while she disappeared from the apartment with the documents? Maybe that was what he wanted to believe. Perhaps his refusal to believe she would actually try to kill him had been an attempt to hang on to one last fragment of his shredded ego. In those last few moments before she had fired he knew Dalgety was right, had saved his life, and he had enough presence of mind to collapse back in the shower, hoping she wouldn't make a closer examination to be certain he was dead.

So he had lain there, letting the water from the leaking shower drip on his body, hating her for making him feel stupidly vulnerable all over again. But for the last time.

He wasn't sure what she'd do, where she would run, or how. He dressed quickly and called Dalgety. They were following her, and as soon as Dalgety received a report he would call back. He shaved, tight with anxiety, trying to cancel out his bitterness with objectivity.

Even revenge was immaterial, although deep down he knew himself better than that. He craved some form of emotional consolation, and he could imagine nothing more satisfying than letting her lead them to Hadaffi.

Finally Dalgety called back. She had taken an Eastern Airlines flight to New York. Mathews and Harper were on board watching her, and they would make another report from New York. Carmody rolled the dice, and decided against running the photographs of Leica in the media. He knew he was gambling in holding off, he was putting everything on this throw, but the pictures could panic Hadaffi into bolting. And he'd take Leica with him. There was nothing on Leica's parents. Agents were out trying to trace them, and there was no guarantee they would cooperate.

They couldn't wait. He and Dalgety and three other agents took another flight to New York. A voice followed him. He couldn't believe it, he refused to believe it; she'd betrayed him, assassinated him, but the voice persisted. *I love you. You turn me on like no other man. Do it, do it, do it.* It made him feel a fool, a weak, ineffectual fool. And any weakness at this crucial stage could be fatal. Not only where Hadaffi was concerned, but also with Schyler. He had the upper hand now, Schyler would be history soon, and he'd left Rick in Washington to be doubly certain Schyler was left impotent.

So he fought the voice, trying to silence it in his mind, all the way to New York. They went to the local office in New York, and waited. That was the worst time of all for Carmody: when the doubts multiplied, and the gamble seemed ill-conceived. And the most horrific thought of all: Could Angela be leading them up a phony path—instead of leading them to Hadaffi, taking them away? Those thoughts he kept strictly to himself, because he didn't want to alarm Dalgety, and he'd lost all confidence in trying to predict how Angela would behave.

All his doubts were dissolved by a call from Mathews. They were in Connecticut, a few miles out of a place called Roxbury. The bug that Harte had placed in the Hertz car had worked to perfection, made it an easy chore, given them a line right to the house where she was staying. They had the place under surveillance. Harte would wait for them on the main road, three miles south of Roxbury.

There was a flurry of maps in the office while they looked up Roxbury. There was an airport at Reynolds Bridge, and that was only about twenty miles from Roxbury. A light plane could get them there inside an hour.

By six o'clock they were there, and by six thirty they had maneuvered themselves into the trees at the rear of the house. If the terrorist leader was inside, then they had him. Carmody rehearsed the vengeful words he would say to Angela when they came face to face again. Then again, maybe he wouldn't say anything at all.

ncluding Carmody and Dalgety, there were eight of them all told. With Harte, Mathews, and Harper were the three agents who had flown up from New York. Carmody had wanted to keep the numbers down, but eight was the absolute minimum as far as Dalgety was concerned. This sort of operation was more an FBI specialty, and Carmody let Dalgety call the moves. If possible he wanted Hadaffi alive, and Leica. Most certainly Leica. He didn't discuss Angela. They gave Carmody a gun, as a precaution, but he was no great marksman, and he handled the weapon cautiously.

He watched and listened as Dalgety issued his instructions. He was a good operator. A small man, about his own age, with balding dark hair, sharp, pointed features, brown eyes almost hidden beneath shaggy brows. Yet in the commonplace features there was a constant expression of alert intelligence that remained, whatever the mood. Eyes that missed nothing. A mouth that could be humorous one moment, then scathing the next. He was almost birdlike in his movements, never still, hands moving, gesturing, instructing, his head darting this way and that, anxious that no point missed his scrutiny. Carmody knew very little about his background except that he had been with the FBI almost all of his working life, a sure progression to the top through diligence and results. And knowing the right people. Contacts were always a part of it. That's what had made it so tough for him. Intelligence was an asset, qualifications were great, but if contacts didn't grease the path for you, then you just had to kick a lot harder.

He wondered if Dalgety had ever known anyone like Angela. Probably not. Very few men ever knew anyone like Angela, and that was their good luck. Or bad luck, depending on the point of view. He could think of some nights that would live in his mind forever, that nothing could cancel out, not even the agony she'd created for him over the last few hours.

No, Dalgety looked like the average family-type man to him. Probably a wife of long standing, with two kids at the best school in Washington.

They had decided to wait until dark, and night was already settling over the hills, turning the brilliant fall hues into one common tonality. It was very still. Somewhere, from a distance that was hard to judge, a dog began to bark, the yapping sound sharp through the trees. He hoped it didn't belong to the house. That was a warning signal that would be difficult to silence.

He slid himself down to the ground, his feet rustling in the leaves, and sat with his back against a tree. He yawned once, then again, his jaw stretching uncomfortably. It seemed like forever since he'd experienced a good night's sleep. Perhaps it would be a long time coming even after this was all over, because he suspected sleep would not be easy in an unaccustomed lonely bed.

The lights came on in the house, two rectangular unblinking yellow eyes staring into the trees. He was fifty yards from the house, but instinctively he shrank down against the tree to make himself a smaller target. He wondered if it was Angela in one of those rooms, perhaps readying herself for bed, and he thought of that marvelous smooth brown skin. He shook his head furiously. For Chrissake, if he went into the house with that sort of thought in his mind, then this time she would kill him. There were no blank bullets to protect him now.

Somewhere above him a night creature skittered about in the tree, vigorously scratching, and a lone leaf drifted down and settled on his shoulder. He brushed it away with an irritable flick of his hand as Dalgety slid out of the darkness and squatted down beside him.

"We're all set to go, Frank," he murmured. "How are you feeling?"

Carmody shrugged.

"I'm having trouble keeping awake, but I'm ready when you are."

Dalgety nodded, his head darting about through the trees.

"Just one thing bothers me that we haven't talked about, Frank."

"What's that?"

"Leica."

"What about him? If he's in there I want him taken alive, that's all."

"It's this psychokinesis thing with his mind, Frank. None of the other boys know about it. What if he turns it on us?"

Carmody stared through the trees at the house, passing the gun thoughtfully from one hand to the other.

"I don't think he could do it to us all at once, Eric," he said slowly. "From what I've learned, I don't think it works that way." He paused again, thinking rapidly. The thought had occurred to him. "Even if there was the possibility, it could only happen to one of us. The rest wouldn't be affected."

Dalgety stirred uneasily and pawed at his chin.

"Fucking nice thought," he muttered.

Carmody shuffled himself into a standing position and patted Dalgety on the shoulder.

"Forget about it, Eric. We've got surprise on our side. If Leica suspected we were here, then something would have happened by now. We'd all probably be running through the trees like screaming idiots."

Dalgety stared at the house as if mesmerized by the yellow eyes.

"Maybe, maybe," he muttered.

He shook himself, as if his fears were like fallen rain on his clothes, spraying them away.

"We'd better move," he grunted. He turned and beckoned with his hand in the darkness, and Mathews materialized out of the trees and joined them. He had a machine gun in the crook of his hand.

"Frank, you go with Howard to the window with the light on at the far side of the house. I'm going in the front with three men. The others will be around on the other side of the house. I just want you there to cut off any escape route."

"You're not going to try and call them out?"

"I don't think it's that sort of situation, Frank. Let's make surprise work for us. If we try and call them out, you know the sort of people we're dealing with. All we'll get for our trouble will be a gun fight." He shook his head adamantly. "Believe me, it's better this way." He held up his wrist, peering at his watch in the darkness. "I'll give you five minutes to get into place, then we'll go in." He glanced at Carmody, then at Mathews. "Okay?"

They both nodded, then Dalgety turned and disappeared into the darkness. They heard his feet rustling through the leaves for a moment, then silence.

Mathews gestured with his head for Carmody to follow, then turned and threaded his way through the trees toward the house, his body in a half crouch. Carmody followed in his tracks, emulating his action, lifting his feet, trying not to disturb the leaves. A bird rushed out of the trees, frantically beating its wings, and soared up through the branches to safety. It startled Carmody, and he almost lost his footing, and he stumbled into one of the trees for support. This was a new game for him. His business was normally behind a desk, directing and planning, not doing. A combination of excitement and nerves sucked the moisture from his mouth, and he tried to swallow the dryness in his throat. His hand felt clammy around the gun, and he gripped it tightly for fear it would slip from his grasp.

Mathews kept going, not looking back, a black shape merging and emerging from tree to tree, and Carmody hurried his feet to keep pace. The leaves beneath his feet felt like a soft carpet, yielding gently under his weight. The air felt suddenly chill, sharp against the skin of his face. It combined with the adrenaline surging through his body to banish his fatigue. His mind was suddenly alive, with a frantic alertness.

Mathews stopped and held up one hand, and Carmody almost blundered into his back. The light from the window threw a yellow outline along the profile of his face. The house was only a few yards away, but here the trees petered out, leaving them exposed.

"Careful from here," whispered Mathews.

Carmody nodded. Mathews went first, almost doubled over until he reached the side of the house. He flattened himself against the wall and peered through the window, the light reflections carving ghostly contours on his face. One hand lifted urgently, and gestured toward Carmody. In a second Carmody was at his side, sharing the view.

He was looking into a small bedroom. A bed, a few odd chairs, a dressing table carrying a small television set. There were two doors leading off the room. A single overhead light with a faded fabric shade hung from the ceiling. A heavy wire mesh was nailed firmly over the window, and he put his fingers on the covering for support, craning to improve his view. There was a woman on the bed reading a magazine. On one of the chairs he could see a small tray, with crockery and the remnants of a meal.

The bed was positioned in profile to the window, and the woman seemed to sit uncomfortably in the bed until he noticed the roundness of the covers, and realized she was pregnant. She put the magazine down and stared momentarily into space, and it gave Carmody a clearer view of her face. His heart suddenly bolted as if someone had needled a stimulant directly into his chest. It was Jo Leica. Her hair was longer now, but he'd memorized that striking face from the photographs.

He wanted to shout, he wanted to sprint through the trees, and scream away the stillness of the hills, he wanted to hug Dalgety. That meant Leica was in the house. And Hadaffi. He could almost feel the warm firm grip of the President's grateful handshake. It didn't even seem to matter about Angela. It seemed to make the agony worthwhile, and God, how he'd used her. It was a warm glow in his belly.

He glanced over at Mathews on the other side of the window with a delighted lopsided grin. Mathews returned an uncertain grin, not really knowing why, and shifted the machine gun about in the crook of his arm.

They watched as Jo Leica threw the magazine down,

put her head back on the pillow, and stared up at the ceiling. Everything about her demeanor, the tilt of her head, her expression, conveyed a sense of depression, of despair. That bothered him, it was something he found difficult to understand. He curbed his impatience, and glanced at his watch. Any minute now, and all his questions would be answered.

They waited. The house creaked by their side.

A door suddenly banged, a small explosion in the still night, and someone shouted, then another voice, then a gabble of voices. Carmody felt his muscles tighten. Footsteps beat through the house like a muffled roll of drums, startling Jo Leica, and she sat quickly upright in the bed. There was a small volley of gun shots, one, two, three, then a fusillade. Mathews readied himself with the gun, and Carmody stirred uneasily, watching Jo Leica. The shots scarcely sounded like a successful surprise raid. He wanted people he could question, not bloodied silent bodies. Jo Leica twisted uncertainly on the bed, her hands down at her sides gripping the sheets, her mouth dropped open, her eyes wide and frightened, staring at one of the doors.

It burst open, and a man lurched through the opening. It was Omar Sharif. Omar Sharif without the moustache, and an ugly red stain across his chest as if someone had emptied a bottle of dye over his shirt. He leaned against the wall, and pointed a gun shakily at Jo Leica. His hand fell away, then he tried again, using his other hand as a lever, his entire body trembling.

Carmody didn't understand what was happening, but it suddenly seemed terribly important to keep Jo Leica alive. The other man obviously was Vilas Daiton, and a Vilas Daiton very close to death; and Carmody didn't want any more bodies.

"Stop him, stop him," he screamed at Mathews.

Mathews was well trained, and adept with the weapon he was carrying. Almost before Carmody's words were out of his mouth, the machine gun was stuttering loudly against his ears. A pattern of small explosions erupted against the wall behind Daiton, the gun dropped out of his hand, and he collapsed to the floor.

Then it was silent again, a silence so intense, the fast running beat of Carmody's heart seemed magnified a thousand times. Jo Leica was looking rapidly back and forth from the window to Daiton on the floor, stupefied.

Dalgety came into the room, glanced down at Daiton, ignored the woman, and crossed rapidly to the window. He put his face against the wire mesh, his nose ludicrously through one of the openings, and peered owlishly at Carmody and Mathews.

"Are you two okay?" he asked. His tone was composed, cool.

"Yes," answered Carmody. "What the hell happened? What was all the shooting about?"

Dalgety extracted his nose from the mesh, and jerked his head back in the direction of the room.

"Come inside," he said. "We're all clear in here now."

This time Carmody led the way, apprehension injecting speed into his gait. If those clumsy bastards had killed Leica and Hadaffi?

He went through the front door, Mathews on his heels, into a small entrance hall. He opened the door immediately ahead of him. It was on old-style kitchen, combustion stove, flagstone floor. There was a squat gray-haired middle-aged woman sitting at a heavy oak table, two agents standing behind her. She glowered at Carmody, and spat on the floor. The acrid smell of cordite ticked at his nostrils. One of the agents jerked his head in the direction of another door leading off the kitchen.

"In there," he said.

Carmody nodded, crossed past the woman, and went through the door. He was in a large living room, old fashioned, beaten-looking furniture, threadbare rugs scattered over a dark-stained floor. There was a body lying over in a corner of the room, face down on top of a bloodied rug. There was another man, dark, flat features, turtleneck black sweater, sitting in one of the chairs, his head down, his elbows on his knees, clasped hands twisting nervously in front of him.

The rest of the agents were grouped around the room, some of them examining the body, the others guarding the seated man. At least none of the agents had been hit.

Dalgety was standing in a doorway on the other side of the room, leaning casually against the frame. He waved Carmody across to him.

Carmody glanced around again before responding to the call. Was that Hadaffi seated in the chair? Or was he the dead man sprawled over in the corner? He was certain neither of them was Leica; even from what he could see of the man on the floor he in no way tallied with Leica's description. And where was Angela? Had she been hit during the melee of bullets? He wondered how he would feel to see her a crumpled lifeless bundle in one of the rooms. Nothing quite added up anymore. The flash of jubilation he'd experienced at the sight of Jo Leica through the window suddenly evaporated.

He went across to the doorway and Dalgety politely stood to one side, his hand outstretched, ushering him through.

Jo Leica was seated on the side of the bed, white-faced, both hands clutching at her rounded belly. She stared at him, and her lips moved, but she said nothing. He turned to a moaning sound to his left on the floor, a thin whining expression of agony, like a forest animal snared by a steel trap, on and on in one continuous wavering tone.

It was Angela, crouched over the body of the man Mathews had killed. Vilas Daiton. Shredded plaster from the ruptured wall lay on the floor and over Daiton's clothes like fallen snow. So much for vengeance for Moccasin. He couldn't see Angela's face, it was buried somewhere against the man's neck, but he'd never heard a sound like that come from any human throat before. Bitter words formed in his mouth, stumbling into each other in their desire to be heard. Bitch, they screamed. Bitch, bitch. Who is that bloodied thing you mourn with such agony? Did you lavish on him all the passion that was only pretense for me? Did he feel more intensely for you than I? Could he screw better than I? Was he more of a man than I?

She suddenly lifted her head and looked at him, and he saw there was blood over the front of her dress, on her white neck, on her hands. She seemed to look at him for a long time, stupefied, a dull glaze over her face. Then she put up her hands and pressed them to her cheeks, and as if in slow motion she lost her balance, tottered on her heels, and fell back against the wall. Her hands fell away from her face, leaving a motley pattern of red fingerprints on her skin.

A thin continuous wail spiraled out of her throat, like a reed instrument held at high pitch. Her eyes were dead, her face expressionless.

"I'm sorry," he said.

He had no idea where the words came from, they seemed so completely in contradiction to his bitterness; they were just there on his lips, and he heard them as if they had been spoken by someone else.

He turned to Mathews standing in the doorway.

"Take her outside," he said.

Mathews nodded and stepped forward, taking her by the arm. She offered no resistance, her face white against the red splotches, and she rose to her feet like a dream walker.

Mathews led her from the room and she passed Carmody without a flicker of recognition, a total stranger she had never seen before.

Carmody stood quite still for a moment, arms folded in front of him, staring at what had been Vilas Daiton, his mind temporarily immobilized. Dalgety coughed awkwardly.

"From the description in the copied documents you sent over with Rick, I'd say it was Vilas Daiton, Frank."

Carmody nodded slowly. The words seemed to be coming to him from the far end of a long tunnel, distorted, taking ages to reach him.

"Yes," he replied. He turned slowly to Jo Leica. "That's right isn't it, Mrs. Leica?"

She indicated agreement with her head, not moving. Carmody went over to the bed, took hold of one of the chairs, and sat down. Dalgety remained where he was, leaning against the wall.

"You are Jo Leica?" asked Carmody.

"Yes," she said. "Yes, I'm Jo Leica."

It was a nice voice, although the tone was low with a slight quiver.

"My name is Frank Carmody." He tried to keep his

voice considerate while his mind screamed impatiently for quick answers. "I'm a government Intelligence agent."

She nodded, and her hands slid down over her stomach and fell loosely in her lap. Her mouth trembled, and tears squeezed out of her eyes and ran wetly down her face. She cried silently, with no movement of her body, sitting upright on the side of the bed, looking slowly from Carmody to Dalgety. Carmody waited, his shoes clicking restlessly against the legs of the chair.

The questions finally came, not from him, but from her, tumbling over each other. "How did you find me? Did my husband tell you that I'd been kidnapped? Where is he? Is he safe? Is he at home? Where am I? Where is this house?"

Carmody held up his hands, warding off the questions.

"One at a time, Mrs. Leica. Let me ask you a few questions first. Your husband isn't here?"

She stared at him, and rubbed at her wet cheeks. She took a corner of the sleeve of the old white night dress she was wearing and dried her eyes.

"Here? Of course he isn't here."

"You know where he is?"

He saw a glimmer of caution come into her eyes and knew she was remembering three years ago. He moved away from her husband for a moment, and glanced toward the wire-covered window.

"You've been held here a prisoner?"

"Yes," she said. Her mouth trembled again. "Please, Mr. Carmody, where am I? Where is this house? Is my husband safe?"

"You're in Connecticut."

"Connecticut? They brought me here during the

night . . . blindfolded. I had no idea where they were taking me." She hesitated, looking beseechingly at Carmody. "But my husband, is he safe?"

"I don't know. Can you tell me where he is?"

He saw the wariness in her face again, and irritation sapped at his patience. Christ, they'd just rescued her, they deserved some cooperation.

"Mrs. Leica, we have to find your husband urgently," he said testily. "I can't tell you how we found out you were at this house, it's a long story, but we do need to talk to your husband." He hesitated. "It's a matter of national importance."

She paused a moment, as if words refused to come to her trembling mouth, and a few more tears wound down her face.

"What have they made him do?" she asked huskily.

Carmody shrugged. He couldn't risk telling her that, she might clam up to protect her husband, and they'd never get anything out of her.

"Just tell me where he is . . . please . . . then we can talk about these people who kidnapped you."

She looked down at her hands, her fingers weaving and interlocking with each other.

"I know he's at our home, I heard them talking." She looked at Carmody. "You know about Brett?"

"The psychokinesis?"

"Yes."

"Yes, we know all about that."

"Is that why it's so important for you to find him?"

"It's part of it, Mrs. Leica."

She dabbed at the fresh tears streaking her face. Her long blond hair was stringy for want of combing, and she pushed it nervously back over her shoulders.

"I know it's why they kidnapped me. I know someone wanted to force him to do something by using me as a lever. I worked all that out, Mr. Carmody. I don't know who these people are, but he's a good man, Mr. Carmody. A good man. He'd only want to protect me."

Carmody shifted his body around in the chair to control a spasm of irritation, and glanced over at Dalgety. The FBI man shrugged and grimaced, then tapped his watch.

"I'm sure he is," said Carmody curtly.

"At first I thought it might have been you people," she said.

Carmody shook his head.

"I know about the episode three years ago, but that's over. Forget it. It was a mistake. Where is he now? Where is home?"

"Kentucky," she answered soberly. "A few miles from a place called Sylvan on Pine Mountain."

Carmody tilted back his chair and grimaced at the ceiling. Kentucky, for Chrissake. He was being led by the nose all over the United States.

"I was kidnapped only a few miles from our house before I was brought here," she added. "But I'm sure my husband is being held prisoner at our house. I'm certain of that, from what they said."

Carmody turned and flicked his hand toward Dalgety.

"The maps, Eric," he said.

Dalgety nodded, and paced quickly from the bedroom.

"What's happened?" she persisted. "What have they forced Brett to do? It has to do with his powers of psychokinesis, doesn't it?"

"Let's rescue your husband first, Mrs. Leica," said

Carmody persuasively. "I want you to show me the location of your house on the map."

"I don't want him to come to any harm."

"We'll protect him," said Carmody glibly.

"Think about what you'd do if something like this happened to someone you loved, Mr. Carmody."

Carmody looked at her, unsmiling. *I've been saving myself all my life to love a man like you,* said a voice. He put his hand quickly to his ear as if to blot out the sound.

"Yes, I will," he said soberly. He stood up from the chair and paced anxiously about the room.

"You know the men who kidnapped you?"

She glanced across at Daiton's body, then quickly averted her eyes.

"There were two men. Vilas was one of them."

"You didn't know the other man?"

"No. I'd never seen him before. He was obviously in command of Vilas."

"What did he look like?"

She paused, frowning, remembering.

"It all happened so quickly, it's difficult to remember details. He was dark, a cruel face, a powerfully built man." She gave an apologetic twitch of her shoulders. "I'm afraid that doesn't tell you much. I only know he was a man who frightened me very much."

"Vilas didn't call him by name?"

"No. No, I don't think so. I think I would have remembered that."

"Not a name like Hadaffi?"

She frowned. "Hadaffi?"

"Yes. You've heard of the name?"

"I don't know. It sounds familiar."

"The international terrorist."

Her eyes widened, and her chest began to rise and fall with rapid breathing.

"That Hadaffi?" she breathed.

"Yes. I think it's possible he was the man with Daiton."

She stirred uneasily on the bed, her hands restless, her feet crisscrossing where they hung down a few inches from the floor.

"You're making me feel very frightened for my husband, Mr. Carmody. What would a man like that want from my husband?"

"I think it's important that we rescue your husband as soon as possible, Mrs. Leica," said Carmody.

He was stalling her. He knew it, and he could see from her face that she knew it too. He could guess at the conflict in her mind, fear for her husband's safety, and fear for what Hadaffi may have forced him to do. But she didn't ask again. Eventually she would have to know, but she gave him the impression that suddenly she preferred not to know. Perhaps fear for her husband's safety had won the conflict. Just as long as it stayed that way until she'd given them an accurate location of the house.

Dalgety came in with the maps and spread them out on the bed. Carmody and Dalgety sat on the edges of the bed and Jo bent forward to join them, all of them poring over the small printed details. Dalgety put his finger down on Lexington. "We can put down at Lexington, Frank." His finger moved on down the main southbound highway, then stopped, tapping, indenting the map with the pressure of his hand. "Here's Pine Mountain right here." He glanced up at Jo. "Now, where's Sylvan, Mrs. Leica?"

Jo peered down and put her own finger onto the map.

Carmody could see it trembling, wavering uncertainly over Pine Mountain. Don't back out now, he thought. Don't back out now!

"They'll kill him if we don't rescue him," he prodded her nervously.

She glanced up at him soberly, then looked away again at the map.

"I know that," she muttered.

Her finger stopped on a small point, and they all craned down for a closer view.

"It's only a small place," she said. "Just there. It's on the road running between Pine Mountain and Wooton."

"Where's your house?"

"Five miles out of Sylvan there is a small side road called Pearidge Road. You have to watch for it, or you'll miss it. It's only a track really, not very wide. Follow it in for about a mile and a half and you'll come to our house. It's a two-story board house. You can't miss it, it's the only one there."

Carmody studied the map thoughtfully, pawing at his chin.

"How long is it going to take us to get there, Eric?"

Dalgety scratched at his head and scrutinized the map carefully, examining the scale, making calculations.

"Maybe two and a half hours by car from Lexington if we push it."

"And from here to Lexington?"

Dalgety flicked over the page to a larger-scale map and made some more calculations.

"Well, we've got to get back to Reynolds Bridge." He diverted his eyes to his watch. "It's around eight now. We'll be lucky to be off the ground by eight thirty. Then to New York. I can phone ahead and have a plane waiting for us, but there'll be takeoff delays.

We'll be lucky to be there by two or two thirty in the morning." He looked up, and jerked his head in the direction of the bedroom door. "What about this mess? We haven't questioned the guy in the other room."

"He won't tell us anything, and I don't want to waste the time. He's not Hadaffi. Hadaffi will be with Leica. The local police at Reynolds Bridge can hold the live ones for us, then come out in the morning and pick up the bodies."

"What about Angela?"

"What about Angela?"

Dalgety hesitated.

"Do you want to talk to her?"

"About what? She won't tell us any more than she already has. She can go with the others." He paused, examining the words briefly. He didn't feel anything. Perhaps the sight of her prostrate with grief across Daiton's body had finally put the ache to rest. He turned his attention to Jo Leica. "We'll want you to come with us, Mrs. Leica."

"To the house?" she asked uncertainly.

"To the house. To your husband. It's going to be important for him to see that you're safe. That you've been released. Otherwise it's possible he may see us as the enemy. All right?"

She nodded and forced a pale smile.

"Of course," she said.

Carmody glanced around the room.

"You have some clothes?"

"Yes, I do."

"Then we'll leave you to get dressed. We have some telephoning to do."

He turned to leave the room, but was restrained by Dalgety's hand.

"Just before we go, Frank," he said quickly.

Carmody paused, waiting. Jo had already slipped down off the bed and stood watching them, her hands folded in front of her stomach. Even in her bare feet Carmody saw she was quite tall.

Dalgety put his mouth close to Carmody's ear.

"Ask her about the subject we discussed before we broke into the house?"

Carmody frowned uncertainly.

"About her husband. About Leica and his psychokinesis. How's he going to know we have his wife safe? What if Hadaffi forces him to use psychokinesis on us?"

Jo Leica leaned forward, her face attentive, catching the muttered questions.

"He would have to see you first," she said. "He would have to know you were there. You'd be quite safe if you took them by surprise."

"But what if we're seen?" persisted Dalgety. "You can never be absolutely sure of these things. We had surprise on our side here, but it didn't stop someone getting killed."

There was a moment of silence. Voices murmured in the living room, and from somewhere outside, the yapping dog fractured the still night again. Carmody guessed they were questioning the man in the other room.

"Well," asked Dalgety, insisting on an answer. "What if he did do it? What if he did use psychokinesis on us? Could he do it to all of us at the same time? Could we all finish up running over Pine Mountain like screaming imbeciles?"

Jo shook her head.

"No," she said slowly. "No, I don't think it would work like that."

"You don't think?" echoed Dalgety derisively. "Lady, I want to know."

"Then I can't tell you for certain," she said defensively. "All I can say is, I don't think it would work like that. In some ways, he's no different from you or me. He doesn't have any magic that will let him know you're outside the house, if he can't see you, or hear you. If you take them by surprise, then you have nothing to fear."

There was a pause while Carmody's gaze alternated between Dalgety's expression of doubt and Jo Leica's white defensive face.

He shrugged and took hold of Dalgety's arm in a tight reassuring grip, urging him toward the door.

"We can handle it, Eric, we've got surprise on our side, like Mrs. Leica says. It'll work for us. Let's move out and let her get dressed."

Dalgety let himself be led without protest across the room, but there was no conviction in his face.

Carmody hesitated at the door and glanced at Daiton's body.

"Does that bother you?" he asked. "I can have him taken out."

She gave him a brief shake of her head.

"It's all right. I'll be quick."

They went into the living room, and Carmody closed the door gently behind him. The body was still in the same position on the other side of the room, but no longer commanding any attention from the agents. Angela was sitting in one of the chairs in a rigid upright posture, her legs together, her hands folded primly in her lap. She could have been carved from stone. her eyes lifeless, her face without expression. She appeared almost in a state of catatonia. The dried blood was still on her clothes, on her face. Carmody went and stood in front of her for a moment, but there was no response. Nothing. Not a flicker of her eyes, not a waver of her head. She'd shut herself off in some other world where no one could reach her, no one could hurt her.

Mathews came over and jerked his thumb in the direction of the seated man. "Dumb," he growled. "Not a sound. He won't even open his mouth to give us a name."

"Forget him," grunted Dalgety. "Anything from the woman?"

"Same thing. They just sit there and look at us."

Dalgety twitched his shoulders.

"Leave her too. We'll drop them off at the police in Reynolds Bridge. Get everybody ready to move. We're going to Kentucky."

"Kentucky? Now?"

"Right now. Move."

He paused a second, looking from Dalgety to Carmody, then shrugged and turned away.

Carmody indicated the telephone with his hand.

"You'd better call the airport and tell them to be ready to take off again for New York."

Dalgety nodded, and shuffled slowly in the direction of the phone. He picked up the receiver, looked at Carmody, then put it down again.

"No matter what Mrs. Leica says, Frank, I'm just not convinced."

"You mean about the threat of psychokinesis to us?"

"That's right."

"What do you want to do? We can't afford to wait. Unless you have any other suggestions, I think we should go in."

"At least we should give ourselves some form of in-

surance, Frank. What if the worst happens and someone goofs, makes a noise or whatever. You saw the
President, not I, so you've got more idea of what actually happens. What if we were put out of action?" He
grimaced, and his hands carved agitated circles through
the air. "I'm not trying to be a pessimist, Frank, and
you know I'm no coward. I don't mind fighting something with a gun in my hand, but something I can see.
Something I can understand. Not what Leica is capable
of doing to us." He paused for breath, eyeing Carmody
warily. "And sometime we're going to have to tell Mrs.
Leica about the attack on the President. That's not going to help us any."

"We can tell her on the plane."

"That's your chore, Frank, and I don't envy you. I'm
not too sure where all this places Leica with the law. In
some ways maybe he's as guilty as Hadaffi. Maybe more
so."

"Let's worry about that later," grunted Carmody.

"Okay, then let's worry about us now." He put out
a hand and placed it on Carmody's shoulder, an instinctive pleading gesture. "Call Martin. Tell him what's
happened. Give us backup if we run into trouble. At
least set some sort of time limit."

Carmody set his mouth down tight in a stubborn
line, folded his arms, and studied the floor. He knew
Dalgety was right, but he revolted at the thought of
taking Schyler into his confidence now. Why the hell
should he let him in on the kill when he'd done all the
work, followed all leads, risked his life, traveled all over
the country? He turned it over in his mind, twisting
and weaving for an alternative.

"All right, you make sense, Eric. I'll call someone and
set a time limit," he grunted sourly.

He decided on a compromise, and called Rick Hamilton. He'd told Rick to stay by the phone until he called, and he wasn't disappointed.

"Frank, where are you? Did you get Leica? Did you get Hadaffi?"

"Not yet, but we know where they are, Rick. I'm in Connecticut now, a few miles out of a place called Roxbury. We're just going to take off for Kentucky."

"For Chrissake, Kentucky?"

"We'll get them both this time."

"I hope so. They're really leading you on a cross-country chase."

Carmody cleared his throat with a surly growl. Dalgety was watching him with a disapproving frown that inferred he thought he should be talking to Martin. He turned his back to the FBI man, put his hand up, and leaned against the wall.

"Rick, do you have a pad to take down some notes?"

The phone clicked in his ear, and he heard a scuffling sound on the other end of the line.

"Okay, shoot," Hamilton came back to him.

"I want to give you an accurate fix on where we're going in Kentucky. We've got surprise with us, so we should be okay, but we've got some . . ." He chewed over the right word. ". . . small reservations about the possibility of Leica using psychokinesis on us. It could abort the entire raid."

"I can understand that," said Hamilton slowly.

"It's only a remote possibility, but I merely want to play safe," said Carmody quickly.

"Understood."

Carmody gave him all the details of the location on Pine Mountain, meticulously repeating each word, then getting Hamilton to repeat it back several times. Finally he was satisfied.

"The earliest we're going to be there, I would say, would be two thirty in the morning. Yeah, at least two thirty, and then if we get no holdups on the way. If you haven't heard back from me by six in the morning, take the documents to Martin and tell him where we are. I think he should contact General Cooper, and he should move in with an army troop. Flatten the house if they have to, and everyone in it. We've only got until midday. Understand me?"

There was a short silence on the line.

"If that's what you want, Frank."

Carmody swallowed noisily, and took a deep breath.

"It's what I want," he said throatily.

There was another hesitant pause. Static whined in his ear like the far-off sound of a high-flying jet.

"Is Angela there?" asked Hamilton tentatively.

"Yes."

Another pause. "It was a good lead?"

"The best. We found Leica's wife here. She was being held prisoner."

"I guess that explains a lot."

"Yes, it does. I'll call you before six, so stay there."

He hung up and turned to Dalgety. "That satisfy you, Eric," he asked aggressively.

Dalgety nodded without answering. He knew of the enmity between Schyler and Carmody, but it was obvious he thought Carmody should have spoken to Schyler.

"Then let's move ourselves," Carmody grunted. "You never know what problems we might run into, and I want to keep plenty of time up our sleeves."

He looked at Angela, but nothing had changed. Her mind had shunted her into a remote corner where no one could touch her, and perhaps she would always be there. Mathews took her by the arms and she went without protest, without a sound, without expression, out to the car.

They drove to Reynolds Bridge, three cars swishing through the night, headlights playfully flickering macabre shadows along the roadside trees. The air felt keen and smelled sweetly of growing things free of smog.

The police had commandeered a private ten-seat jet, and it was waiting for them at the airport, fueled and ready to go. It meant they didn't have to go back through New York, but could fly direct to Lexington. It put them on the road leading up to Leica's house at just twenty minutes after twelve, instead of two thirty. Such are the slim gaps that sometimes decide the fate of nations.

Noel Zambretti was an ambitious young man, a man in a hurry, and every breathing moment was directed toward upward mobility. Except that in the last few months that upward drive had been disturbed by a nagging insecurity.

He felt like a bettor who had wagered all his resources on a certain winner and then experienced the chagrin of watching an outsider overtaking his choice near the finish line. Yet in the beginning his selection had seemed so obvious, completely devoid of risk, so he'd bet everything on Schyler. The fact that he was related helped, of course, but it was not the only factor responsible for his decision. Schyler seemed the surest way up, so he made himself indispensable. No job was too small, too menial, too unethical, and he applied himself with the diligence of a beaver.

But his feelings of insecurity began to multiply at the same rate as Carmody's rise in stature and power with the Agency. The whisper around the Agency that Carmody would eventually replace Schyler grew to thunderous proportions, and his sense of futility increased accordingly. But his bets were down, there was no time to change selections, and for a time now he had felt the sour taste of being on a loser.

He was an intense individual, of chunky build, fair, with hair swept forward in a youthful style, rimless spectacles. He was the same age as Hamilton, but he seemed older. He walked with a peculiar anxious gait, hips pushed forward, head held high, like a runner perpetually poised for the sound of the starting gun, ready to flash out of the blocks at a second's notice.

He had needed no second bidding from Schyler to join the "Get Carmody" team. Perhaps Schyler believed it was blood affection, but Zambretti saw the assignment in much more personal terms. Schyler had given him a deliberately vague brief, so as to leave him an open field of operation, all the maneuvering room he wanted, and no questions asked. Schyler didn't want to know how or why; he wasn't interested in details it might have been dangerous for him to know, he just wanted results; he wanted Carmody flat on his ass.

It left Zambretti in the enviable position of being

unrestrained in pursuit of a dirty-tricks operation, of being responsible to no one. It took time, and it had only come to fruition that night, but he managed to put a tape on Carmody's phone, on Rick Hamilton's phone, and on Angela's phone. And being a diligent eavesdropper he returned to the office that night to see if any gems of information had been recorded for him to hear.

There was a reward waiting beyond expectation. The entire conversation between Carmody in Connecticut and Rick Hamilton was down on tape.

He took it straight to Schyler. And Schyler went to Hamilton. It was tough on Hamilton. He was trying to be loyal to Carmody, but Schyler was his top superior, and he was put on a spit, turned slowly, and roasted, until he had no alternative but to hand over a copy of the Stanford documents to Schyler.

Schyler went to General Cooper. Not to inform him anything about Carmody, but to show him the documents that *his* men had turned up. And that he, Martin Schyler, also knew without question where Hadaffi was, where the man responsible for the psychokinesis was, plus a glib additive that there was suspicion that Hadaffi and Leica were set to vacate the house in Kentucky by early morning. They had to get them now, tonight. Cooper made some urgent phone calls. They could put a computer fix on the house in Kentucky. They could have planes in a strike position over the house by about one fifteen in the morning.

Schyler bobbed his head with elated satisfaction, and grinned at Zambretti. Zambretti grinned back, both their faces expanding almost to a splitting position. It was a night to remember.

When Carmody got to the Kentucky house, there would be nothing but smoldering embers.

Schyler picked up the phone, dialed the White House, and asked to speak to the President.

There was a strong wind over Pine Mountain, whipping at the trees, giving voice to the mountain. The pines rolled and threshed, and beat at each other as if alive, filling the mountains with the roaring sound of their agony. It was a good night for surprise. This time even the weather seemed on Carmody's side. They drove the two cars well into Pearidge Road, slowly, the engines muffled by the sound of the wind, lights out, feeling their way along the track under Jo Leica's guidance. She still had no knowledge of the psychokinesis attack on the President. The moment to tell her on the plane never seemed to come because she gave Carmody no opening, no encouragement, until finally he concluded it was what she wanted; for the time being at least she just didn't want to know. Perhaps she was too frightened to know.

The clouds scudded across the sky, propelled by the wind, occasionally permitting the moon a few brief seconds' glimpse of the mountains.

For the moment, the flashes of white light were a guide in negotiating the narrow track, but Carmody hoped they would be snuffed out by the time they reached the house.

Jo Leica was seated beside Carmody, and he could

feel the rigidity of her body against him. She gestured ahead of them, along the track.

"Just toward the rise there is a small opening at the side of the road. You should be able to turn the cars in there."

Carmody leaned forward and tapped Mathews, who was driving, on the shoulder.

"Did you hear that?" he murmured.

Mathews crouched over the steering wheel, peering uncertainly into the blackness. On each side the trees probed at the body of the car with snapping branches, producing a continuous scratching sound, as if resenting an invasion of their privacy.

The car was scarcely moving, creeping forward under the impetus of the automatic with no applied acceleration. It was more of a drunken stagger, lurching from one scoured scar in the road to the next.

"Can't see a bloody thing," muttered Mathews.

The wind beat around them, gently rocking the car. They seemed to be in a vast auditorium of sound orchestrated by the wind, with the trees as instruments, running up and down a scale that varied from a low moan to a high-pitched screeching whine.

"Watch for it," urged Carmody.

The moon peeped abruptly through a keyhole in the cloud cover, and the mountain was suddenly in sharp, hard-edged black and white.

"Just there," said Jo quickly, pointing ahead again. "Just past that large pine."

Carmody squinted in the direction of her pointing finger. There did seem to be something there, an uninviting black hole set in the wall of the forest. She stirred beside him, her hands agitated, propping herself against

Carmody to counter the roll of the car. He wondered what was in her mind, how far he should trust her. It was hardly the type of question to form in his mind when they'd come this far. Maybe she didn't quite trust him, didn't quite trust any of them, but fear for her husband was a motivation he was sure he could rely on.

He craned his head against the window of the car, and peered up anxiously at the sky. The brief flashes of moonlight bothered him, they could give them trouble when they made their approach to the house. A bank of clouds blocked out the keyhole, the light faded, a gray fuzz replaced the sharp monochromatic landscape, then all was blackness again.

"I saw it," grunted Mathews.

He swung the car slightly right to make a turn, and something sharp and rigid bit into the side of the car and scrunched along the metal with a rasping sound.

"Shit," muttered Mathews.

"Never mind that, just keep going," grunted Carmody.

The car swung left, crawled up over a small embankment with the underside of the car rubbing abrasively against the gravel, and lurched into the black hole.

"I hope to Christ the others can see us making the turn," muttered Mathews.

"Keep going, they're right on our tail," grunted Dalgety, from the other side of the car.

Mathews went on in from pure instinct, seeing nothing, the car swaggering over the uneven surface, the high grass hissing against the metal body, expecting any minute to be jolted to a halt by the impact of a tree. When he thought he was far enough in to allow room for the other car, he stopped, and cut the engine. Carmody glanced quickly back through the rear window. He could dimly make out the shape of the other car stopped behind them.

"Nice work," he grunted to Mathews.

"Christ, talk about blind-man driving," replied Mathews.

The wind rushed through their cavern, and branches flailed at the hood of the car with a metallic slapping sound. They must be very close to a tree.

"Let's move," said Dalgety.

There was a new edge in his voice that Carmody had not heard before. He knew it was Leica. It was psychokinesis. It was fear of the unknown. He understood it, and he knew Dalgety enough to know that he would contain it, but he wondered why he wasn't as deeply affected himself. Perhaps his fatigue desensitized fear. He had slept on the plane, but there was a nagging ache in his muscles that persisted like an infected tooth needing to be pulled. And there was an anticipation, an excitement, that Hadaffi was so close, that Leica was so close, that in the next few moments all his efforts would come to fruition. Maybe they all combined to deaden his fear, to erase from his mind the memory of the President writhing on the desk of his White House office.

"What about Jo?" he asked, looking at her.

"What about me?" she asked testily.

"I think you should stay here, in the car. There may be some shooting, and I don't want you to come to any harm." He glanced down. "Or your baby," he added, with emphasis.

"I agree," put in Dalgety.

She hesitated uncertainly, and even in the darkness

Carmody could sense her mistrust, like an odor rising from her body. She knew they spoke sense, she didn't want to put her baby at risk, but what would they do when they found Brett?

"I think I should come with you," she said slowly. "You'll need me to show you the layout of the house, and the best way to approach it without being seen."

"We can't afford to have a pregnant woman staggering around out there in the darkness," said Carmody firmly. "I'm sorry, you have to stay in the car."

"I won't stagger around. I know the area too well."

"No, I'm sorry," persisted Carmody, in a more conciliatory tone. He put his face close to hers, trying in the darkness to impress her with an expression of honesty. "I'll look after your husband. I'll make sure he comes to no harm. Trust me. Give us a brief outline of the layout of the house, then leave it to us. Believe me, it's better that way."

He gave her little option. It did nothing to relieve the tugging anxiety creating the feeling of emptiness in her body, but she told them all she could. She didn't trust Carmody, but there were no alternatives for her, and all she could do was pray, for the three of them, with the baby moving restlessly under her hands.

Carmody opened the door of the car and eased himself out. The wind gusted through the opening and swirled around inside the car. It chilled Jo, and she hunched her shoulders and drew her arms tightly about her.

"I'll be back to get you as soon as it's over," Carmody promised. "Don't forget, Hadaffi is the man we want." He was lying, but he tried to make it sound convincing. How much forgiveness there would be for Leica would be for the law to decide, and he had a feeling the law wouldn't quite see Leica's life as being of more importance than the Presidency.

They gathered in a small knot between the two cars, the wind tugging at their clothes, whipping their hair about their faces, listening to Dalgety's murmured instructions. Now they were out of the cars the wind had more than a dimension of sound; it had a dimension of feeling, of chill feeling, that probed at the gaps in their clothing and made them shiver and stamp their feet in the damp grass.

There were six of them this time. Carmody had left two agents behind in Reynolds Bridge at the police station with Angela and the others. It was a deliberate choice on his part to cut down the number of participating agents. Surprise was all important, especially where Leica was concerned, and the smaller the number involved, the better the chance of surprise. It was a dangerously small force, but Carmody considered it the lesser of two evils.

As in Connecticut, he left the planning of the assault to Dalgety. But this time he wanted to be in the forefront where the action was, not to play hero, but to put a cautionary damper on any quick trigger fingers. He wanted Hadaffi alive, he wanted Leica alive, he wanted live trophies to parade before Washington, trophies that could answer questions that could reflect his glory.

There was a brightness in the sky now, not enough to betray movement, but enough to create shapes of trees and contours of the land, instead of an inky, all-enveloping blackness.

They set off in single file, keeping to the side of the road, following Jo Leica's instructions. They came to the rise where the road turned abruptly to the right, and halted in the shadows of the trees, Dalgety leading, Carmody directly behind him.

"The house is only three or four hundred yards down there," said Dalgety. Carmody paused, breathing deeply, and glanced back down the road.

"Pity we couldn't get any closer with the cars, it'll be a good fifteen-minute walk to the house."

"Too risky, Frank," Dalgety shrugged. "We wouldn't have got this close without the wind deadening the sound of the engines." He gestured ahead with a quick movement of his hand. "The track Mrs. Leica spoke about should be just ahead of us, on the other side of the road." He turned to the other agents at the rear. "All of you keep low, and in the trees. Put your hands out and touch each other if you have trouble keeping in touch. Quiet as you can, and no talking."

Dalgety turned sharp left and merged into the trees, Carmody and the rest of the line of agents following closely on his heels. They padded noiselessly over a soft carpet of pine needles, shadows flitting from tree to tree. The wind moaned around them, rushing through the gaps in the pines, buffeting their clothes, chilling their faces.

Carmody sought to keep his emotions strictly in check this time; he didn't want to think about any other possibility, because it would almost be like starting all over again, and he didn't have time for that.

At least for now Angela's voice was silent in his mind, but the memory would take a long time dying. The memory of what she had been, and what she was now, that vegetable back in Reynolds Bridge.

Dalgety turned right again, weaving through the pines, moving quickly, then came to an abrupt halt.

The others shuffled forward and formed a tight knot around him, huddling together for protection against the sharp needles the wind was driving into their bodies. They were on a narrow track scarcely wide enough for one man.

"I guess this is the foot path Mrs. Leica told us to look for," muttered Dalgety, looking at Carmody for confirmation.

Carmody hunched his shoulders and peered ahead at the steep incline weaving through the forest in front of them. He could just discern the sharp tree-pointed horizon cutting across the sky.

He waved on impatiently with his hand.

"Well, it's the only path we have, so let's follow it," he grunted. "According to Mrs. Leica it should bring us out around the back of the house."

They moved on again, Dalgety still leading, bodies craned forward to counter the steep incline, like birds scouring the ground for scattered seed. Occasionally someone's foot would slip on the soft mountain soil, and there would be a muttered curse, followed by a scrabbling at the side trees to regain balance. The wind generously blanketed all such sounds. They came to the apex of the incline and the path curved away and down just as steeply as the climb. The clouds allowed another brief spasm of moonlight, and at the bottom of the incline they caught a flash of a two-story wooden house, nestled into the pines.

Then the light fuzzed out again, and it was all black forest once more.

"Did you see that?" murmured Dalgety over his shoulder.

Carmody grunted a reply. The wind slapped hair around his face, and he brushed it out of his eyes with an irritated flick of his hand. Somewhere at the rear he caught the faint sound of a safety catch clicking off, and he felt a fresh surge of irritation. He leaned forward and put his head close to Dalgety's shoulder.

"I don't want any unnecessary bullets flying around down there," he muttered anxiously. He jerked his head in the direction of the men behind him. "Do they know that?"

"Yes, they do," said Dalgety curtly.

They moved forward again with the ground firmer underfoot for the descent, and they made faster time, ignoring the branches overgrowing the track that snagged at their clothing, and whipped antagonistically at their faces. The bulky shape of the unfamiliar gun in Carmody's inner coat pocket clumped awkwardly against his ribs. He wondered vaguely if he would ever use it. He'd never considered a human target, never shot at a human being. How did a man like Hadaffi, with an expressed contempt for human life, respond when asked to freeze at the point of a gun? Would that contempt extend to his own life? If it did, then the thought of taking Hadaffi prisoner might be an impossibility.

Dalgety slipped around the trunk of a large pine and raised his hand in a signal to halt. They were on the outskirts of the rear fence of the house, a neglected construction of leaning posts and loose tangled wire. The moon was still a prisoner, locked above the clouds, but there was sufficient brightness in the sky to disconnect the house from its surroundings. There was a small shed in the left-hand corner of the yard, and a narrow gravel path meandered up from the door to the rear of the house. About the halfway mark there was a huge solitary pine, a shovel leaning against the base, and a few feet away a mound of freshly turned earth, almost like a small grave. A faint pale-yellow glow was framed in one of the downstairs rear windows, probably from a light somewhere in the front of the house.

Dalgety gestured silently toward the side of the fence. His pistol was in his hand, and he used it as a pointer.

"Over there," he murmured. "There's more cover."

Carmody nodded agreement and followed Dalgety's example, taking out his own gun. It slipped easily into his hand, with a feel made more comfortable by the Connecticut experience.

They went out around the side of the shed, still in single file, threading through the trees, following the line of the fence up to the house. There was a carport at the side of the house sheltering an old-model Mustang, and in front of that, pointed out in the direction of the road, a recent-model Buick.

They gathered in the carport, crouched against the cars, and listened. There was nothing but the wind slamming around the building, creating a canopy of threshing branches overhead. Somewhere on the other side of the house it probed at a loose board with an insistent knocking sound, like an impatient caller.

Dalgety put his hand out on Harte's shoulder and put his mouth close to the other man's ear.

"Stay by the cars," he said. "Just in case anything goes wrong in the house."

Harte nodded mute agreement, lifted his gun, and checked it in the dim light. They left him and filtered one by one along the rear of the house to the center set door. It was too risky for words now. Dalgety made a quick impatient gesture at the door and stood to one side as Mathews sidled forward and bent to the lock, manipulating by feel in the darkness. Carmody could see the grave more clearly now, the newly turned earth in sharp contrast to the mounds of grass shivering frantically in the wind. Somehow it bothered him, it didn't seem to have any place in what they were doing, didn't seem to connect to Hadaffi, or Leica. He shrugged it away as immaterial.

Mathews straightened with a grunt of satisfaction and pushed the door slowly inward. Over his shoulder Carmody could see the shapes of doors and furniture, softly outlined by the wan light coming from the other room. This would be the workroom Jo Leica had described, cupboards to the right, workbench and chairs to the left, and straight ahead in the direction of the light, the large living room.

They mushed through the opening, and paused a moment, staring owlishly toward the source of the light. Dalgety lifted one leg off the floor and tapped against his shoe with his finger, glancing around at the group. Then he quickly slipped off his shoes and put them gently to rest by the wall. They all rapidly followed his example.

By the time Carmody had his shoes off, Dalgety had reached the door across on the other side of the workroom, watching cautiously, softly brushed with yellow light. Carmody hastened to join him, and somewhere under his feet a loose board creaked a warning. It drew a furious glance from Dalgety, but Carmody ignored it and peered past his shoulder into the room. The wind was creating a symphony of creaks around the house, and one more from him was of little consequence.

It was a large room, somehow the sort of room he mentally associated with what he'd learned of Leica. Scattered rugs, large casual comfortable chairs, small timber-stained tables, a book-lined wall, rough exposed wooden beams running across the ceiling, paintings on the walls. It exuded a warmth, a style, but it was a couch set like an island in the center of the room that drew his attention. A large red-shaded lamp perched on a table at the end of the couch was the source of light, which revealed the sleeping figure of a man, a rug drawn up over his body, one hand clutching the end of the covering, partially hiding his face.

Dalgety made a silent gesture with his hand and moved into the room, Mathews close on his heels, Carmody bringing up the rear, the other two agents remaining at the doorway. To their left was a banister-lined stairway, leading up to the first floor, and Carmody hesitated, cautiously surveying the head of the stairs. There was another weak light source up there somewhere, identical in intensity to the lamp in the living room, throwing pale uncertain shadows about the top of the stairs.

Was Hadaffi up there? Was Hadaffi the man on the couch? He turned as a huge-fisted gust of wind punched against the side of the house, and he felt the floor tremble under his feet. Dalgety and Mathews were already at the side of the couch, the man still sleeping, the muzzle of the gun in Mathew's hand resting gently against the forehead of the comatose figure. Dalgety gently pulled back the blanket from the man's face, and Carmody felt a sliver of disappointment. He was too young, it couldn't be Hadaffi. Then suddenly he was awake, eyes wide, head twisting about in fear until he was staring up at Mathews' gun, exaggerated to the size of a cannon by the closeness to his face.

Dalgety made a fast warning gesture of silence with his finger, but it was ignored, his mouth snapped open in preparation for a warning scream, but just as quickly Mathews' gun slammed down forcefully against his head. The man's head dropped back soundlessly, his mouth still wide, the only thing coming from the opening a thick trickle of saliva that dribbled slowly down his cheek into the collar of his shirt.

Carmody tightened the grip on his own gun, his fingers taut against the butt, suddenly excited by the demonstration of violence. That was one of the bastards, that was one closer step to the President's side. Now where was Hadaffi, and Leica?

He jerked his head toward the top of the stairs, and Dalgety crossed quickly to his side, a cautionary expression on his face.

He paused, one foot on the bottom step, and even above the wind Carmody could hear the sound of his breathing, rapid and shallow, a man under stress, containing his fear, taking great care not to let it show in his face. Carmody knew it was Leica, the psychokinesis, and it triggered an instant memory rerun of the President's face that day in the White House, and this time he did feel the same tang of fear. He moved away quickly, up the stairs ahead of Dalgety, anxious not to be infected by the virus.

They paused at the top of the stairs, hearts pounding, the board floor cold against their shoeless feet, four of them, Carmody, Dalgety, Harper, and Mathews, with one agent left below to guard the unconscious man on the couch. They could see the other light source now, at the end of the corridor, a door partly open and a shaft of bright white laid out in a geometric shape on the dark stained floor.

The wind seemed to have grown in strength and was louder up there, battering at the roof; and a tree set close to the house added its contribution, the branches raking back and forth across the tiles.

They moved together, almost in unison, padding silently, an eight-legged insect probing its way. Carmody was first to the door, his instinctive caution overwhelmed by his anticipation, his eagerness to be certain Hadaffi and Leica were there. He flattened his back against the wall and peered through the opening, Mathews behind him, Dalgety and Harper on the other side of the door. It was a bedroom, a large bed with bookshelves set into the head, the blankets rumpled as if someone had recently slept there. There was a chair at one side of the bed with a man seated, black hair, back of his head to the door. On the other side of the room another man moved into the framed viewing area, hands clasped behind his back, bespectacled eyes glowing at the man in the chair. It was Leica.

Carmody felt a surge of elation identical to when he'd first seen Jo Leica, only it was more this time, because this was the ultimate moment for him, this meant the end of the trauma for the Presidency.

He edged across for a clearer view, but the movement betrayed him to Leica, and he lifted his eyes and stared at Carmody as if he were an apparition. It was too late to move back, Carmody was stranded, and he put his finger to his mouth in a warning signal of silence.

Leica merely stood where he was, staring, his arms hanging loosely at his sides. It was an attitude as much a betrayal as Carmody's overexposure at the door, then the dark head over the back of the chair was suddenly alert, twisting around toward the door. He was young again, like the man downstairs, only faster, and Carmody caught the flash of a hand, and a gun, while his own gun hung stupidly down at his side.

Then something thrust him forcefully to one side, and two shots roared in his ears, almost simultaneously, and he heard the thwacking sound of a bullet impacting into the frame of the door. He blundered into Dalgety, stumbled into the wall, and hung there a few moments regaining his balance.

Mathews was standing at the door, his gun in his hand, waiting, peering through the opening. Carmody shook his head, shaken by the near death, struggled to regain his composure, and stumbled back toward the door.

The man in the chair was dead. He was slumped across the arm of the chair, his arms hanging down, the dark hair matted with red. Leica hadn't moved, paralyzed in the same posture, his eyes moving uncertainly from the dead man to Carmody.

"Thanks, Mathews," whispered Carmody, his lips trembling.

"My pleasure," said Mathews phlegmatically.

Carmody edged past Mathews, and stepped slowly into the bedroom until he was positioned beside the chair holding the dead man. He never took his eyes away from Leica's face. Leica still appeared stunned, his head cruising slowly from side to side, his eyes moving from Carmody to the dead man, on to Mathews at the door, over to Dalgety, then returning to Carmody. The overhead light reflected in his lenses, tiny moving white spots that made it difficult to see his eyes clearly.

Carmody wanted to see his eyes, wanted to be able to gauge their expression, wanted desperately to feel safe.

"Where's Hadaffi?" he asked warily.

Leica found his voice, inaudible at first against the wind thumping about the house, then gradually moving up to a scale of strength, repeating the same question, with variations, over and over.

"My wife? Where's my wife? My wife, Jo? Where's Jo? Is she safe? If you don't know where she is, you've killed her."

Carmody nodded his head slowly, eyes still on Leica, trying to control his anxiety.

"We're government agents," he said. "We have your wife, and she's safe. Where's Hadaffi?"

Leica sagged down onto the bed, as if the power to his last reserves of energy had been abruptly severed, his head drooping down onto his chest. He removed his spectacles, closed his eyes, and pinched at the bridge of his nose with forefinger and thumb.

"Thank Christ," he murmured wearily. "Thank Christ, thank Christ."

"Where's Hadaffi?" repeated Carmody harshly.

He turned to Dalgety for support, then realized he was alone in the room. Mathews watched carefully from one side of the door, the gun still in an upraised position in his hand, and Dalgety across from him, his eyes fixed on Leica with a hypnotic stare, a thin film of moisture glistening on his forehead.

Carmody glanced down and realized he was still holding his own weapon, useless though it had been, and he felt foolish, thrusting it out of sight into his inside pocket. He shuffled several steps closer to Leica until his knees rested against the side of the bed.

"For Chrissake, where's Hadaffi?" he demanded fiercely.

Leica looked up at Carmody, red-eyed, the tips of his fingers damp from suppressed tears.

"Downstairs," he said vaguely, as if he'd just heard the question. "There's another man there also, young like this one was."

"We got him. Where's Hadaffi?"

"He was there twenty minutes ago. I saw him."

"Well, he's not there now."

Harper poked his head around Dalgety at the door.

"No one in the other rooms, Frank."

Leica shook his head in bewilderment.

"I tell you I saw him. If he's not down there, then I don't know."

"Jesus Christ," spluttered Carmody furiously.

"Someone coming, Frank," called Dalgety from the doorway. The FBI man seemed unable to force himself into the room, as if someone had drawn an evil line across the entrance, and he found it a physical impossibility to lift his feet across.

Mathews swirled around, the gun up and ready to kill again. The quick patter of footsteps rat-tatted along the bare boards in the corridor, competing with the wind, growing louder as they neared the door.

Two people surged through the door, Jo Leica and Stevens, the agent they'd left down in the living room.

Leica glanced up from the bed, his eyebrows pushing up tightly into a wrinkled brow, his mouth open, taking in his wife, his eyes wide with wonder.

"I thought I told you to stay in the car," cried Carmody angrily.

"It's Hadaffi, Frank. She saw Hadaffi," said Stevens breathlessly.

"Where? Where?" roared Carmody.

Jo Leica went slowly across the room to her husband, not looking at Carmody.

"He went past me in a car," she said. "Heading down toward the main road. I came to the house as fast as I could."

She sat down on the bed opposite her husband, and Leica put out his hands and began to touch her, starting with her hair then her face, moving down over her shoulders and arms, until they were cupped as if offering a prayer over her swollen pregnancy.

"What?" screamed Carmody. He took Stevens by the arm and propelled him violently toward the door. "What happened?" he shouted. "Where the fuck is Harte?"

"He's dead, Frank," answered Stevens tersely.

The fury bubbled in Carmody's throat, words momentarily stifled.

"What?" said Dalgety in disbelief.

"Down in the carport," said Stevens. "Hadaffi must have taken him by surprise from behind. I think his neck's broken."

"Oh, Christ," said Dalgety.

Carmody felt a fresh spurt of adrenaline through his body, and his mind began to race. Grief was for later, all that mattered for now was Hadaffi. He wanted a double trophy for Manningham, not just Leica.

He put his hand out and grasped Dalgety fiercely by the arm.

"Eric, you take Harper with you in one car." His head swiveled quickly to Mathews. "You take Stevens with you in the other." He glanced swiftly toward Jo Leica. Her husband was bent forward, his forehead resting on her rounded stomach, and she was stroking his hair.

"Did you see which way he turned?" he asked abrasively. "Back toward Sylvan, or on toward Pine Mountain?"

She shook her head without looking, her hand still stroking.

"No," she said. "He didn't have his lights on. It was too far away for me to see which way he turned."

"It's a wonder we didn't hear the engine," said Dalgety.

"The wind," said Carmody. He pushed them urgently toward the door, one hand on Dalgety, the other on Mathews. "Move . . . as fast as you can. He won't go far, but you'll have to split up, one car toward Sylvan, the other toward Pine Mountain. I'll wait here."

Then they were away from him, running for the stairs, stockinged feet muffled against the floor, Dalgety leading, taking the steps two and three at a time.

"I'd like him alive, but kill him if you have to," Carmody roared after them. He leaned against the door frame, suddenly exhausted. He heard the back door slam violently and wondered if they'd paused to retrieve their shoes. A fierce gust slammed at the house, and somewhere there was a cracking sound as a tree surrendered to the force of the wind. He turned wearily in his tracks, feet shuffling awkwardly, and looked back into the room. Leica and his wife were still as he last remembered them, on the side of the bed, his head against Jo. It would be nice to be like that with someone again, but Carmody wondered if that sort of trust would ever be possible for him now.

All Leica could feel was relief. Relief that Jo was safe, relief that Hadaffi had lied to him over the baby. Vaguely he wondered about the identity of the unfortunate foetus that Hadaffi had used as a lever, now buried in his backyard. He was aware of the confusion at the door, of the angry words, and for a time they washed over him, failed to penetrate his involvement with Jo. Then gradually the words filtered into his mind, took shape and meaning, challenged the new strength he had found. He lifted his head, took Jo's hand gently away, and stared at Carmody watching him from the doorway. He sat up and away from Jo.

"I'll take care of Hadaffi," he said steadily.

Carmody watched him, eyes narrowed.

"Leave me," urged Leica. "Take Jo with you. I'll take care of Hadaffi. Not for you, but for me."

Jo looked at him for a moment as understanding came into her face, then she rose to her feet, walked unsteadily across the room, and took Carmody by the arm.

"Leave him, Mr. Carmody. You know what he means."

He turned uncertainly under the pressure from her hand and back-stepped out of the doorway. It was ironic justice, but was this what he wanted? What if by some chance Dalgety or Mathews failed to pick up Hadaffi on the road? Anything was better than facing that risk.

"Yes," he said slowly. "I know what he means."

He joined with Jo and went out of the room, closing the door gently behind him.

For a long time that night sleep had eluded Hadaffi. There were chinks of concealed doubt in the brash confidence he exhibited toward Leica, and they forced him to toss and turn in his bed until he finally had abandoned the idea of sleep.

Everything was going so well, the ultimate power he wanted was so close to his grasp, but it all revolved around Leica. That was both the strength and the weakness of the plan.

He knew how much Leica hated him, reveled in it because it was good to be hated and feared by a Jew, but the man was near the breaking point. What if he revolted at the last minute, refused to go through with the final psychokinesis on the President, accepted the fact of his wife's macabre death? Would he really accept such a horrendous fact, because Hadaffi had every intention of carrying out the threat? There was no place for idle threats in his plans. The foetus, yes, that had been a bluff, a successful bluff, but if it had failed then he would have had Jo Leica aborted and gone through the same process. But it was those icicles of doubt that froze out the possibility of sleep.

He decided on a walk. Everything in the house seemed in order, and he had gone out the front door and turned left into the trees, trying to contain the devils loose in his mind. He liked the feel of the wind; sensed an empathy with its uncontrolled violence, the determination to inflict its will, the sounds of the trees quailing submissively about him.

It was the way things should be, the way he was, a dominating force as natural as the wind. He paused, leaned to a tree, and lifted his face to the sky, his hair flailing wildly, his ears filled with the roaring cacophony around him. It soothed his fears; brought peace to his mind.

Then he looked back to the house and saw the file of men moving toward the door, crouched down in an assault posture, the shapes of machine guns in their hands, and his peace exploded like shattered glass, into a multitude of tiny irretrievable pieces.

The vision of ultimate power disintegrated like a

mirage that had never existed. He had been betrayed. It was the only thing his mind could grasp, the only thing that made any logical sense, and he felt a raging fury in perfect kinship with the wind. He stood there, crushed, helplessly savoring the taste of a lost dream. He would find the betrayer, because someone had to pay dearly for a lost dream of this magnitude. But who? Daiton? Nerida? Fardrin? And Jo Leica had to die the way he had threatened her husband, people had to learn that he made no idle threats.

He was tense now, his body wound tightly into a co-ordinated attacking machine. For now escape was all that mattered; retribution was essential for the brotherhood's survival, against Leica, against his wife, against his betrayer. There was nothing to be done for those inside, they were immaterial anyway.

He waited a moment, not moving, blending with the frenzied darkness around him until the last man had entered the house. Then he moved, swiftly, silently, until he was cloaked in the shadows cast by the house at the corner of the carport. There was a man guarding the cars, but he would be easy. Hadaffi wasn't armed, but Americans relied too much on their weapons; they were soft, and easily broken. This sort of violence came easy to him, it was a challenge, a well-rehearsed, precise drill, and the man never knew what happened: one powerful muscled arm encircling his neck, a savage wrench, a snapping click, and he was dead.

He laid him down carefully by the side of the house, took his gun and placed it in his pocket, then went to the Buick. He opened the door, put it in neutral, then began to rock it gently to gain momentum. It started to move, slowly, and he slipped behind the wheel as it rolled out of the carport and down the slight incline to the road fifty feet away. He started the engine, judging the sound to coordinate with a strong gust of wind, and drove slowly down the road to the turn, no lights, feeling his way. There was no elation about his good fortune at not being trapped in the house, at his chance of escape; his mind boiled with anger and frustration. So close. So close. But he wasn't done yet, they would all know Hadaffi had been in America before he was finished. He had to survive. It was imperative for the continuance of the brotherhood that he survive, because there was still so much to be done, so much that could be achieved, even though Leica was now a lost cause. There were still the well-tried methods, the kidnappings, the hijackings, and he would be totally ruthless, totally contemptuous of life. Nothing mattered, not a single life, not a dozen lives, not a thousand lives, only justice for the Palestinians.

He reached the main road without incident, hit the light switch, thumped the accelerator hard to the floor, and swung the car brutally toward Pine Mountain. The car responded with a screech of tires, and bolted down the road with a surge of power. There was no clear plan in his mind, only the desire to put as much distance between himself and the house as fast as possible. He began to try and think his way out of the disaster. He would try and make New York; there were friends there who would shelter him until he could reorganize. Connecticut was too dangerous, maybe Daiton was a prisoner, even dead. And Nerida. But how? How? Had they set Leica's wife free? No matter, he would find her, and kill her. The brotherhood would insist on that, an example had to be set for any further operations.

He kept his foot down hard, slewing the car through the curves, the engine throbbing with a frantic beat like an animal running for survival. The tires bit hard with an anguished scream of savaged rubber. The headlights bored a white passage down the road, and he hunched over the wheel, concentrating fiercely, fighting every curve. The trees rushed past on either side, and for a moment he had the eerie feeling that he was stationary, and the forest was fleeing around him, roots became legs, and every tree in panic-stricken flight.

How much start did he have? How long before they found the man dead in the carport, and realized the Buick was gone? And where were their cars? He had seen nothing. They were questions he couldn't answer.

He was not running totally blind. In his caution he had planned an escape route, but for himself, without mentioning anything to his companions. They would expect him to go back through Sylvan; that's why he had turned to Pine Mountain. He could head for Bledsoe, then follow the road right around back onto the main highway. But it was a long way to New York. Maybe it would be better to try and hide out in Lexington, and get word to his friends in New York to organize an escape route.

For a brief second he thought his eyes were deceiving him. He came into the curve fast, holding the wheel down, and the figure seemed to burst from the trees and hurl itself in front of the car. Then his reaction was pure instinct. He swung violently left, slewed across the road, the wheels hit side gravel, refused discipline, and took their own course, slithering and skidding through bushes, over rocks, making their own road. Hadaffi froze over the wheel, his eyes wide, mouth dribbling, his foot punching helplessly on the brake. The car slammed into one tree, ricocheted into another, then plowed into the embankment, gouging a deep gash that eventually brought it to a halt. The engine was still running. Hadaffi leaned forward and switched it off with trembling fingers, and he crouched over the steering wheel, his body shaking with the intensity of the trees around him. He put his hand to his face and controlled the trembling with a massive effort of self-discipline.

He was still alive, that was all that mattered, and he would need to assess the damage quickly to see if the car was still drivable. Who before God was the maniac who had leaped out of the trees into the path of the car, and by what miracle had he avoided hitting him? He cursed his instinctive reaction. He should have kept going, straight through, and swept the fool out of the way. He switched awkwardly in the seat and fumbled at the door lock. A large indentation thrust into the car on the driver's side, and there was a similar distortion on the opposite side where he had bounced from one tree to the other. Maybe he would be lucky. These large American cars were like tanks; they could absorb a lot of punishment and still keep going. He clambered out of the car, his feet unsteady in the loose gravel, and fumbled his way toward the front of the car. Miraculously, the lights still worked; most of the damage had been absorbed by the sides of the car. The forest whined around him in the darkness, and the chill wind beat fiercely against his face.

"Hello, Haddy," said a voice.

For a moment he disbelieved his ears; he thought it was a distortion of the wind through the pines, and he refused to react to the voice.

"Hello, Haddy," said the female voice again.

He turned slowly, one hand resting on the twisted fender of the car. It had been years since he had heard that pet name, and the user was now long dead. There was a figure standing by the side of the car, watching him, then she began to move, slowly edging forward until the light revealed her features. It was as if someone had reached into Hadaffi's heart and slowed the beat, restricting the flow of blood to his brain, making him giddy, and for a moment he was unable to focus, and his surroundings swirled and blurred before his eyes. He shut his eyes, opened them, and stared again.

"It's me, Haddy," she said, and smiled. A slow smile that bloomed and faded, laced with sad memories.

Then Hadaffi understood. It was his sister, Soyra. Soyra whom he had executed those long years ago for marrying a Jew, for betraying her people. And of course it couldn't be his sister; it was Leica, burrowing into his mind, and it meant they knew he was gone, and he had to make haste. He tried to ignore the apparition, and attempted to move to the front of the car to examine the damage. There was something wrong with his feet. Maybe they had sustained injury from the accident, but he couldn't force them to move.

But he was stronger than Leica; he had boasted he was stronger than Leica, his mind was more powerful, more disciplined than that weak fool, and now he would prove it.

"Go away," he said hoarsely. "You're not real. Go away."

He turned his head and tried to look down at the damaged side of the car, his fingers nervously caressing the ruptured surface.

"I've brought Irwin with me, Haddy," she persisted.

She dragged his eyes back to her again, as if there were some magnetic force operating that was impossible to resist. There was a man standing beside her now, dressed casually in slacks and an open blue shirt, a young good-looking man, with dark curly hair, and sharp, even features. He looked at Soyra with a sad smile, then at Hadaffi, and the smile went out of his face and was replaced by glowing hatred. Hadaffi had forgotten how young his sister had been, still with her teen-age chubbiness, the full lips, the dark eyes, the expression of constant innocence.

Her husband lifted up his hand to the light so that Hadaffi could see he held a coil of rope.

"I have come for justice for your sister, Hadaffi," he said.

Hadaffi stared at the rope, then at his sister. She smiled, and shrugged.

"I have to do what Irwin wants, Haddy," she murmured.

Hadaffi clenched his teeth to the point of pain, and fought to set up steel shutters in his mind. He would not submit; it was beneath his dignity to succumb to a weak fool like Leica, he was stronger than that, he was stronger than all of them. He thought of the crazy gyrations exhibited by Oxley in the hotel in New York, and it inspired his determination. He was more than that ludicrous traitor, he was the master of his own mind.

He resolved to face the situation out, not to flinch away from the apparition in front of him. Time and pursuit were suddenly inconsequential, this was what mattered, Leica's challenge to his mind, and he would win. Soyra and her husband did not move; they remained in their posture like inanimate waxworks, his sister still with the stupid half smile on her face, Irwin his hand still upraised, the coil of rope swaying in the wind. They began to blur like an out-of-focus screen, fading in and out from three-dimensional solidity to ghostly transparency.

The distortion of the vision excited him; he interpreted it as a sign of a superior mind gaining ascendancy, and he increased his concentration, his eyebrows tightly knit, his eyes wide with a fixed, penetrating stare. He knew he should be away, testing out the car, but this was something he had to do.

Then abruptly, taking him by surprise, his mind switched the attack to his body, and it was as if a plug had been inserted into his flesh, sucking all the energy from his limbs. He was overwhelmed by a debilitating weakness draining him, and he grasped at the side of the car for fear his legs would buckle and drop him to the ground.

His concentration fell apart, it was the end of any phase of transparency, and the two figures in front of him were terrifying solid reality again, moving reality, and he could feel himself slipping into a void, down and down, clawing at walls coated in slime. He struggled to regain control, then he was gone, lost, enmeshed in Leica's created world.

The man Irwin was at his side, his fingers pincered into his arm. Hadaffi tried weakly to pry himself free, tried to reactivate the physical strength paralyzed within him. Dripping sweat suffused his body with a humid stench, defying the chill mountain wind, and Irwin lifted the coiled rope to his eyes and let it hang there, slowly swaying.

His sister's body began to sway in time with the rope, her eyes closed, keeping time to music he could not hear.

"I'm sorry, Haddy, I'm sorry Haddy, I'm sorry

Haddy," she murmured, over and over again, as if it were the chorus of a song. "I loved you and you destroyed me."

Hadaffi could feel his legs moving as if they were independent appendages free from any control of his brain; he was being led, stumbling, like a senile invalid, terror finally seeping into his mind. The man's fingers bit deeply into his arm, and the limb began to tingle, as if the grip were cutting off the circulation.

"You betrayed your people," he screamed at his sister.

The accusation made no impression on his sister; her body swayed to the same silent beat, her eyes remained closed, her mouth still tilted at the corners in the same forlorn smile.

"I'm sorry, Haddy, I'm sorry Haddy, I'm sorry Haddy," she repeated again, in the same singsong voice. "I would forgive you, you know that, but Irwin is different, and my husband knows what's best."

"Traitor, traitor," he screamed hoarsely.

Irwin led him into the forest, and he would have fallen but for the other's grip of his arm. This couldn't be happening, he was stronger than Leica, he knew he was stronger than Leica, his mind was an all-powerful machine, but now it refused to function. And the nightmare was that he knew it was happening; could feel himself being led like a docile idiot, as if he were an outsider, a viewer watching it happen to someone else on a remote screen.

Then he was standing up on an old tree stump, the rope around his neck, the end thrown up over a branch and secured tightly on the other side by his sister's husband. The man he'd hunted to kill.

"Good-bye, murderer," said Irwin softly.

"No," said Hadaffi.

It was absurd. All he had to do was lift his hands and remove the rope from around his neck, but his arms stayed locked at his sides.

"Step off the stump," demanded Irwin.

Hadaffi commanded his legs to remain where they were.

"No," he said again.

He could feel his feet shuffling about on the stump, preparing for a violent act of insubordination. The wind rushed over his body, flapping his clothes, making him feel alive.

"Step off the stump, murderer," persisted Irwin.

"No," screamed Hadaffi.

His feet took polite note of his request, hesitated, twitched, shuffled, decided for Leica, and stepped off into space.

When Dalgety and Harper found him he was dead of an unexplained wound, his face ugly and contorted, angry red weals about his neck.

When it was done Leica went down into the living room to Jo and Carmody, and fell wearily into a chair. There was a tension in the room, a strained silence that he failed to grasp at first.

"It's done?" asked Carmody.

"It's done," murmured Leica.

"Is he still alive?"

"I would be surprised."

Carmody was silent for a moment, observing the other man. Leica had dressed before coming downstairs, heavy cords, thick check shirt, boots. He was tall, six foot three or four, his feet splaying out awkwardly from the chair. He sat with his eyes closed, his head thrown back, his spectacles glinting tints of red from the lamp.

Carmody fumbled for words to say to him. He'd been through a horrendous experience, but then so had the President. What would he have done in similar circumstances if it had been Angela, the way he had felt about her, how long ago? Yesterday? A year ago? Should he try and put Leica under arrest? That would be dangerous, here on his own, and he had no idea how the man would react. While he was ferreting about for a direction, Jo Leica stepped in the breach for him.

"Mr. Carmody has told me about the President," she said soberly.

Leica lifted a hand to his head and slowly massaged his forehead.

"Yes," was his only comment.

"I know you did it because of me," she said.

"Yes," said Leica again. And now I'm a different man from the one you knew, he could have added, but he let it pass. That was for later, when they were alone. If there was going to be a later. He opened his eyes and rolled his head in the direction of Carmody. His eyes were heavy-lidded, and splotched with red. "How is the President?" he asked.

Carmody shrugged. "Recovering," he said shortly.

"I'm sorry about that," said Leica.

Sorry, thought Carmody. Could he really go back to Manningham and tell him that Leica was sorry for his brush with insanity?

"There was another man," muttered Leica. "In the Taft Hotel in New York."

"Oxley?"

"I never knew his name."

"He's dead. He fell out of the window."

"Oh," said Leica. He closed his eyes again and went back to massaging his forehead, his fingers pushing deeply, reddening the skin.

"They threatened to kill your wife?" asked Carmody, feeling his way.

"They threatened lots of things. Hadaffi was an animal." He took the hand from his forehead and waved a finger in the direction of the rear yard, then returned to his massaging again. "There is a small grave in the yard I dug myself. Hadaffi brought me a foetus in a cardboard box. I thought it was my son, that they had aborted you, Jo."

"Dear God," muttered Jo.

Carmody studied the floor, his hands fidgeting. Did anything matter except the Presidency, was any coercion justifiable?

"They were going to send you back to me, Jo, by piece. Amputation by amputation. A leg. An arm. I couldn't fight that. I grew to hate Hadaffi with a hatred I didn't think I was capable of, but I couldn't fight that," said Leica.

Jo Leica went across and sat beside him, put her hands about his shoulders, and cradled him in her arms.

"It's over, it's over," she whispered soothingly.

Leica was silent for a moment, taking pleasure in the feel of her arms, the warmth, the safety. Then he lifted his head, set himself free of her arms, and looked at Carmody.

"No, it's not over, is it, Carmody?" he said.

Carmody met his gaze but didn't answer, holding down tight on the flicker of alarm in his spine.

"I know you people too well. I should, you're the reason I spent three years on Pine Mountain, almost too timid to leave the house."

"That was a mistake."

"The only mistake was yours, when you let me slip through your fingers and disappear. I'm different now, Hadaffi forced me to be different. In a way he taught me something. I'm not running anymore."

"That's good," said Carmody vacantly. Was it good? Could they ever lock up a man like this? At least he felt safe, he knew he would be spared the horrors of any psychokinesis.

"I did what I did because I couldn't see any alternatives," said Leica aggressively. "Surely you can understand that?"

Carmody nodded slowly. His body ached with fatigue, but he forced pace back into his mind. There was opportunity here, exciting opportunity. He could stand by Leica, go to bat for him with the President if necessary, infiltrate the man, put him in his debt, then subtly wean him over to work for the Agency. It would be a master stroke. Not the blunt stupid approach they had tried to use three years ago.

"I can understand, Leica," he said. "And I'll help you. Every way I can."

Leica studied him silently, red eyes staring out suspiciously from behind myopic lenses.

"I don't trust you. I don't trust any of you. I trusted Vilas once, and look where that led me."

"I wasn't involved three years ago."

"I don't trust you."

"I rescued your wife. I brought her here, back to you.

I could have just dropped a bomb on this house and left it at that. I would have been justified."

Leica hesitated, glowering.

"I promise to go right up to the President on your behalf," added Carmody. "Believe me, I can appreciate your dilemma, I would have reacted in the same way. The President's not dead, he's recovering. Maybe there are ways you can develop this ability of yours to be beneficial to mankind."

"There are," said Jo. "Oh, there are. Many ways."

"Yes," agreed Leica. "There are many ways. I would like to do that."

"Then we can use that as a basis," said Carmody persuasively. "I'm sure I can persuade the President to waive any charges."

There was silence. Leica stared at him moodily, his mouth moving, tongue brushing his lips, his hand out and resting on Jo's stomach. Carmody smiled reassuringly. He could see that Leica wanted to believe.

"Hadaffi is dead," he added. "That was the threat we wanted removed." And he meant what he said, he would go to the President.

Leica hesitated indecisively. Perhaps the man was sincere, or was he being influenced by an overpowering urge to believe? Was this the way the new Brett Leica should react? Perhaps he should just stand on his feet, take Jo, and drive away in the Mustang. There was no way that Carmody could stop him. But that would be running again, that would be a recycle of the last three years, and he didn't want that. Not for himself, not for Jo, and certainly not for the baby.

"You can help?" he asked cautiously.

"I give you my solemn word," said Carmody. "I'm very high in the Agency. After this I may even be heading the organization. I can assure you, I'm not without considerable influence. You deserve some sympathy."

He put his head to one side, studying the effect of his words. He was winning, it showed in both their faces, and he was sure he could bring the President to his way of looking at the problem.

He caught a new sound from outside the house, something divorced from the howl of the wind, and for a moment he thought it was the cars returning from the hunt for Hadaffi. But it was a different sound from a car, whining, high-pitched, coming closer, making itself heard above the thrust of the wind. It was a jet, surprisingly low, probably a commercial flight heading for Lexington.

The Leicas heard the sound too, and glanced toward the ceiling. The sound drew no words.

"Thank you, Mr. Carmody," said Jo simply.

Leica nodded agreement, a half smile on his lips, but his face still wary. They were all slippery bastards, but perhaps this man was an exception. He had to have someone he could trust; anything was better than running again. Perhaps they would let him work, as Carmody was suggesting.

The sound of the jet grew in strength to equal the wind, perhaps there was more than one, and the intrusion could no longer be ignored.

"They're low," observed Carmody. "Is your house on a commercial flight path to Lexington?"

Leica shook his head uneasily.

"No," he murmured. "I've never heard them over here before."

Carmody had a sudden premonition of disaster and it propelled him to his feet, and he stood there, elbows cocked, staring up at the ceiling.

The sound swelled to a howling scream, defeating the wind. Then there was a cracking, whooshing explosion in the trees to the left of the house, as if the forest had suddenly disgorged eons of growth, spattering it violently over the mountains. A vivid yellow light flared in the front windows, blinding in its intensity.

For a moment Carmody was stunned; his first thought was that the plane had crashed, and then he heard the sound of the jets again, thundering away across the mountains. And then the sickening realization that they'd be back. Schyler. It was the first word that flashed into his mind, an instant reflex that challenged belief. He didn't know how, he didn't know why, maybe someone had got to Hamilton, yet he couldn't make himself believe that Schyler would actually have him killed, joined with Hadaffi and Leica in mutual carnage. It seemed impossible, it was an obscenity his mind rejected. If Schyler was responsible, then he was insane.

Leica was on his feet, white-faced, his arms around Jo beside him.

"You bastard, what the hell was that all about?" he snarled.

Fear took hold of Carmody, freeing his mind of everything but survival, and he started for the door, flailing his arms wildly in the air.

"Get out of the house," he screamed. "They'll be back, they're aiming for the house. Get out. Get out."

He didn't wait for either of them, but bolted for the door, flung it open, and plunged through onto the path. His foot missed the first step, and he fell, rolling, coming back to his feet in one unbroken motion, then running for his life, away from the house, his breath sobbing in his throat. The forest was alive with an eerie dancing yellow light, the crackle of hungry fire, and the air was heavy with smoke that reeked of the smell of scorched green timber, stinging his nostrils.

He half turned in his flight, searching for the two Leicas, but all he could see was the shape of the house, starkly outlined by a stretch of yellow flame. Christ, oh Christ, they must be using napalm, the bastards were trying to turn him into a roasted ember. He couldn't believe Schyler was trying to murder him, there had to be another explanation, it was all crazy. He kept running, head down into the wind, his hands beating in front of him, trying to carve a path of escape.

He heard them coming again, sweeping in from the other side of the mountain, the roar of the jets tuned with the wind, then gradually losing altitude as they drew closer. He had almost reached the turn in the road when exhaustion won the battle with his fear, and dropped him down on his knees, and he felt the sharp impact of the coarse gravel into his skin. Then it came again, a whooshing crump behind him, and the forest flashed with the brightness of a yellow day, and there was a sharp outlined shadow cringing on the track in front of him, painted jet black against yellow gravel. There was a second explosion, then another, then another, until they mingled together to form one giant roaring sound, and the air was full of smoldering shredded leaves, caught in the wind and swirled along like helpless fireflies.

He rolled over until he was sitting upright, leaning back on his hands for support, facing back toward the house. Or where the house had been. All he could see now were scattered clumps of fire, trees that seemed to be alive with yellow vines licking up their trunks, and here and there the shattered outlines of fragments of the house, a section of roof, a piece of wall, a twisted door, and other parts that defied identification, all connected with one common yellow glow.

He clambered to his feet, and the smoke wafted over him, clearing fast, setting him coughing, and his eyes sprung leaks sending tears coursing down his cheeks.

He wandered slowly back down the road toward the site of the house, stumbling, not looking down at the ground in front of him, but staring at the flames already dying, dabbing at his wet cheeks.

He could only see one thing moving, apart from the flames, and he groped his way in the direction of the figure. He weaved a path drunkenly through smoldering pieces of glowing timber, and peered across to the site of the house. The building had totally disintegrated, leaving only a blackened scar on the ground as evidence it had ever existed. The ground felt warm beneath his feet, the grass crisp and tinder-dry. The flames crackled at the forest with greedy relish. It was the dominating sound now, the jets were gone, and the wind had suddenly died, as if overawed by a force as powerful as its own.

The figure kneeling on the ground turned to him as he drew closer, and he saw it was Leica, his face blackened, his hair singed and tangled about his face. He stared at Carmody, his face malevolent in the yellow light, a frightening complex amalgam of grief, anguish, and anger.

There was something lying on the ground in front of Leica where his hands rested, and Carmody averted his eyes. He didn't want to look; he knew it was Jo Leica.

He stopped several feet short of Leica, swaying on his feet, the heat from the fire reddening the side of his face. The President wasn't going to like this; it would make them all look bad, but it was Schyler's debt to pay, not his. Perhaps he should try to keep it from the President.

"I'm sorry," he murmured.

Any moment he expected his legs would revolt against the pain in his muscles and spill him to the ground again, perhaps near to Jo Leica, and he didn't want that. He cringed from the thought of being close to the charred body, and he shuffled back as if fearing contamination.

"I'm sorry," he mumbled again. It was the only word his brain seemed able to find.

He looked back toward the fire again, frightened to expose himself to the expression in Leica's face.

"You're shit, Carmody," Leica spat at him. "Stinking evil shit, murderer, liar." His voice sounded garbled, straining out of a volcano overlayered with thick phlegm. Carmody's hands pawed at the air in a weak attempt at defense.

"I wasn't responsible for that . . . I wasn't responsible," he stuttered. "They tried to kill me too."

"You're all one of a kind," continued Leica, deaf to Carmody's words. "You care nothing for anybody, not for their lives, not for their innocence." His hands gently caressed the shape in front of him. "All of you, all liars, all murderers. You. Hadaffi. You're no different. You carry misery around with you like disease, infecting everyone you touch. You move over the earth leaving a polluted trail of filth, sewage running through your veins instead of blood. No conscience, no compassion, no anything." His eyes seemed to glow with the ferocity of the flames in the forest, as if they could drill charred holes through Carmody's body.

"I'm not responsible," muttered Carmody, stupidly,

as if repetition of the words would somehow transmit life back to Jo Leica.

"Go with Hadaffi, you bastard," snarled Leica.

Then Carmody's legs did give way, and he fell backward, slowly, without tension, his muscles relaxed, and he hit the ground like a soaked sponge, his body loose with exhaustion.

The ground felt warm and comforting, enveloping him like a heated blanket, and he closed his eyes. He was sorry, he was sorry, but there was nothing he could do. He was certain he was apologizing for Schyler, and why should he apologize for that bastard. All he wanted now was peace, he wanted to let his mind hang out to dry until all the pain had evaporated, and not use it again for a long time. He tuned out and let blackness slide over him.

"It's what he would want," said Dalgety.

They were the first words Carmody heard when he opened his eyes. He was still lying on his back, and he could still feel the warmth of the ground against his body, and the tang of green wood smoke in his nostrils.

But he couldn't see, there was a shadowy blur over his eyes, with chinks of light showing through, and he could feel something soft brushing back and forth over his face. He turned his head and caught the sweet aroma of pine. It was the branch of a pine tree across his face.

He wondered if he was in the hospital, but his mind

was still in the forest, although he couldn't imagine why it would be reluctant to leave.

He wondered what Dalgety's words meant. Surely they could see his eyes were open, and he lay there, waiting, trying to assemble some sort of order into his mind. Footsteps shuffled around him, and he could hear the sounds of objects being dragged along the ground, an abrasive scratching sound, then something being thrown across his body. Although not on his body, but above it, an addition, and he was suddenly conscious of a weight pressing down on him. He tried to move, to raise himself to a sitting position, but the weight pressed against him, and it had the form of various shapes, lying over his legs, over his chest, over his arms. He managed to lift his head slightly, and he could glimpse the darkened outlines of a collage of small trees and branches pressing against his body.

"I guess this means that Schyler is going to remain in charge of the Agency," he heard another voice say. He thought it was Mathews, yes, it was Mathews, from somewhere above him, and another piece of timber clumped onto the pile holding him down.

"Forget Schyler," Dalgety growled. "Let's concentrate on doing this for Frank. We don't want those bastards to take care of him. He deserves better than that."

Better than what? What the fuck were the crazy bastards doing to him? He began to struggle, violently, threshing his head about, trying to move his arms, his legs, but the weight against him was immovable.

Then his hand touched something, not the moist feel of grass, nor the coarse texture of earth, nor the patterned hardness of timber, but something soft, yet firm, a human feel.

He craned his head around, and it was Angela, beside him, lying on her side, still wearing the same dress as when he'd last seen her in Connecticut, her eyes wide and smiling at him. The weight of the forest gatherings enclosed them tightly together in a cocoon of leaves and timber.

"It's better this way, Frank," she murmured softly.

He jerked his head away from her, feeling his neck wrench with sudden pain, and the sweat of panic oozed out over his body in a flood. He shut his eyes again, clenched his hands into tight fists, and tried to discipline his mind. He was still unconscious, it was as simple as that. This was a dream, a nightmare, engendered by strain, and in a moment he would wake and shake his head in wonder at the intensity of the experience.

He felt Angela's fingers touch his hand, soft and caressing, and he flinched as if it were a touch of hot metal.

"It was a mistake in the apartment, Frank," she said gently. "I really loved you. You know I really loved you, Frank. You want me to love you, don't you, Frank. But I was terrified of Hadaffi. You don't know the sort of man he is. Forgive me, Frank, darling. Love me. Love me."

He refused to turn his head again, because he told himself she wasn't there, and he tried to concentrate on forcing his mind back to consciousness. There must be great things waiting for him, the President, the cabinet, gratitude, reward, security, position.

"It's better this way, darling," she murmured. "They'll lock me up forever otherwise and I'll never see you again. This way we can always be together. You know you want to be with me, Frank. You know you want to love me, no matter what I did to you."

"Go away, you bitch," he gritted through his teeth. "Go back to Daiton."

"I can't love a dead man, darling. You killed him, remember, back there in Connecticut. I'm like you. I have to love someone. Don't you know how hard it was for me to shoot you."

"I guess that's about it," said Dalgety.

"I guess he really loved her, Eric," said Harper.

"Yes, I suppose so. Sometimes it's like that. It wouldn't have mattered what she did to him, he was always going to go on loving her. He was a good guy, Harper."

The disembodied voices floated down to him, some of the words broken and indistinct, as if being strained through a filter. The weight on him was oppressive now, thrusting down against his chest, making it difficult for him to breathe. And because fear was making his heart run over at such a rapid rate, forcing his breath in fast gasps, the pain was more intense. Perhaps he should try to call out, to tell them that he was still alive. It was ridiculous, it was only a nightmare, and he would wake any moment, but perhaps he should try.

Angela's hand came down over his mouth as if she had read his mind, small and lightly boned, but like a suffocating band in his helpless state.

"They're only trying to do their best for us, darling," she soothed in his ear. "You'll hurt their feelings if you cry out. Leave them be."

He swirled his head about trying to force her hand away, but she clamped tighter with surprising strength. Christ, please let him wake, this feeling of totally trapped helplessness was terrifying.

And he didn't want to love Angela, or whatever it was beside him, not her memory, nothing. That was pain, and he shied away from the thought of that sort of perpetual pain. He couldn't allow it to interfere with the future head of Intelligence. It would disable him, make him incompetent, vulnerable.

"The President won't like it," said Mathews.

"We won't tell him," said Dalgety.

"What about Schyler?"

"The hell with Schyler. We'll just tell him that Frank disappeared along with Leica. He can think what he likes."

Leica. Of course, that was it. Leica. Revenge for Jo, revenge against all of them, that's what was happening to him. But that wasn't fair, he was serving penance for Schyler, why should he be here and Schyler probably back in Washington congratulating himself over the bombing of the house. This was what it was like, this feeling of total reality, this was what Manningham felt that day back there in the White House.

He tried to still the panic that was forcing him to arch his back desperately against the ground, to stop twisting his head about to dislodge Angela's persistent hand, to bring some composure to his mind.

Leica was doing this to him, it was all in his mind, and it would pass. Surely to know what was happening was the perfect antidote; it wasn't like Manningham taken unawares, if he could just relax, hang on to his sanity, then he could survive. Manningham survived.

Almost immediately the thought was canceled by another. But the others died. Oxley died. Hadaffi died, and he must have known what was happening.

His attempted composure was abruptly swept away, the accelerator pedal in his system thrust down even harder, and his heart began to race as if every beat was a thunderclap in his chest. His eyes filled with water, his skin felt clammy, alternatively flushed with heat, then just as suddenly chilled.

"It's away," Mathews called.

"Okay, okay," cried Dalgety. "Stand back, stand back."

Carmody swiveled his head around in panic. What was away? Why did they have to stand back?

"Relax, darling," came a sibilant whisper in his ear. "It won't take long, then we'll be together forever. No more Hadaffi, no more grief, just love."

The sound of crackling surged into his ears, and smoke drifted down through the tangle of foliage, scented with the sharp bite of singed pine. Christ, they'd set it alight. They were going to burn him with some macabre ceremonial warrior's funeral. He began to struggle again, violently, throwing his body around in the confined space, all thoughts that this was merely a nightmare erased from his mind. This was reality. This was horror. This was death.

The wood was dry, maybe already smoldering from the bombed forest, and it caught rapidly, roaring in his ears, and the smoke came down in suffocating clouds. He retched horribly, but Angela's grip held firm, forcing the vomit back into his throat.

"Soon, soon," she shrieked in his ear.

He reached up with his head and caught her hand against a branch, and wrenched it free of his mouth. He could feel the heat, unbearable, blistering his skin, and sanity gave way, and he opened his mouth and screamed and screamed and screamed.

They kept him in the hospital for three weeks. He didn't remember much of the first week, staring up at the white ceiling, occasionally an unexpected scream escaping from his lips that would bring a nurse running, and he would feel stupid and grimace an apology. They gave him a small rubber ball to squeeze in his hand for when he felt that sort of tension, and it seemed to help. He slept badly, but that was more from fear of sleep. Sleep meant dreams, macabre images, certainly not with the intensity of the attempted cremation, but still to be avoided. He would lie in his bed at night, fighting sleep until it would creep up on him, take him unawares, and he would drift off. But only for a short time, maybe thirty minutes at a time, then he would wake with a start, staring at the ceiling, at the fretwork of shadows that seemed to collect there at night, and he would be staring up again at his funeral pyre, and he would groan and struggle as if straps were holding him down on the bed.

Then the night nurse would come running, shining her flashlight into his wide eyes, asking if he needed anything to make him sleep. He would shake his head and try to smile, and lie there for the rest of the night, determined not to succumb to sleep again.

He thought about Angela. He thought about Leica and his wife. He wondered about Schyler and Dalgety and the President, because for the first week he was allowed no visitors. The blisters on his skin quickly healed. The doctors assumed they were from the forest fire; he knew better, but how could he explain it to them? So he let it pass.

After all, it was the blisters on his mind that concerned him more, they would be a long time healing, and maybe the scars would remain forever. The days passed slowly, and a semblance of balance began to return to his mind, the passive deadness faded, his isolation began to bore him, questions formed in his mind that needed answers. He began to look at the Leica experience with some form of objectivity, trying to understand what had happened to his mind, how he had survived.

The nurses fussed, the doctors examined him, nodded their heads, and smiled with satisfaction at his progress. They talked about shock, and the trauma of his brush with death, but no one mentioned Leica, and as far as Carmody knew, they knew nothing of the man, or of Hadaffi, or psychokinesis. Certainly he had no intention of raising the subject.

Toward the end of the second week they allowed Dalgety to come and see him. The FBI man sat on the edge of the bed, exchanging small talk, feeling his way, studying Carmody with his shrewd eyes.

They moved around the point in ever narrowing circles until finally impatience provoked Carmody into direct bluntness.

"You can stop treating me like an invalid now, Eric," he said brusquely.

"You've been a sick man, Frank," grunted Dalgety.

Carmody shrugged away the obviousness of the comment.

"Where's Leica?" he asked.

"Are you sure you want to talk about it?"

"For Chrissake, yes. Where's Leica?"

"Gone. Vanished."

"Just like that?"

Dalgety squinted his eyes, and they almost disappeared into his brows.

"Yes, just like that. When we got back to what was left of the house there was only you, and the remains of Mrs. Leica. There was no sign of Leica. We searched, we thought he might have been killed also, but . . ." He spread his hands. "Not a sign. Almost as if he'd vanished off the face of the earth."

"I'm sorry about her," muttered Carmody.

Dalgety grimaced and shook his head.

"Yeah, that was bad. Real bad."

"Where's Hadaffi?"

"Dead."

"From Leica?"

Dalgety frowned, and rubbed his hands slowly back and forth along the edge of the bed.

"Yes, I guess so, but don't ask me how."

"It was Leica. He applied psychokinesis at the house before the bombing," said Carmody.

"That explains part of it, but we still don't know how he died. He wasn't a pretty sight when we found him by the side of his wrecked car. It looked as if someone had strangled him with a rope."

Carmody sighed, his hands moving nervously about the bed, twitching at a corner of the blanket. He did want to talk about it, there were things he had to know, had to resolve, but the memories frayed at his nerves. He looked up and saw Dalgety watching his nervous fingers, and dropped the blanket. He placed one hand over the other as some sort of physical control against any sign of agitation.

"You want to go on?" asked Dalgety solicitously.

"Of course," said Carmody irritably. "I've been isolated here long enough. It's time I had some answers, Eric." He cleared his throat with a gravelly rasp and edged himself up higher in the bed.

"It was Leica, wasn't it, Frank?" asked Dalgety. quietly.

Carmody drew a deep breath before answering.

"Yes, yes it was."

"Want to talk about it?"

Carmody thought about the question for a moment. He thought of the President pouring out his horrific experience of the operation, and decided against telling Dalgety. What had happened in his mind would remain his own private nightmare. Perhaps he had guilt feelings about Angela, perhaps many things, but the experience would always be a private preserve.

"No," he said quietly. "Just let's say it was an experience I wouldn't want to share with anyone."

Dalgety gave a nod of understanding acceptance.

"Because of what happened to his wife?"

"Yes. He blamed me for the bombing. He thought I'd tricked him."

"You can chalk that one up to Schyler," said Dalgety acidly.

Carmody shrugged and looked up at the ceiling, his face blank. He would take that up with Schyler and the President later. He wanted badly to know how that happened.

"I wouldn't worry too much about it," grinned Dalgety.

"What do you mean? Where is Martin?"

"Let's say he's gone on extended leave. Very extended leave. There's a very vacant office down at your department."

Carmody nodded slowly, his face expressionless, waiting for a jolt of exultation, but it didn't come. He wondered about that. Perhaps it was his surroundings, his state of mind, but it was a culmination, and he should have felt something.

"After what happened to Hadaffi, I wonder how I managed to survive," he said instead.

"I can't answer that," grunted Dalgety. "When we found you, you were in a bad state, writhing around on the ground, screaming your head off. You didn't recognize any of us. You fought us, called us obscene names." He grinned at Carmody. "I thought I knew them all, but you taught me some new ones." He paused, and his face flattened out into a serious expression again. "Maybe we disturbed him, coming back too soon for him to finish you off. The murderous bastard, he's in the same league as Hadaffi."

Carmody shook his head, rustling against the pillow, and made a negative gesture with his hands.

"No, no, I don't believe that. Hadaffi screwed the poor bastard into the ground, and he just cracked, that's all. I was unlucky enough to be in his way when it happened. I guess he loved his wife a great deal. I can understand that."

It sounded magnanimous, but he didn't mean it that way. He didn't feel magnanimous in the slightest about the experience Leica had subjected him to, but he did understand about Jo. He looked at Dalgety, and saw Angela in his face.

"Yes, I guess so," said Dalgety musingly. "But I'll feel a hell of a lot safer when we pick him up. If we ever do pick him up."

They talked idly for a few more minutes, then Dalgety shook his hand and left, with expressions for his continued recovery. Carmody was sorry to see him go. He liked the man, it had been good to share the Hadaffi operation with him, and he had a lot of guts.

Hamilton came the next morning. Shamefaced, and mumbling, but he told Carmody all he wanted to know about Schyler's involvement in the bombing, and the taped telephone conversations in the office. Carmody listened with weary forgiveness. It was over, there was nothing he could do about it, it had cost Jo Leica her life, and been directly responsible for his experience of psychokinesis. He couldn't blame Hamilton, he couldn't feel any anger. But when Hamilton had gone, he lay there for a long time thinking of the fresh beauty of Jo Leica and the last charred sight he'd had of her.

On the weekend the President came with Secretary of State Dan Wenkell. Early in the morning Carmody sensed something was up by the flurry around the hospital. Nurses scurried around the ward, placing flowers, polishing, tidying, exchanging whispers, smiles, sideways glances at Carmody, flinching from sharp-tongued matrons. They converted the ward into a regal reception room, Carmody perched in style on the bed as if preparing to meet royalty.

There was only Manningham, Wenkell, and Carmody in the room. Manningham shook his hand firmly. He looked almost like his former self, his pallor still tinged with gray, but the old political spirit was twinkling in his eye again.

"If the nation knew what we knew, then they'd be as grateful as I am, Frank," he said warmly.

It sounded pompous, a little like the opening catch phrase of a political speech, but Carmody knew he was sincere.

"Thank you, Mr. President," he smiled.

Wenkell cleared his throat loudly to indicate agreement with the President's sentiments.

"It's just a pity about Leica, that's all," he growled.

"I'm sure we'll pick him up sooner or later," said the President easily.

Carmody nodded, and the smile stayed rubber-stamped on his face, but he was certain the President was wrong. Leica was gone. He'd hidden himself away for three years before, this time he would vanish forever. He suspected they could put the entire country under a microscope, but they wouldn't find a hair of his head.

"We have the doubtful honor of sharing a unique Leica experience, Frank," said the President solemnly.

"We must compare notes one time, Mr. President," said Carmody.

Manningham extended a fatherly hand and gripped Carmody by the shoulder.

"Don't worry, you're going to be all right, Frank. It takes time, but you can see I'm getting back to normal. You won't forget the experience, I know I won't, but you will learn to cope with it, believe me."

"Oh, I feel better now," answered Carmody. "The first week was pretty grim, but I'm coming around."

"Fine, fine," said the President effusively. "We want you out of here as soon as possible, Frank. Intelligence needs a man like you."

Carmody allowed a hesitant smile. He waited for a mention of Schyler's name, but it didn't eventuate. He knew that was Manningham's style. Nothing would be said for a time; there would be insinuations, innuendos, unconfirmed reports, speculations, then Martin would fade gradually into obscurity. He guessed Dalgety's report would have put the finishing touch to Martin.

It was a short visit. Manningham went through all the formalities, and his gratitude would take solid form; but Leica and Hadaffi were already history, yesterday's problems, and now there was an election to be fought, and won.

The rest of the week dragged for Carmody. He began to sleep again, sweet dreamless unconsciousness, and the lines of fatigue and apprehension in his face gradually softened and disappeared.

On Friday he was released, and he went back to the apartment. It was like returning to a tomb, a musty, airless crypt that had lost the feel of living human warmth. It wasn't the pleasant place he remembered, but a cage; not a place to live, but a place from which to escape.

He went through the place thoroughly, removing every trace of Angela he could find, padding from room to room, garments, nail polish, a comb, a hair clip, a trace of powder, every minute detail that could spark remembrance. He knew he was still scouring his mind more than the apartment, and it was more difficult removing the evidence from there.

He slept badly again, the bed was like a wide field, and he roamed all night searching for a corner to find peace.

In the morning he came to a decision, moved out, called on the agent to cancel his lease, and asked him to find a new place to live. It was all done with surprising speed, and within a few days he was established in a new place in Arlington. From the first night he slept in dreamless, untroubled sleep.

The next week he went to the office. He sat in Schyler's chair, and made phone calls and tried to marshal his concentration, but there was little for him to do. No one mentioned Schyler, but they all deferred to him as if he were sitting in his rightful place. Hamilton grinned a welcome, and people kept putting their heads through the door for the remainder of the day with individual greetings. There was nothing on Leica.

Someone had subtly altered the configuration of Angela's office, and there was a new girl sitting there, at a new desk, in a new chair, surrounded with new furniture, and displaying a bright new smile. It was the sort of thing that Hamilton probably arranged, but he offered no comment. She was attractive and called him Frank from the first, which was good, and he smiled a welcome at her.

Gradually over the next few days the pace began to pick up, and he found he could gear himself to meet it—conferences, appointments, minor decisions. There was still no mention of Schyler, no communication, no letters, no memos. Someone had waved a magic wand and he had disappeared in a puff of smoke. He discussed Leica with Dalgety, and they had a wanted description out all over the country, but there was nothing.

It was good to be busy again, and he began to slip into the feel of Schyler's office and the power it automatically generated.

On the following Friday morning he received an urgent summons to the White House. He put the phone down with a satisfied grin. It was probably concerning Schyler, an official confirmation of his role over Intelligence. The President would probably want to make an announcement to the press, and there would be reporters, but he could cope with that now.

He could not have been further from the truth. When he was ushered into the President's office it was as if he'd stepped backward in time: he was staring at a rerun of a past episode, all the same characters, the same expressions, the same foreboding atmosphere. For a moment he stood at the door, his feet anchored in position. There was the President, Dan Wenkell, Harvey Schultz, General Cooper, Bob Rand, Dalgety. Mort Helder and Schyler were painted out of the scene, but the others were in the same chairs, with the same grim expressions, the same tense postures. For the first time since the Leica experience his mind floundered again in attempting to define reality. Was this reality, or was his mind playing tricks and recycling past experiences?

He felt the initial tingle of panic, and he smiled woodenly in an attempt to cover the feeling. No one said anything, they all stared at him, then turned back to the President, each in turn, as if connected together with a timing device.

Manningham acknowledged him with a tilt of his head and motioned to him to sit down. Carmody moved across to a chair, his shoulders hunched in a subconscious protective gesture. The atmosphere enveloped him with the clamminess of a heavy fog, almost with a tangible solidity, blinding him, chilling his spine with apprehension.

This was certainly no confirmation of his position at Intelligence; this was a wake, and the only thing missing was the corpse.

He sat down and fidgeted about in the chair, the soft leather creaking beneath his weight, and waited. The President made an imperious gesture of clearing his throat to guarantee attention. His color seemed to have deteriorated since Carmody had last seen him at the hospital, the gray had deepened again, and there was an alarming tension in his manner, not something motivated by grief, or anger, but something much deeper, holding him in a strangling knot. Leica? Surely not?

Yet that was the type of expression Leica created, and Carmody shivered as if a chill draft had swept through the room. Surely that was impossible?

The President confirmed his fears. He held up a piece of notepaper for Carmody's attention, and waved it about slowly in the air. The President braced his elbow against the top of the desk, as if the piece of paper had weight out of all context to its appearance.

"We have received a communication from Brett Leica, Frank," he said. There was a forced harshness in his tone to cover a soft nervous trembling in his body.

Carmody opened his mouth to say something, but nothing happened. There was a sudden vacuum in the deepness of his belly that denied speech, and he stilled an urgent demand created in his bowels by the announcement.

The President put the paper down on his desk, adjusted his spectacles, glanced at Carmody, then to the paper, back to Carmody, then to the paper again, an admonishing teacher to pupil.

"The others have seen the contents, but I want to read it out for your benefit, Frank," he said. "For an innocent victim of circumstances, he has learned well from Hadaffi. He has proved an adept pupil."

The President paused, and lifted his eyes to Carmody again for comment, but there seemed no words Carmody could find. He inclined his head to the President and waited. The tingle of panic gathered momentum like an injected anesthetic, moving slowly up his body, numbing his legs.

The President returned his eyes to the paper.

" 'President Manningham,' " he began. " 'There was

a time when I believed I could hide myself away from the world, and be safe. Hadaffi taught me differently. Carmody taught me differently. You are all insane cannibals who will consume each other and the world if left alone. My personal safety has now become immaterial. I call on you and the Premier of Russia to reconvene a new disarmament conference immediately, and to draw up an agreement to make massive reductions in your mutual nuclear insanity. An identical message has already been read by the Russian Premier. Failure to agree will result in the application of crippling psychokinesis to both of you. Brett Leica.'"

The President placed the note carefully down on the desk, removed his spectacles, and peered grimly at Carmody.

"A schoolboy message," he said harshly. "The man is dangerously insane. He has obviously become unbalanced by his wife's death. He has illusions of grandeur which have no relationship to the realities of international politics. This sort of nonsense would only destroy the security of this country."

"The Russians would never buy this," growled Wenkell.

"The bastard's lying anyway," said Cooper belligerently. "I don't believe for a moment that an identical note has gone to the Russians. Leica has defected, sold out to the Russians. No one is going to convince me that Leica is capable of producing psychokinesis halfway across the world for a start. So forget it. We can't knuckle under to this lunatic demand, Mr. President, any more than we could surrender to Hadaffi."

There was a period of silence, while a mélange of anxious eyes bored in Carmody's direction. They were all waiting on him, he realized, waiting for magic words of reassurance that this new threat from Leica was merely bluff, merely the ravings of a deranged man.

"You knew Leica more than any other man here, Frank," asked the President anxiously. "Spoke to him, got some idea of what the man was about. Would he carry out a threat like this? Surely he's not a man in the same mold as Hadaffi?"

His pink tongue made agitated sweeps across his mouth. He wore the stunned look of a condemned man who has just been informed that his reprieve was only the handiwork of a practical joker.

Carmody glanced hopefully at Dalgety for support, but the FBI man stared fixedly down at his tightly bunched hands.

"Christ, you had the man in your hands, and you let him slip through," said Cooper harshly.

The remark was too ridiculous to warrant a reply, but it needled Carmody. He had the feeling that they were intent on levering him up onto a crucifixion cross over this, and for Chrissake, were their memories that appallingly short? Remember me, I'm the man who got Hadaffi for you, he felt like screaming. Schyler was responsible for Jo Leica's death, not I.

"I'm sure he's bluffing," Carmody blurted out finally. "I think he only wants to frighten us. He believes we killed his wife, and he wants to make us sweat for a while."

"Rubbish," snarled Cooper. "He's doing it for a price. A Russian price. We're going to have to get him the same as Hadaffi. Kill him. No government in this country is going to be safe while he's loose."

"No, I believe his wife's death has temporarily unbalanced him," insisted Carmody. "I just don't believe he's the type of man to step into Hadaffi's shoes like this. I'm convinced of that."

"But you saw him with his dead wife," persisted the President. "How can you be so sure, Frank? Look what he did to you. A man can get very twisted by revenge after an experience like that."

"I still believe I'm right," said Carmody stubbornly.

Abruptly the President smashed his clenched fists down on the desk, as if trying to force some of the tension out of his system.

"No, I'm with General Cooper, Frank," he said angrily. "I think Leica is out of his mind with revenge for what he thinks we did to his wife, and that revenge has taken the form of a sellout to the Russians. He could destroy the Presidency as effectively as anything Hadaffi threatened. We leave a madman like this on the loose, and he will try and dictate the policies of this or any other government."

"He hasn't set any time limit," added Carmody hopefully.

"Immaterial," grunted the President savagely. "You have to find him all over again. And quickly."

He stared at Carmody, as if trying to pry some hidden secret out of his mind, as if he half suspected that the Intelligence man knew where Leica could be found. He waited an impatient moment for some response, then switched his direction abruptly toward Dalgety, as if Carmody had somehow failed him.

"Eric, what do you have?" he demanded. "You've been working on Leica for the last few weeks. Any leads? Anything at all? What about his parents?"

Dalgety glanced up quickly at the President, his fingers kneading at each other as if in conflict.

"To be perfectly honest, Mr. President, nothing, I'm

afraid. His parents have been interviewed extensively, but they can't tell us a thing. They haven't seen him for years. The man has vanished. We have information on him with every enforcement body in the country, but it's going to take time."

"We haven't got time," thundered the President. He paused, gulping air, and glared around the room. This was more of a personal stake for him than for anyone else in the room, it was his personal sanity that was under threat again. Like an escaped prisoner who has tasted freedom, the new incarceration seemed more unbearable than before, and he was reacting accordingly, ready to slash out in every direction.

The telephone began to ring, an insistent jangle demanding attention, another needle into the frayed nerves of everyone in the office. The President glared at the offending instrument as Harvey Schultz moved hastily to silence it.

"I've had just about all I can take of this situation," said the President cryptically. "And I demand the absolute protection of all the resources of the enforcement bodies in this country. The total resources. Do I make myself clear?"

He was noticeably wilting under the renewal of the threat of psychokinesis, from the regurgitated memory of Leica's previous assault on his mind, and the foreboding gray pallor was flooding back into his face.

"You're getting it, Mr. President," protested Dalgety.

Rationality was deserting Manningham, and Dalgety's words failed to penetrate.

"And I want . . ." He stopped and glared savagely at Schultz, who was standing with the phone delicately to his ear. "For God's sake, Harvey, I thought I gave specific instructions against any incoming calls."

Schultz hesitated, and jiggled the phone about in his hands as if it were scorching his fingers, then reluctantly held it out to the President.

"Yes, I know, Mr. President. It's Tom Knowles from the State Department. He says it's vital he speak to you, or the Secretary of State."

The President hesitated, made an impatient gesture with his hands, and seized the telephone from Schultz. Schultz sat down with a strained expression of relief, took a handkerchief from his pocket, and patted at his forehead. It was a tough day, and there was no joy to be had in standing in as whipping boy to Manningham's apprehension. Perhaps the change Leica had wrought in the President's natural affable demeanor was now irrevocable.

The room was hushed with a tense, polite silence, individual doubts and fears ticking over in individual minds. The President spoke little, listening with brief grunts of affirmation, and it seemed to Carmody that his face shaped to an even sterner mold, the grayness in his face deepened, and his lips drained to a bloodless hue.

The President removed the phone from his face, stared at it, weighing it in his hand, then replaced it carefully back on the cradle as if it had the fragility of an egg.

They all waited for him to resume.

"We have just received a communication from our embassy in Moscow," said Manningham. His voice was slow, the words measured, but from somewhere deep in his throat phlegm crackled the tone. "The Russian Premier has been hospitalized with what can only be described as a massive mental collapse. There are unconfirmed rumors that some unexplained traumatic experience has reduced him to a state of insanity." He stopped, and his mouth snapped shut, as if the issue of any further words were too painful to bear. He placed his hands together on the desk in front of him, and even the interlocking of his fingers failed to disguise completely the trembling. His eyes moved slowly around the room, pausing briefly on each face for some response, then moving on. No one spoke.

Dalgety coughed nervously, reddened, and glanced anxiously at Carmody. Bob Rand shifted his bulk awkwardly around in his chair, crossed and uncrossed his legs, and scowled an expression of intense concentration to compensate for lack of words. General Cooper placed his fingers carefully together into a tent structure, placed them to his mouth, and stared ruefully into space. Wenkell leaned back in his chair and studied the ceiling, as if seeking spiritual guidance.

The President's eyes came to Carmody, but he looked away, down at the floor, scrubbing nervously at the carpet with the heel of his shoe. He felt a sense of desperation. He kept his head down. He sensed that all the eyes in the room had followed the President's lead, like venomous darts aimed at his body. Where the hell could he start? For all he knew Leica could be out of the country and a million miles away. It would take a miracle to find him again.

The silence seemed as if it would extend on into eternity.